604 30p

PARADISO

Bermuda is a paradise; sea, sand and sub-tropical flowers in abundance under a blazing sun. To Abbott, the money-man, survivor of a lost marriage, it offers a haven of peace and rest, an idyllic background to his passionate affair with the golden-skinned Angel. To Angel it is merely a stepping stone to Shaftesbury Avenue and Broadway. To Snow, black and local-born, but with an overnight international reputation as a director of musicals, the Island is a political symbol, the farthest-flung colony of Empire. To his mother, Happy, it is simply a place in which she has always lived. Nothing has changed on the Island for a long, lazy time but can such a paradise be allowed to exist in the nineteen seventies?

Against this setting Allan Prior tells his story of Abbott and Angel as they grapple with the task so dear to Angel's heart, of persuading Snow to take on the musical which Abbott is prepared to back as long as Angel has the lead. On the face of it, the situation is one not uncommon in the world of the theatre. But beneath the surface run undercurrents stretching back through 300 years of the Island's history.

This dramatic and absorbing novel looks at a glamorous but little-known location, seven hours' jet-flight from London, two hours from New York, where time has stood still, where white and coloured live amicably together while the tourists provide money for everyone; a happy island where violence and protest are almost unknown. But Snow is no longer one of the contented majority. His horizon has long since been extended beyond Bermuda and his contacts could be a threat to its peace and security. For Abbott and Angel the undercurrents prove treacherous indeed.

Novels by Allan Prior

A FLAME IN THE AIR

THE JOY RIDE

THE ONE-EYED MONSTER

ONE AWAY

THE INTERROGATORS

THE OPERATORS

THE LOVING CUP

THE CONTRACT

Paradiso

A NOVEL BY

ALLAN PRIOR

CASSELL

LONDON

CASSELL & COMPANY LTD
35 RED LION SQUARE, LONDON WC1 4SG
Sydney, Auckland
Toronto, Johannesburg

First published 1972

I.S.B.N. 0 304 29089 0

Printed in Great Britain by
The Anchor Press Ltd, and bound by
William Brendon & Son Ltd, both of Tiptree, Essex

F.772

1

The money had done it, of course.

Abbott knew that.

Until the money arrived his life had been uneventful and, despite all the work, placid. The need for the money had made him keep his head down—exactly why he could never be sure, certainly not simply to get rich; but it had happened. The money had come, like an involuntary sexual climax, and everything in his life had abruptly and violently altered. The need to work had gone, and with it a whole way of life. Instead of there not being enough hours in the day, the very minutes dominated by the tyranny of the desk-diary and the company car, there were suddenly too many hours, all to be filled in a new and alien and sometimes frightening way. The money had come and the work had gone, and with the work had gone the old props and stays, home and family— God, Helen's face, when he told her! And with the money had come the new ways, the new needs, the new and seemingly inescapable life-style.

With the money had come Angel.

She stirred amongst the huge silken pillows, propped herself up on her elbows and swung off the bed. She padded nude, golden and firm-breasted, to the window, and surveyed the grey and smoggy New York morning through two panes of glass.

'Shit, what a city,' said Angel.

It was her first visit to New York and she had not been as enthusiastic as Abbott thought she should have been. After all, they *were* staying at the Regis and they *had* been to lunch at Twenty One, and supper at Sardi's, and for drinks at the Four Seasons. They had sailed round Manhattan on the steamer and they had been up the Empire State Building and to Radio City Music Hall. It had been a strictly tourist trip, all right, but Abbott still felt that she might have shown a little more appreciation. Instead, she had stood outside St. Pat's, and looking up and down the dramatic sweep of Fifth Avenue, declared, 'But I've seen all this on the movies.'

Abbott had recognised the disappointment in her voice. It was the tone she used when a promised celebrity had not turned up for drinks after one of her shows, had excused himself and run, probably from her dramatic beauty. Angel's looks scared people off, unless they were very famous or very confident or very rich, and sometimes even then. Poorer, less talented men did not feel they deserved her, Abbott had noted. He would never have dreamed of approaching her himself, before the money.

'I thought you said we'd be meeting Snow in this town.' Angel turned from the window, and Abbott, looking at the small but perfect breasts, the sloping, tiny waist and the dark V of pubic hair (above all the angelic, golden face, the strong white teeth, the afro hair style) thought : I have no right here with her, she's too beautiful, we don't belong together, we have nothing in common except our flesh. He sighed, and stretched out his hand. 'Come back to bed.'

Angel did not get back into bed. She padded sulkily into the bathroom suite and left the door open so that she could talk to him. As she made water she called, above the splashing sound, 'I don't know why we stopped off in New York.'

'Because you wanted to. And I had to talk to his agent. You know that. Don't worry. We'll get everything fixed on the Island.'

'I hope so.'

'We'll see him today, after all, darling.'

'I dunno. He could have waited for us, maybe he's gone cold on the idea.'

'If he had done that he wouldn't have asked us to fly over. He's just gone ahead to get some sun.'

The splashing sound stopped and Angel came back into the bedroom, still naked. 'Do you think it's bread that's worrying him?'

'Anything but. Morris said he'd take no fee, just a large cut of the profits. If he decided to go ahead with it.'

Angel sat on a chair, ignoring, possibly not even seeing, Abbott's newly outstretched hand. She crossed her legs exactly as if she had clothes on, and said, 'The bastard probably never even heard of me.'

'Well, of course he did. Anyway, we sent your tapes, didn't we?'

'If he bothered to listen to them.'

'Why should he talk to us unless he was interested?'

'Fellas like Snow, big dealers, they never mean a word they say.'

'How can you know—you never met the man?'

'I've met plenty like him.'

The truth was, Abbott thought, she probably had. Small-time, of course, but the type did not change, it was international. He sighed. 'Angel, we are over the big hurdle. We are going to talk to the man today. Come to bed.'

Angel ignored that. She moodily inspected her toenails, which were painted silver. 'You sure you sent him the right photos? The Bailey ones?'

'Of course I did.'

'Not the others, those ones that made me look *thirty*?'

She made it sound obscene.

'No, the Bailey ones. Don't worry. It'll be all right.'

Abbott recognised in his voice the tone he had used when talking to his children, when they were young and distressed. The comparison saddened him. He missed them (and Helen too, sometimes) and the house. And even the garden, which had been simply there, as far as he was concerned, to walk in, but which Helen had tended lovingly, delicately, as she did everything she touched. It astonished him now that occasionally he looked back to it as to a haven, whereas when he had been imprisoned there (Helen's word to him at the final tearing break-up, 'You always thought of it as a prison, you always hated it!') he had forever fretted about what was happening to other men on the other side of the hill. A needling, fortyish ache for a different life, dismissed as a regretful pipe-dream by most men his age. Not, in the end, by him. The money had brought the dream real. He was now, this minute, actually on the other side of the hill. Abbott checked his thoughts : what was this ridiculous nostalgia for smoky suburbia all about? The world was his to choose from, and he had chosen. He smiled at Angel's golden body, and told himself, I like it in this place I have chosen.

'He'll flip when he sees you.'

Angel said, a trifle mollified, but still anxious for reassurance, 'Snow's used to big stars. I'll be a nobody to him.'

'No, you won't. He isn't all that used to big stars either. He takes unknowns and makes stars of them.'

'In his last big Broadway musical he had a top star.'

'It flopped.'

The remark cheered her, as he knew it would.

'You're right, Mister Snow had a flop! That's good, I like that, that makes him human.'

'Everybody has a flop sometime, everybody has a disaster,' Abbott said, gently. He did not want to be there on opening-night, if ever this whole project came real, and find himself staring into Angel's eyes, the show truly a flop.

But Angel laughed and got to her feet and danced round the room, her breasts so firm that they hardly shook, and called out, 'Not me, I'm never gonna have a disaster, never, never, never!' and he knew it was no use talking about failure to her. She had come from too unlikely a place. To get to this point was almost as much a miracle for her as the money had been for him. Perhaps there was something else besides the flesh, after all?

He reached for her wrist. 'Come to bed, there's time.'

Angel pirouetted around the bed, showing to him first her trim bottom and then her flat belly and the dance (perfectly executed, she *had* been a dancer, after all, if only in a chorus-line) took her to the bathroom door. She stopped there, a little breathless and smiled at him, lips parted. His groin stirred, and he got out of the bed and made for her.

'You bloody tease, you!'

'No, no time, we have to go at nine, right?'

And the bathroom door slammed, just as he reached it.

Abbott hammered on the door. 'Hey, come out!'

Inside, water flushed and roared.

'I'm having my bath now. You'd better pack. You're the one always saying we haven't much time.'

Abbott laughed, gave the door a last thump and threw himself down on the bed. He did not wear pyjamas with Angel (with Helen he always had, buttoned up, right from the beginning) probably because his skin was brown now, after a month at Cannes in October. His fingers explored his waistline, feeling for the roll of fat that had been there a year ago; hardly any. The expensive course of slimming, at the best clinic in the Home Counties, had got rid of it, and the workouts at Jack Solomons' gym had put muscle in its place. He had not been so fit, or looked so good, since he had finished his army service. While he was married to Helen he had always been starting on a slimming course, or a keep-fit course, and abandoning it after a few days or weeks. For a very good reason : there had been no need to go through the punishing routines for Helen. She had always laughed at his efforts and kissed him, and said, 'I love you, fat or thin.' The remark had irritated him then, as the recollection did now. The memory of himself, twenty pounds overweight, the collar straining at his throat, the waist-band of his trousers tightening after each too-large meal, was a ridiculous one. He had tried to drown himself in food, and in work, and in Helen. None of it had been enough, in the end, when the real test came—the money.

It had not happened all that quickly, simply he had not expected it to be so much, when, finally, he rested to count it. The buy into television shares, when the companies were first formed, had been a slice of astonishing good luck. The group had wanted an accountant who understood show-business dealings and he had happened to be around. There had been no money to spare to pay his fees. Any there was had to go on the 'presentation'—the document that would decide whether the consortium would be given the priceless franchise, or get nothing at all. His own work had been easy enough, simply to make sense of their possible assets and to check that they would have backers in the City of London, if their application should succeed. There was nothing to that—any banker would come in with a big smile and an open cheque, once the consortium had the franchise; but the members, mostly showbiz people, producers, actors and directors, had not known much about that. Abbott was personal accountant to several of them (working, as he did, for a big showbiz agency) and they trusted him. They had offered, in the casual, easy way of such people, a seat on the board if they were successful, and a hatful of shares in the company. All that, old Jack, as one of them had said, arm round Abbott's shoulder in the Savoy Grill, all that but no cash now; what say?

Abbott had said yes, what else could he say?

It had been the best decision, anyway the most momentous decision, he had ever taken. Against all the odds, the unlikely consortium had been given the franchise—a licence, as another lucky applicant had once said, to print your own money—and Abbott had simply, overnight, become very, very rich.

That had been four years ago. Three of those years had been taken up with work. Then he had met Angel. Of course, he knew who she was, the moment he met her at the party. Her face smiled from the television screen every Monday evening, in a popular advice-giving panel game. She was on it, the producer had told Abbott tipsily and confidentially, because she had wonderful tits and wonderful teeth. The producer had, in the user's manner of such people, thought her just another beautiful scrubber. He had

5

never expected her to come up with any good advice. But she had, salty and funny and practical advice, based, Abbott supposed, on experience, although she was only twenty-four, or so the publicity handouts—which Abbott sent for the next day—insisted. Angel's commonsensical replies to the fatuous questions had become mildly famous. She had been the first woman to use a four-letter word on British television. It had come out so smoothly and naturally that most viewers had not really registered it, at the moment. Abbott had registered it. He had watched her say it, and from that moment he had wanted her, sexually. The scandalous incident had created a sensation in the British press and the show had been taken off the air, for, as everybody at the Network piously insisted, a rest.

'Why the hell do we need a rest?' Angel had demanded. 'The people want to hear me say it again, they'll switch on in their millions in the hope I might.'

Abbott knew that she was right, but although the publicity had been useful to her, it had landed her without a job. She had told Abbott, at the party to celebrate the last show, that all she had been offered was a nudie part in a horror film. He remembered the conversation word by word, because from it everything had stemmed.

'What will you do? Take it?'

He had kept his eyes from her golden, unsupported breasts with great difficulty.

'Hell no, it's a rubbish movie. I can't see the billing, Angel da Sousa in *Vampire Virgins,* can *you*?'

'No, but you have to do something?'

'I suppose.' She was wearing a dress cut to her thigh and three men—all much younger than Abbott—were standing around, holding drinks, just staring at her. Abbott found this offensive, but she did not seem to mind or even notice.

'Nothing else in sight, nothing at all?'

Angel opened her huge dark eyes and looked straight into his. 'Well, I do have a script for a musical.'

'Oh yes, what's it called?'

'*Paradiso.*'

'Is it good?'

'It would be good for me, if I could find anybody to put it on.'

That had been the moment to withdraw, into the smoking, sweating crush, to move on to the next, safe group with a grunt and a smile, to allow the quickest of the joyless young men eyeing her to step in and make claim. Abbott had not taken advantage of the moment. Instead, he had said, somewhat astonished at himself, 'I'd like to read it.'

'I didn't know you were on the production side?' The dark eyes widened. 'What do you do exactly, Mister Abbott?'

'Jack.'

'I don't like Jack. I like Abbott.'

'Then call me that. I'm the company accountant.'

'A money-man?'

'Sort of.'

'I have a copy of the script at my place.'

Angel had smiled then, and Abbott could have wished the smile had come earlier, when she didn't know who he was, but what the hell, if a man was somebody, then he had to expect that. Women gravitated towards success; it wasn't new, when hadn't they? It was in their natures. Unless they were new women, denying it all, protesting too much. Anyway, those kind of women had never appealed to him. But he did not mind the aristocracy of real talent. His work in the agency had brought him in contact with enough of it to recognise it, when he saw it. He smiled back at the black-haired girl, and said, happy and suddenly reckless, 'Then I'll come and read it.'

'Now?'

'Why not, the party's nearly over?'

She looked round. 'Yes, it is, isn't it?'

Abbott had left with her and a lot of people had noticed. He had not cared.

It had all started then, the return to life, or more likely, since Abbott had been studying textbooks and account books since he was sixteen, his first real crack at living. The other lucky men, who had won the money with him (he still thought of it as a gambler's throw), had fared no better than himself. Some had taken to drink, one or two to illness, a couple to megalomania. He had taken to Angel. Helen had seen it happening, and had not understood. Why was it that the only women who knew anything about men were the whores, actual or temperamental? Ordinary nice women never knew, which was why they had to be protected. That, at least, had been the theory, except that he had not been able to protect Helen, in the end. He had not been able to protect himself.

So it had all begun, the parties and the air-flights to Paris and Rome and the drinking (it always seemed to be champagne, he had discovered quite a taste for champagne) and finally the large Mayfair apartment rented for Angel, in his name, and the late-night visits straight from the office, his mind reeling with figures (Christ, the money they were all making!) and then the falling into bed, the frenzied outpouring of his sexual want for her. It had, from the very first night, been a physical relationship, and he had not wanted any other. Not until it was too late, after Helen's discovery of the keys to the apartment, the lipstick marks, the scent, the telephoned reports from girl-friends who had seen him with Angel in public places. He had become very careless, a part of him—the deprived lust-for-life part—wanted Helen to know, to end the deceit, to set him free; and another part, the accountant part, said no, what kind of emotional book-keeping is this?

Emotionally, he had gone into the red with Angel, the dark reds of desire and need, and he had been helpless to stop himself. No more, he thought, than he could now. He was still in the middle of it, there had been no slow-down. Adroitly (he supposed) Angel gave him no chance to become used to her. He had never lived with her in any permanent place. She insisted on keeping her own apartment, and that Abbott lived somewhere else. It hurt him a little that she didn't seem to care where he lived. In the end he had moved out from Helen into a small service-flat near his office.

'Do you love her?' Helen had demanded, at the end, still anguished and shocked.

'I think I must.'

'Surely you know?'

'No, I bloody well don't know. All I know is I must be with her.'

'And for *that* you'd give up everything? The house, the children, me?'

'What do you mean, for *that*? You say it as if it's nothing! I married you for *that*, and now you talk as if it's dirty!'

'So it is, so it is, you and her! She's only a . . .'

'Shut up, Helen.'

'Oh go and screw her, it's all she's *for*. You'd throw us all away, and your job, for *that*!'

'It won't affect my job!'

Of course, it had. Finally, he had requested a year's leave and the chairman had not asked any questions. Probably he knew the facts about Angel by then, they were common enough property.

'Jack, you don't need to come back if you don't want to, you know that. We've got fifty good accountants now.'

Abbott had shaken his head. 'Maybe I won't.'

That was the day Snow had telephoned from New York, the dark brown voice faint over the transatlantic telephone.

'Mister Abbott, I got the tapes and the script you sent, through Morris Simons.'

'Oh, good.'

'I like them, I think there's maybe something here.'

'You like the script?'

'Quite a lot, yes. Mainly I like the tapes.'

'Would you be interested in doing a production, I mean in directing it?'

Snow had hesitated, coughed politely, faraway and wary. 'Well, I tell you, Mister Abbott, about that I haven't made up my mind, I'd like, y'know, to talk to you about it?'

An electric joy had coursed through Abbott's limbs. He thought of Angel's ecstatic face when he told her such news. But he had merely said, in what she called his accountant's voice, 'Why don't we do that?'

Snow had coughed, again. 'I don't know that I have any plans to come to England at this time.'

'We could both come to New York?'

'You could?'

'Yes.'

'You and Miss er . . . ?'

'Da Sousa. Angel da Sousa.'

'When?'

'Next week maybe?'

'Great. You'll have to talk to my agent first, of course.'

'Naturally.'

There had been a pause. 'One thing, Mister Abbott . . . ?'

'Yes?'

'Had you thought about backing?'

'If need be, I could find the backing.'

'You could?'

'If it wasn't a huge extravaganza. And it isn't that, is it?'

'I don't know, I haven't thought about costs yet.'

'Well, I was thinking of Shaftesbury Avenue first, Broadway later.'

'We'd need a top impresario.'

9

'I've talked to Cowan . . .'

'Rex Cowan?'

'He said if you liked it, he'd handle that end of things.'

'He did?' Snow's voice had been suddenly respectful. 'Then let's meet very soon. You'll cable my agent to confirm?'

'Right.'

'Oh, and I look forward to meeting Miss da Sousa. Great pictures you sent.'

'Thanks, goodbye.'

Angel, when he told her, had flipped. Her arms had gone round his neck, and they had waltzed around her apartment, Abbott carrying the bottle of Brut he had brought to celebrate, and she had cried out, 'Snow! New York! Next *week*?'

'That's right.'

'Oh, Abbott, you're so good to me.'

'I thought we might go down to the cottage for the weekend?'

'Oh, yes, fine, great, let's do that!'

And so they had gone, and walked in the woods, tweeded and suèded, not talking much, Angel throwing away the hard, professional mask of capability and eagerness and, sometimes, manic enthusiasm. Here, in the country, hand-in-hand, soft turf underfoot, it was difficult to believe she was the same girl. The excitements of town, the drinking, the spiced food, the late hours, the slam of car doors and the falling asleep at dawn—all that was as if it had never been. Here Angel was kindly, where she was irritable in town. Here she was loving, where in town she was offhand and preoccupied. Here she found time to be womanly. Their sex was leisurely and natural, and not the frantic, exhausted thing it was apt to be at the end of a long restless day of conferences and late drinking and eating. They ate plain food at midday, steaks and eggs and coffee, and went to bed early and slept late. With her soft young body in his arms, rested and happy, Abbott would waken to birdsong and the waft of sharp, pure air from the open windows.

'We ought to come and live here one day.'

Angel stirred, took his hand and put it on her breast. 'Um, it's great.'

'No, I mean, really live here.'

She opened one eye. 'You'd hate it.'

'No, I wouldn't. I want you all to myself.'

Angel opened the other eye. 'Do you mean it?'

'Of course.'

'I couldn't. Not yet.'

Abbott kissed her. 'I know.'

'I have to work, Abbott.' Her tone was serious, and she looked at him as if she cared.

'I know you do.'

'I have to!'

'I know.'

'I've got to do it, to make it, or bust trying!'

'You'll make it, don't worry. You have a real talent.'

'Do you really think I will? I mean really?'

Her voice was very soft and tentative, and nothing like the voice she used in town, in the studios and agents' offices and in the fashionable restaurants. All that was armour, Abbott knew. This was the real, soft, vulnerable flesh. 'Of course you will.' He added, 'Then you'll fly away.'

'I won't, Abbott, I won't, honestly. I won't leave you, ever.'

Abbott ran his hand down her soft belly. 'I know, I know.'

'But I won't!'

'All right.'

'You don't believe me.' Her voice was sulky. He had reminded her that there was sixteen years' difference in their ages. It was unfair. He should not do it, it was self-indulgent. 'You think all I care about is being a success, that I'll go Charley Star if I do, and nobody will be able to talk to me.'

'It happens to most people.'

'Not to me, I've seen it too often.' Her tone was sad, wondering, and Abbott knew that she did not know, any more than he did, what success, if it were to touch her, would do to her. Her arms went round him tightly, and her mouth was on his, and then he was in her moist body and the reds and blacks of desire drowned them both. Afterwards, the sheets thrown back, she said, drawing on his cigarette, 'Abbott, I know what you gave up for me. I wouldn't be a bitch to you.'

'I didn't give up anything for you.'

'You did, I know you did. Your kids . . .'

'No. If it hadn't been you it would have been somebody else.'

Angel pouted. 'Charming!'

'No, I mean, it was coming, that's all.' He kissed her. 'But it was you, and I'm glad.'

'Why?'

'You know.'

She touched her smooth belly, the bush of coarse black hair. 'Not just this?'

'No.' He smiled at her. 'Not just that.'

'Why then, I mean really?'

How could he tell her that she excited him, that it was all in that one word? He said, 'Because I love you.'

That was easier.

'I don't like to say that to anybody.' Angel frowned. 'It's too much, y'know?'

'It's all right. I don't expect you to say it.'

Angel passed the cigarette back to him. 'I'm a bitch to you. I spoil your life and I won't even say I love you.'

'You didn't. And I don't care.'

Her dark eyes brooded. 'I meant what I said, Abbott. You've been good to me. You're good *for* me. I'm happy with you.'

'Don't promise. Those reasons . . . Sometimes they aren't enough.'

'Oh, Abbott, I really am a bitch sometimes, but . . . I have to be like that, oh, I mean hard-shelled and like tough, or else I'll get trodden under, I'll just be another scrubber from nowhere who thinks she can sing.'

'Never.'

'It could happen.'

'No, it couldn't.'

'Who could stop it?'

'I could.'

'You have your job. You'll have to go back to it sometime?'

'No, I have you. I want . . . ' Abbott was careless, he said more than he meant to. 'I want to see you make it, I want to be there all the way.'

'All the way?'

'While you want me.'

'I'll always . . .'

' . . . Don't say it.'

'Well, I will.'

'All right.' Abbott laughed. 'To prove it, why don't you do one thing?'

Her fingers touched his body. 'Anything.'

'Get up and fry eggs and bacon.'

'God, you're asking a lot, aren't you?'

'Yes.'

'Just to show you, then.' And she had leapt out of bed and gone downstairs and made breakfast, and he could hear her singing (a throaty, beautiful voice, better, surely, than any other of its kind he had heard?) and then she came back upstairs, nude but for a tiny apron, with coffee, eggs and bacon, on a tray. They had eaten with enormous appetite, and at the end of it, drinking their last cups of coffee, she had said, 'Abbott, I need you. You're good for me. And I wouldn't be going to such exciting places without you. New York, wow!'

And so here they were, in New York, and Snow was in Bermuda, waiting for them. His note to Abbott had said that he was going before them to 'think out a few ideas', and would they care to follow on, as his guests? Abbott supposed that this was the way people like Snow worked, but it did not matter, really, how he worked, so long as he was prepared to direct the musical. 'The action of *Paradiso*,' Abbott had told Angel, 'takes place on a sub-tropical island. Bermuda is such a place. What better than to discuss it there?'

'So long as he isn't running away from us,' Angel had replied sulkily. Abbott had reassured her, and thrown in the sightseeing trip around New York while he talked with Snow's agent. He was sorry that Angel had got very little from the trip, but not surprised. Her mind was a truly creative and ambitious one. She felt that any action that was not in some way work was a waste of time and energy. He did not mind that now. He had grown used to it. The idyllic episode in the cottage was forgotten. This was business.

Abbott lit a cigarette and got up from the bed and looked out of the window. Tiny figures, way down, walked around in top-coats. It was still cold in New York in April. Bermuda would be warm, that was something to look forward to. He slammed on the bathroom door again.

'Come on, darling, you've been in there hours!'

'Okay, coming!'

The door opened and Angel, in a towel, stood there smiling. She seemed to have recovered her good humour and rewarded Abbott with a kiss in which her tongue was prominent. He put his arms around her and the towel dropped to the floor. Half-looking at his watch, Abbott bore her back towards the bed. As he did so there was a rap on the door and a Spanish-sounding voice called, 'Breakfast, sir!'

Abbott grabbed the towel and disappeared into the bathroom.

He opened the door again, quickly. 'Put on a robe!'

Angel turned smiling. She hadn't.

'What?'

'Put on a robe or something!'

She could have forgotten. It was possible.

'Oh sure.' She slipped into his bathrobe.

'And give the boy a dollar.'

'Huh?'

'Change on the side table.'

'Oh. Right.'

She opened the door to the smiling, elderly Puerto Rican. Abbott closed the bathroom door smartly, and got under the cold shower. The icy water stung his body and cooled all thoughts of sex. The day took on the perspectives of work, or what passed for work in his life nowadays: the promotion of Angel da Sousa. Abbott turned the water to 'hot', soaped himself liberally, and sang. On the whole, he felt optimistic. The proposition he had made to Snow on the telephone in London ten days before must look good to the famous director. 'A hard man maybe, a little chip on the shoulder,' Morris Simons, the famous agent, had told him. 'But who wouldn't be if they were as clever as he is, and black?' Morris had smiled his wise smile, and pulled on his cigar and said, idly, 'This girl's good, is she, I mean not just in bed, but a good artist?'

Abbott had sweated, but kept his voice level.

'She's a personality, but I don't swear to talent, because I'm not good enough to know it when I see it. All I can go on are opinions and you've seen her press notices? They couldn't be much better if she'd written them herself?'

'That's a careful answer,' Morris had said.

'Let's say, I think she has great potential.'

'You're not a production man, Jack, you'll pardon me asking but how do you know?'

'You've talked to her. She has a quality of her own. She's an original. *And* she can sing.'

'Is that the lover or the accountant talking, Jack?'

Abbott had looked out of the Savage Club window, across St. James's to the Palace. 'Both, Morris.'

'I like that answer.' Morris had settled deeper in his leather arm-chair. 'And I like this club.'

'I'll put you up for membership, if you like?'

Morris shook his head. 'Not in London enough to be worth it.

But thank you, Jack, you're a nice guy.' Morris had gestured with his havana, 'And I'll have another port, okay?'

'George, two large club ports,' Abbott had told the club servant, adding, in the English manner, 'If you will be so kind?'

The port had come and Morris had mused, and, finally, he had said, 'Jack, could you stand a little advice?'

Abbott held up his hand. 'Are you going to tell me that just because I've left my wife and kids and I'm shacked up with this girl that's no reason to lose my wallet as well?'

'All right.' Morris had shaken his balding head. 'All right. Forget I spoke.'

'Gladly,' Abbott had said, 'because *Paradiso* could make money.'

'For everybody's sake,' Morris said, with deep professional caution, 'I certainly hope so.' But he had taken the tapes and the Bailey photographs and, by so doing, given the business his blessing. That had influenced Snow, must have. Now all they had to do was convince him some more. Abbott got out of the shower, towelled himself dry, and began to shave, using a new electric razor, a present from Angel, bought the previous day at Macy's. Angel often bought him small presents and it touched him, in an absurd way. Also, it seemed to give her pleasure. The mirror showed him a face that was handsome, in a fair-skinned Scandinavian way, a little heavy around the chin, but with abundant fair hair. For that, he was grateful. He ran a comb through the hair. He was wearing it long these days, and without pomade, for it was not possible to be around Angel in anything but the conventional style of the day. He went out of the bathroom—Angel was sitting at the table drinking coffee and reading the *New York Times* show-page—and rummaged in his wardrobe. Abbott still hated sitting down to breakfast half-dressed. He supposed it was a hangover from his puritanical days, before the money. He pulled on a cream shirt and selected a large-knot Macclesfield-silk tie, in a dull bronze. Angel had changed his tastes. A suit, and collar and tie of an English cut, such as he had always worn, when he was living with Helen, would be ridiculous now. He compromised by wearing blazers and slacks, and suits in suède and corduroy. These were young in style, but did not make him feel foolish. Or not very. Until now he had avoided extreme fashion. No silk scarf had yet been wrapped around his neck. It was, he thought, only a matter of time.

'Come and sit down, darling, your coffee will be cold.'

Angel's clothes of the previous day were still scattered all over the room, but she made no move to collect them together. Abbott knew that she would leave everything to the last minute. She always did. He drank his coffee, and chewed on his toast and jelly a trifle sadly. He was always sorry to leave New York, despite the feeling of insecurity it always gave him, in the darkness hours. It had taken him quite a long time to convince Angel that some central streets in the city were not safe after sunset, that the whole metropolis changed character, abruptly, once darkness fell. So they always took a cab, and he felt easier. Angel had no sense of fear of this kind. 'If you were born where I was, it would take more than a mugger to scare you.'

Abbott never followed up such leads. When Angel wanted to tell him the facts of her childhood she would tell him. That they had been hard was obvious. She had talked to him about Stepney, and the old slum house in which she was born, no father there either, just an uncaring and feckless mother, now dead. Or Angel sometimes said she was. Other times she said she sent her money. Abbott did not know what to believe. It did not matter. Angel was herself, that was all.

They had finished their coffee when the desk-clerk rang, to remind them they had a plane to catch. Abbott swiftly packed his valise. He never carried anything he could buy at the other end, like spare shirts, one small consolation of being rich. It took the ministrations of two chambermaids to get Angel's two large cases finally packed. She had shopped a lot in New York, out of boredom perhaps, buying trendy clothes and boots she might never wear.

'You'll be overweight again at the airport,' he said.

'Does it matter?'

Abbott smiled, ironically. 'Not really.'

The cabby was impressed by Angel, who had elected to wear purple hot-pants and a white leather maxi-coat with long thigh-length white boots. He looked often in his mirror, and finally managed to open the conversation.

'You Briddish, sir?'

'That's right.'

'The liddle lady too?'

'Right.'

The cabby chewed his gum. 'You showbiz folks?'

'In a way.'

'The liddle lady sing or sumpin?'

It was amazing how they always knew.

'She sings *and* dances.'

The cabby navigated them on to the airport route. 'I tort so. She looks like it, y'know?' He chewed. 'Been on any television, lady?'

Angel said, 'Only in England.'

'Not in the States?'

'Not yet.'

'Gonna be, huh?'

'I certainly hope so.'

Angel always took trouble, always to Abbott's surprise. The cabby was her potential public, anybody was her potential public. So she was nice to them. It was as simple as that. If wanting and effort stood for anything in the realisation of Angel's kind of talent, and they did, then sooner or later, one way or another, she would make it.

'Whaddya say ya name was, miss?'

'Angel da Sousa.'

There was a hesitation. There always was.

'That would be?'

'Spanish.'

'Spanish?'

'Spanish name, but British.'

The cabby's work-worn face, which looked as if it had been bloodlessly gashed by a thousand razors, creased into a rare and terrible smile.

'I'll look out for ya.'

'Thank you.'

'My pleasure.'

Angel leaned back in the car, her face slightly warm, as always after an encounter with somebody about her work, even at such a ridiculous remove as this. Abbott was, none the less, touched. His hand went out and covered hers. She turned and looked at him in surprise. He withdrew his fingers. The dream was a private one. Nobody could share it. He did not feel sad, only a little sorry.

The cab swished (it was raining now, a persistent drizzle) into Kennedy airport. 'Where you going, sir?'

'Bermuda.'

'You're a lucky fella.'

'We hope so.'

'Some people get born lucky,' the cabby sighed to nobody in particular, tooling to a stop outside the flights entrance. Abbott realised that it was a compliment. He got out of the cab, tipped the cabby two dollars, and looked around the airport. Kennedy always excited him. Like the city itself, it was overcrowded, over-populated, over-busy, but alive. They found a sky-pilot for their baggage, and checked in. For once, they were on time, Abbott having told Angel that the flight left half an hour before it actually did. Otherwise, he knew, they would have been sitting in some traffic-jam at that very moment. Angel was untidy, and unpunc-tual, she lived off the cuff. Abbott had seen, in her London apart-ment, underclothes thrown to the ground and, quite simply, left for days on end. After Helen's compulsive neatness it had outraged him, but he had rationalised his horror. It simply did not matter that Angel lived that way. It was part of her, like the desire to win acclaim. It almost certainly stemmed from the same training, or lack of it. People from very well-run homes, like himself, rarely made good artists, he had noticed. Art was the business of making a pattern out of disorder. To do that you had to know something about disorder. A suburban upbringing, like his own, was abso-lutely no training for the arts. He watched Angel, as she opened her Mappin's lizard bag (fifty guineas, he'd bought it for her) and rummaged amongst the chaos inside. Lipstick, keys, cigarettes, she never could find anything in a hurry.

'What are you looking for, darling?'

'Tickets?'

'I have them.' Abbott presented the tickets to the girl clerk in the large but quiet lounge. Not too many people were going to the Islands today, it seemed. He remarked on it.

'No, sir. You are early season, but the weather's good, so the reports say. If you take a seat you'll be called in about twenty minutes.'

'Hey, we're early!' Angel looked at him accusingly.

'For once.'

'You lied to me about the flight time.'

'Right.'

She deliberately kissed him full on the lips, and the girl clerk did not avert her gaze. Abbott felt embarrassed, and not a little proud, as he always did when Angel did things like that.

'What was that for?'

'Being you.'

They sat down and people stared at them, as people always did. Abbott was almost used to it by now, but at times he flinched. Angel was showing rather a lot of leg, as usual, and two young men on a form opposite gazed at her hotly, their adolescent faces flushing.

'Pull your skirt down.'

'I don't have a skirt on.'

'Then cover your legs.'

'Why?'

'Those two young men are almost ejaculating on the spot.'

'Ah, let them enjoy themselves.'

'But they aren't, that's the point. They're in pain.'

'Huh?'

'Helpless pain.'

'Abbott,' Angel said, tolerantly, 'you do talk some awful crap sometimes.'

The two-hour flight was uneventful. The aircraft was only half-full, mostly of New Yorkers escaping to the sun. Angel closed her eyes and slept instantly, rejecting the plastic food and drink. Abbott ordered a gin and tonic, which turned out, as usual, to be a lot stronger than he was accustomed to. American liquor, he reminded himself (not for the first time), was thirty-over-proof stronger than European spirit, and the measure larger. So, take it easy. There was no point in breaking the rigid diet-and-exercise campaign just because he was anxious for Angel. If Snow wanted to do the thing he would do it. Drinking large anxious gins on aircraft would not help him make up his mind. He left half the drink, feeling very righteous, and closed his eyes. When he opened them, the aircraft was losing height, and, looking out of the window, he saw, as if by a trick, jewelled in the poster-blue sea, the Island.

It was shaped like a croissant, and lay golden-fringed and green, shimmering in the sun, which was now hot on the observation-window. They lost height rapidly, and now he could see the small houses, stuccoed pink-and-white, with tiled roofs, nestling back from the sharp greens of the lawns. There was something curiously English about it all, at first he could not think what. Then he realised it was scale. The houses were small, and mostly stood in sub-tropical gardens. Whoever had originally landscaped these places had thought in small plots, had based it on the English yeoman tradition. The houses themselves had a Spanish look, with their verandahs and wooden shutters, but the scale was implacably English. Abbott smiled. A small sub-tropical England, three thousand miles from home.

They landed smoothly, and suddenly they were on the postage-stamp airfield, released from the aircraft, to walk, with hand-luggage, the hundred yards to the customs building. Angel was barely awake; one of her talents was the ability to sleep anytime she liked. Now she stood on the airfield and breathed the soft, balmy air, and turned her face to the sun, and said, 'Abbott, you bring me to some lovely places.'

Abbott felt absurdly pleased, and he must have shown it, for she added, distantly, 'You should cool it a bit with me, you really should.' Then she walked on.

Abbott thought, walking through the customs shed behind her, into the car park, a porter staggering under the weight of Angel's trunks, that he had never been able to cool his feelings from the first time he had seen her.

'Your hotel, sir?'

'Royalty, Hamilton, please.'

They got into the cab and were instantly impressed by the smile of the middle-aged, negro driver. 'Takes twenty minutes, sir.'

'Don't rush it. We want to look at the place.'

'I can't rush it, sir. Twenty-mile speed limit.'

'That so?'

'Your first trip?'

'That's right.'

'It won't be the last. Folks always come back, that's what they say.'

The taxi droned out of the airport. Abbott looked out, with interest. As they drove along towards the river-bridge they never, at any time, seemed to be free of the sea's presence. It loomed through sea-dune, and fringed palm-tree. Abbott said, 'Why do I see so many people on these small motor-bikes?'

'If you ain't a resident, you can't have no car.'

Abbott was dismayed. 'You mean I can't hire one?'

'No, sir. 'Gainst the law. Island's only twenty-two miles long, see? 'Till nineteen-thirty-seven, no cars allowed at all. All horses and cabs. It was real nice and quiet then.'

'It's pretty quiet now.'

The driver shook his head. 'Bit more hard to walk. Sometimes I think we spoiled now!'

Abbott saw what he meant. The roads were small and winding, like rural English roads, and like England every turn brought a fresh, miniature view, but of sub-tropical gardens, of bright plants and soft, shadowed, crabgrass lawns. In this climate the lawns would need great and loving care. He thought of how Helen would love it here : the lavish greenery of the place, the sudden jungle blooms, nature's wild paradise tamed. He said to Angel, 'Lovely gardens, don't you wish you . . . ?' And stopped.

'What?'

'Nothing.'

He had spoken to her as if to Helen.

'You said don't I wish *what*?'

' . . . Oh, that you lived here?' he said, off-hand, quickly.

'It's great, sure,' Angel said, 'but what do you *do* . . . ?' She paused.

Abbott knew she meant, with her talent? He patted her arm. 'I know, just wondering.'

'Lovely place to settle down to die, anyway.'

Her voice was sober and he was surprised.

'Nowhere's a lovely place to die.'

'This would be.' She seemed serious.

The cab drove on, through the lanes, occasionally passing the odd tourist on his bicyclette, face reddened or bronzed, the whole exercise taking place at never more than twenty miles an hour. Abbott leaned back, and relaxed. This was going to be pleasant, on a physical level at least, this was a pace that could be lived with. He thought of the blaring, relentless traffic of New York or even London, and smiled at the cab driver's idea of spoiled. He sat back and took in the panorama of lane and sea and sand, and the occasional fin of white sail against the water.

'Just coming into Hamilton now, sir. We don't get into the town really. Your hotel's this side.'

The Royalty loomed majestic and pink out of lawns and fronded trees. The foyer had a real waterfall tinkling down from the roof. Angel stood and gazed at it.

'You throw money in for good luck, miss,' said the porter, smiling. 'Especially if you is on honeymoon.'

Angel laughed. 'I'll throw some in anyway.' She fumbled in the chaos of her purse. 'Does it matter if it's British?'

'In this Island, money's money, like any place else, I guess.'

Angel showered coins into the water.

'There!'

'Good luck, miss.'

'Thank you!' She turned to Abbott, delighted. There was something very childlike about her. It was as if she had had no childhood, that these kind of experiences were absolutely new and to be prized, as a child might prize them. He waved, then turned to the desk, and signed the hotel book.

'Two adjoining singles, sir?'

'Yes.'

The clerk, who looked absurdly English, paused. 'Yourself and Miss . . . da Sousa?'

'That's correct.'

The clerk glanced briefly across the lounge at Angel, who was still throwing small coins into the waterfall.

'Her name is Spanish, her passport is British.' Abbott held up the small pasteboard book in an irritable gesture.

The clerk blinked. 'Of course, sir. For one week? That will be fine.'

He pressed a bell and Abbott sighed. *That* was over.

Their rooms were large and opulent, and gave out on to a balcony overlooking a central courtyard, with the pool at one end of it. The sea encroached, as always, at the end of the courtyard, and on the three sides of the headland on which the hotel stood.

'Isn't this great?'

Angel was on the balcony, looking far out past the flags on the three main flagposts facing out to sea. The Union Jack, the Stars and Stripes and the Maple Leaf.

'What's that flag?'

'Canadian.'

'Why?'

'A lot of people fly down here from Nova Scotia.'

'Do they?'

'It isn't far and it's probably got something to do with precedent, like most things. This island is the oldest British possession in this hemisphere. It has links with Canada and the States, going way back. And the South, for that matter. It's just an accident it's still British.'

'Let's swim, huh?'

'Might as well. Snow will contact us, he said.'

They went down to the pool and there the resemblance to anything British was not in evidence. Most of the other swimmers (or rather sunbathers) were American, and in many ways it reminded Abbott of another great hotel of the world, the Beverly Hills—only here there were no telephones at the side of the pool. This was not a place of business, at any remove, and just as well, he thought. He settled down in a low chair (he had changed before they came down) and smeared oil on his body. The tan must be preserved, and with it the desirability. He smiled, it did not sound like Jack Abbott, accountant, the hard-working suburban boy, sweating on exams and possible promotion. He put on dark glasses. The truth was that Jack Abbott was dead, or he hoped he was.

There was a stir around the pool and Abbott opened his eyes. Inevitably, the source of interest was Angel. She stood, golden bronze, utterly relaxed, on the diving-board. Angel slowly and deliberately adjusted her pink bikini. The men's heads around the pool were all up, by now. Several had removed their sun-glasses to get a better view. The women around the pool kept theirs on, staring implacably at the dark-haired girl. It was impossible to guess their thoughts; but when Angel's body had broken the water, they turned to each other and conversed in low tones, glancing back towards the girl from time to time. Abbott sighed. It was always like this. Until Angel revealed that she was an entertainer, until she put herself forward for their love, the women would hate her. Once they could discuss her, criticise her performance, feel free to have a point of view about her, then the resentments would fall away. Until they did, it was something she had to live with, and Abbott, because he was with her, had to live with it, too. He closed his eyes and let the sun caress his body. They had not been in the sun for three months (at Tenerife for two weeks in January) and he had missed it. Nowadays, he was learning to live in the sun a good deal of the time. When he had been living with Helen it had been difficult to get him away at all. He had always found travel very tiring in those days, probably because he had been work-exhausted before he went. Now his life was devoted to himself. And, of course, to Angel. *This* was all very restful, but sometimes the pursuit of pleasure was exhausting. A gentle weariness came over him, and he dozed.

'Mister Abbott?'

He wakened sharply. A black man, of short but very muscular stature, was looking down at him. He was dressed in a T-shirt and slacks, both black and of shiny material, and his head was close-cropped and woolly. The arms were extraordinarily long and at some time or other the nose had been broken and badly re-set. Dark glasses protected the eyes, but there was no reserve in the stance, which was alert and birdlike. Abbott knew the man from his photographs in the newspapers.

'Mister Snow?'

'Right.'

'Did you ask at the desk ... ?'

'Hell, no, I asked one of the waiters. I'm a local boy.'

'I thought you were from New York?'

'Spent my grown-up life there, but I was born right here, in this iddy-biddy little paradise, man.'

Abbott decided that the gone-coon thing was an act and ignored it.

'Sit down.' He indicated a striped chair. 'Let me get you a drink.'

Snow did not sit down. He looked around the pool, his eyes flickering behind the glasses. Abbott beckoned to a waiter. 'Two planter's punches? That's the local drink, all right?'

Snow smiled, showing beautiful teeth. 'It's the local drink, so long as you ain't local. It's the local drink for tourists. Those ole locals like me just has plain ole rum.'

Abbott began to signal again, but Snow slumped down in the chair.

'Don't bother. I can drink what you ordered. I can drink anything.' He glowered round the pool, Abbott thought, a trifle defiantly. Certainly a few of the tourists seemed to be looking in their direction, but Abbott reasoned that tourists would look at anything that moved.

'I still don't understand,' Abbott said, 'about your waiter friend knowing where we were. We told nobody ...'

'Waiters know everything that happens in a hotel,' Snow said. He lit a cigarette, American fashion, from a soft pack, without offering it to Abbott. 'It's their business to know. You ever been a waiter?'

'No.' Abbott laughed.

'I have.' Snow did not laugh. 'Now, Mister Abbott, you talked to Morris and he talked to me. So I know what the proposition is.'

'Fine.' Abbott smiled. 'End of the business end of the business?'

The drinks arrived, and Abbott sipped his cautiously. As he suspected, it tasted potent. He debated gesturing to Angel, who had got out of the far side of the pool before Abbott dozed off. He had seen her sit down on a mat, after an exhausting four lengths at top speed, a device which had left her admirers breathless, and reduced to sitting on the edge of the pool, gazing at her with faint longing but some wariness. Any woman who swam like that was a surprise, and maybe best left alone. Now she lay face down, at the far side of the pool.

Abbott tasted his punch again, and smiled at Snow. 'You get used to it quickly.'

'Sure, it's for Western tastes, don't taste like liquor, tastes like a fruit drink.'

Abbott wasn't sure what Snow meant by 'Western tastes' but he did not pursue the point. 'You've been here a few days, Mister Snow?'

'Just call me Snow, everybody does, yeah, it just came to me that if I wanted to think about this *Paradiso* idea, well, why not go home to paradise to do it?' His tone was obviously ironical, but Abbott merely smiled. Artistic people, in his experience, rarely enthused about their homes. They had usually suffered too much there, being sensitive and ambitious, and, in recollection, harsh sentiments often came easily to them.

'Very good idea. I'm glad you did. I think I'm going to like the place.'

Snow looked at him a long moment. 'I guess you would, ole buddy,' he said.

'I hope that's a compliment?'

'Just a guess.'

Snow had not touched his drink. He still seemed to be looking round with a faint apprehension, despite his tone of certainty and confidence. Abbott decided that it was time for introductions. Snow forstalled him.

'You got your girl with you?'

'My girl?' Abbott reddened. 'I'm not sure . . .'

'You're in connecting rooms, right?'

'How . . . ?'

Snow put a finger along his nose. 'Once a waiter, always a waiter.'

'Angel and I . . .' Abbott said, playing it for the joke, 'are simply very good friends.'

Snow laughed at that. It was a very loud and deep laugh, and it was full of life and merriment. When he stopped, there was a silence around the pool and a great many people seemed to be looking their way. The silence lasted a long time; and then the people began talking amongst themselves again.

Snow stood up. He still had not touched his drink.

'Look,' he said, and his voice grated, a very different tone from the laugh of a moment before, 'I'll get transport and meet you at the front of the hotel. We'll go somewhere and talk, okay?' Before Abbott could reply he turned and began to walk quickly out of the pool area.

Abbott stood, nonplussed, a moment. When he recovered, Angel was at his side, the water-and-oil globules glinting on her golden skin.

'Is *that* him?'

'Yes.'

Angel kept looking in the direction Snow had taken.

'What a great-looking fella.'

Abbott looked at her sharply. Then he called for the check.

2

Snow waited at the front of the hotel with three motorised bicyclettes.

Abbott said, 'What's wrong with a cab?'

'Nothing, except you have to get back.'

'Where do we go?'

'Up the Island a ways, okay? Can you ride this?'

Abbott took his bike gingerly. 'Just about.' He got on, and wobbled. 'I think!'

Snow grinned. 'Easy when you get the hang of it.'

Abbott said, 'How . . . ?'

'I told them in the mechanics' shop back of the hotel, I said book them down to you, okay?'

'Just these two, or all three?'

'Just these two. I've got my own.' The third bike was rusty and showed signs of wear. Snow patted the saddle. 'My ole Mammy keeps it in good condition, like maybe she runs a cloth over it every six months.'

'Your mother is still here?'

'Where else would she be?'

Abbott hadn't thought of Snow as having relatives. He seemed like one of those people who are so self-sufficient that any senti-mental family connection would somehow devalue him.

'How far do we go on these things?'

Snow did not reply to the question. He was looking past Abbott.

Angel emerged from the swing doors of the hotel under the admiring, paternal eye of the uniformed doorman. She wore a new pair of hot-pants, and a sweater caught across her breasts so tightly that it stayed up on its own, leaving bare her firm and fleshy shoulders. Angel carried no handbag, except when travel-ling. She would have cigarettes in her hip pocket; no money. There was really nothing else at all except off-white gym-shoes, and large oval sun-glasses. Simple and stunningly effective, Abbott thought; but what he thought did not matter. Snow's opinion was the only one that counted. All this was for him, and for him only.

'Wow!' Snow said, and his tone was distinctly ironical. 'So this is the little lady?'

27

The words were loud enough to carry to Angel, and they seemed to slightly unnerve her (a very difficult thing to do, as Abbott well knew), for she came forward rather quickly, in a businesslike manner, the grand entrance thrown away like a match that had not struck.

'What do we do with these?' She indicated the bikes. 'Ride them or frame them?'

Abbott said, quickly, 'Angel, this is . . .'

'Hi!' She looked frankly at Snow. 'You'll have to show me how they work, I've never been on one.'

'You'll need something else besides *that*.' Snow indicated the half-on sweater. 'It gets cool later.'

Angel behaved as if he had not spoken.

'One gear, you kick-start it, and then there's just the brake?' Snow nodded.

'Then what are we waiting for?' Angel threw a long golden leg over the saddle of her bike, and kicked the starter, hard. The motor erupted first time. She twisted the handle-grip and the bike shot forward down the hotel drive towards the road.

'Keep to the left!' Abbott yelled, as Angel turned out on to the road. He hastily kicked his own bike into life, taking three efforts to get it going.

Snow had not moved. 'Some chick,' he said. Again his tone was ironical, but, Abbott thought, slightly less sure than before.

'Here we go!' Abbott twisted his hand-grip. The bike moved off, far too fast. He corrected, and turned carefully out of the grounds in the direction Angel had taken, the road up the Island. The sensation of speed was considerable and he wondered how it would feel to fall off. Unpleasant, he decided, seeing the road come swiftly past him. He noticed that other riders, going in the opposite direction, were wearing hard-hats and that one was strapped to his own saddle-bag. He would put it on, he decided, at the very first opportunity. He zoomed up the road. Angel was two hundred yards ahead, and he was not gaining on her. He twisted his handlebar-grip, but no extra speed came. He was flat out, and so, apparently, was she. He wondered if it was her first time on a moped, but decided that she would have behaved like that whether it was or it wasn't. Angel worked to her own rules, which were, briefly, to surprise people. Abbott did not, for a moment, think that she worked it out, as some pushful, unpleasant people of his acquaintance did. With Angel it came naturally.

Snow passed him, on the outside. 'I'm souped up a little. Can she ride that thing?'

'I don't know.'

'She seems to be doing okay.'

The distance between Snow and Angel narrowed, but Abbott could not make better speed. He settled for droning along behind the two of them, keeping station at a respectful distance. Angel turned, as Snow finally reached her, and he plainly asked if she needed assistance, for Abbott saw her shake her head. After this short exchange, Snow zoomed past her and they all continued in line-ahead for twenty minutes, passing a large golf-links, with perfect crab-grass lawns to the right of them, and sand dunes to the left of them, with a practice cricket match (played on concrete wickets) thrown in. Abbott would have liked to stop and watch, but the idea, in this company, was ridiculous, so he contented himself with a promise that he would look later. It was one of the things he missed in his new life : the slow contemplation of the most subtle physical game in the world.

The odd tourists faded away as Snow took a left-fork towards the sea, and finally he could hear the surf, very loud indeed. He turned after the others and found that Snow and Angel had left their bikes on the grass fringe and were walking over the dunes towards the beach. They did not seem to be talking yet, as Snow was still a dozen paces in front of Angel. This seemed to irritate her, and she ran to catch up; but Snow must have been conscious of this, for he merely increased his stride. She mustn't try so hard, Abbott thought. I must tell her that. He sighed. She would not listen. Angel had got thus far by her own efforts. She did not need anybody's advice.

He trudged through the brilliant sand, across the dunes, and there, suddenly and dramatically, was the sea, smashing itself against huge black rocks, five hundred yards in front of him. Abbott stopped and surveyed the scene. Golden sand and blue sea and sky, it was like a travel poster come real. They were the only people in the cove. The sun was hot, but there was a breeze to take the edge off it. Abbott made his way, but slowly, towards the two figures on a high dune. When he got there, they were each drinking beer direct from a can. Snow pulled a third can from his shirt and tossed it to Abbott.

'Where did these come from?'

'I told you, I used to be a waiter. You learn to live off the land.'

Abbott opened the can. The beer was American and slightly warm. He swallowed and said, 'Where are we?'

Snow pointed far across the water. 'That's Spanish Rock. Where the first men who ever came here landed. Carved their names on it. Nobody on the Island at all then. They let a few hawgs loose and they multiplied, y'know, like hawgs I guess do?' He looked side-wise at Angel, but she was drinking her beer and studiously looking anywhere but at Spanish Rock. 'The very first fella ever set foot on this Island was a sailor from one of them Spanish ships. The captain man, he couldn't get in close so he sends this sailor in at night, with a lantern. Alone. The birds crowded round him, all colours, hundreds of them, attracted by the light, but tame see, they'd never seen humans before, didn't know they was dangerous.' His voice took on a deeper, amused note, the gone-coon act, Abbott thought, was here again. 'This first fella that them Spaniards sent on the Island, why he wasn't no Spaniard, I tell you that. He was a negar—that's how they spell it, n-e-g-a-r, that was one scared black boy when all them birds come at him in the night. The Spaniards thought the Island was inhabited by spooks. But there was only the tame and trusting old birds.'

Angel said, idly, 'What happened to the black boy?'

Snow smiled, lazily. 'They got him back. Wasn't that nice of them, to get him back?' He leaned back against the rock and smiled. 'I call that real nice of them to get that poor shivering ole sonofabitch back, probably not long outa the African jungle that boy, strictly expendable to them Spaniards, yes sir.' He closed his eyes. 'Da Sousa? That's a Spanish name, isn't it?'

Angel stood up, abruptly. 'You going to swim?'

The remark was addressed to Abbott.

'Later maybe.'

Angel slipped off her hot-pants. She wore the briefest of bikini swim-pants under them, blue this time. 'What about the top?' Abbott asked.

In answer, she peeled off the sweater. A thin, bikini bra gently held the perfect breasts. Abbott was surprised at her preparation. 'How did you know we'd be swimming?'

'I didn't.' Angel kicked off her fashionable dirty-white gym-shoes, and walked down from the rocks towards the water.

'Tell her to watch the rollers. They can be big.' Snow had not opened his eyes.

Abbott called, 'Watch those rollers!'

Angel waved, without looking back.

Abbott watched Angel closely, as she ran unhurriedly into the sea. When she broke through the first wave safely, he said, 'Is she right for the part, do you think?'

'I dunno, I don't know her yet.' Snow did not open his eyes.

'You must admit she looks right?'

'She looks very right, I will *admit* that.' Snow's eyes were still closed. 'I'd have to work with her, in a rehearsal hall. Talk, listen, watch. For a stage-musical you have to know a lot. I mean technically. You can't con the way you can in movies, I mean you can't *edit*, it has to be a finished, shaped performance.'

'She can sing. You heard her voice on the tapes.'

'Yep, that's a help.' Snow's voice, Abbott noted, had lost the 'jest-a-little-colour'-boy' style. He sounded like any other New Yorker, except that somewhere there was a touch of Old England pronunciation, a heritage, probably, from his childhood days on the Island.

'It's a big help. A lot of so-called musical stars can't sing these days.'

'It's all down to publicity,' Snow said. His voice was mildly disgusted. 'Poor old film-star biddies the public know and love from way back, exposed on stage, singing songs they don't understand, never ever having been singers in the whole of their lives. The stuff the public will take, I tell ya.' He opened his eyes. 'Yes, she can sing, if the tapes you sent are anything to go by. Yes, she also looks right. But she needs a lot of work, she's unknown and raw, and I don't know, I really do not know, that I can face all that work. Like I say, if it was a movie it would be easier, if it was a movie I could maybe trick it. On stage I couldn't, on stage you have to have it, I mean the performer has to have it.'

'She'll work at it. You can rely on that.' Abbott felt his voice falter. All this was so very important to Angel. Every word counted, or it should; but something about Snow told him that a hard sell was no good. This man would make up his own mind, in his own time. He was probably very used to resisting pressure, anybody in his position would be.

Abbott tried another tack. 'Do you think the script is all right?'

'No.' Snow closed his eyes again.

'Oh?'

'But I could get it rewritten. I'd want to do that, some of the music too.'

'I only have an option on the thing,' Abbott said, carefully. 'I don't know if the author . . .'

'He'd jump at it all, film possibilities, all that, why wouldn't he, it's no use to him as it stands, just a lotta words on paper?'

'If you think that . . .'

'That ain't my worry.'

'No?'

Snow opened his eyes and took off his sun-glasses. The eyes were very large and very black. He looked much younger, and harder. The sun-glasses, against all the rules, actually softened him. The black eyes searched out Angel, found her a hundred yards from shore, deep in the white breakers. Her head bobbed in the surf, was lost for a long moment, bobbed again. Snow said, 'That girl sure works.'

'She's quite safe. She's a marvellous swimmer.'

'That right?'

Abbott forced himself not to look out to sea again. 'She's got quite a personality. She did very well on British television.'

'I believe that,' Snow said, in the style of a man who will believe anything about television.

'The standard's high over there,' Abbott said.

'I know, I've seen it, I was in London last winter with *Moon Girl*.'

'I know.'

'Do you?'

'I even know the box office returns and the net profit.'

'You're really some money-man, aren't you, Mister Abbott?'

Abbott said, 'I'm a lucky man.'

'That's what all the rich people say.'

'I'm not rich enough to back a movie, so it has to be a small musical. With your record of a London success, with *Moon Girl*, and by carefully packing good professionals around Angel, I think we could have a good *small* musical—which this is. I know the fashion is for big musicals, costing God knows what. . . .' Abbott paused, making the words count, it was a speech he had rehearsed many times. 'But I think London might take to a small musical, like this, always provided it had real quality. We can handle the financial end, as perhaps Morris explained to you?'

'He surely did.' Snow nodded his head three times, took his eyes from Angel's head still bobbing in the surf, and replaced his dark glasses. 'All I'm not sure of, is it right for me?'

32

'That's what we're here to talk about.'

'Mister Abbott . . .'

'Call me Jack.'

'She calls you just Abbott.'

'Do that if you like.'

'No.' He looked at Abbott steadily. 'I think Jack. Look, Jack. You're a money-man, no matter what you say, and hell I respect a money-man, but if I come in on this, I say if I do, then there has to be one boss and that has to be me, no room for associate producers or any of that crap, I run the whole thing. I have to say this right off.'

Abbott said, stiffly, 'Mister Snow . . .'

'Just Snow, I told you, everybody does.'

'I know my limitations,' Abbott said. 'I worked in a top agency as an accountant. A lot of showbiz rubbed off on me but I'm no kind of an artist and thank God I'm not, having seen a few of you. I'm strictly a commercial fella, and all I ask is you talk to me from time to time about mundane, unimaginative things like costs. That and nothing else. I'll keep my mouth shut, even if I feel like screaming.'

'I've heard that one from backers before.'

'You're hearing it from one who means it.'

Snow looked at him soberly. Then he smiled. 'I believe you.'

'Then you'll . . . ?'

'I'll consider it.'

'That is good enough for me.'

Abbott leaned back and let the sun soak into him. He had done as much as he could, for now. The sales-pitch he had kept deliberately low-key, and if it had done no good, it had certainly done no harm. Angel would have to do the rest of the work herself. He was simply on the sidelines to cheer, or cry foul if she got hurt, which was always possible. Angel's ability to survive bad shocks was a constant surprise to him. She had taken two or three since he'd known her, including the saga of the nudie horror part, which she had tried for, after all, but which had turned out to include sleeping with the producer. He was a bigger horror than anything in the movie, Angel had reported to Abbott. She had shown unexpected fire on this occasion. 'If he doesn't like me for my work he can go screw himself,' had been her exact words, biting on a reefer, in Abbott's apartment. She smoked them rarely, only when she was very tense. Abbott could have wished that her reasons for

33

not sleeping with the producer had been different ones, but he had to be grateful that they existed at all. 'I don't screw around to get work from anybody,' Angel added. And, of course, that meant she didn't do it with him for that reason. Abbott liked that. The sun was pleasant. He grunted and shifted, and kept his eyes closed. Soft waves of sleep came over him for the second time that day. At some point he heard Angel's voice, and Snow's, lower and deeper. Their voices were still droning on as he wakened. He was very hot now and knew that he had taken too much sun, but he kept his eyes closed, behind the dark glasses. If Angel was making headway, that was fine.

'This negro that came to the Island first, I mean,' Angel was saying, distantly. 'Was he really the first man on this place?'

'The first recorded. After him the Spaniards came, one or two, you know, like claimed it in the name of the King of Spain, all that. But they didn't stay, maybe it was the spooks they were afraid of, maybe they were on their way to South America and it didn't seem like worth the stop.' Snow paused, as if he wished he had not said so much, but Angel's voice prompted him, gently, interested. Abbott, who knew her so well, could not tell if it was genuine.

'Who, I mean, *lived* here first?'

Abbott wondered if Snow thought she was conning him.

'A boat went aground here. A big white fella captain, he brought his boat inshore in a storm.' Snow was doing the nigger-boy act again, whether out of embarrassment or malice Abbott could not guess. 'That boat was just about coming apart with these here white settlers on their way to ole Virginey. And this white capt'n, he bring that boat ashore, losing but very few lives. Right through those very waves there, but in a storm, baby, and if you never see a Bermuda storm you never see a storm.'

'What was his name?'

'Sir George Somers, that his name, chile. Y'see, we know his name but nobody know the name of that pore ol' negar who first come ashore all on his lonesome, in the dark. No, sir. His name done gone.'

Angel said, gently, 'What happened?'

'To the colour' man?'

'No, to Sir George Whatsit?'

'Sir George Somers, well, he just naturally grabbed him this Island for God and the King of England. Built a new boat from the cedar trees back there and sailed him to Virginey. But in ole

34

Virginey they all starving. So he come back here for hawg-meat and vittles. Then he died, one year later.' Abbott waited for Angel to ask another question but she said nothing.

There was what seemed to be a very long silence, and then Snow said, 'That man, Sir George, he's buried in England. They took his body back, likely pickled in brine. But 'fore they did, they buried his heart on this here Island. Nobody knows where.'

The sea washed softly against the rocks and the sun beat down.

'That's very sad.'

'Sad about the poor ole negar as well?'

'Yes, sad about him too.'

'There were lots more like him later. Only they stayed here and worked.'

'Slaves?'

'They didn't like to call them that.'

'But they were?'

'Sure. Only the white settlers weren't workers. The ole-time ones. Didn't need to be. There was plenty of water, anything you planted just naturally grew. Plenty of hawgs. All the fish you could be bothered to hook. So slaves, yeah, but they called them servants, and they took their masters' names, like Snow.'

'Is that how . . . ?'

'Josiah Snow, first took a passel of land on this Island, seventeen-twelve. A Plymouth man. He owned my great-great-great granpappy and his woman. Not his wife. His woman. My great granpappy was a buck.'

Angel said nothing, just kept looking at Snow.

'I don't mind his name. A name don't mean nothing.'

'I think you dig this Island, just the same,' Angel said.

Snow laughed, the deep brown laugh Abbott had first heard over the transatlantic telephone. 'If I don't, I should, because my ancestors built every stone wall in the place. Tilled every field. Only they don't own the walls and the fields.'

'Not any of them?'

'Hell, they own their own houses now, most of 'em. They got their own little livings and their own little ways. They as well off, lady, as any colour' man anywhere in the world, probably better. They don't want it no different, you go ask 'em, baby.'

'The Island's prosperous, looks like.' Abbott opened his eyes. Snow's voice was getting an edge on it. 'They're in on the tourist boom, I suppose?'

35

'That's right,' Snow said, in a final-sounding voice. 'The tourist boom is absolutely what they are in on. Driving hacks, waiting table, they do pretty good all round.'

'Then they aren't grumbling?'

'They surely ain't.' Snow smiled. ' 'Course, not many of them own sailing boats or belong to the Royal Bermuda Yacht Club, but like you say, they ain't grumbling at all, not one little bit.'

Angel sat up straight, in the sand. Her body was a wondrous dark gold, the sun made no impression on it. 'You sound as if you are?'

'Why should I be, lady? I work here as a waiter, before I hitch myself to New York because . . .'

'You hated it so much here?'

'You said that, lady, I didn't. No, sir. I got a nice sweet reference to a hotel in New York City. And I worked in that hotel one week. Then I went and I got a job, dancing. I walked in and asked the fella for a job dancing. And he gave it to me.'

'How long after you arrived in New York?' Abbott asked.

Snow allowed the sand to dribble through his fingers. 'One year, Daddy-o.' He smiled crookedly at Angel. 'The money-man is smart.'

'You don't have to be very smart to know that nobody just walks into a job as a dancer. Even in New York, where most things are possible.'

Snow threw the sand in the air and it drifted away from them on the breeze. 'I got another job washing dishes. I washed cars too. That's nice work, washing cars. Only morons do it. I found them pleasant company.' The act had gone, this was not serious stuff, Abbott thought, there was no need for a cover-up. 'All the time I washed dishes and cars, I saved money for dancing lessons. I wasn't a great dancer but I had lots of ideas. Nobody wanted the ideas but I got the job as a dancer. Like you say, money-man, after one year I got it. And then I danced and danced and danced. In night spots, in off-Broadway rubbish that I had to pretend was great. Starving? Sure, but I had my actor's card, I was with the great people, the dancers, actors, writers, whores, spongers, wasters, drunks, bums and queers. I was respectable, I could starve in good company.'

Angel laughed. There was something in the tone of the laugh, a sympathy, that made Snow suddenly look up. His glance was sharp, hard. Then, as she looked back directly at him, it softened

36

and his voice was lower, throwaway, as he said, 'Well, in the end I went to the Actors' Studio, and I did some choreography under Robbins, and I tried to write a little. In short, I was ready to direct, knowing a little of everything. Musicals, in my case. Always able to read music. Taught myself on this here Island, sometimes sitting on this very beach, on this very spot. And so, finally, I got *Moon Girl*. And she took off. Then I had a big bad bomb. I guess you know about that. And why then I went to the Coast to the movie pot before it finally spilled over, and that was no good, only money, and I've been bumming ever since, waiting to do the really big one.' Snow turned his dark eyes (he had pushed the sun-glasses on to his forehead) and said to Abbott, 'But you knew all this, didn't you, Mister money-man?'

'I did,' Abbott smiled. 'I like to know who I'm ...'

'Doing business with?' Snow grinned. 'Like the guy said, it's a fine art we're doing business in?'

'Simply we have to work together, I hope,' Abbott said.

'Well, all I know about you is what Morris told me. He said you ...'

'I don't want to know what he said.'

'He said you had worked in a showbiz-agency looking after their money, got lucky in television, that you knew a lot of people, that like most Englishmen when you said a thing you meant it, and that ...' Snow's gaze travelled very slowly over Angel's body but he merely added, 'You were one hell of a nice fella.'

'I'm very grateful to Morris for that,' said Abbott, feeling irritated, for the first time. Some of it must have shown, for Snow jumped to his feet with the loud laugh he had sounded earlier, at the bathing pool. He pulled off his black T-shirt, slipped out of his slacks, and stood, in jock-strap swim-briefs, sturdy, muscular, dangerous. He grinned at Angel. 'Come on, baby, I'll show you how to ride the waves!' Without waiting for an answer, he loped off towards the water, head down, moving very fast across the fine white sand, kicking up a spray behind him.

Angel did not move. She hated people giving her orders.

'I don't dig him at all.' Angel stared resentfully after the speeding figure. 'I don't know if he even likes us.'

Abbott watched Snow belly-flop into the first row of white breakers. 'I'm not sure he even likes himself.' He stood up. He felt a little dizzy, and he swayed.

'You've had too much sun.'

'I'm all right.' Abbott slipped off his shirt and slacks. 'Let's get at it.'

'You sure?'

'I'll be fine.'

He wasn't. The large rollers took expert riding, and at once, in an attempt to emulate Snow, Abbott belly-flopped on to the first white horse to reach him. The undertow pulled him down and he swallowed a lot of water. He turned turtle and fought for the surface, found it, only to take the next roller smack in the face. He went down again and this time he thought, if *that* happens again, I will drown. It was a very calm thought, and it was accompanied by a sudden weakening, a letting-go, and he did not mind, for it would all be over . . . and then Snow's voice was in his ear, and he was struggling hard for the shore and gasping huge lungfuls of air; then the water was shallow and the sand firm beneath his feet, and he was retching. Sea-water came sharp into his mouth and as his head at last ceased to spin, he thought, ironically : I'm with Angel, it could only happen to me when I'm with her. I'd be too cautious, otherwise. Snow's arms went around him, doubling him up, forcing him to cough up more bile. At last, Snow stopped the pumping process.

'You okay now?'

'Yes . . . don't worry . . .'

'You don't look it, fella.'

'I'll be . . . all right.'

'Sit there a minute.'

But Abbott felt a fool sitting in six inches of water (by now he could hear Angel's voice, 'Is he all right, what happened?') and he tried to get to his feet, but staggered again, the bilious sea-water dribbling out of his mouth.

Angel ran over and took his hand, gently. 'Sit down a minute, you'll be okay.' But Abbott shook himself free and ploughed through the shallow water to the dry, hot sand. There, his head still spinning and the salt-water flooding his mouth, he sat and tried to breathe normally. The other two looked down on him.

'He sure don't look too good,' Snow said.

Abbott kept his eyes closed. He felt humiliated and foolish.

'He looks awful.' Angel was concerned.

'It's the sea-water,' Abbott managed. 'Don't bother about me. Get on with . . . your swimming. I'll be fine.'

'You do look sick,' Angel repeated.

38

'I'm okay, I tell you!'

Snow said, in a surprisingly soft voice, 'You just sit there a while. Take it quiet, okay?'

Abbott refused to look at them further, and in the end they turned and ran back into the sea. He sat exactly like that, for what seemed a very long time, until the worst of the sickness had passed away. When he looked up, Angel and Snow were still swimming, far out past the long line of rollers, in the smooth, calm, water before the surf began. Abbott got to his feet and slowly walked back towards the pile of clothes, pausing to retch twice on the way. Nothing came up. He very slowly pulled on his slacks and shirt. A feeling of bone-chill came over him; he sat in the hot sun, and shivered.

'Hi, Jack, how you feeling now?'

Abbott looked up at Snow, who stood black and glistening, the water spraying off him as he moved.

'I'll live.'

'You look green. You ain't got it all up.'

'Maybe we should get him a taxi and go back to the hotel?' Angel suggested.

'How would we get a taxi out here?'

'Telephone?'

'Where from?'

Angel looked annoyed. 'How would I know? A house? Anywhere?'

Snow seemed to be debating. 'We could go round to my place?'

'Your place?'

'My mother's place.'

'Oh, is it near?'

'Just up the road.'

Abbott noted that Angel was still challenging Snow, still weighing his every action. If she wished to get on with him, she would have to look as if she was prepared to bend the knee. Maybe that was why she was being defensive, because she knew that? It could make Snow's necessary, eventual domination even sweeter to him. Perhaps, Abbott thought, she knew what she was doing.

They all got dressed and began to walk from the beach. Snow wheeled Abbott's bike and his own, one in each hand. Abbott took Angel's arm and walked behind, feeling a very considerable fool. The sickness was still there, the salt-water sour on his stomach. Snow led them up a lane, off the main road, bounded by one of the stone walls that were a feature of the Island. He did not look back at them at all, and Abbott mentally thanked him for that.

'You were in the sun too long,' Angel said. 'And you need to be a good swimmer in those waves.'

Or just young, Abbott thought, but said nothing.

The road was unmade, but deep hedges thick with oleander sprang up; they turned a sudden bend in the track and faced a small stone-built cottage. It was obviously a hundred years old, but with a curious, half-finished look. It had an open door, shutters in the Spanish style, and in front of it stood a large tamarind tree. All around the house, blossoming roses grew wild and seedy. There was no sign of life, but loud pop-music issued from inside the place.

A large red-parrot-like bird flew out of the tree at their approach.

Abbott started. 'Good God, what's that?'

'A redbird. Some call them cardinals.' Snow stood in the doorway. 'Come on in.'

Abbott eased himself from Angel's solicitous hand, and walked unsteadily into the cottage. It was dramatically dark inside. A fat, jolly-looking woman wearing a very white apron sat in a rocker-chair with her hands in her lap. Her teeth showed white in the gloom, as she smiled her welcome. 'Come in, come in. My son tells me you not too good now?'

'He's still got a bellyful of sea-water,' Snow said. 'Folks, this is my mother, call her Happy. Mister Abbott, Miss . . . da Sousa.'

The woman got to her feet. 'Sit you down there an' rest a minute, Mister Abbott. I'll find you sumptin' fix you up.' Angel she neither smiled at nor nodded to, but seemed to take for granted, simply indicating that the girl sat in the chair she had vacated. Then she went out into what looked like a small kitchen. An old brass-faced grandmother clock ticked very loudly in the sparely-furnished room. A table, some hard chairs, a mat, some cheap ornaments, the clock the only object of any value, apart from a new-looking record player, from which the music came. Snow switched it off.

'She liked you,' Snow said to Angel. 'Nobody, but nobody, gets to sit in that chair.'

Angel sat, and rocked. 'I like it.'

'Came from the Barratt house, like the clock.'

'Lovely clock.'

'Very old. Happy used to work for the Barratts. When they left, they gave her the clock.'

'Left?'

'They were one of the oldest of the original white settler families. Only a couple old aunties left. They sold up and went to live in California. They were as English as you can think, but English weather would have killed them. So they sold the old house and land for a hotel building, and they left. My Mammy's folks had worked for their folks for nearly three hundred years. They got to live in California and she got that clock.'

'Is she unhappy about that?' Abbott asked.

'I dunno, you ask her.'

Abbott swallowed. He still felt very queasy.

'A little bicarb would be fine . . .' he called.

'She'll get you something better than soda,' Snow smiled. 'Around here she's got quite a reputation.'

'This *is* a beautiful clock,' Angel said, inspecting it.

'A fella came in, tourist fella.' Snow sat on a hard chair, relaxed, subtly different from the insecure, international man of the hotel-pool. 'This fella hummed an' hawed, talked about this an' that, finally he says to my Mammy, "Y'know, I might just take that ole clock off your hands, lady, got a corner it would just go into, I'd be glad to give you twenty-five U.S. dollars for that clock." Happy says nothing, and finally he says, "Well, what d'you think of that?" And she's sewing in that chair, an' she just looks up and says, "I say there was only one brass-faced booger in here before you came in." '

'I never said that.' Happy came bustling back into the room, carrying a small glass containing a green mixture. 'An' if I did, I ought to be ashamed of myself. Anyway, I wouldn't sell that clock, not for anybody or anything.' She proffered the glass to Abbott. 'Now you just drink that down, Mister Abbott, and you're gonna feel just fine in a few minutes, I know.'

The mixture was noxious and seemed to contain, amongst other things, a good deal of mustard. Tears started to Abbott's eyes. 'It's out back there,' Happy said. 'But hang on as long as you can, then you'll get rid of it all that way.' Abbott felt his stomach turn, but he sat still, as the woman had instructed him to, in her business-like, motherly way. She was still talking. 'Yes, that's a wonderful little ole clock. I reckon it's worth five hundred dollars of anybody's money.'

Snow exploded with a laugh. 'Not that you'd sell it?'

'No, but it's worth five hundred dollars. At least.'

'Happy, it's worth a lot more.'

'Five hundred dollars would do, I don't want a lot more.'

'She can think in dollars now, don't let her kid you, she was brought up on British pounds.'

'That's true,' the fat woman said, smiling, 'but you gotta move with the times, don't you?' She turned to Abbott and patted his hand and said, 'I think you can go now.'

Abbott was on his feet before her words were finished. He found the outside Elsan a moment before the rest of the sea-water (and the noxious mixture) came into his mouth. Behind him he could hear Snow's laughter; when it was over he sat there, weakly, for a few, long, blank minutes. Then he got up, and unlocked the door of the closet; and found himself suddenly face-to-face with a tall young negro in a check shirt and jeans. The man wore granny-glasses and he was as surprised to see Abbott as Abbott was to see him. Plainly, he was going into the closet and Abbott supposed it to be a communal one, possibly serving another house across the dirt road.

'It's all yours,' he said, awkwardly.

The man nodded, and went inside. Abbott heard a bolt shoot home. The cardinal bird cawed in the tree, and Abbott stood in the air a moment, to clear his head. He felt much better. Slowly, he walked back into the house. In the kitchen, cups were on a tray, and there was a smell of coffee beans in the air.

Happy came to meet him, in the small kitchen.

'You feel better now?'

'Yes, thanks.'

'My grandmammy taught me that. An' a lot else. Now you drink this.' She pressed another glass in his hand. Abbott shook his head.

'Coffee would be fine.'

'Not yet. This first. Put a lining on your belly.'

This mixture was of milk and oil and had a mint taste. Abbott swallowed it in a gulp. The fat woman smiled and patted his arm. 'You'll be all right now.'

'Thanks.'

'That your lady in there?'

'In a way.'

'Only in a way?'

'Well . . .'

'She's pretty.'

'She is.'

Happy took the glass back. 'Go and talk to her. I'll fix the coffee.'

Abbott went back into the room.

'Yes, but what do you *want*? To be a success?' Snow was asking Angel the question and his voice was sharp. Angel obviously did not like it. Abbott knew that she was trying, with difficulty, to keep her voice level. He wondered what had happened to get the conversation on this non-productive level.

'Yes, to be a success! Who doesn't?'

'Yes, but what kind of a success? Financial? Artistic? Personal?'

'I want to be a good artist.'

'Good dancer?'

'Right.'

'Good singer?'

'Right.'

'Big success on Broadway and Shaftesbury Avenue?'

'Right.'

'And that's it?'

'Huh?'

'That's the whole scene?'

Angel's lovely eyes closed in irritation. 'Of course it's not the whole scene. But it's the part I want first. The rest, the personal happiness bit, comes later. I mean, I need that kind of human-being happiness last, I have to do well in my profession first.'

'It's the least of it. The other's more important, eh, Jack?'

Abbott still felt faint, but convalescent. He sat down.

'Don't ask me, I'm no artist.'

'You had your work.'

'Yes.'

'Do you miss it?'

'I suppose I do.'

'Often?'

'Enough.'

'Want it back?'

'It was only figures.'

'But you enjoyed it?'

'I was conditioned to like it.'

'You got rich quick?'

43

'Right.'

Snow smiled. 'Then you're still in shock?'

'Maybe.' The thought had not occurred to Abbott.

'That kinda shock I could use.' Snow was only being polite. Abbott knew that. The object of his quiz was Angel. Abbott knew the symptoms among unhappy, creative people. He had seen it before. Take them away from their work, set them down in a place like this, and they became dissatisfied, invented truth-games, probed and upset each other. Something like this, he guessed, was happening now.

Snow turned back to Angel. She had curled her long legs under her, in the chair, and her posture was defiant. She refused to meet Snow's amused gaze.

'So you just want success?'

'Right.'

'You want the stage and then later movies and your name in *Variety* and the big penthouse and the cover of *Time*?'

'If I can get it. Who doesn't?'

'It ain't enough, baby.'

Angel said, 'Don't give me that crap, mister.'

Abbott said, 'Where's that coffee, I could . . .' but Angel was still talking.

'You've had those things, I mean all the success and publicity and you've forgotten how it is to want it, to really hunger for it.' Snow began to say something but she overrode his words. 'I know you talk a lot about how success doesn't mean a thing once you have it, but I don't believe that either. I didn't train myself to get somewhere, work hard at singing lessons, talk nice to fat old men who could do me some good, show my knickers to producers, all the rotten lousy bit, just to get it and sit back and say it's all too sodding boring, I can live without it, now I'm gonna worry about bigger things.' Angel's eyes were staring and there was a fleck of sweat across her upper lip. 'And neither did you, mister, so I repeat, don't give me that crap because I don't believe it!'

There was a long silence in which Snow just stared at her, a slight smile on his face, then Happy's voice broke in, 'That's telling him, girl. I don't like language—but God forgive me—*I* swore when that ole Yankee wanted to buy my clock for twenty-five dollars, so why shouldn't you when this boy gets clever?' She put the tray on the table, and began to pour large mugs of strong black coffee. 'Everybody take sugar, do they now?'

'Thanks, two lumps,' Abbott said, finding Angel's eye and signalling to her to drop it. Possibly no real damage had been done, it was Snow's fault for needling the girl. Snow said nothing, just sat and sipped his coffee and looked at Angel, who turned away from him, and refused to meet his gaze. Abbott knew her well enough to know that she would be in a turmoil now, hating herself for having said as much as she had.

Surprisingly, Happy picked up her cup and slipped her arm through the girl's. 'Come on, I'll show you the place. We'll drink our coffee outside, let these two big men talk bizness, that's all they good for, eh?'

Angel looked up at her and suddenly smiled, and they went out. Abbott drank his coffee and said nothing. They sat in silence for a long minute. Abbott broke it.

'This was your home?'

'That's right.'

'You miss it?'

'Hard to believe I ever lived here.'

'That so?'

'You know what home's like. It's the place you can't go back to.'

Abbott had not had that experience. His father and mother were still alive, retired, living in the same suburban house they had always lived in. He was always glad to go home, and they were always glad to see him. Of course, it was different now, since the money, and Helen. They had loved Helen, and the children. They had never understood about that.

'You didn't need to push Angel. She's been travelling a lot, and she's tired.'

Snow turned to Abbott. 'Mister, when I said earlier that I was to be in charge of my end of things, the artists, I meant exactly that, no interference, none or it doesn't *begin* . . .'

'It hasn't begun and it won't unless you sign some papers in New York.' Abbott was angry now, despite himself. 'Then, and then only, do you have official permission to taunt and upset what you call the artist. Not before. I mean that.'

Snow smiled, the slow sad smile. 'Man, she's sure got you hooked, hasn't she?'

'Now, look here . . .' Abbott began, but Snow was standing up and listening to the sound of a car coming up the dirt road. Abbott was surprised at his intensity, but grateful for it. He had no wish to fall out with Snow, at this point. Too much depended on the man. He lit a cigarette, cursing himself for revealing his feelings for Angel. The depth of them was something that he would rather have kept to himself.

Snow opened the front door and stood there, waiting.

Abbott relaxed in the rocking chair. The sickness had quite gone and he felt surprisingly well. Outside, at the back, he could hear the voices of Angel and Happy. Angel seemed to be laughing quite a lot, and the laughter had a girlish quality, quite unlike the polite, social noise she made at showbiz cocktail-parties in London.

The car's engine suddenly cut, the door slammed, and there was the sound of gravel crunching underfoot as somebody walked across towards the front door. Snow said, 'Excuse me a moment. Maybe you'd like a little music?' He bent down, switched on the record player, and went out to meet the newcomer. Abbott did not get out of the chair. He listened to the music from the player, which was of an English folk-group, Steeleye Span, singing about life in an English village three hundred years before. It was pleasant, and obviously Snow's choice. He would be in with every new development, anywhere. A pile of other discs—Dylan, The Stones, Led Zepplin—testified to the catholicity of his tastes. Abbott closed his eyes, and listened to the folk-songs of Old England. This, he thought, was the kind of music the first settlers brought to the Island with them. The fancy amused him. Outside, he heard a man's voice, faint, but it carried over the music. 'Have you seen him?' and Snow's answer, indistinct, 'Why should he come here?' and then the man's voice, deep, and British-sounding, authoritative, a voice you listened to, but did not argue with. 'You know the position as well as I do. If you see him, I want you to . . .' The rest of it was indistinct, as the musicians began a louder chorus. Then a car door slammed shut, the engine re-started, and the car was driven away, down the dirt road. It had a harsh note and to Abbott sounded rather like the Land Rover he had out on his cottage in Dorset.

Snow came back in. He closed the door quietly, and looked questioningly at Abbott's face. Abbott showed nothing.

'Good record?'

'Yes, I like it. I think we should have some songs like that in our show.'

Snow smiled. 'If we do it.'

Happy and Angel came in from the back. Angel was smiling

now and seemed relaxed, and the two women were arm-in-arm.

Abbott had never seen Angel arm-in-arm with a woman before.

Happy said, 'Somebody call?'

'Just a fella.'

Happy looked quickly at Snow's face, but asked no more questions. 'I just showed Angel the place where they throwed the witches. I tole her they throw them in an' if they float, they guilty an' hung. If they drown, too bad.' Happy laughed deeply, a dark brown laugh, like Snow's, but her eyes were on her son's face. He showed nothing at all.

'I like this here Angel,' Happy said. 'She feels at home here.'

'So she does,' Snow said, smiling at Angel, freely, as if he had known her a long time. 'So she does.'

3

'This place is kinda dreamy, timeless, y'know? It's like living under water.' Angel looked across the harbour at Hamilton, towards the soft green hub of the Island. She laughed. 'Made for love, like the old song says.'

'You mean sex?'

She shook her head. 'Everything's so slow. No poverty that you can see. Everywhere you look it's all beautiful, all clean, all calm. It's not loud and noisy enough for sex.'

'I had noticed,' Abbott said, drily. Angel had gone straight into her room after dinner the previous evening. She had fallen silent, since they left Snow at the cottage. Abbott put it down to travel-tiredness, and the worry of how Snow felt about her, whether she had impressed him or not.

'I was just tired last night.'

Abbott said nothing to that except, 'Don't worry about Snow. He's sold on you. It'll just take him time to say so.'

'Do you really think that?'

'Certain of it.'

Angel leaned back against the rail. 'Nice to be away from the rat race!'

'Looks pretty competitive to me.' Abbott indicated the small black boys fishing for red snapper from the rail on Front Street. The sun glinted on the water, across the harbour. Behind them, the modernised shop-fronts (always tastefully restored, and some showing the Royal Crest) stood foursquare to the sea, as if waiting for profit.

'This Island has been a market-place for three hundred years,' Abbott said. 'Don't let the picturesque look of it fool you. Some of the smartest businessmen in the Western hemisphere sit in those offices. The Island has always been a staging-post for vast enter-prises. In the American Civil War merchants from these very offices supplied both sides, North and South. They could do it, because the Island was quite genuinely on both sides. Some of the people supported the South. Some the North. Being careful to stay under the British flag all the time.'

'How do you know this?'

'My friend O'Hara told me.'

Abbott had cabled David O'Hara that they were arriving. David was an accountant, like himself, an old friend, or perhaps it just seemed that. Anyway, they had been juniors together, at Auerbach and Hope in Regent Street. Abbott had virtually forgotten that David was in the Island. He had cabled back warmly, and they had met for coffee that morning, in the hotel. David had seemed delighted to see him, and had told Abbott a few things about his job (working for a big local bank) and the Island's way of getting a living in the twentieth century. He had also invited them both to the Royal Bermuda Yacht Club for lunch. Abbott gathered that David was doing very well. He had told Angel all this when she wakened. Angel always slept till noon if she could, whereas Abbott was an early riser. Even the money had not changed that.

Now, bathed and rested, she stood, expectant of the day, the most arresting figure on Front Street. This time she was wearing a square-cut but very low gingham dress, with, Abbott knew, no bra beneath it. He sighed, wondering if it would be all right for the Royal Bermuda Yacht Club. David O'Hara had seemed to hint that it might be stuffy. Abbott himself was wearing one of his blazers and a Savage Club tie.

'What's he like? Your friend O'Hara?'

'He's like an accountant. He's careful. He's discreet. He's a man of his word. He's also like an Irishman, which means he wishes he was doing something else, like sailing boats six days a week.'

'Who does he work for?'

'Local bank. This place is a tax haven, it's also a hive of commerce. Lots of international companies have offices here.'

'I don't know what an accountant's going to think about me.'

'When I met you I was an accountant.'

'No, you weren't, you were a director of a television company.'

'David's fine. You'll like him.'

'Is he married?'

'No.'

'What did you tell him about me?' Angel looked interested and suddenly radiant. She always did at the idea of two or more people discussing her. Abbott was entranced by it.

'Just that you were a singer, and beautiful, and all that.'

'Had he heard of me?'

49

Abbott nearly said, 'Out here, you have to be joking,' but he compromised with, 'He said your name seemed very familiar to him.' So David had, but it had been merely politeness, Abbott knew, an obeisance to his own anxious eyes. Angel seemed satisfied with his reply, and adjusted her hat, a very large white straw, with a broad brim and a dangling ribbon. Abbott supposed that it would be all right at the Royal Bermuda Yacht Club. Presumably there would be men there. He looked at his watch. 'We should be walking along.'

Angel fell into step with him, tucking her arm into his and walking close, so that her breast touched his bare elbow. It was impossible, Abbott knew, for her to do anything that did not have sex in it, but this was a natural rather than a deliberate thing. Helen had not been at all like that, much more English and tweedy and dignified, but he had never felt quite the same walking with Helen along a street as he did now with Angel. On the credit side, he felt proud that every man who passed looked hard at her. A tourist in dark glasses and jazzy shirt and bright red trousers of an English cut, obviously bought locally; a local businessman, wearing the distinctive shorts and dark jacket and American rimless glasses affected by the commercial community on the Island; a black man on a pedal-bike, with a load of green farm-produce wobbling on his handlebars. They all looked first at Angel, glanced but briefly at him. The policeman on traffic duty smiled, from under his cupola, at Angel. He wore a British policeman's navy helmet, and white duck uniform, which gave the salutation an official style. Angel smiled back, delighted.

All that was, Abbott supposed, credit, the envy and approval of men wherever they went. The debit was that no man seemed to think Abbott might *like* her, too. The unspoken male consensus seemed to be that Abbott must be having sex with her in ten minutes' time, or had done so ten minutes before. It was all there, in the smiles that were sometimes leers, and the touch when no touch was needed, from taxi drivers, head waiters, airline pilots. That was the debit side.

They walked out of the small sleepy town, along the winding Pitt's Bay Road, towards the Yacht Club. Tourists, many of them American, walked by, be-goggled and Bermuda-shorted, and the accents were mainly of the Canadian plains and New York. 'Few British come here,' David O'Hara had told Abbott. 'Too far away from home, and too expensive, just for the sun. There isn't even

50

a casino.' David's accountant's itch had shown. 'You have to go further south to Nassau for that.'

'Casinos bring all sorts of trouble.' Abbott knew that much. He'd once handled a casino account in London.

'Protection and prostitution mostly, in this hemisphere. They go together.' David had sighed. 'You won't find either in this paradise.' His tone was regretful. Abbott remembered that David, being Irish, liked to gamble.

Now Angel and Abbott were at the entrance to the club, a low brick building surrounded by a lawn, at Albouy's Point, a small and pretty harbour. The sails of many vessels spiked the sky above the building.

Abbott said, 'I'll go in and find David.'

'What about me?'

'Hang on a minute. They may not allow lady guests in this way.'

'Oh, all right,' Angel pouted. 'But don't be long.'

Abbott went inside, and felt instantly at home. It could have been any sailing-club in the West of England. Members sat about drinking and talking, and the atmosphere was restful and familiar. A club servant came forward, but by then David had already seen him, and crossed from the bar.

'You're on time, Jack.'

'My old business training.'

'I have a table reserved, on the terrace. Where's ... ?'

'Angel is outside.'

'Let's get her, walk her round?'

'Fine.'

David O'Hara hesitated, looking as if he was about to say something. Abbott knew that David wanted to ask him what his situation was with Angel, his domestic, social, even his sexual situation, but lacked the nerve to do so. They had been good friends in the old Regent Street days, and David had met Helen once or twice. At their meeting during the morning Abbott had simply told David that they had split up. David was obviously wondering about Angel. Abbott gloomily decided that he was in for the usual male-envy nonsense. David, after all, was thirty-six and not yet married. He was probably beginning to get neurotic about it, except that the Irish always married late, a fact he had been pointing out as long as Abbott had known him.

Angel was sitting looking out to sea, the white bulk of the Bank of Bermuda building looming behind her, at the end of the ancient lawn.

'It's like having a skyscraper on a village green,' Abbott said.

'I know,' David grimaced, 'but so many of our members work there. It's one of the few tall buildings on the Island. An edifice to Mammon. Is this the fair lady?'

Angel got to her feet, holding on to her hat with one hand, her dress whipping around her legs in the fresh breeze from off the water.

'I say,' David O'Hara sounded almost masochistically gloomy, 'isn't she something, though?'

Abbott had rarely heard him talk so enthusiastically about anything except boats. They walked across the lawn. 'David, this is Angel da Sousa.'

'Delighted.' David held her free hand—the other was holding on to the hat—for what seemed to Abbott much longer than absolutely necessary. 'Da Sousa? Portuguese?'

'Spanish name,' Abbott said, adding, 'British passport.'

'Of course!' David let go the hand reluctantly. Angel smiled at him, delighted, as ever, with admiration of any kind, from, it sometimes seemed to Abbott, any quarter. 'Shall we go round, I have a table on the terrace? And how do you like the Island?'

'I've hardly seen it yet.'

'It's best seen from the water. I must show it to you. I have a boat.'

'Oh, do you?'

They swept on, chattering, and Abbott followed, with a sigh. It was clearly going to be that kind of lunch. David would talk to Angel without cessation, probably about boats, and Abbott would be left to enjoy his food and drink. It would be useless to try to break in. Angel had heard most of what he had to say anyway, and Abbott was sensible enough of the stupid male demand, made on loving women, that they listen again and again to the same stories. She could have a treat today and listen exclusively to David.

The table was on the terrace and in close view of large and splendid ocean-going boats, both cabin and sailing, the whole a panorama of blue sea, white sail and fresh gleaming paint. Most of the people dining and drinking were locals, or what passed for locals, bronzed, sun-tanned, Bermuda-shorted, English of haircut, manner and (often) voice. 'With land at three hundred thousand dollars an acre, you need to be well-britched to come and live here,' David observed, in a low voice.

'How do ordinary people live?'

'Ordinary? You mean . . . ?'

'Black people?'

Angel asked the question innocently, but it sounded to Abbott like a bomb going off. There was not a black face to be seen. David O'Hara received it cheerfully enough. 'Oh, they're quite happy. Got to do a couple of jobs, y'know, hacking and waiting on tables, something like that, to get your own house. The jet, the tourist boom, that changed the Island. It's brought the packaged holiday, the commuters from New York and Nova Scotia. It's our tourist miracle, and the blacks have had their share of it. If you work, you can buy your own house.' He grinned and sipped his rum and coke. 'Not in the middle of Hamilton obviously, but you'll make out. Black people are better off here, I mean materially, than anywhere else in the Western Hemisphere. I mean, the people you were asking about, ordinary black people.'

'Do you really mean that?'

'Of course. Education's decent. Or anyway it's improved. There's no poverty.' He shrugged. 'In fifty years, who knows? Now, two black people to every white person on the Island. Sixteen seats out of forty in the House of Assembly. It can all change, like it has in the Bahamas, only I hope not.'

'Why?'

Abbott had never known Angel take much interest in such things. He put it down to the influence of Snow.

David debated. 'Well, it's all gone wrong down there. Casinos and boom-time and Mafia and black-power politics instead of white. Of course, it's a bigger deal than this but the problems are the same. They have a black prime minister but he has a ten per cent annual rise in the cost of living to cope with, and at the same time to provide for his people, I mean the social advancement they've got to have, I mean to even catch up. No, I hope it's slow here.' David's voice took on a sad note. 'It's a little like Ireland. Nobody understands it, except the people who live there. Everybody wants to leave but those who do always come back.'

'Somebody else said that yesterday,' Angel mused.

'The cab driver,' Abbott supplied.

'Oh, was it?' Somehow, she seemed annoyed that it was the

cabby. Abbott wondered if she would have rather it had been Snow.

'Anyway, can I order for you?' David waved to the waiter. 'You both like seafood?'

'Oh yes, lovely.' Angel smiled and looked around, conscious of the admiring glances of the members and the less admiring ones of their womenfolk, who had that expensive, international, leathery look, the result of too much wind in the face. They all looked extremely healthy, and like the native English of the same class, Abbott noted, their voices were cheerful, but somewhat too loud.

David was looking at his menu. 'Most of the food's flown in from the States, obviously. But we do have lobsters, very good, and a local fish, red snapper. So, cold lobster and salad, yes, and wine? Chablis? Splendid.' He looked at Angel with immense interest. 'And now, young lady, I want to hear your life story.'

'But Abbott is your friend, you must have lots to talk about . . .'

'Abbott?'

'She calls me Abbott.'

'Oh? Does she?' David look uncomprehending, then turned back to Angel. 'Begin with you were born?'

'That's too long ago.'

'Well then, tell me how you met this character? When I first knew him the only language he spoke was Double Entry.'

'Just because I actually worked !'

'He used to hate it, really.'

'So did you.'

'Ah yes, but I didn't get out and you did.'

'I was lucky.'

'You always were.'

David's voice had an edge of impatience on it. For a very good reason. To him, it was true. Here I am, Abbott thought, sitting in the sun, sleeping, obviously, with Angel, and stinking rich, to boot. He didn't seem to be doing too badly himself, Abbott thought, but then he wouldn't *feel* lucky, nobody ever does.

'Tell me how Abbott was always lucky,' Angel said.

'He won all the sweepstakes in the office. If he bought any shares they doubled . . .'

'Simple study of the markets.'

'If he went racing he'd back one horse and it would win.'

'I simply looked up form and did a few sums.'

'If we needed a new deal for a client he always came up with the answer.'

'I used to actually think about it, instead of chasing dolly birds all over Chelsea.'

'Well, you had Helen. . . .' David flushed and said, with enormous sincerity to Angel, 'Did you want another drink or anything at all?'

'Nothing,' Angel smiled. 'Tell me more about Abbott?'

'Well, I don't know much about him really, after he left the old firm. He got into that showbiz agency, by a large slice of good luck . . .'

'A good recommendation and a wonderful interview.'

'And the last I'd heard he was into television. Glory be to God, if he steps in shit it turns to gold.'

Abbott knew that David had said that to break the tension he thought the mention of Helen's name had created, and he liked David for it. David wasn't to know that there was no tension at all. Angel did not care about Helen. She had never cared about Helen, or any other woman in Abbott's life, one way or the other. Abbott supposed it was simply tolerance, but sometimes it troubled him. 'Do you want me to be jealous, darling?' she had once asked him, lying back in her low chair in her Mayfair flat, showing her thighs casually, for his inspection. 'I'm not. I'm never jealous. If you want somebody else, you'll go. I'll cry for a bit. Then I'll stop crying, and start living again.' Abbott wasn't sure he'd liked or understood that, either. But he had respected it. And, there was no denying, it made life simpler. Not that there had been any other woman since Angel. She was enough for any man.

The lobster was good, and they ate with appetite. David plied them with wine, and they talked easily, as it took hold. He seemed sobered and contrite about his gaffe, and occasionally looked at Abbott with something nearer sympathy. He was a Catholic, of course, and for him any union would have to be for life. Abbott thought he knew now why David had not yet married.

'The ice cream's American and the coffee's American too, so they are both very good,' David offered.

'Just coffee for me,' Abbott said.

'A brandy for mam'zelle?'

'No thank you, but maybe a Cointreau?'

'Lovely idea. Three?'

Abbott nodded. Why not, what was a waistline when you met

55

an old friend unexpectedly? The Cointreau tasted good and he sipped it slowly, savouring the oily orangeness of it. The boats rocked, at anchor, white and blinding in the hot sun, and Abbott's eyes closed. Goddamit, he thought, I'm going off to sleep again. He forced his eyes open with an effort and sipped his coffee. As David said, it was excellent.

'Hallo, David, how are you?' A thickset, gingery, fiftyish man, dressed in a dark shirt, and white Bermuda shorts, was regarding them with a smile, especially favouring Angel.

'Oh, hello, Tony.'

David waited, but the man did not go away, simply stood there, smiling, so he said, 'Tony Waters, Miss da Sousa, Jack Abbott. Join us for a drink?'

'No, I couldn't, you're lunching.'

'Don't be silly, old boy. Sit down and have one.' David snapped his fingers. 'Usual for Mister Waters, please, John.'

'Ah well, if you put it that way.' Waters sat next to Abbott and said, 'First time, Mister Abbott?'

'Here, or on the Island?'

'Both.'

'First time both.'

Waters smiled, accepted a large whisky from the club servant. 'Your very good health, David.'

'And yours, me old son.' David was deep in conversation with Angel, his back half-turned to the two men. Abbott could hear the words, 'Fifteen-footer, light as cork, strong as iron,' and he could also see the glazed look beginning to set on Angel's face. Serves her bloody well right, he thought, although for what he could not say, unless it was the closed bedroom door of the previous night.

'Staying long?'

Waters was a reddy man. Reddy hair, reddy complexion, reddy hairs on his arms. He seemed amiable, but there was about him, Abbott thought, something deeply sceptical. Abbott had dealt with enough clients in his time to spot the odd one who would always ask awkward questions, would always want to *know*. For some reason, and on little evidence, he put Waters in this category.

'Booked in for a week.'

'Should give yourself a bit longer. Lovely spot.'

'It is. You a local?'

Waters looked faintly annoyed, nothing, just a flicker. He isn't used to answering questions, Abbott thought, he always does the asking.

'I'm from the Islands. A bit south of here.'

'Oh, where?'

'Born in Barbados, actually. Went to school in England.'

'Ah. Which one?'

'Rossall, actually.'

'I was at Kirkham. We played you at cricket.'

'Did you?'

'Yes, I'm sure.'

'I wouldn't know. I don't play. Never liked it.' Waters drank the rest of his whisky at a swallow. 'You?'

'No, thanks.' Abbott held up his Cointreau. 'I'm toying with this.'

'Nearly met you yesterday,' Waters said.

'Oh, how was that?'

'Called on your friend Snow.'

'Snow?'

'At his mother's house. You were there, I think?'

'Yes, I was. Did you . . . ?'

'Known Snow long?'

'Only met him yesterday.'

'Business?'

'Yes.'

'Theatrical?'

'That's right.'

'You were in television, I think, Mister Abbott?'

'How did you know that?'

'Heard it somewhere.'

'Did David . . . ?'

'Funny man, Snow.'

'Oh, is he?'

Waters squinted into his glass. '*I* think so.'

'How?'

'Well, made it very big, hasn't he?'

'Yes, I suppose he has. You know him well, do you?'

'Yes, I think I can say I know him well.'

'A friend, then?'

'Oh, I wouldn't exactly say a friend. How long have you known him?'

Abbott was wide awake now and fast becoming irritated.

'I'm not sure, if you're not a friend of his, that we should be talking about him.'

'Why not? It passes the time.' Waters' mouth smiled, but his eyes did not. 'He's a very interesting man. Clever. Talented. I envy talented people. But it's the simple ones I like. Know where you are with them. Like his old Mum. One of the old school. If they were all like her the world would be a better place.'

Abbott was surprised. 'You know her, too?'

'Oh my word, yes. Great old girl. Brews a wonderful cough mixture. Made from juniper berries. Old Island recipe. Doesn't cure your cough, but by God it makes you pissed, drink enough of it.' Waters laughed. 'Odd thing, Snow coming from her.'

'Why not, she's as good as anybody else.'

'That's what I said.' Waters looked patiently at Abbott, as if waiting for him to say something even more foolish. 'Salt of the earth. Snow's all right too, in his way, just keeps funny company.'

'Meaning myself and Miss da Sousa?'

Waters laughed again, very loud and spontaneous. Nobody turned and looked at him, as the people had turned to look at Snow in the Royalty Hotel pool the day before. 'My dear Mister Abbott, I would not call Miss da Sousa funny company.'

'No?'

'A charming young lady.'

'I agree,' Abbott said. 'But then I would, wouldn't I?'

'Yes,' Waters replied, slowly, 'I suppose you would, sir.'

'Don't trouble to call me Sir. Unless you're a public servant?'

'Sorry, just popped out.'

'Army?'

'Air Force. A long time ago.'

'Oh, R.A.F.?'

Waters looked half-uncomfortable, half-proud. 'I worked for Vickers as a boy, after I left school. Came the war, they sent us to Norway in civilian suits, getting people home from Stavanger.' Abbott pictured that cold, northern airfield. He had not seen it himself until the 'fifties, when a Swedish jet had stopped there *en route* for Oslo. He had been on his way to sell the Norwegians some old television repeats, or anyway to talk money, for his company. He looked at Waters carefully, and put him there, in the blazing summer of nineteen-forty, the work, the sweat, the stink of high-octane fuel, the parachutists, the danger coolly coped with, and it all fitted only too well.

'You're a policeman?'

Waters looked mildly affronted. 'Whatever gives you that idea?'

'Well, you are, aren't you?'

'I think you need another drink.'

'No, I don't, but I'll take one, if only to give you a job explaining it on your expense account.' Abbott tapped David on the shoulder. 'We're having champagne cocktails.'

David looked dubious. '*Are* we?'

'Why not?'

'Oh. All right.' He turned back to Angel. Abbott's question had merely interrupted his flow. Angel nodded her head, dumbly, wordless.

Serve her right, Abbott thought again, and snapped his fingers. The club servant appeared as if by a trick.

'Four champagne cocktails, please. For Mister . . . ?'

Waters' face seemed a shade redder, but it was hard to tell. His voice, however, was very steady. 'Make it three.'

'Three, sir. Coming along in a moment.'

Abbott sat enjoying the sun for a moment.

'Why didn't you tell me you were a policeman?'

'I would have.'

'It wasn't an accident you talked to us here, was it?'

'No.'

'Mister Waters, I don't like you much.'

'Mister Abbott, I don't give a sod.'

'But I will enjoy your drink.'

'I hope you do.'

'You must have a very curious idea of me if you think I will discuss my friends with policemen.'

'I don't know very much about you, Mister Abbott.' Waters leaned back in his chair and studied Abbott. Then, slowly, he looked at Angel, a long, searching look, taking in her mock-interest, as she leaned forward to listen to David O'Hara's possessed words (it was still boats), her breasts pushing against the flimsy dress, a mistake, Abbott reflected, after all, for this place. Waters' mild gaze returned to Abbott, but he let the silence say it all.

'I'm glad to hear I'm not in your dossier,' Abbott said, uncomfortably. 'You seem a very nosy old chap, to me.'

'I don't know you,' Waters' gaze returned to Angel, and then to Abbott again. 'That doesn't mean I don't know *about* you.'

'Do you actually mean you have been making enquiries?' Abbott could feel his temper rising. He wondered if he was being wise. He had been out of boardrooms for months, but that did not mean he was out of practice at the business of male mock-cut-and-thrust.

'I think I have some friends in Whitehall who might think that irregular.'

Waters briskly wrote a chit for the champagne cocktails. 'Mister Abbott, I'm not interested in you. Or the young lady.'

'I'm very relieved to hear that.' Abbott sipped his drink. It tasted very good. He was a fool to drink it after the Cointreau, he thought, but what the hell? The gesture was worth it. 'Who *are* you interested in? Snow?'

'Not really.'

'Oh, I rather thought you were?'

'No. He keeps, as I said before, funny company.'

'Then it's his company you are interested in?'

'In a way, yes.'

'This drink,' Abbott said, 'is excellent.'

'I'm very pleased to hear that.'

Waters leaned forward, in what Abbott at first thought was a conspiratorial way. He half-expected the man to grin. Waters did not grin, and his voice seemed sober and serious. 'Was there anybody else at the cottage yesterday, while you were there?'

The drink and the sun conspired Abbott to further idiocy. 'You mean Rowley?'

A bead of sweat appeared on Waters' reddy brow. 'You saw him?'

Abbott drained the glass.

'I heard you ask about him.'

'What?'

'I was in the cottage at the time. I heard you ask Snow about some person called Rowley.'

'I see, I see. Mister Abbott, you are a very funny man.' Waters looked at Angel again. 'And everything I heard about you is true.'

'What *are* you talking about now . . .'

But Waters had got quickly to his feet. He laid his hand on David's shoulder. David was saying, 'The bloody backstay had broken—would you believe it!—and the mast was heading forward like a fishing pole, no, you wouldn't believe it unless you'd seen it, I swear to God!' and Angel was still nodding, a fixed smile on her face.

'Sorry, old boy, got to go,' Waters said.

'Oh, so soon?' David turned, smiled and turned back to Angel.

'Nice to meet you, Miss da Sousa.' Waters almost came to attention. 'Interesting to talk to you, Mister Abbott.' He walked out of the place, his back very straight and his reddy hair close-cropped, his profession more obvious than ever.

David swung back reluctantly to take Abbott into his field of vision. 'I must say it was decent of old Tony to buy those drinks.'

'Wasn't it?'

'I mean, he'll buy his round and all that, but what in this world made him think of champagne cocktails?'

'What does he do?'

'Oh, didn't he say, he's some kind of civil servant.'

'Policeman?'

'Well, I suppose so, in a way, but very loosely.'

'There's no loose way of being a copper.'

Angel said, 'I don't like policemen.'

'Be careful,' David said, 'most of my uncles are in New York's Finest.'

'Well, we used to have one on our television panel game. He was big and tough and quite nasty. I think he had a thing for me.'

'The man was a fool,' David said, gallantly, 'if he hadn't.'

The champagne cocktail was obviously affecting him too, Abbott reflected. The lunch had now dragged on until three o'clock. 'We don't kill ourselves here,' David explained, reluctantly getting to his feet. 'But it's the usual thing to be in the office by two-thirty, even if you do nothing when you get there.'

'In that case you're late.'

David kissed Angel's hand with a flourish. 'Angel tells me she'd like to go sailing.'

'Oh, does she?' Abbott looked at Angel, who was nodding politely.

'I'll fix something. That's mine, the *Rawalpindi*.' David pointed into the flock of sailing boats nestling along the pier. 'Sunday any good?'

'Yes, I imagine so.'

'We'll make a day of it.' David shook hands with Abbott, and said, in a low voice, 'I'll ring you, you lucky old bugger.' And with that he was gone.

Angel slumped. 'Boats! What a drag.'

'Then we refuse politely.'

'Oh, no. Talking's the drag. I don't mind the boats, if they're like these.' Angel surveyed the superb craft moored to the club jetty. 'Do you suppose he owns that one?'

'I suppose he must.'

'He's nice, isn't he?'

'I told you he was.'

'What was the policeman really like?'

'Oh, he was all right.'

'You seemed to be having a long chat with him?'

'Our schools used to play each other at cricket.'

'Oh, did they?' Angel turned away. Abbott smiled. He had expected that she would. She knew him well enough not to have to pretend interest when she didn't feel any.

There was a message from Snow waiting for him at the hotel. *I'm tied up until tomorrow but will be in touch then.*

'Well, I'm just as happy.' Abbott flopped on the bed. 'Chablis and Cointreau and champagne cocktails are altogether too much.' He closed his eyes drowsily.

'Darling, unzip me, will you?'

Angel was presenting her back to him. Abbott sat up, yawned, and pulled the zip down. She was wearing nothing underneath and his hands cupped her breasts.

'Abbott, let me go, I'm going down to the pool.'

'Later.'

'No. Look, Abbott, we have to stop behaving like this.'

'I thought you liked it.'

'I do, but . . .'

'But you want to be free to think about your bloody work?'

It was cruel and true and Abbott felt sorry he had to say it.

'Don't tell me you're jealous of Snow?'

'Of course I'm not jealous!'

'Not much!'

The sight of her standing there, half-naked and golden, was too much for him and he reached forward with a groan : and the groan seemed to work where the angry words had not, and they were suddenly in each other's bodies and Abbott felt peaceful as he always did with her. It was, often, a gentle thing between them, not the rushing passionate coupling that everybody probably imagined. Angel did not always like what she described as 'piston pokes' and asked for, nay demanded, gentle, easy movements, only giving way entirely towards her climax. She never, at any time, took over the mechanics of the act. Abbott found this a wonderful blessing, and was grateful for it. He was not interested in adolescent male anger, or the even more bitter tyranny of harsh satisfaction for the woman. It was, for him, a revelation, unexpected and new each time, and he only hoped that it would never end.

Abbott found cigarettes and lay back.

'Nice?'

'Great.'

'Ciggy?'

'No thanks.'

Abbott smoked and closed his eyes. At some point he heard her moving about in the bathroom, but the food and wine and the sex worked their magic easement on him, and he slept. When he wakened (suddenly, with a sense of loss) the room was empty, the shades drawn against the sun's glare. All that could be heard was the faraway cries of the bathers down at the pool. Abbott put on a dressing-gown, rang for tea, and when it came, drank it very slowly, recovering, he was not sure from what. 'Blast the bloody man,' he said, wondering who he meant, Waters or Snow.

The tea finished, he lay back on the bed and closed his eyes. He would, he decided, really have to do something about this continual drowsiness. What was he trying to blot out? Helen and the kids? The possibly uncertain future with Angel? He threw himself to his feet, put on his shorts, and went down to the pool. The shock of sunlight, the bright-coloured shades under which the people sat and sipped their drinks, the brown rows of flesh, young and old, that lay inert around the pool, Angel amongst them, cheered him. The water was cool to a body not yet baked by the sun, but it revived Abbott, and because he was a Northern European, exhilarated him, in a worthy-feeling way. He swam several lengths, in the racing-crawl he had perfected as a boy, to the consternation of the other swimmers, mostly tourists, who regarded the pool as something to float in. He climbed out of the water, and sat, exhausted but cheered, next to Angel. She stirred, in her low chair, and said, without opening her eyes, 'What do we do tonight?'

The night club at the Royalty was large and unexpectedly full. To obtain a good table Abbott had adopted the American tradition of putting two dollar bills in the head-waiter's palm as he entered. The grimly humorous fiscal attitudes of New York, most commercial of cities, had simply been transported here, along with the tourists. The waiters, Italian to a man, would never have thought of it for themselves. It was their natural tradition to give service, and be rewarded at the end. Their handsome features, as they moved swiftly in the half-dark, wore an expression comically compounded of equal parts greed and pain.

Abbott was given a good table, in the first row. 'Nice, eager, tourist crowd,' he said, looking round. 'Out to enjoy themselves.'

'They'll be lucky.'

'Oh, I don't know. Somebody said the acts were good.' Luigi, the waiter, had said so, in the restaurant, his dark eyes gleaming at Angel.

'I don't expect much.'

Angel had not made a stir with her entrance, despite the daring of her dress, a sensational black silk, slit almost to her thighs, but high in the neck. Abbott had never seen it before. The entrance had been a failure for a very good reason: nobody had seen her clearly. The place was very dark indeed, and all attention was on the acts. From time to time a flash-bulb popped, something Abbott was never to get used to.

'Fans,' Angel said disdainfully.

Abbott smiled to himself. Angel had nothing against fans, provided they were her own. He shook his head and sipped his drink. The workings of the creative psyche were a constant mystery to him. Why should Angel knock herself out for the applause of any audience, when all she had to do, with her looks, was sit still and take her pick of anything that was going? But Abbott had learned the foolishness of saying anything like that to her. Angel knew that she was beautiful, and that she could have most things (and most men) for the asking, but it was nothing like enough. There had to be applause and adulation, and not for her looks alone. Abbott supposed it was some emotional displacement from her muddled childhood, a compensation for the lost (or dead?) mother. Whatever it was, he did not find it in himself to be jealous of her talent. It did not seem to give her happiness, quite the reverse, except on the rare occasions of towering triumph. Relatively speaking, that was, she hadn't done much yet; but the time she had been praised in some theatrical weekly for one of her folk-rock songs had been a high. Then, there was a sort of modest ecstasy. It was all very childish, really, but Abbott was used to these

64

displays, from his years at the showbiz agency. He did not love Angel because she was a performer. He thought perhaps he loved her in spite of it.

Angel sipped her drink. 'This band's far too loud.'

'Everybody likes everything too loud these days.'

A flash-bulb popped behind him and Abbott jumped. The band *was* very loud, but good, in a very competent and dated style. Piano, lead clarinet and sax, second sax, and drums, with a girl singer—young, hardworking, sexy in a bland, blonde way. They played hits from Broadway shows of the 'sixties, and sang inoffensive pop-classics to an audience that really did understand them. Abbott was reminded, again, of the difference between American and British audiences. Americans had been *reared* on pop, old and new. They knew when a band was playing well. A British audience of the same age group (thirty to fifty, with a few honeymooners thrown in) would not have reacted anything like so knowledgeably. The band finished (very loudly) with 'Sweet Sue' and bowed, sweating. Applause and more flash-bulbs. Angel yawned.

'It's not even modern pop.'

'This audience wouldn't want that.'

'Yes, God *what* an audience—I'm sorry for the band.'

Angel stood up. 'I suppose we might as well dance.'

Abbott knew she was bored and that, dancing, she might be noticed.

A local five-piece (white) band came on and played well enough, while the tourists danced slowly, close together, old-style. One or two danced the modern ritual way, standing well apart, but Abbott and others cannoned violently into them and they, too, were finally reduced to the double-shuffle of the majority. The floor got very crowded and Abbott finally suggested they sat down. He ordered two more brandy and sodas; they came double-strength, with ice, in tall glasses, and the ice took away the taste of the brandy, as usual. They sat in the loud, dark room and Abbott felt rested, even amongst the noise and the popping flash-bulbs of the tourists, who were, after all, simply imprinting a mobile memory to look at on dark winter nights in Calgary and Brooklyn. The tourists were sunburned and happy and healthy and they probably *were*, in Angel's terms, a terrible audience. That was to say, an audience composed of people of no exalted or special tastes, not likely to take to any extreme kind of talent or expertise, but somewhere, deep down, vastly prejudiced in favour of anything simple and good, like common audiences anywhere. These temporary residents of the Island were as much part of it as Snow was himself. They brought their hard-earned dollars and spent them prodigally and harmlessly in the place. Their faces shone with sweat and good health and enjoyment.

The new act was, Abbott guessed, almost obligatory in any Caribbean island show. The limbo dancers (inevitably) sang 'Yellow Bird' and Angel grimaced, but Abbott noticed that her fingers began to tap the table as the bongos stepped up the rhythm, and as the lead player began to take long solos on his own, his muscles gleaming and coal-black, the showbiz patina lost now in the jungle rhythms, survivors of an eighty-day journey from Africa three hundred years before. The girls in the act wore long skirts cut high to leave their legs free; bare midriff and handkerchiefed breasts, and straightened black hair. The men had shirts open right down the front to their jeans, and nobody wore shoes. The lead man cleverly cut the tension by introducing honeymooners into the act, calling them out by name (more flash-bulbs) and cajoling them into trying to dance, often falling clumsily backwards, under the low pole, adjusted by the youngest and most sulky girl in the troupe.

'Oh God,' Angel said. 'Not *this*!'

She was, Abbott knew, irritated by any act playing to the gallery, by being too obviously commercial. She had the true performer's necessary need for an audience's love, but she was not prepared to beg for it.

'They like it.'

'Do they look as if they like it?'

A fat young honeymooner from Detroit was trying very hard to get under the pole without falling on his back. His face grew steadily purple, as he shuffled forward, and it was only the judicious supporting hand of the lead dancer that got him under at all. The flash-bulbs popped particularly loudly at that, and the honeymooner was roundly cheered. He reported back to his seat, his fists clenched above his head, in the style of a boxing champion.

'He's enjoying it.'

'This audience would stand for anything.'

But, again Abbott noticed, Angel's long fingers tapped on the table-top as, the crude comedy over, the limbo dancers really began to work. The lead bongo player upped the rhythm until the noise grew almost intolerable and even the waiters stopped serving drinks. The girls moved their hips disdainfully, as if sorry to be doing this for mere tourists, but they too got caught up in the beat, and by the time the leading girl dancer (Marie by name; plump and sexy) was bending far backwards to shuffle under the two-foot pole, now set alight by a tarry substance, everybody in the room, audience and act, were part of the happening; and although Abbott guessed the performers had done the thing a hundred times before there was still, he thought, a half-genuine feeling of relief when the girl, Marie, came slowly, to the ever-faster beat of the bongos, through the mock-flames to safety. The applause was deafening.

When it had subsided, the limbo dancers left the stage, the waiters began to serve drinks again, and only the leading bongo drummer, very handsome and African, stayed on, wiping his face and body delicately, bobbing and smiling, and rolling the bongos with his huge spatulate fingers.

'Surely,' Angel said, 'he isn't going to try to top that?'

Abbott looked back across the crowd. In the darkness, standing at the very back, behind the waiters, he thought for a moment that he saw a familiar face. Then the bongo drummer hit a long roll and the spotlight stayed on him. The huge white teeth gleamed at his audience. 'Ladies and gentlemen, we have a celebrity in our audience tonight!'

At the hallowed word there was instant silence.

The drums rolled again. 'Yes, sir! Here tonight we got a real London star . . .'

Angel whispered, 'Oh, no . . . !' and her whole body went taut, but whether in anger or pleasure Abbott could not tell.

'Miss Angel da Sousa!'

The bongo drum rolled, the spot searched for Angel, found and held her. Abbott leaned back to be out of the searing pool of light, and Angel got to her feet and smiled.

The audience did not know her, and there was a slight slackening of attention. The reception was merely polite. Angel's face softened, as if she had been struck. Then she smiled again and sat down. The spot, to her obvious irritation, stayed on her.

The bongo player rolled his drums, again.

'Miss da Sousa . . . I was wondering if Miss da Sousa could possibly give us a song . . . Folks . . .' He appealed to the audience. 'I hear tell she sings pretty good, done a lot back on the television in London, England. Give her a big hand, folks!'

The audience applauded, again, merely politely.

'How did he know?' she hissed.

'In an hotel everybody knows everything, remember?'

The bongos rolled again, in salute, and Angel got up and walked out to the platform. She walked very well, not too fast and not too slow. The audience's attention was caught. A walk like that, looks like that, promised something.

'Welcome,' the bongo player grinned. 'Come on, people, show appreciation!'

The audience applauded, more warmly.

'What will it be?' the bongo player asked, lazily.

'I'll sing something nobody here will know.' Angel took the mike firmly and aggressively, adjusted it skilfully with one hand, detaching the mouthpiece with style, and stood holding it in her left hand. The bongo player looked respectful. 'It's a ballad, from a musical I may do one day, called *Paradiso*.'

'Do you want a piano?'

'No. It's very simple. I'll do it unaccompanied.'

The audience stilled, respectfully, but without great expectations. Something they didn't know, such a song, could hardly be a hit? But Abbott had heard Angel sing this song and he knew that it suited her voice very well. Without a good voice it was a song impossible to sing. Without breath control of a decent order the verses could not be sung clearly. It was a ball-breaker of a song. That was why, Abbott knew, she had chosen it.

The quartet had come out for the dancing that was plainly to follow, but when she began to sing, low, throaty, but with great power and conviction, they fell quiet and still. Like all musicians, they were profoundly cynical of talent, and, like all musicians, talent was the only thing they respected.

> 'I know what it's like to go hungry,
> I know what it's like to go short.
> I know what it's like to live daydreams,
> I know what it's like to be less than the dirt.'

The audience was silent now. Not a glass chinked, not a plate was touched, nobody coughed. Angel barely acknowledged the piano player, who had slipped into his seat and taken up the melody.

'Yes, I know what it's like to be shut out,
Yes, I know what it's like to be hurt.
I know what it's like to be a shadow on a wall,
I know what it's like to be treated like dirt.'

When she had finished, standing there alone in the spotlight, and the banal, theatrical, touching words had died away, there was a silence.

Then the applause came.

It came in waves and it did not stop for more than a minute. A little of it, Abbott thought, had to do with the fact that she had kept the song short, had not tired or bored them; and some of it came from the fact that she had been a lot better than they expected. But most of it came, he knew, from the fact that she had, instinctively, chosen to sing a song that touched them, in this place, at this time. It had been an inspiration; and she had put emotion and power into it, and yearning, and sincerity. For the moment she had made the simple sentimental little ballad real. Abbott was very proud of her.

Angel bowed, refused, correctly, to do an encore, and came back to the table. The spotlight left her, the band began to play for dancing, and before the tourists came crowding up for her autograph (on anything, menus, drink price-lists) she said, quietly to Abbott, 'It was a fix with the bongo player. Snow was at the back, he's gone now. Auditioning me!' Her face closed up. 'I like his bloody nerve.'

Then she signed an autograph with a smile, asking the woman's name, in a soft and pleasant voice.

4

'You go and talk to him,' Angel said.

She was sitting toying with coffee in the gazebo restaurant. It was morning and Abbott felt well and rested. They had got up too late to catch breakfast in the main restaurant, and had to make do with coffee and toast. Abbott was momentarily irritated by this : he liked his bacon and eggs and coffee. No bread nowadays, naturally, but he had learned to live without bread. If you were rich, you learned to live without a lot of things. When he had lived with Helen, and worked in the city, he had simply rushed for his train on a cup of tea. Now, he felt disinclined to move. A swim in the pool, a laze in the sun, lunch to look forward to, it was all too pleasant to disturb.

'He'll come and talk to us when he wants to.'

'I want to know what he thought he was doing—oh, certainly !' Angel broke off, crossed her legs and smilingly signed yet another card, for a lady tourist in a large pink sun-hat. It had been like that since they sat down; this was the sixth request. They would stop, Abbott knew, if Angel did not perform again. For the moment, she had become a celebrity, and was free to be admired, and if possible, approached, by the tourist audience. Abbott supposed that this worship of a celebrity, odd but endearing, came from not having an aristocracy, an ascending order of inherited merit. If having an aristocracy stopped this kind of silly adulation, perhaps it was a good thing? On the other hand, celebrities were usually celebrated for being good at something, which had a decency about it that the European worship of mere rank basically did not have.

Angel gave the autograph book back to the lady tourist in the pink sun-hat.

'Such a lovely voice. It's so rare to hear one these days.'

'Thank you. Glad you liked it.' Angel smiled and the lady tourist went on her way, along the glassed-in corridor down the side of the hotel. Outside, the sun shone brightly and the flags above the pool whipped in the slight breeze. Abbott looked forward to his swim.

'I want you to go and talk to him. Please.'

'I advise you to leave it, darling.'

'He set that thing up last night! I want his opinion, I'm entitled.'

'He may not have made up his mind yet. It's weak.'

'I don't care if it's weak.' She did care, Abbott knew, which was why she wanted him to go, rather than herself. He understood, and he sympathised.

'All right. I'll go up after lunch.'

'Why not now?'

'Because I want a swim and a laze.'

'Oh, for God's sake! Are we here on business or not? You're the one who's always going on about not letting anything go . . .'

'In this case,' Abbott said, sharply, 'I'm very much for letting it go, I'm for taking no notice, I'm for ignoring the whole episode. If Snow wanted to find out whether you could sing to a live audience or not, all right, he found out that you could. Let him digest the knowledge.'

Angel brooded, childlike, on that. 'I want to know,' she said, simply, at last.

Abbott tried again. 'People like Snow—you should have sussed him out by now—use all kinds of gambits to gain ascendancy over anybody they work with. It's almost more important to them than the work itself, in fact it almost always is. It's why they're doing what they do in the first place. Oh, not *all* of them, of course there are a lot of absolutely genuine, concerned people around. But you've seen Snow, he's young, he's unsure, he thinks there's only one way to do a thing—his way. Once you bend the knee to him, you'll belong to him. You'll have to do anything and everything he says.' As he spoke the words, Abbott recognised the futility of them. Angel had to bend the knee, that was the truth of it. There was no other way to work with a man like Snow.

'We'll sort that out when it comes to it.'

'I told you yesterday, I think he's sold on you anyway. Why not leave it?'

Angel chewed a long fingernail, and sipped her drink. Then she turned to him and said, 'Please, Abbott.'

Abbott, sighed and got to his feet. 'Go and enjoy yourself in the pool. I'll be back when you see me.'

'Check at the desk in case he's telephoned?'

'I will. Don't worry.'

'And don't chat too much.'

'I'll handle it. Just enjoy yourself.'

'Don't say I sent you . . .'

'No, I won't.'

'Don't let it seem, y'know, too obvious?'

'I won't.'

'If he asks did I see him last night, say I didn't.'

'I'll say *I* did.'

'Will you?'

'Of course.'

'That's smart.'

'I know.'

Angel stood up and kissed Abbott on the cheek. 'Thank you. You're too good to me.'

Abbott felt a thrill of pride and service, but all he said was, 'Rubbish.'

'You are, you know you are, and I don't always seem as if I appreciate it. But I do.'

'I know.'

'I don't always show my feelings.'

'I know that. I'm off.'

'Don't forget to check at the desk?'

'I won't.'

There was no message at the desk. Abbott walked out into the bright sun and found his bike, parked where he had left it, at the front of the hotel. This time he put on his helmet, and feeling very self-conscious, under the regal eye of the doorman, kick-started the machine, and buzzed sedately out on to the coast road. There seemed to be a deal of local traffic around. It was Saturday morning, and the Island people would be coming into town to shop, to gaze, they would themselves be on holiday today. It was possible that Snow was amongst them. There was no certainty that he would be at the cottage, which, of course, had no telephone.

The road was quieter once he got out of Hamilton, and he remembered the way well enough. Today, instead of the unrelenting heat of the sun, there was occasional cloud building up, breaking the heat, and the wind against his face was cool. Abbott felt refreshed by it, the relaxing atmosphere of the Island was too much for him, showing itself in his persistent drowsiness. Or was the weariness simply a reaction from the emotional events of the past year, the break-up with Helen, and the constant pushing-away of guilt and worry? He had swallowed many sleeping pills, and

72

drunk a great deal of liquor, during that unhappy period. Neither had helped, possibly only time would. His pitch of idealisation must have been high, he thought. He had never expected at any time that he would leave Helen, he had never ever thought about it. It was all as if some other hand had arranged it, except, of course, that it hadn't. The hand had been his own. Gloomy, but half-satisfied by this explanation, Abbott turned up the dirt road towards the cottage. It had the same unfinished but permanent look, as if it had been built by hand, stone upon laboured stone.

Snow appeared at the door, warned, obviously, by the noise of the engine, wearing only dark jeans and a shirt, nothing on his feet. He waved his hand. Something about him seemed unsure, surprised. 'Hi. Didn't expect you today.'

Abbott parked the bike. 'I bet you did.'

'Oh that?' Snow laughed, showing the beautiful teeth, stood barring Abbott's way into the cottage. 'So you sussed it?'

'It was pretty obvious, I would have thought.'

'I had to see if she could really sing. Tapes can be fixed.'

'Those tapes weren't.'

'I know that now, I didn't then.' Snow still barred Abbott's way into the cottage. 'She sings as good as she looks. Now, I have to know can she act?'

'Not in any obvious way.' Since Snow did not move, Abbott rested on the small stone wall. Snow sat on the doorstep of the house. 'Angel has no classical dramatic training or anything like that, but, as you saw last night, she has a personality of her own. She makes audiences watch her.'

'I noticed.'

'Then you're satisfied?'

'She send you?'

'I'm her adviser. Let's say I came on her behalf.'

'Couldn't wait to know, eh?'

'It was my idea to come.'

Snow stretched his legs in the sun. 'Not you, mister money-man, you're too smart for that. You let the other fella move, that's more your style, let him make the mistake, am I right?'

'I think it was Allenby who said, "When in doubt do nothing, it's usually the best thing".'

'Who the hell is Allenby?'

'British general. Now dead.'

73

'Sounds like a lot of people on this Island. Dead, only still walking about.'

Abbott said nothing to that, except, 'What do you want to do next?'

'In what way?'

'About Angel?'

Snow debated. 'Like I said, find out if she can act.'

'How?'

'Take her through the book.'

'Of *Paradiso*?'

'Correct.'

'Here?'

'I can't think of a better place.'

'Just Angel, on her own?'

'More or less.'

'Where would we do it?'

'I'll fix something.'

'When?'

'Next day or so. I want to think about it a little, read the script some more, give it all time to jell.'

'It can't be tomorrow, I promised to go sailing with a friend.'

'Who's the friend?'

'Nobody exciting, I'm afraid. A man I used to know in London. He's an accountant here.'

'Doesn't sound my bag.'

'Well, accountants know other accountants, it's a natural law.'

'Where's he taking you?'

'Oh around, nothing fixed. We leave around ten.'

Snow squinted at the sky, leadened by grey, sullen cloud. 'Funny you should say that. An old buddy was promising me a trip but I dunno, it could blow up tomorrow.'

'You're a sailor?'

'Here everybody's a sailor. They used to say, in the old time, this Island lived on salt, cedar and sailors.' Snow shielded his eyes, and looked at the sky again. 'Yes, it could just blow up tomorrow, if it had a mind to. You going out in some big sailing job?'

'No, small sailing boat, down at the Yacht Club.'

'The Yacht Club? Your friend a member?'

'Yes, he is.'

'You run with the right people, Mister Abbott.'

'I don't run with anybody. He's just an old friend, that's all.'

74

'Your friend's boat . . .'

'It's called the *Rawalpindi*.'

'Think I know it.'

'You do?'

'Don't look so surprised. Like I said, the sea's our business on this Island.'

'Well, it means tomorrow's off. Unless you insist?'

'Oh no,' Snow said, softly, 'I never insist.' He raised his voice. 'Come on in, have a glass of Happy's lemonade.'

'Well, I don't know . . .'

'Come on here.' Snow stood up suddenly and ushered Abbott inside. Abbott went into the soft gloom. Nothing seemed to have changed, except that the record player was not on. Happy sat in the rocker-chair, as before, and behind her the brass face of the grandmother clock gleamed. A door slammed suddenly at the rear of the house and there was the sound of footsteps in the yard at the back. Nobody spoke, as the steps grew fainter, and then Happy switched on the record player. The room filled with Dylan, and Happy got to her feet, slowly and with a gasping effort.

'I'll just get you a glass of lemon.'

'No, please, don't trouble.'

'No trouble.' She went off into the kitchen, calling back, 'And how's that Angel girl?'

'She's fine. Left her at the pool.'

'She worry a lot, that girl.'

'Well, she's ambitious.'

'Don't do no good for a woman, don't bring her no happiness.'

'My mother,' Snow said, with a tight smile, 'hasn't yet heard of Women's Lib.'

'I have so heard of Women's Lib.' Happy returned with a glass of what looked dismayingly like pure lemon juice. 'It's the same as any other kind of lib, it's all right if you know what to do with it when you got it.' She gave the liquid to Abbott, who took it gingerly, and sipped. It *was* pure lemon juice, but somehow sweetened, not only with sugar, but mellowed in some way, molasses perhaps, Abbott could not tell. Anyway, it tasted good.

'You like that?' Happy asked, settling back in her chair.

'Delicious.'

'Perk you up. You work too hard.'

'I don't work at all now.'

'You chase after that girl. That's work.'

'I don't exactly . . .'

'Now, that Angel, she's liberated.' Happy laughed comfortably. 'She knows what she wants. She mean to get it, I tell you.'

Abbott smiled. 'I think you're right.'

'I usually am.'

'My mother is an old reactionary,' Snow said. 'An old Aunt Thomasina.'

'That is true,' Happy said, rocking gently. 'I don't see any point in change if you all right as you are.'

'Happy,' Snow said, 'I could use some coffee.'

'If I was Women's Lib,' Happy said, 'I'd tell you to get your own coffee.'

'Could I wash my hands?' Abbott asked.

'You really mean wash them, or use the john?'

'I really mean wash them. I had to mess about with the bike coming up.'

'Go through with Happy, she'll find you a towel.'

Abbott went into the kitchen. Happy poured warm water from the kettle into a bowl. Abbott looked out of the window quickly, but he could see nobody at the back of the house.

'Sumptn' in what he say, but don't tell him I said so.' Happy found an unused tablet of soap in a cupboard. 'When I was a girl, the women waited hand and foot on the men, hand and foot.' She tested the heat of the water in the bowl with her finger, unwrapped the new cake of soap and gently dropped it in, moving it around with one hand to make a gentle lather. 'I take your jacket, you'll be more comfy with it off, while you wash.'

Abbott took off his jacket. Happy hung it up behind the door, on a wooden hanger.

Abbott began to wash his hands and Happy watched him. 'Yes,' she said, 'in those days the men expected you to run around after them, dawn till dark. Them Women's Lib people, they won't have that. That water right for you?'

Abbott said it was fine.

'Yes, sir, I tell you, they expect you to wipe their bottom for them in the old days, they sure did!'

Abbott washed his face, reached blindly for the soiled roller towel behind the door, only to find that Happy had placed a dry, white towel in his hands.

'This here one is clean for you,' she said.

Abbott dried his face and hands, and gave the towel back to the waiting Happy.

'I tell you, Mister Abbott,' she said, folding it, 'in the old days all the men do is a little farming, a little fishing, otherwise they sit around all day, black and white no different, never mind what anybody . . .' She raised her voice so Snow could hear, 'Never mind what *anybody* say.'

'Thank you,' Abbott said, as she held his windcheater for him.

Happy deftly poured away the dirty water. 'Them fellas, they think a woman no good for anything but waiting on a man,' she grumbled. 'Them Women's Lib, they got their number.'

She brushed the back of Abbott's windcheater with a clothes brush from a drawer, and handed him a comb. Abbott gravely combed his hair in a small mirror, and gave the comb back to her.

'Yessir,' Happy said, 'they wanted us to wait on them hand and foot in the old days, and we fool enough to do it.'

Abbott looked out of the window again, longer this time. The backyard and the field behind it were empty. 'Thank you, I feel a lot better,' he said, and went back into the living room.

'No trouble,' Happy called, beginning to breadcrumb some red snapper taken from a larder. 'Just holler when you want a little more lemonade. That drink come from lemons growed out back in the yard there.'

Abbott sat down, and called back, 'Sorry to disturb you when you're about to eat. I'll be gone before you start.'

'No, you won't,' Happy called. 'You eating with us.'

'I can't . . .'

'You in a hurry?' Snow asked, quietly.

'Well, not exactly.'

'Then you have a treat in store. You like fried fish?'

'Yes, I do.'

'Then relax and wait for it.'

Abbott wondered how fast to push along the business end of the deal? Was Snow ready for him to ring New York and talk to his agent? At what point did Snow get businesslike? Abbott decided it was useless to put any pressure on the man. He had already advised Angel not to do so. It could wait.

'I talked to somebody who knows you, yesterday.'

'A lot of people know me on this Island. I'm one of those who got away. Who was it? Some porter at the hotel?'

'Man called Waters.'

'Waters?' Snow's face was expressionless. 'What did he say?'

'Just that he knew you.'

'He said more than that, Jack.'

'A little more.'

Snow took a reefer from a shiny tin kept in his hip pocket. Abbott couldn't smoke the things, he'd tried once, but it had simply made him feel dizzy and rather sick. Snow lit it, and inhaled, leaning back in his chair and closing his eyes. It was the first time Abbott had seen him retreat, and he was surprised. There were slight lines of worry and fatigue around the eyes, and Abbott realised that Snow was probably four or five years older than his publicised age, which was twenty-eight. Snow inhaled again, and his whole body relaxed, limb by limb, his hands and arms, then his shoulders, his torso, finally the outstretched leg, as the room filled with the sickly scent of pot. It is the will, not the cannabis, Abbott thought. It's yoga or something like it, it's the sort of thing you can do if you use your body like a machine; if, like Snow, you are a trained dancer.

'All righty,' Snow said, not opening his eyes. 'What little more did he say?'

'He asked about a man called Rowley?'

Snow's eyes opened.

'Rowley?'

'Yes.'

'Just that, what about him?'

'He asked had I seen him?'

'Where?'

'At the cottage here.'

'And what did you say?'

'I said I hadn't.' Abbott let the words hang. 'As far as I knew.'

Snow looked up sharply, then drew deeply on his reefer and held it in front of him, between thumb and forefinger.

'Rowley is an old friend of mine.'

'I guessed that.'

'Waters is a sorta cop.'

'I guessed that, too.'

'Waters has it in for Rowley.' Snow seemed to Abbott to be picking his words carefully. 'He has it in for anybody . . . anybody he don't . . . instinctively . . . approve of. You follow?'

'Not exactly.'

'Well, take me.' Snow got up, poured Abbott a measure of rum from a bottle on the table. 'Have a real drink.' Abbott nodded his thanks. 'Take me,' Snow said, again. 'I got off the Island and I did well. I got written up in the papers. New York papers. London papers. I'm like famous. Everybody—well, a lot of people anyway —knows my name. Nobody knows his name. He's like an apparatchick, y'know, a bureaucrat, a functionary?'

'Yes, but not one you'd want for an enemy?'

'The day I worry whether fuzz love me or hate me, I'm dead,' Snow said, harshly.

'Any of them?'

'Any of them.'

Abbott could not resist it. 'Do you mean that, or are you just talking fashionably?'

Snow's eyes widened in anger, but to Abbott's surprise he held it in.

'Jack, you're getting at me?'

'Not exactly. I just hear a lot of this kind of loose talk around showbiz and the arts and I know that most of the people who talk that way are yelling for the police two minutes after somebody steals their milk from the front doorstep.'

'You're talking about white intellectuals and that type of person, the sort we all know, theatricals, actors, directors, that kinda person, right? Their experience is to be protected by fellas like Waters, right? So they would holler for him if they got into trouble, what more natural?'

'Then they shouldn't talk crap . . .'

'Meaning I do?'

'Not meaning anything, except you seem to have it in for him, just because he's a policeman. I didn't like him much myself . . .'

'Man,' Snow said, 'I don't have it in for anybody. They have it in for me. I tell you, if you'll listen . . .'

'All right, sorry, go on.'

Snow took a deep breath, debated, poured himself a measure of rum, and sipped it. Abbott, who did not have a lot of knowledge of these things, wondered about the matching qualities of pot and rum. Maybe it did not matter, to Snow. Any sensation, however induced, was different and, therefore, valid. It was the life-style of a lot of people Abbott had met.

Snow was talking. 'Waters knew me when I was a little fella. I got into a mite of trouble on this Island in 'fifty-nine. In the riots.'

'Riots? About what?'

'Segregated cinemas.'

'Riots about *that*?'

'May not seem much but it was big to us at the time. I got arrested, got a bloody nose. Gave one, an' all, I was fast with my fists. Yes, I hit one fella flush in the face, pow! And he's not even in uniform, but I know him, and pow! An' he's down, man, blood and snot everywhere and I'm in the cooler, my feet not touching, yes sir.' Snow sipped his rum. 'People thought I was political. I wasn't, I was just young.' Snow shook his head. 'Then, I got thrown off a few beaches for swimming there when tourists were around. Private beaches, y'know? I got fined a coupla times, name in the paper, all that. So Waters knew my face. Knew my name. I was on the books. Nothing much, nothing big, just a lot of scrapes and bother and trouble.' Snow sat down again, stretched his long legs, sighed. 'All a lotta fuss about nothing, just a young kid showing off. So I need a job. I've no father to speak for me. My old man was a labourer at the docks, he died when I was a kid. A cargo fell on him in a ship's hold, crushed him.' Snow finished his rum in one easy gulp. 'I don't recall him. Happy says he was a drunk, okay, so I guess he was, but I dunno that he had any reason to be anything else, humping stuff around all day for pennies, when he could find the work. So all righty, I'm a wild kid, but what kid isn't if he's worth a damn?'

Abbott said nothing to that, because he had not been a wild kid himself, and he knew hardly anybody who had, in his neighbourhood, at home. His own adolescence had been one long grind at textbooks, and the fear of failing examinations.

'So, okay, I'm on the books.' Snow poured himself more rum, swilled it round in his glass, looked at it. 'And I need a job. I need one very, very bad, man. I apply here and there, but word goes before me. This fella's a troublemaker. This fella's a pretty bad boy. Why employ him when you can have a nice docile boy who never swam from the wrong beaches, and didn't demonstrate, and wasn't fined by the court? So I need a job as a waiter, and the hotel needs a recommendation, and on this Island that means somebody who carries a little weight, right?'

'It means that anywhere in the world.'

'Okay, I take the point, sure. So I go along and see guess who?'

'Waters?'

'Jack, you are no fool. Waters is the man I see. I say to him, all nice and humble, 'cos I'm only seventeen, Mister Waters, I say, an' I tell you he's all surprised that I go to him, he can't believe I have the nerve, y'know?' Snow laughed loudly, the uninhibited dark brown laugh. 'You see, *Mister* Waters is the guy I hit in the face at the demo.'

'You bust his nose?'

'Right.'

Abbott said, 'I can see how he wouldn't like that.'

'Walked around with a plaster on it for a week. Had to have it re-set.' Snow grinned. 'Jesus, I certainly hauled off and let him have one. Anyway, it was like maybe a year later, I asked him for this recommendation. I mean, most people don't know where he works, he don't have an office at any official place or anything like that, he's like a sort of undercover guy, I s'pose. So, I see him on the street, right out there on Front Street and I say to him, what about signing this recommendation for me?' Snow got up and walked around the room. 'Jesus, the cool of that guy, I have to hand it to him. He just says well, if I'm gonna sign it I'd better read it first, hadn't I? Just like that.'

'They teach them that at Rossall.'

'Rossall? I'm not with you . . .'

'Go on, please.'

'Well, he reads it in the sun, just like standing there, and when he's finished reading, he just looks up at me over his sun-glasses for a long time, just looking, y'know that stare all the fuzz get, looking right through you, or want you to think they do, what's the difference? Anyway, when he's done looking, he just says to me, okay, turn round, and I say why turn round, and he says, if I'm gonna sign this bloody thing I have to have something firm to sign it on. And I turn round, and he takes out his pen, and holds the paper against my back and he just signs it, and says good luck. Then he turns and walks away up the street, just like it happens every day.' Snow shook his head. 'Sure was cool.'

'You had no trouble at the job?'

'No, sir. I was clumsy — I'm a rotten waiter — but I smiled, and ran around the people, and took my tips and saved them. I talked to folks in showbiz, on the Island on vacation, and I asked questions, and I listened, and I thought, if these people can do it why not me? They're no smarter than I am, they're no fitter and healthier than I am, they aren't any more hardworking than I am? And so, I got into a group of limbo dancers, like you see at the hotel last night, but I only last two weeks because I take the chick belonging to the lead guy, and he finds us in bed together and I'm out, back waiting table again.' Snow smiled, crookedly. 'I'm always doing that, gettin' in the wrong bed, I made a few enemies like that.'

'It's easily done.'

Snow laughed. 'Yes, sir! So anyway, I decide what the hell, I'll get to New York somehow. And so, I go. And like I told you, finally I make it good. It takes me time, and the sweat, man, oh, the sweat, walking that big, cold unkind city, trying to find a way in, nobody wanting to know. Getting an introduction to an agent, so he'll get you an introduction to a secretary, who might fit you in with the boss, and half the time it is all a waste of energy. And the other half somebody wants something outa you 'cos you're young and good-looking, and you don't know your ass from your elbow. Men *and* women, you know how it is? So you oblige when you half-want to, y'know, some gal with hot pants wants to help a struggling artist, all that balls? Till you learn that all you have in this world is your reputation and then you stop it, and get like integrity, 'cos if there's one thing they like in showbiz it's integrity. A little pretension, Morris tells me, when I get to him, when finally I'm working as a dancer, wanting to get in as a choreographer, going to the best people to learn, sleeping six hours a night, maybe five, still living in this cold-water walk-up, spending every penny I got on dance tuition or books, living, y'know, like a monk, and Morris says to me, y'know that way he has, leaning back with his cigar going and looking like all the cares of the world are on his shoulders, and he says, "A little pretension, Snow, it never did any harm".' Snow laughed and slapped his knee. 'And so I get pretension. I talk crap about the musical being an art form and wanting to bring folk art to the people, and all of that.' Snow made a self-disgusted snort and shook his head. 'The crap I talked, at parties, at first nights off-Broadway. In bars. In beds. Boy, I sure did give out with a lot of plain stupid artistic-soul bullshit. I still do it now, for the papers and the columnists. You ever hear anybody sound as stupid as a performer when he's talking about his work? Or an actor? Nobody knows *how* they do it, act, dance, sing. Nobody. So what's the wild scene *for*? Well, I tell ya. People like to think artists are different, when all that's different is they do a different job and that makes them different. But all the talk isn't about being different in a professional way, it's about being different in some sorta deep *special* way, and I know that's crap and you know that's crap, but it's what they want to hear. Morris is right, the old shrewdie, a little pretension never did any harm, and so I gave them that, oh man how I gave it to them.'

Snow stopped talking and sipped his rum. Happy singing to herself in the kitchen; a chink of plates, and the hiss of frying fish, were the only sounds, apart from the slow tick of the brass-faced clock.

'Man', Snow said, reminiscent and faraway, 'I sure gave it to them.'

'And so you made it?'

'And so I made it.' Snow came back to the room, from whichever bar or bed he had been in. 'And then I came back home, for like, y'know, the applause, the curtain, all of that?' His voice was light, but there was a catch in it. 'I got interviewed, sure, written up, sure, in the local paper, sure, and everybody stopped me in the street and shook my hand and said great. But I tell you Jack . . .' Snow leaned forward and his eyes were tender and regretful. '. . . I behaved like a shit. I'd got the big head by then, y'know, the really big swollen head, oh man.'

'Understandable,' Abbott said. The rum was getting to him, and he was feeling drowsy again. 'Young man, back home, big success, perfectly understandable.'

'Sure it was,' Snow agreed. 'To me, to you, to my mother maybe. To the world, especially to some people on this Island, strictly *not* understandable.'

'In what way?'

'Well, like they don't *say* anything. Nothing direct. I mean, I see Waters on the street and he shakes hands right there and he says, "I dunno what kind of dancer you are, Snow, but I hope you're a better dancer than you are a waiter", y'know, like joking, like referring back to when I used to be a waiter and he comes and sees me not doing too well, 'cos I'm just scared a little, see, this job is important to me, and I say, "Man, I sure know I'm a better dancer than you a cop, because it ain't clever to get your nose busted if you're a cop, especially not by an itty-bitty fella like me," and at that he kinda gets cold and he shakes my hand again and he says, "Good luck", just like that, good luck, and he walks off, and I'm full of this kinda stuff, only stronger.' Snow patted the reefer-tin in his pocket. 'And I just call out, "All cops are pigs anyway!" I don't really mean a damn thing by it, I mean, all the people I'm like balling around with in New York

83

City that time, well, to them that is just like a harmless remark, it don't mean anything at all . . . but I'm forgetting where I am, or maybe I'm not forgetting, maybe I mean it, I dunno, the dope's kinda getting to me, and maybe he guessed that. But like I say he just stops in his tracks. He don't turn round. He just like stands there, absolutely still, with his back to me, right there in the sun on Front Street, with all the rich people going past him into Trimingham's to buy their English cashmeres, and all that scene. I know he's heard and he's wondering what to do about it, if anything . . . and, finally, he decides nothing, which is smart of him. He just walks on down the street. I stand watching him, and I want to call out to him, "Mister Waters, no offence" . . . but the words just, y'know, stick in my craw and I can't get them out. Then he's gone and it's too late to say anything.'

Snow brooded over his empty glass, got to his feet, refilled it, and sloshed some into Abbott's half-full tumbler.

'You ain't drinking, man.'

'Should you be?'

'Huh?'

'Well, that?'

Abbott indicated the small, shiny tin. Snow laughed loudly. 'That won't hurt me. This is simply cannabis. I've been on big trips. I trip the acid now and then. I was on it, on the Island, the next time I talked to Waters. I mean, I had this show going in New York by now, and I was back in the Island to see Happy, take her to New York maybe, but she wouldn't go, ain't never been off the Island in all her life. So I was a little tight about that. I mean, she was my own mother and I wanted her to come and see my success and all. But I might have known with her, 'cos all she ever says is "Are you content?" And I know how that's the right question to ask, I mean I know it sitting here and talking, I don't know if I know it when I'm running about working on a show, because then if anybody says are you content I'd yell balls at them, y'know? So, I'm feeling down when I run into Waters again and he walks past me. I mean just like that. In the street. Down Queen Street. Straight past.'

'Did he see you?'

'Couldn't miss me.'

'Were you alone?'

'I had a chick with me. It's okay. Black.'

'You were on . . . acid at this time?'

'I was on acid.'

'Ah, well.'

'You say ah well, but could he have known, I mean could he have known, walking up to me, not getting a good look, just a glimpse in the street, could he have known I was on it?'

Abbott said, 'The man I met yesterday could have known. Maybe he did you a favour by ignoring you?'

'Never thought of that.'

'I don't say he did, I say it's possible.'

'Never thought of that,' Snow said again, slowly.

'If drugs are a problem on the Island . . .'

'The young kids look for them, like they do everywhere in the like Western world, okay, why not, it's a drug-culture now, the young scene, it's not alcohol and aspirin any more, it's hash and speed and acid, it's got to be here like it's anyplace else, sure. You see,' Snow said, 'if a kid has hash on his person, even if he ain't smoking it, it makes him feel somebody, it's an act of defiance against the establishment, it's the first step on the road.'

There was a silence, then Abbott said, 'If Waters saw you with that?' He pointed to the shiny tin, 'Would he do something about it?'

Snow looked surprised. 'Sure he would. He'd have to.'

'Then it's likely he *was* doing you a favour.'

Snow shook his head. 'Why should he?'

'He signed that recommendation for you.'

'He did. But . . .' Snow looked philosophical. 'Anyway, it don't matter one way or the other. We never spoke again till they held the Black Power conference here in 'sixty-nine.'

'Here? That's pretty liberal of them.'

'Man, they are liberal. That's the trouble.' Abbott looked disbelieving. Snow saw the look. He hunched forward, earnest. 'Some guys I know figure that this liberal bit is worse to deal with than the other stuff, the hard stuff. You can face that, deal with it, it's blow for blow, but with the liberals, man, it's like punching thin air. . . .'

'Do you *believe* that? I mean, yourself?'

'Sure I believe it.'

'There's two ways of . . . your friends getting what they want. Talking about it, or trying to take it.'

'They aim to take it. All over the world. A lot have taken it already.'

'But these people here let your . . . friends run a conference?'

'Hell, they'd let you run a conference on child-murder on this Island, so long as you paid the hotel bills. This is the conventioneers' paradise.' Snow relaxed, his good temper had returned. His accent was still of the Island, and this made Abbott wonder. 'Anyway, I see Waters hanging about, sussing everybody out, and he's in his civilian clothes and all that, smoking his pipe, looking innocent, and I tell my friends, I tell everybody who he is, and some stupid guy goes over to him and spills a drink right down his shirt-front. Y'know, like accidentally on purpose? I mean, I didn't know this joker was gonna do it, but when I look across the bar, there is Waters and it's happening to him, and he is looking at me, 'cos this guy who done it has just come from my group. Waters knows I've been talking to him and that he's come right over and done it. I dunno what Waters thinks, but I see him in the street a coupla times since, and he never speaks to me, not good morning, good evening or kiss my ass, not one word.'

'I can't say I blame him.'

Snow roared with laughter. 'Jack,' he said, 'you another goddam liberal.'

'I don't think Waters is a liberal.'

Snow laughed louder than ever.

'You didn't tell me about Rowley yet,' Abbott said, equably. 'Rowley?'

'I've enjoyed your life story, told in Uncle Remus fashion. But I did ask about Rowley.'

Snow stopped laughing. 'Jack, you think I've been putting you on.' Abbott smiled. Snow sighed, and said, 'Well, he's a friend of mine. It's guilt by association, see? I had this cannabis on me when I came in the last time, and there was a fuss . . .'

'And was Rowley . . . ?'

Happy came in carrying a large dish on which lay several whole, fried red snapper. The scent was delicious, and the fish tasted like all fish just taken out of water, of the sea itself.

'Delicious.'

'They were swimming this morning,' Happy said.

'Who caught them?'

Happy looked at Snow, just a flicker of hesitation, and Snow said, forking in a mouthful, 'Fella down the road.'

'Off the rocks or out in a boat?'

'Boat, you won't get much off the rocks.'

'Small boys in Hamilton do.'

Snow laughed. 'I used to fish off Front Street there, when I was a kid. It's just good practice 'cos you ain't got a boat.' They ate in silence and Abbott was glad of the food, which was greasy but delicious. He was not used to rum at midday; the liquor was making him sleepy again. When the plain but ample meal was finished, and Happy had given them large bowls of coffee, they retreated to their chairs.

'How was the red snapper, Massa Baas?' Snow asked.

'Fine, Uncle Remus,' Abbott said.

'I done tole you, man.' Snow curled himself up on the old leather sofa, and closed his eyes. In a moment he was asleep.

'He could always do that,' Happy said. 'When he was a little boy he could do that.'

'Odd, in a boy?'

'He had jobs from being so high.' Happy lowered her hand from the table. 'Running errands from the hotel, an' such, anything. He slept when he could. We needed the money.'

'He told me.'

'He was a good boy.' Happy got up from the table and sat down in her rocker. 'You got him to talk, he must like you. I know he plays the fool, imitating old coloured people with that damn fool voice, but most of what he tells you is true.'

'I don't know if he likes me,' Abbott said. 'He hardly knows me.'

Happy rocked, gently. 'If he talks about them first days in New York he likes you. I reckon he did a lot of things he wishes he hadn't.' She looked at her son's form, curled like a cat on the sofa. 'Still, he got what he wanted in life and that's better than not getting it.'

'I suppose so.' Abbott wondered why Snow had elected to switch off. If he slept at will, that was what it amounted to. Talk probably, he decided, too many old memories dredged up. Abbott wondered. He had had a feeling of things held back in Snow's torrent of talk, of something important . . . not said.

'You don't sound too sure, Mister Abbott.'

'I'm not.'

'It has to be better,' Happy said, gently, 'or you never satisfied, is you? I mean, you always wondering.'

'Yes, there is that, I expect.' Abbott felt his own eyes closing. It was warm in the room, and stuffy. The cottage did not have air-conditioning, and he longed for the chill of the hotel room.

87

'You know, don't you, Mister Abbott?'

'I'm sorry?'

'I say, you know. You found out what it was like? To get what you want?'

'I don't know how you mean . . .'

'That girl, Angel. I like her, but she's only twenty-three or four, am I right?'

'Twenty-five, actually,' Abbott said, stiffly.

'Lord, I ain't correcting you, Mister Abbott,' Happy said. 'You do a lot for Miss Angel, right?'

'I do what I can to help her career.'

'That what she want?'

'I think so.'

'Not children, home, all that?'

'I don't know, I haven't asked her.'

'I think you knock yourself out for her, Mister Abbott. No woman really want that, deep down in her heart.'

'I don't know how you can say that. You don't know Angel.'

'I know women, Mister Abbott, becos I am one. An' I know that I like a man that takes charge, y'know?'

'All that's changed now.' Abbott felt himself getting irritated. 'Like your son was saying, all women don't want to be tied down all their lives to one man.'

'I heard what he said, dunno if I believe it. Not sure you do either.' Happy smiled broadly. 'You a man of forty, I bet, you not one of those fellas who grown up with Women's Lib, like my boy here. I mean, before you meet Angel you had a wife, right?'

Abbott nodded, reluctantly.

'Yes, I know you was that kinda man. Children?'

'Yes.'

'Boys or girls?'

'One of each.'

'What age, like?'

'Seven and thirteen.'

'Your wife still with them?'

'Yes, she is.'

Happy sighed and rocked in her chair, keeping her eyes on Abbott. He suddenly did not feel sleepy any longer. He had a feeling that he had stayed too long in this place. He stood up. As he did so, there was a soft knock on the back door of the house. Snow woke at once, his eyes going to Happy, in question.

'Sit down,' she said to Abbott. 'Just a neighbour.' She waddled out into the kitchen. Abbott sat down again. He looked round at Snow, but the heavy-lidded eyes were closed again. Abbott could hear Happy's voice, but could not make out the words. Another voice, a man's, replied, but that, too, was low, and indistinguishable. He got to his feet and went out into the kitchen, but the door had closed, and there was only Happy, her back to him, drying her hands (or pretending to dry them?) on the soiled roller-towel behind the door. Abbott could hear quick footsteps in the yard outside, but as he moved across to the window, Happy somehow impeded him.

'Did you want to wash again, Mister Abbott?'

'No . . . I wanted the john.'

'Oh, okay, you know where it is.' She stood aside and Abbott nodded and went quickly out, into the yard. The wind had fallen and all was still, apart from the far-off wash of sea against rock. The cardinal bird cawed grumpily in the tamarind tree. The heat was sudden and almost brutal, the drifting sun hemmed in by low, metallic cloud. Abbott went across to the john, sure of Happy's eyes on his back, and pulled at the door. It was locked.

Abbott said, 'Sorry.'

A man's voice inside mumbled, but Abbott could not make out the words. He waited, but the man said no more.

'Neighbour in there.' Snow was unexpectedly at the back door. 'Come inside and wait, okay?'

'No, thanks,' Abbott said. 'I'd better get back. Angel will be expecting me.' He went across to his bike, and kick-started it. 'Tell your mother thanks for lunch.'

'And you tell Angel,' Snow said softly, 'I'll be seeing her.'

'I will,' Abbott said, and rode carefully out of the yard. It was very hot and dusty on the road and the heavy grey clouds seemed to be pressing lower than ever.

5

The *Rawalpindi* was a trim little sailer, built on the lines of the original old Bermuda sailing-ships, to a design original to the Islands and developed by the shipwrights of two centuries before. Or so David O'Hara told them. 'She's a bit slow and heavy, but she has character.' To Abbott's unspoken question, he added, 'I rent her.' Abbott was doing his best to crew for David, in the most amateur way, since he had not sailed for years, and then only on English lakes and around the small estuaries of the West Country. The Great Sound looked a very different proposition indeed, a vast expanse of grey-green water stretching back to Two Rock Passage and beyond. The boat seemed a brave but tiny speck on that vast expanse of slightly choppy water, and Abbott was glad that David had decided not to go out too far. Squinting up at the sky, with the grey, metallic cloud thickening, Abbott had been somewhat surprised that David thought it safe to go out at all.

'There'll be a storm, but it'll be tonight.'

'I'm glad you're so confident.'

'My dear old Jack, I've read the weather reports.' David had smiled at Angel, asking her to witness Abbott's old-maidish fussiness and David's slight advantage of years (no more than five or six, as Abbott recalled) and Angel had smiled back. She was in a good humour, for Abbott had told her of Snow's willingness to try a rehearsal. He had said nothing of any other matter. Angel had dressed for the occasion sensibly and demurely, in a thick white Aran sweater and faded blue jeans. She did not need telling more than once the kind of place the Bermuda Yacht Club was— conservative and British and no need to shout, whether it was the clothes you were wearing or just your voice. Anyway, one or two people had smiled at her in the bar (that was, apart from the usual male sex-stares) and David had said to her, sipping his Scotch (rum *was* a strictly local drink), 'It seems you had quite a success night before last?'

'You heard about me? I only sang one song.'

'People said you were first class.'

David, again, was playing the old game of talking directly to

Angel, forgetting Abbott's existence for minutes on end. Abbott hoped that David would not fall for Angel, even in a small, silly way. Angel was not interested in conventionally handsome men. 'They're always so vain,' she had told Abbott, when he asked her why she kept away from the obvious people, why, in fact, she preferred him. Staring at herself with comical concentration in her looking-glass, she had said, 'I knew one once, he was an actor, great looker, y'know, the hair, the eyes, the body, the whole bit? That man was an exploiter of women. He wanted me to run around after him, all day and all night, and I mean both those words. I stuck him for six months then heave-ho!' Abbott had not asked the actor's name, in case it was somebody he knew.

Angel reclined in the boat, and said, 'Isn't it great? I never was much for the sea, y'know? But this is something, isn't it?' She looked happily at Abbott, and he felt the warmth he always experienced when she was happy. Her mood had lasted from the evening before. Even at breakfast she was still asking, 'Did he really say that? Was he really knocked out or was he just talking? God, if he was just talking...'

Abbott had said, 'No, Snow doesn't just talk. He meant it.'

'You were there hours. He must have said more.'

'Yes, but not about you.'

'What about, then?'

Abbott had turned the question aside, and they had gone down to dinner. They had an excellent view from their table, right across the harbour, and the lights were on in the houses across at Paget. The candles on their table were lit by Luigi, the Italian waiter, who smiled at Angel as if she was dining with *him*. The art of shutting out, Abbott decided, was one much practised around Angel. Angel had been entranced by *everything*, the food (mostly American-sized portions but superbly cooked) and the wine, very expensive on the Island. However, Abbott had long since given up looking at menu prices. In fact, he often lunched in London at a small club frequented by film and television people, where no prices were printed on the carte at all. Even so, his accountant's mind made him automatically check dollar against sterling, and the prices on the Island, for many things, were high. But only by British standards. By American ones, it was a buyer's heaven, most things were duty-free, and the tourists seemed to make the most of it. With nothing but cedar and sweet water to start with, the settlers had done the best they could. Many were rich, and, in addition, they lived in a paradise. Looking past the candles, across the harbour to the lights in the houses on Paget, Abbott had fallen sad and silent. Suddenly, inexplicably, he felt the need of a house, a place of his own, to be shared with some loving woman. It seemed, at that moment, that he was an exile, a man who has not been back home for a very long time, one who may never go back again.

'What's the matter? Your tummy playing you up?'

Angel looked concerned, her arms shapely and soft in the candle-light, another dress he had never seen before (or, if he had, he had forgotten it), cut low across her beautiful breasts.

'No, I'm fine.'

'You sure?'

'Yes, of course.' He was touched by her concern, and put his hand across the table, over hers. In the shadows Luigi sniffed and made his way across the restaurant for the next course. Abbott was reminded of Maugham's words: 'Anglo Saxons are sentimental and emotional, but not amorous. Latins are amorous, but not sen-timental or emotional.' No doubt Luigi had seen the sentimental—as distinct from sexual—expression on his face and had thought it unbecoming to a man.

'You seem sad.'

'I'm all right.'

'Oh, isn't it lovely here?'

'Wonderful.'

'You're good to me, Abbott. You are. You really are.'

'Nonsense.' He pressed her hand again, holding it there even when Luigi came back. To Abbott, for just that moment, all things had seemed possible. It had seemed possible that Angel would have a short, fabulously successful career, say five or six years, and then retire, and come to live at such a place as this. Perhaps he could buy a house like the ones with the lights across the harbour—and they could sail and sunbathe and live life easy, possibly even have a child? He would only be in his middle forties, she would not yet be thirty. Abbott finished his glass of wine, and poured another to take the nostalgia away. He was missing Patrick and Maria. It was as simple as that. The distant lights of home across the bay had done it. He had become sentimental, and in his case, because of his long domestic training, sentiment always took, finally, the form of woman and house and child. He swallowed his wine. It was all nonsense. He'd had that dream. It was over, and, anyway, it was out of date, finished, unnecessary in the world as it now was; besides Angel had told him she did not want children. She had not said *ever*, but it had sounded final enough. Another thing that Abbott hated about the way they lived was the lack of privacy. He decided that he would have to get her to live with him in London. He would buy a house for them both and have her live in it whether she liked it or not, or married him or not. The business of separate flats was nonsense. If *Paradiso* was a success he felt, somehow, that it was possible she would agree to move in with him. He did not know why he had this feeling, simply that he had it.

After dinner they had walked on the beach. Angel had hung on to his arm, their feet heavy in the sand, and she had said, 'Oh, I'm happy with you, Abbott, I really am.'

'Are you?'

'You settle me. I don't want to rush off and do things. I'm glad to just be with you.'

'That's nice.'

'Believe me, Abbott. I mean it.'

'I know you do.'

'You never take me seriously when I say things like that. What's the matter?'

'I don't know.' Abbott had kicked up sand. 'I suppose I'm insuring, in case you go one day.'

'But I won't go. Ever.'

'Don't say that. Nobody can say that.'

She turned him round to face her and reached up, and kissed him on the lips. His arms went round her, and her breasts were soft against him. 'But I mean it. Why should I leave you?'

'Because you're lovely, and men chase you, and one day you might give in to one of them.'

Angel thought for a moment, and then said, gravely, 'No. I've had enough of that. That was all right when I wasn't going anywhere, felt despair, wasn't sure. Now I am. I don't need one-night stands. I'm happy with you.'

'People's sexual patterns don't change,' Abbott said. 'They like to think they do, but it doesn't happen like that.'

'Oh, you're always so bloody pessimistic.' Angel smiled and kissed him again. A couple of guests from the hotel passed by, looked at them curiously, smiled, and walked on, close to the moon-lit sea. 'I used to sleep around, all right. Coming from where I did, that wasn't unusual. I haven't slept with anybody else since I've known you.'

'I know that.'

'And I'm not going to. All that kind of sex ever meant to me was despair.' Angel reached up and touched his face. 'Despair and maybe, now and then, a wild release.'

'That's what I mean.'

'I haven't felt it since we met. For anybody else.' There were, to his astonishment, tears in her eyes. 'I don't want those kind of people, Abbott. They destroy you, the one-night-stand people, all they do is use you, and all you do is use them. It's okay, it's a fast exciting screw, and then it's over, and you feel lousy, and dirty, and I don't want to get back on that scene. You saved me from it, from the sudden, half-drunk impulse. Like, y'know, after a rehearsal, in the middle of an afternoon? Why, I'd find myself in bed with some guy I didn't even like, and it was only seven in the evening, and we'd done *everything* and the problem was, how to get through the rest of the evening before I could tell him goodnight and goodbye.' Her arms clung to Abbott, tighter. 'You've saved me from all that, Abbott, and I'm grateful.'

'Don't be.'

'But I am. And I'll show you how much. Let's go back to the hotel, huh?'

They had gone back to the hotel, and she had shown him her gratitude, and there had been no mistaking the genuine nature of it, the beginning gentleness and the ending passion, and her last words, as he was falling asleep, his hand on her soft breasts, had been, 'Believe me now?'

On their way down to meet David that morning, as they walked along Pitts Bay Road, she had said, 'Last night was wonderful.'

'It was for me.'

'Me, too.'

'No, you did everything.'

Angel had disengaged her arm. 'Abbott, you're sometimes so bloody stupid.'

And Abbott had felt it.

'Sorry, I'm a bit touchy.'

'You still thinking about that husband-lover, that Helen?'

'No, of course not.'

'I bet you are.'

'No.'

They walked on, down the hot, shaded street, past the pink-washed bungalows and the discreet tourist shops. Angel put her arm back in his. 'Anyway, forget her. She'll forget you. She's written you off by now.' Abbott felt a pang, but said nothing. 'The way she lives, she needs another fella to look after her children. She's not a bad-looker. She'll find one. You'll see.'

Abbott said nothing to that, and Angel added, hurt in her voice, 'Look, if you want to go back to her ever, all you have to do is like say. I'm not gonna beg you to stay with me, I don't want any fella that bad.' And she had taken her arm away, again.

'I don't want her. Besides . . .'

'Besides what?'

'Nothing.'

'Besides, she wouldn't have you back?'

Abbott was stung. 'Who knows, she might.'

Angel laughed. 'Not Helen. She's too suburban. She'd never be able to explain it to her friends. You going, yes okay, in her little row of highly desirable residences, okay, that is fine, a lot of fellas leave home, it's join the club, dear, down at the local golf links. You did say she played golf?'

'To competition standard,' Abbott said, coldly. Angel knew bloody well Helen played good golf. It was a thing he used to boast about, especially to other men.

'She isn't going to take you back unless you go on your knees, offer to take her away to some place nobody knows her, start life all over again. And, besides, your kids are both at boarding-schools now, aren't they?'

'You know they are.'

Abbott had always hated boarding-schools. It had been one of the things Helen knew he cared about. When she had declared, in the dusty lawyer's office in the Inner Temple, that she intended to send them away to school, Abbott had detected nothing in her direct stare. He looked away, guiltily. It was really to give her elbow-room while she looked around for another husband, he had decided, and had only contested the thing in a token way. 'No objections to any of this?' the lawyer, a public-school man (inevitably) had asked, peering over his old-school tie. And Abbott, a day-boy himself, at an ancient grammar-school at that, had replied, 'No, of course not,' and avoided Helen's now openly triumphant eye. At that moment he had known the hurt was deliberate. Helen did not intend to marry again, or at least not until somebody went very much out of his way to ask her. Helen did not, and never had, chased after men. They did not chase after her either; not as a rule; but if one did, he meant it. Abbott knew, with an absolute certainty, walking down the sun-hot road towards the sea, that Helen would marry within a couple of years. He felt oddly sad, and deprived, at the thought.

'You'll have to forget her, you know. Or else go back to her.'

Angel's voice was soft and understanding-sounding.

Abbott said, 'Don't be bloody stupid, I love you.'

Angel stopped and looked into his eyes. 'Do you? Really?'

Abbott was embarrassed. 'Of course I do. Stop behaving like an idiot. Come on.'

'But *do* you?'

'Yes!'

'Just because you left her for me, doesn't mean you love me. It could be just vanity? A change? A new look at life, and I was the excuse?'

'It could be, but it wasn't!'

'You sure?'

'Yes, I'm sure, now here we are at the club, shut up, do!'

Angel had squeezed his arm and touched his lips with the tip of a long finger, all her good spirits returned, and had gone ahead into the club. David had come to meet them, looking very tanned and fit in white T-shirt and jeans, and, Abbott thought gloomily, they made a handsome pair. He sat now and stared at the expanse of green water, the Island riding in the background, and waited for David's next order.

'Keep an eye on the leech, will you, Jack?'

'Aye, sir!'

Abbott obeyed clumsily but David pretended he had done it expertly, smiling at Angel. 'I didn't know Jack was as good as this.'

'Don't be such a bloody show-off, David,' Abbott said. 'Anybody would think you hadn't got a girl.'

David reacted as if stung—that was to say like a good Irish boy who loved his mother too well. 'I'm waiting for Miss Right,' he said, but he reddened.

'I'll bet.' Abbott found his good humour restored. 'Biggest ram in Regent Street. Chased the typists all round the office.'

'Bloody liar!' chanted David. 'Now *do* watch that leech. . . .'

'Aye, aye, Capt'n.'

In this fashion, they sailed mindlessly on. The cloud lay in thick grey banks between them and the sun, but the hot rays percolated through. The wind was very warm. Angel took off her sweater and jeans and lay stretched out in her black bikini, a study in gold and jet. She seemed to be asleep.

'Sorry about that,' David said, in a stage-whisper. 'I was getting a bit carried away. She's such a dish.'

'I would have thought you could get all the lady tourists you wanted?' Abbott smiled. 'In the holiday mood?'

'I can, but I don't fancy them.' David shrugged. 'Too keen, I suppose.' He looked at Angel, rather sadly. 'You'll be marrying her, will you?'

'No idea,' Abbott said.

'You live with her, don't you?'

'Oh that. Yes, of course.'

David looked at him with respect. 'Will you be helping her, in this show thing?'

'You mean financially?'

'Well, yes.' David looked awkward. 'I suppose you could, now?'

'Yes, I could.'

David looked enquiringly at him. 'And will you?'

'Yes, but I'm not rich enough to do it all on my own, nobody is, and, besides, it would be stupid to do that. If the thing has to have a chance a lot of professionals have to believe in it, too, and that includes the impresario and the money-men behind him. If they think she has a chance, then so do I.'

'That's pretty realistic.'

'I don't live on another planet.'

David looked out across the water. The ferry from Watford Bridge was crossing their way, far ahead. As it came near it hooted, and David waved his hand. The ferry chugged on, charged with tourists at all rails, waving and taking the inevitable pictures. The sailer bobbed in its wash.

'How much did you make out of the television thing, Jack?'

Abbott had been anticipating the question for a long time. David, after all, was an accountant, too. He would want everything straight. He answered the question frankly.

David whistled. '*That* much?'

'I'm afraid so.'

'How does it feel?'

'Upsetting.'

'Surely you're used to it by now?'

'Beginning to get used to it.'

'But you've had it a couple of years . . .'

'Just the same. It takes time, David.'

David looked up front towards the sleeping girl. 'You'd made it when you met her?'

'I'd made it, but I hadn't realised I'd made it. I was still working on, as if nothing had happened. You know, going into the office every morning, taking work home in my brief-case, all that.'

'And after you met her you stopped?'

'Not all at once. Eventually.'

'And now . . . what?'

'Now I'm drifting. Like this boat.'

'Take the helm and pull her to starboard a quarter,' said David. Abbott did as he was bid.

David pointed. 'Spanish Point that side, Ireland Island over there.' The points were smudgy and shimmered, far-off in the heat.

Abbott took in deep lungfuls of air. He was beginning to feel very fit and well. The drowsiness of the last days seemed to have left him, at least for the moment.

'I wouldn't mind living out here,' he said.

'You're serious?'

'Of course.'

'Property's very expensive.' David shrugged and smiled. 'But that wouldn't matter to you. Even by expatriate standards, you're loaded. Lots of people buy a house here, and live just some part of the year. You'd have to like sailing, there's not much else.'

'Well, I do.' Abbott had felt the helm under his hand for the first time in ten years or more, and a little of the dream of the previous evening filtered into his mind. 'I've had my go at the market-place. I'd settle for this.'

David looked at him, curiously. 'Would you? I mean, really? Oh, it's great for a fella like me, I mean for the time being, I don't suppose it will last at all. They'll transfer me to New York or Philly or somewhere. But I'll have had my good times by then. I suppose I'll find a good Catholic girl, settle down, get married, have four kids, do all the things they tell me are out of date. But I'll do them because I've always expected to do them. It's finding the girl.'

'Your trouble,' Abbott said, meaning it, 'is that you're too handsome. It's too easy.'

'With the chicks in London and New York, sex means nothing

these days,' David said, an aggrieved tone in his voice. 'It doesn't mean they've fallen for you or love you or *anything*.'

'It hasn't meant that with men, ever.'

'I know, but bloody hell!' David looked comically indignant. 'Anyway, you were telling me about this place.'

'I work all day in an office. I'm busy. I'm telephoning New York and London and Tokio and everywhere else you can think of. When the day ends I'm ready for this.' His gesture took in the silence of the Great Sound, the slap of water, the heat, the small, hot wind. 'I don't know if I'd like to do it all the time, I mean with no regular job.'

'I'll have no regular job whatever I'm doing.' Abbott had not meant it to come out sadly, but it did. He smiled quickly, and added, 'I don't see how I can go back to the office now. I'd just be an embarrassment to everybody.'

'But you'll be working on this show with Angel?'

'Yes, I'll be doing that.'

David looked at Abbott a long moment, then his eyes flickered to Angel, lying still and golden. 'Is that her real name or is it a stage name?'

'It's the only name I know her by.'

'Oh? I see. Then you think that she changed it at some time?'

'I've never asked. It's the name in her passport and on any documents I've ever seen.'

'Doesn't she tell you things, I mean . . .'

'All I know is that she's been very poor. Anything she's got, anywhere she's going, she's done it all by herself.'

David looked as if he did not believe that Abbott was telling him everything he knew. Which was true; Abbott wasn't. He did not believe in idle gossip. His father had told him once, 'Never gossip, your guard is down and you are apt to say what you mean.' It had seemed good advice, then as now.

David, added, as if a postscript, 'But you didn't meet her until you came into the money?'

'No,' Abbott said, smiling, despite himself, 'I didn't.'

David nodded, in a satisfied way, and picked up Angel's sweater from the deck. He made his way forward, and wakened her by gently touching her wrist.

'Put this on. It's going to get cooler now.'

Abbott looked up at the clouds. They seemed dramatically lower of a sudden and were moving faster across the sun, breaking up in a sudden whipping wind. He shivered, and pulled his own jersey up over his neck. David was right, it was cooler. 'I think maybe we should head home?'

'Nervous?'

'Matter of fact, I am.'

'All right. Pull her hard to starboard.'

Angel came and sat down next to him. She was shivering. The light was suddenly beginning to go. David passed over his hip flask. 'Try that.'

Angel swallowed, grimaced. 'It's neat!'

David passed it to Abbott. 'Jack?'

'No thanks. Why don't we move?'

Abbott was beginning to feel vaguely apprehensive. They had been out three hours and there had been no hint of any sudden change in the weather until now. He looked all around him and saw only the small white heads of the waves, as they slapped with increasing urgency against the side of the boat. David let out more sail, and shouted, 'Here we run for home, this wind will blow us right back in.' The sailer swung round, and they swept, for minutes on end, through the rising chop of the waves.

The sudden squall hit the *Rawalpindi* like something solid. Abbott hung on, wet and shaken. Angel laughed, her even, white teeth a gleam of youth against the golden skin. She's enjoying it, Abbott thought, she's really not at all afraid. He sat tense, and soaked, obeying David's calls as they came, fast and sometimes lost in the wind, his wrists aching and his arm screaming for release from the sharp pain of unused muscles. The sweat began to stand out on his face, despite the sudden cold (the hot wind of only ten minutes before had now quite gone), and he called to David, 'You've left it a bit late, haven't you?'

David, working at the sail, merely grinned at Angel, and Abbott swore under his breath. That, again, was what it was all about. They were at risk because of simple male vanity. 'You're a bloody fool!' he shouted, but David did not seem to hear him, but only grinned back and called, 'Keep her steady! I'll do this.'

The solid wall of wind behind them bellied out the sails, and for a long time they ran in front of it, making the kind of speed Abbott would not have thought possible in such a small craft. David was a good sailor. When the wind got too strong, he called to Abbott to tack and take less of it, in a very expert way, and Abbott was glad to see it, but scarcely relieved. The ache in his wrists and arms grew worse, but he tried hard to ignore it, only glancing from time to time towards Angel. Her expression had changed now, the afro hair was holding clear globules of water. She glanced up at the black and threatening clouds scudding behind them, as if in deliberate pursuit. The smile had quite gone from her face.

'Anything I can do?' she called, as the second squall hit them.

'Put this on.' David threw a yellow oilskin at her. She struggled into it, half-standing to do it. *'Don't* stand up!' he yelled. She sat down quickly, thrown by the swing of the boat, and hung on. Her eyes found Abbott's. She was scared now.

Abbott smiled at her, and said, 'It'll be all right, we'll be home in no time,' and cursed David O'Hara's virility-proving exercise, yet again. Another squall hit them, and he was soaked through once more with rain and spray. After that the wall of wind and water struck them regularly, until Abbott thought it would never end. The salt stung his eyes, and he could barely hear the urgent calls of David, which now, he ironically noted, had an apprehensive bravado about them. Abbott himself was too tired and angry to feel any fear. He knew that if he stopped working, and really looked at the sudden high seas bearing down on them, he would feel terror, rather than fear : but the work kept it at a distance, as if it was unimportant, as if the only thing that mattered was to hear David's last order. He worked on, desperate, chilled and sweating by turns, and the seas around them grew large and looming, and the wind became icy and his fingers were glued by freezing spray to the helm.

'Get in the cabin,' he yelled to Angel, the spray filling his mouth as he opened it, but she simply shook her head. Abbott worked, numbed past any kind of feeling, until suddenly the wind dropped. He looked up, blearily, the salt-water running from his eyes, creating a distorting-mirror effect.

'What . . . ?'

'We're in lee of Marshal Island.' David pointed to the small, uninhabited rock behind them. It formed a natural harbour, which acted as a wind-break for them.

'How long do we stay here?'

'Till we get a lull in the weather.'

'How long will that be?'

David looked up at the solid grey sky. 'An hour, maybe less. Of course, it won't be over. This is in for the night.'

'You know, David,' Abbott let his muscles relax and they hurt so much he almost cried out in pain, 'you are a very considerable fool.'

'I'm sorry,' David said, stiffly, 'but how the hell did I know it was going to blow up like this?'

'You *knew* . . .'

'Somebody's here before us,' Angel interrupted. A large cabin cruiser lay off the island, nestled close in, avoiding the worst of the squalls. It rode easily on the swell, and a man on the deck waved to them. Abbott waved back as they got nearer. The *Rawalpindi* drifted up very close to the cabin cruiser, and Abbott could see that there was a man in the cabin, at the wheel, in addition to the man on the deck.

Angel stared. 'Hey, I think it's . . .'

'What?' Abbott's eyes were still half-blinded by salt. He could not recall when he had been so tired.

'It's Snow!'

'What?'

'It's Snow! On the boat!'

'No!'

'It is!'

'Who?' David called.

'A friend.'

'The black fella?'

'He's . . . the famous . . . yes. The black fella.'

'Is that his boat?'

'I don't think so.'

David studied the craft. 'I don't know it. Looks as if it's from Florida or down south somewhere. Big ocean-going job. What's he doing on *that*?'

'I don't know. He did say something about friends with a boat. I expect they picked him up earlier today.'

'Lovely job. Very fast. Didn't see her in Albouy's this morning, though.'

'Maybe she went out early.'

'Didn't see her last night.'

'No?' Abbott was so tired he let go the helm. 'Hey!' He grabbed it again.

A call came from the cabin cruiser, through a megaphone.

'Hey, that you, Jack?'

Abbott waved. It cost him a great effort.

'You going into Albouy's?'

Abbott waved again.

The deep voice drifted across. 'See you in there, okay?'

Abbott waved a third time.

'Keen guy,' David observed.

'Oh, he's all right.'

'Is he a sailor?'

'Of sorts, I think, like everybody on the Island. Or so I've been told.'

'Bit odd.' Before David could say more a sudden gust of wind struck the *Rawalpindi* and they were struggling again. They ran her as close into shore as they safely could, put down an anchor, and David passed his rum around. This time Abbott did not refuse. The neat spirit burned his gut, and some of the chill went out of him. The cigarettes in his jeans were ruined, but David had a waterproof case and a patent lighter, and they drew heavily on their Camels. Angel was quite suddenly sick over the side. When they clambered towards her she waved them back and they turned away, courteously, as all sailors do, until she was ready to talk to them again.

David O'Hara said, worried expression on his face, 'I'm sorry about all that, Jack. Honest miscalculation. You can't know, with these storms out here. One minute pond-like, the next a bloody windy whirlpool.'

Abbott said nothing. He did not trust himself. He was now shaking with reaction. David chattered on, 'Of course, you must have heard the story of how Somers happened on this place? In the worst possible storm on the worst possible night. Just like tonight will be, probably. The old records say his ship's timbers were boiling, whatever that means, possibly that the pitch holding the timbers together distintegrated. Anyway, the old boy navigated her in, and discovered the place before his ship blew up. Must have been a great sailor.'

Abbott did not trust himself to reply.

After an hour's wait the wind dropped appreciably, the cabin cruiser hooted, and began to chug her way out of the small, natural harbour.

'He's making signs,' Angel reported. She looked wan and pale, and Abbott's chest hurt, just looking at her.

David waved, and Snow called through his megaphone, his voice barely carrying, 'Go ahead. We'll follow you in.'

David waved again, and said, 'He's a decent wee fella, he's keeping us in view. 'Course we aren't in any danger now, but still...'

The gale hit them again as soon as they left the lee of Marshal's and Angel was suddenly sick once more. Abbott called out encouraging words to her, but she did not reply. The sinews of his arms and wrists screamed agony, all the way into the port. Various vessels hooted at them, once they were in safe water, and David waved back, his red face streaked, childlike and gleeful. Abbott could cheerfully have struck him.

'Home safe and sound!' David shouted, as they came into berth, at the quayside. The cabin cruiser had pulled in alongside. Snow had already thrown off his oilskins, and was at the side to help Angel ashore. She took his hand with a wan smile. She was shivering violently.

'Lady,' Snow said, grinning, 'you sure picked a day for it.'

'*She* didn't pick it,' Abbott said.

David refused to look up, other than to call, 'See you this evening? Drinks at the club, okay?'

'Maybe,' Abbott said, shortly, putting his arm around Angel. She closed her eyes and swayed.

'Let me find you a taxi?' Snow was dry and looked as if he had never been on a boat. He wore a seaman's black sweater and black jeans. 'Hey, hold this for me, will you?' He put a small duffle-bag in Abbott's hand. It felt surprisingly heavy. Snow walked quickly up the jetty. Abbott followed, more slowly, Angel clinging to his arm.

'I feel a proper bloody nana,' she said.

As far as Abbott could see, there was only one other man on the cabin cruiser, and Abbott, in passing, did not see his face. There was radio equipment rising from the cabin, and deep-sea fishing tackle on the decks. Abbott followed Snow along the jetty, very slowly, feeling wet and wretched. Several people offered help, but Abbott waved that he was fine.

'Go into the club, get dried out,' David called, still tying up behind them. 'I'll see you in there in a minute.' Abbott ignored him, and passed the club building.

'We'll get back to the hotel and dry out there,' he said.

'It wasn't his fault.'

'It bloody was. Trying to impress you.'

Angel said, seriously, 'Do you think he was?'

'Don't you *know*?'

Snow turned back to them, at the end of the green. He called out, 'I'll have to go to the road to get a cab. You stay here . . .'

At that moment a Land Rover, driven very fast, turned from the main road, and stopped with a jerk in front of Snow. Waters got out. He stood, just looking at Snow, and then he said, in an even voice, 'Just got in?'

'That's right, Mister Waters.' Snow's voice was careful, vaguely hesitant. 'Just this minute.'

'Come in with Mister Abbott here?' Waters' glance took in Abbott, and the unsteady Angel.

'No.'

'In what boat then?'

'The cabin cruiser back there.'

Waters studied him curiously. 'Perhaps you'll be good enough to accompany me back to it.' It was not a request and as he said the words he nodded towards the vehicle. Two very tall, fair-haired English-looking men in their twenties got out. They walked, in a soldierly fashion, towards the cabin cruiser.

Snow looked at Abbott, raised his shoulders. 'I ring you later, Jack, okay?'

'Yes,' Abbott said. 'Of course.'

'You got caught in it, did you?' Waters asked, not unkindly.

'We certainly did.'

'Out with David?'

'Never again.'

'It's the luck of the Irish.'

'They can have it.'

'You get back to your hotel, Miss da Sousa,' Waters said, with what seemed genuine concern. 'Get hot baths. Hope to see you both tonight at the club.'

'Maybe,' Abbott said. 'See how we feel.'

'Mister Snow?' Waters turned, but Snow was already halfway back towards the boat. Waters sighed, knocked out his pipe on his palm, and followed.

At Pitts Bay Road, outside the looming safety of the Bank of Bermuda building, Abbott hailed a cruising taxi, the duffle-bag still in his hand. There was, he noticed, a heavy lock on it.

6

The storm began with the night.

At first it was simply a continuation of the vicious squally wind that had driven them ashore in the afternoon. The sky had darkened, the cloud thickened, as they dozed on the bed, refreshed by hot baths and hot drinks. They wakened violently, at eight o'clock in the evening, to the first darkness and a clap of thunder so loud that it seemed it must be false, like a badly done off-stage effect in a theatre. The lightning that followed it was, again, a seeming confection, a white sheet of electricity so fierce that the large bedroom, still in darkness, was lit like an under-exposed camera negative, the shadows of objects in the room black, the surfaces a searing white.

At that moment the telephone rang.

'Jesus God!' Abbott reached for the instrument. 'What a noise!'

Angel was awake too, but she simply lay there, her eyes just opened, an expression of wonder on her face.

'Was that *lightning*?'

'Was it *not*? Hello . . .'

It was Snow on the line. 'Jack, hi.' He sounded friendly. 'How are you now, recovered?'

'Yes, fine.' Abbott felt disorientated, the storm had emphasised the strangeness of waking in yet another unfamiliar room. 'We're fine. We had baths, and we've been flaked out for a couple of hours.'

'Angel all right? She looked pretty chilled down there on the landing?'

'Tell him I'm fine,' Angel hissed.

'She hisses me to tell you she's fine,' Abbott said, in a normal voice.

'Don't play games,' Angel added loudly, annoyed. The look of wonder at the lightning had gone from her face. This was work.

'I'm glad of that,' Snow was saying. 'What are your plans?'

'We were asked to the Yacht Club by David O'Hara, but I don't think I want to look at him for a day or two, even if he is an old mate.' Abbott spoke with feeling. 'He gave me the shock of my life out there today.'

'You should never have gone out in that stuff, anyway not in that sailer.'

'I know that now,' Abbott said. 'How did it go with friend Waters?'

'I'm not with you?'

'Waters? You went back to the boat with him, didn't you? Wasn't there some trouble or something?'

'Oh, that?'

There was a pause. Abbott waited.

'I can't talk on the telephone, Jack. I'll tell you when I see you.'

'When will that be?'

Snow's next remark seemed to be spontaneous, but somehow Abbott had a feeling that it was not. 'Why not tonight?'

'Tonight?'

Angel sat up, catching the intonation of surprise. She pushed her hands through her black hair. She was wearing only a slip, and Abbott's hand reached out and cupped her breast. She did not move away, but put her hand over his. Abbott felt his body stir, but Snow was still talking.

'Why not come and see how the other half lives?'

'Where?'

'There's a kinda party at a neighbour's up the road from Happy's place. Why not come out?'

Abbott could think of all sorts of reasons why not, but Angel's fingers were touching his chest, delicately probing, her sharp fingernail a tiny razor of delight against his skin.

'Where are you now?' He pushed Angel's hand away.

'I'm with a friend, but I'll meet you both at Happy's. Just take a cab there from the hotel.'

'I don't know, that lightning just now . . .'

'That was nothing. You'll hear it really go, later.'

'It was enough. Let me ask Angel . . .'

Snow's voice on the other end of the line was suddenly muffled. 'Hold on a moment, Jack, willya?' He seemed to be talking to another person.

Angel put her hand on Abbott's groin, and stroked. He pushed the hand away. 'What are you doing, for God's sake?' Angel rolled on to her face on the bed, and laughed softly.

'Listen, Jack, change of plan.' Snow was back on the telephone, his voice brisk. 'It seems this party don't start till late. I'm with a little gal here and she says she wants to go to the cinema, like fill in time till then. Oh, and we eat at the party. Real Island food, you'll love it. Can you last out till then?'

'We've done nothing but eat since we came to the Island. Of course we can last out.'

'Tell you what then, Jack.' Snow's voice was more careful. It had lost none of the warmth, but the words were very clear, as if he was speaking to a child. 'Why don't you come to the movies?'

'Movies?'

'The theatre's in Hamilton. Any cab driver will take you.'

'Well, I don't know . . .'

Angel looked up as he touched the soft flesh on the inside of her thighs. She nodded. Her instinct was always to say yes, to anything, in case later it might turn out she had missed something.

'All right,' Abbott said, reluctantly. 'Do we meet you there?'

'Inside, okay?'

'What's showing that's so good?' Abbott asked, but Snow did not seem to hear the question.

'We'll be there before you, back of the balcony. We'll see you there.'

'All right.'

'Oh, and Jack?'

'Yes?'

'Do me a favour and bring my duffle-bag, will you?'

'Duffle-bag?'

'I gave it to you this afternoon.'

'Right.'

'Great. See you both. You're going to enjoy tonight, I promise. 'Bye now.'

Abbott put the instrument down thoughtfully.

'What was all that about?'

'We're going to the movies.'

'I gathered that.'

'And afterwards to this party, or whatever.'

'What will I wear, did he say?'

Abbott kissed her neck. 'Nothing.'

'You're very sexy this trip.'

'No.'

'I think you are. Any special reason?'

'No, and don't push it all on to me. You began it.'

'Yes. I did, didn't I?'

'Yes, you did.'

Abbott never knew why making love to her was different from the other women he had known. Many of the girls he had known as a young man, before he married Helen, he had wanted desperately. Then it had been a business of self-gratification, not far removed from a purely functional act. There had been no heart in it, the pursuit of unwilling girls, in taxis, cars, and bed-sitters. Like most other young men of his time, he had chased more often than he had caught, and in the end it had all got too much. The girls were not worth catching (the ones you *could* catch) because they were still conditioned, even in London, to think of marriage as the ultimate goal. It was still fairly unusual in the 'fifties to find a girl willing to sleep with a young man without a ring in mind, sooner or later, preferably sooner. Helen had been one of them. Also, she had owned a flat of her own, off the King's Road — even more unusual. Further, she had been a virgin. And when he asked her, *why,* she had simply said, 'It was time. And I wanted to.' *That* had put bands of steel around him, coming from his background, and he had asked her to marry him a month later. She had been unsurprised, and had handled the arrangements (the meeting of parents, the finding of a small house, the wedding itself) with a poise that astonished him. Had she expected him to marry her? 'Of course,' she had told him coolly, on their wedding night. They went to Majorca; it was just beginning to get popular. Helen would have been very disappointed if he hadn't married her, she said. And sex, after that, had been Helen. Youthful, violent, without subtlety, but basically good and satisfying. Or so it had seemed. The edge had finally gone off it, he thought, but naturally enough. He had not lusted, as many of the young men he knew did, after the dolly-girls in the offices, who became more sexually 'obvious' (his mother's phrase) as the 'sixties wore on. He had been working too hard to notice them; and there had always been Helen. Their sex had been a silent thing, private, performed mostly in the darkness hours, in a bed, and with little of the day, or the room, or the place, anywhere in it.

With Angel all that changed.

It was as if the whole business had been liberated, had become not so much natural as unimportant. Certainly Angel did not consider it important, not in the same sense that he did. For Angel her body was something to enjoy, and there were no fetters on place or time. It had happened between them in various cars, many strange hotel bedrooms, the woods outside the cottage in Dorset, once in the day-compartment of a French train. It happened with their clothes on, and with their clothes off, by day, night, and, fairly often, in the afternoons, on beds, chairs, often on floors. It was a thing of surprise, and there was no pattern to it. Yet, for the most part, it was a tender thing between them. Or was the tenderness his? Was the difference between Helen (all need and love?) and Angel (sly, unpredictable, hardly moving sometimes, at others all teeth and nails and writhing flesh, satisfying yet never quite satisfying) something within *himself*? Had he changed so much?

He could not know.

'Darling, that's nice,' Angel said drowsily.

He touched and moved gently, with her. Now he did not feel the frenzy, only tenderness, and some wonder that she was partner to him in this.

'Oh God, that's great.'

He moved gently, very gently.

'Ah, Abbott, you lovely man. Now, please.'

But he did not.

'Abbott, now.'

Still he did not.

'Ohhhhh . . .'

He waited for her to say, I love you.

She did not say it. She never did.

None of them did now, he knew that.

He moved inside her.

'Oh, *darling*.'

They rocked together, gently, in small, tender embraces, alternating the position of their bodies, kissing in a soft fashion, until suddenly everything exploded and they fell back, not exhausted, but merely breathing deeply. It was the way Angel liked it most.

'That was great.'

'Yes. I thought so, too.'

They lay on the bed, smoking, for several minutes. They did not talk. Angel never talked afterwards. When Abbott, conditioned by habit, had tried to do so, she had put her finger on his lips and said, 'Shush. Don't verbalise.'

'Verbalise? You mean talk. Who talked to you about verbalise, and in what bedroom?'

Angel had laughed at that, but he had not pressed her for an answer. For a very good reason. She might have told him.

Angel was the first to get up and shower. Abbott finished his cigarette, pulled on a dressing gown, and took the duffle-bag out of the wardrobe, where he had thrown it when they returned, soaked and exhausted, that afternoon. He sat looking at it. It was a perfectly ordinary duffle-bag, with a lock. Abbott hefted it in his hands. It still seemed heavy. He gave up, went into the bathroom and showered, slapping Angel as he passed her.

'Hey, don't *do* that! What do you think I am, some tart?'

Her eyes flashed, she was really annoyed.

'Sorry, I forgot you don't like horse-play.'

'No, I don't. It bloody hurts. Besides, it's putting me down, that stuff.'

'Rubbish. All I did was smack your lovely ass.'

'It's all the male chauvinist thing.'

'Oh, come on, Angel, what crap!'

'I don't like to be slapped.'

'Why?'

Her eyes welled. 'Never mind why, I just don't.'

She looked so childlike, standing there, hurt. He was touched.

'Sorry, I'll try to remember.'

'I'm not a chattel, Abbott. I'm a person. You don't own me. Nobody owns me.'

'I don't want to own you,' Abbott lied, painfully.

Angel dusted herself with talc, only a little mollified.

'All that one man owning one woman stuff, it's over.'

Abbott got under the shower. 'So I'm told, on all sides.'

'Your trouble is, you don't believe it.'

'I believe what I see, which is often very different from what I'm told.'

'You've been too long with that Helen, running about after you.'

'Balls.'

'No, I mean it, seriously.'

'Go and put your clothes on, we're late.'

'You see, all the time it's orders. Do this. Do that.'

'You *are* a silly girl. I love you.'

'I don't want soppy old love.'

'What do you want?' Abbott asked, and it was a mistake. 'A meaningful relationship?'

'Yes, I do, with give and take both ways, not the man being the daddy all the time and the woman the daughter, yes daddy, no daddy all day and all night.' Angel sulked. 'You can stuff that dated old scene.'

'All right.'

Angel said, 'And sex doesn't make any difference.'

'I know it doesn't.'

'Just because you bang me and it's great, it doesn't make any difference.'

'I heard you.'

Abbott got out of the shower and wrapped the towel-coat around him.

'You think it does, though.'

'What?'

'You think that sex is everything.'

'No, I don't.'

'Yes, you do. You pretend you don't, you hide it up with all kinds of nice feelings, but you think it's everything.'

Abbott towelled, briskly. 'You're wrong.'

Angel shook her head stubbornly and climbed into her pants. 'It's the most important thing in the world to you, it is to most men. . . .' Abbott could have sworn she was going to say 'your age' but she didn't. She just shrugged. 'To me, it's not all that big. I could do it with a mate and it would mean just as much and no more.'

Abbott hated the phrase 'mates' when it meant friends between girls and men. 'That,' he said stung, 'is a lot of cock. . . . Girls might think that way, young men never do. They're out for a dirty quick bang, my dear. Mates? What sentimental old corn. But if you want to call it that, they won't mind. They won't care what you call it so long as you let them bang you. Now, get dressed and let's go. We are very, very late.'

His voice must have had an edge on it, because Angel let it go, and went into the bedroom consoling herself by muttering, 'Forty years old, you don't suss the young scene, you're so *dated*.'

Abbott shouted, 'Crap!' and much cheered by the exchange sang loudly, as he shaved and combed his hair. Outside the thunder rolled again, louder than before, and the whole Island seemed to be waiting for the lightning. It came, far out across the sea, a sheet of incandescent flame. Angel watched it from the window. She seemed, to Abbott, very small and young and vulnerable.

'It isn't raining yet.'

'The storm's still out to sea. Snow says it'll get worse.'

'Not possible.' He put his arms around her.

Angel kissed him. 'Sorry. Just I hate being smacked.'

'Any reason?' Abbott asked.

'I'll tell you one day.'

She always said that, when he asked her about the past.

The feature film was half-over when they got to the cinema. The girl in the booking office was surprised.

'It has only forty minutes to go, sir.'

'That's all right.'

'But I'll have to charge you full price.'

'That's all right, too.'

They went up the stairs to the balcony, Abbott carrying the duffle-bag. The cinema was very dark and small and there was no attendant to show them to their seats. It was stuffy and close in the balcony, and Abbott was struck at once by the lack of air-conditioning. Rows of faces, mostly black, were turned towards the screen, washed silver by the glare. Suddenly, the audience laughed. Very loud, and without reserve, several hundred people laughing as Snow had laughed at the Royalty pool two days earlier.

It was a sound that Abbott recognised. It had a simplicity that belonged to the England of the 'thirties, to the flea-pit cinemas he remembered as a very young boy of seven or eight years old. This audience was identifying closely with the characters, *living* the story, childlike, utterly absorbed. In that it was like the Depression audiences he remembered from his early childhood. The difference was, this audience sounded happy.

'Jack—over here!'

Snow was leaning towards them, from an aisle seat in the back row.

They moved across. Snow stood up to let them pass, retaining the end seat for himself. As they pushed past him, Abbott had a glimpse of a black girl in a white linen suit, sitting next to Snow. There was something familiar about her.

'Sorry we're late.'

'All right,' Snow whispered. 'This is Marie.'

'Hello.'

The girl nodded, without looking at them, her gaze on the screen. Abbott pondered for a long moment, then remembered where he had seen her. She was the leading dancer in the limbo group that had performed in the hotel night club. He settled back, and tried to pick up the threads of the movie, a tale of the New York waterfront, starring Sidney Poitier.

Angel whispered, 'I think I know who the girl is.'

'Yes, I know.'

Snow leaned across. 'Jack?'

'Yes?'

A man in front turned round, and said, 'Hush, back there!'

Snow said, 'The duffle-bag?'

Abbott groped under the seat. 'Do you want it now?' Abbott manhandled the bag across the girl's lap, into Snow's arms. Snow nodded his thanks, and put the bag down in the aisle. Then he lit a cigarette and turned back to the screen.

Abbott offered Marie a cigarette.

'Don't use that kind.'

Still she did not look at him. Her eyes were fixed on the screen.

'Sorry we were so late.'

'Forget it, mister, it's okay.'

Her tone was impatient. Abbott shrugged and turned to Angel. She also was immersed in the movie. Abbott had always hated to enter in the middle of any story, and he fretted, shuffling, and gazing around at the audience. From time to time they erupted into one of the loud hoots of laughter. The sheer force of it was unnerving. It had an untapped power that disconcerted him, and made him wish the film over. He smoked stolidly, until it was. Sidney Poitier got the girl in the end, it really wasn't at all a bad story, it touched on the universal subjects of labour and love in a reasonably honest way. Certainly, it was popular here. The lights went up, and a long sigh of satisfaction came from the people. They stood up and smiled, and waved and called to each other. It was all very warm and stuffy and friendly, like being a member of a large and easy family.

Snow led the way out. As they were in the back row they were among the first people into the streets, which were quiet, save for a group of afro-headed black youths standing around at the entrance, presumably lacking the admission money. There was an electric closeness in the air, and, as they left the cinema foyer (even that was tiny, and carpeted and, again, took Abbott back to his childhood), a shaft of lightning flashed along Church Street, illuminating the City Hall a startling white.

'What a great building!' Angel said.

'Modelled on Stockholm's City Hall.'

'For God's sake, why?'

'Who knows, it just is.'

'Still, it looks good.'

One of the afro-haired boys called out, 'Snow, we minded your car.'

Snow surveyed them, tolerantly. 'You did?'

Their leader, tall, frizzy of hair, brilliant white of teeth, sporting a large buckle-belt and jeans, grinned. 'Sure thing!'

The whole gang stared at Angel and Marie hungrily. Marie sniffed. She was small, and had a puggy attractive face and a sturdy body. Against Angel's leggy, thoroughbred look she seemed strong and durable. 'Sod off,' she said, amiably. 'Dirty-minded brats.'

The boys laughed, delighted.

Snow flipped a coin. Then another.

They scrambled, the tall boy shouting, 'Okay, okay, it's mine, divvy up, come on!'

Snow turned back.

'Joey,' he called.

'What?'

'When you give an order, don't shout it.'

The boy looked sullen.

'You hear?'

'Yeah, okay.'

'That way they take notice.'

'I said okay!'

Snow took a pack of Camels from his pocket and flipped them to the boy. 'Be lucky!'

'Gee, thanks, Snow!'

Snow got in the car. It was a battered Chevvy, of indeterminate age, rusty and none too clean. It smelled of old tobacco and a woman's scent. Marie got behind the wheel, and started the engine, which was noisy. Abbott and Angel got in the back. Marie adjusted the driving-mirror, and had a good look at Angel as she did so. Abbott realised that the girls had not spoken one word to each other.

'Did I introduce Angel da Sousa?' Abbott said, ironically.

'Hi,' Marie said, without enthusiasm, putting the car into gear, and moving out on to Queen's Street.

'I saw you dance,' Angel said. 'You were good.'

'For this place, you mean?' Marie answered, briefly and contemptuously.

Angel looked at Abbott and shrugged, but her mouth twisted in disdain. She did not like people who put themselves down. She had once told Abbott, 'All they want is for you to tell them they're great.'

Snow leaned back over the front seat, using his gone-coon voice. 'We are going to show you the Island tonight, folks. You won't regret not having taken up that ole invitation to the Yacht Club, I promise.'

'Yacht Club?' Marie laughed, a sudden, wild, high-pitched eruption. 'They was going there?'

'They sure was, honey!'

Marie shook her head. Thunder rolled again, louder than ever, nearer. The inevitable lightning hit the silent streets of the small settler-town. Nobody was about, apart from a few people hurrying from the cinema.

'We didn't pick much of a night for it.'

'But you did. The very best kind of night.'

Again Marie laughed. Angel glanced at Abbott, ironically. Abbott pressed her hand. She said, in a whisper, barely audible, 'I can see I'm going to love *this*.'

The Chevvy took the Front Street road out of Hamilton, coasting along the sea-front. The few ships at anchor in the harbour seemed to be riding high on the heavy swell, and waves were crashing against the sea-wall, sending spray curving, white and high, over the rails. The streets shone black with the rain that had fallen while they were in the cinema; but now all was still and silent, as if the Island was barricading itself against the final assault to come. Marie turned the Chevvy towards the South Road, keeping well inside the statutory twenty miles an hour, and as the verandahed-offices and shops of the town fell away, the Island was suddenly pitched into darkness, with only the headlights of the car to guide them, or an occasional blink of lights in a lonely cottage; and the white flash of the lightning. They turned off the main road at some point, making towards the sea. The roar of surf seemed, of a sudden, very loud indeed. Finally, they were on a dirt road of some kind. Marie stopped the car, abruptly, and sat still in the seat, saying nothing.

Snow got out. 'Here we are, folks.'

'Where?' Angel peered into the night. The wind howled and

came cutting keen through the door of the car, as Snow opened it.

'You both have coats? I'd bring them.' Snow squinted up at the black sky. 'She'll really blow any minute now.'

Abbott said, 'I have a light coat, Angel has an umbrella.'

'Umbrella?' Marie laughed again.

'Yes, an umbrella,' Angel said, coldly. 'What's wrong with an umbrella?'

The girl laughed again, high-pitched and loud. Snow said, 'Shut up!' and she stopped in mid-laugh, looked at him sulkily while he stared back, his eyes unblinking. She took the key out of the ignition, and got out of the car. The wind outside was very strong now, and they had to lean into it.

Snow said, 'This way, folks, won't take us but a minute or two,' and led them on a path across sand-dunes, and down a rocky lane towards the sea. Abbott had by now lost all sense of direction, but guessed they were on the south side of the Island, somewhere west of Spanish Rock. The rocky lane petered out, and then they were walking on soft, wet sand. Angel stumbled, her arm in his, but Marie walked ahead like an explorer, her thick dancer's legs sturdy and sure as a guide's. The noise of the surf grew louder; and then, mingled with it, a sudden, insistent music.

The sound of bongos came from a large stone cabin (it could hardly be called a cottage) nestling under a bank of rocks, so close to the sea that they could feel the spray on their faces. The cabin was blacked-out in some way, for no light penetrated the windows. Abbott noted that there were many pedal-bicycles and mopeds piled all around the small courtyard of the place. At that moment rain began to fall, solid, heavy, tropical.

'This the place?' Abbott shouted.

'It surely is,' Snow yelled back.

They fought their way against the wind, to the door, and Snow hammered on it. There was a noise of bolts being unshot, and the door opened a few inches, on a heavy steel chain. Bongo music flooded the air.

'Who's that?'

'Snow and friends.'

The largest black man Abbott had ever seen replied, in a deep, easy voice, 'Didden know you had any, man.' And the door opened wide. The man was dressed in jeans and shirt, and he seemed surprised to see them. He looked questioningly at Snow.

'They're all right.'

'If you say so.'

'I do.'

'Okay. Come in everybody.' To Marie he added, 'Hello, chick.'

'I've got a name,' she told him. The big man grinned, not put out.

The door closed behind them.

The light inside the cottage was bright, and the music deafening, shutting out the driving of the rain upon the roof. The whole cabin was alive with sound, and there were people packed solid, dancing, in the main room through from the hall, and in what seemed to be the kitchen, beyond. A three-piece bongo band was playing on steel drums in the main room, and Abbott, who normally liked the sound, found it harsh and disorientating in such a confined space. The men were all dressed in bright shirts and jeans. Some of the older girls wore thin, coloured dresses; the younger ones, their shape apart, could have been young men. All were wearing the world-youth uniform of shirt and jeans. Even here the merging of the sexes was happening, he thought, the same look, the same style. It made him feel rather sad. The average age in the room seemed to be around twenty, although a proportion of men seemed to be in their thirties. There were many bottles of rum standing on tables and chairs, and there was the sickly, recognisable scent of pot in the air. Nobody else in the room was white.

Marie said to Angel, 'Do you want to freshen up?'

Angel had dressed in a Quant mini-suit, simple but plainly a model. There was nothing in the place remotely like it.

'Why not?'

'This way.'

Marie disappeared into the wall of softly-moving bodies and was lost in the noise and smoke. Angel, with a quick, sceptical glance at Abbott, followed her.

Abbott turned to Snow. 'They mostly seem very young. Is it our scene?'

'I don't mind young people. Do you?'

'I don't mind them. I just hate their noise. And why keep all the windows closed?' Abbott fought his way through the crush, behind Snow. 'There's no air in the place.'

Snow smiled blandly. 'If you open the windows you'd let the storm in.'

Abbott struggled behind Snow towards a table. The barely-moving dancers gracefully made way for them, without seeming to pause in their private movements. The heat in the room was intense. Abbott tugged off his jacket, and fell gratefully into a chair against a wall. The dancers surrounded them in a solid mass, moving hardly at all, the beat of the bongos coming to an intolerably high pitch, as they repeated the chorus, again and again. It had as little to do with the commercial performance they had seen at the night club, Abbott reflected, as modern jazz had to do with African jungle music. He said as much to Snow.

Snow nodded, his eyes glazing to the beat. 'Sure, this is the real thing, boy.'

'What's the party *for*?' Abbott yelled. His voice came out as a whisper in the ear-punishing din.

'Huh?'

'Somebody's birthday or what?'

'It's a storm party.' Snow gestured to the roof: a deep base note of thunder could be heard, above the strident pitch of the steel drums. 'When a storm like this blows up, somebody always throws one.'

'How do they know to come?'

Snow looked round at the mass of moving bodies. 'They're here, ain't they?'

'Who are *they*?' Abbott saw a sudden olive face or two in the crowd.

'Portuguese,' said Snow. 'They came to the Island as indentured labourers, when the slave supply ran out. Y'know, coupla hundred years ago. Came from the Azores. They keep to themselves as a rule, they're the only Catholics on the Island, they dig their own life. But sure, there's some of them here, they're human, they like to dance.'

'What does everybody do for a living?'

Snow's mouth twisted wryly. 'Why, they're like I was, they're in the service industry. They tend shop, or they wait on tables, or maybe they tend bar, or they work on bikes in some garage, or maybe they work in the dockyard.' He smiled. 'Yessir, they hew wood and draw water, like the good book say!'

'They look happy enough on it, anyway.'

'Oh, sure. They're happy. That's one half of the trouble, Jack.'

'What's wrong with being happy? It's all most people want in life.'

'That,' Snow said, 'just has to be true, it's so simple it just has to be.'

Snow leaned over and took a large tumbler from a passing tray. The carrier, a fat, cheerful bald man, stripped to the waist, and with rolls of fat around his belly, called, 'Snow, you bastard, I heard you was home, how's New York City?'

'Dirty, dangerous and full of nooky.'

The fat bald man looked regretful, balancing his tray of glasses protectively, as the dancers moved around him. 'Wish I was back there.'

'Not you,' Snow said. 'You come home. You wouldn't of done that if you hadn't hated it.'

'It was my wife hated it, not me.'

'Your wife's never been to New York.'

'She hated me being in it, is what I mean. She thought I was chasing skirt all the time.'

'You were.'

The fat, bald man shrugged. 'Maybe a little. It ain't like here.' He sighed. 'Your friend drinking?' He handed Abbott a tumbler of the dark spirit. 'That's the best Jamaican, believe me. I bought it myself.'

Abbott accepted the glass respectfully.

'How come you working, Harry?' Snow asked.

'Can't get outa the habit. Besides, it's my party, ain't it?'

'You the host?' Abbott asked. 'Thank you for . . .'

'Think nothing of it,' Harry said. 'Gee, I wish I was in New York City again, chasing the women.' He brightened, addressing Abbott, but nodding in Snow's direction, 'I knew this boy *when,* you know that?' Abbott sipped his rum, and nodded politely. 'Yes, sir! Those were the days, eh?'

Snow said, pleasantly, 'They still are, Harry.'

'For you maybe. Not for me. Not now I'm married, buying the house, moonlighting on two jobs, tending bar and driving cabs, I tell you, I don't know ass from grass these days.'

'Wasn't much of a job we both had in New York City,' Snow said.

'Washing dishes in a big hotel, would you believe?' Harry told Abbott, earnestly. 'But what a time we had when we was off duty, I kid you not.'

'When we were off duty,' Snow said, mildly, 'we were sleeping.'

'Yeah, I know that, but it's who with that counts, okay?' A

group of people on the next table called impatiently to Harry, and he sighed. 'I tellya, it's harder work than work, throwing this party, but it was my turn.' He made to move, then turned back. 'Snow?'

'Yep?'

'Some of the kids . . . they're a little . . . y'know, high?'

'There'll be no trouble. Who knows we're here?'

Harry looked round the room. 'I don't want any, I'm past all that.'

'Harry,' Snow said, patiently, 'you're the same age that I am.'

'*I* know that, but my wife don't know that!' He laughed loudly, the rolls of fat shaking. 'My wife feeds me good to make me fat and slow. And you know something? It works.' He said to Abbott, 'Enjoy the party, any friend of Snow's. *Coming*!' He was gone into the wall of dancers, the tray held firm and high in a vice-like professional grip.

Snow laughed and shook his head. 'To Harry, New York City was like the army was to other fellas. A male dream, y'know, all women and song? In fact, we never picked up any decent nooky. Who'd want us? We stank of grease from the washing-up water, it got in our hair, it got down our fingernails, it got in our mouths. Boy, I can taste that fat now. Who'd have us? Nobody. It's all a dream.'

'He seemed happy with it.'

'Jack, you're gone on this happy stuff.'

'Like the poet says, you've got to be dumb to be happy.'

Snow smiled. 'Dumb you ain't. Drink up!'

Abbott grimaced, and sipped the lethal spirit.

The bongos stopped, and the dancers, as if at a signal, squatted on the floor. Angel picked her way through them, catching plenty of glances, and it amused Abbott that the girls here resented her, too.

Snow took the shiny tin from his pocket, and leaned forward. To Abbott's surprise Angel accepted one of the thin roll-ups with only the slightest hesitation. Snow provided the light, his eyebrow lifting ironically. Abbott felt a rush of annoyance, then repressed it. Angel's gesture was deliberate, it was to demonstrate to Snow that she was no different from any of his friends. Again, he was impressed at Angel's reading of a situation. It was basic and obvious, but in the end it could count. In the end, as Abbott well knew from his agency experience, people only worked with people they liked. It was the way her world worked, and Angel knew that. The point was, Abbott thought ironically, whether Snow knew she knew it. If he did, the gesture was wasted.

'Ah, food, now this is the *real* food of the Island.' Snow hailed a stout and determined-looking woman (obviously Harry's wife) carrying a tray of plates loaded with food. She looked pleased. 'Hello, Sammy, how are you?'

Snow said, 'I'm fine, Bertha. You?' She was the first person who had called him anything but Snow.

'Great. These your friends?'

'They sure are.'

'Enjoy yourselves, folks.' Bertha handed them each a loaded plate, and a fork. 'I brought these over to you, specially. Everybody else is having to queue. Some don't want food.' Bertha sniffed. 'I don't mean the ones that have been drinking.' She sniffed again. 'I mean, the *others*.'

'It's a free country, Bertha,' Snow said.

'It isn't,' Bertha said, harshly. 'Nowhere's free, not in this world. Not for any man. I'd like you to talk to these young people, tell them . . .'

'Bertha, it's their life.'

'I know, I know, but . . .'

Snow waited. Bertha said, 'I want to help, anyway I can, but . . .'

Snow still waited. Bertha shrugged, and her shoulders fell. 'Anyway, enjoy your food, folks.'

'Thank you,' Abbott said. 'Delicious.'

'*Is* Sam your name?' asked Angel.

'It is,' Snow replied. 'But don't tell anybody.'

They laughed. Now the music had stopped, Abbott felt pleasantly relaxed. It had been a long day, starting with the sailing incident; stilled with the act of love, in the hotel bedroom. This party was an end to it, and he was not sorry. Soon they would apologise and leave. If Snow didn't want to go too, they could doubtless telephone for a taxi. He had seen an unexpected telephone in the hall. The food, rice and peppers and seafood—mostly fish, but some lobster and prawn shredded into it, and slices of sharp lemon to garnish—was delicious, and had plainly been cooked on the premises. Even the best hotel food lacked that kind of sharp freshness. Abbott ate, and felt a sudden pull for house-cooking, for the small culinary enjoyments of home : hot scones, and

Irish stew, and roast beef and Yorkshire pudding hot from the oven. Angel was no cook, she never even tried, pleading work and lack of interest. The kind of meal he was reminiscing about belonged to another era in his life. It belonged to Helen. He was unlikely to eat a meal of that kind again, unless he ate one at home in Surbiton, with his parents.

'There's a lot of hash being smoked,' Angel said. 'As if this is their first time, at that.'

'No more than at most parties where there are young people.' Snow forked his food down steadily. 'How's the food?'

'Great,' Angel said. 'A lot of kids here look way out?'

'They get the British and American mags. They copy stuff.'

'Must be funny for them, cut off out here.'

'Not funny.'

'Strange?'

'Strange I'll buy, except it's all they know. They just sense there's something else, something better. Hence the gear.'

Abbott stared gloomily at the lace-up Victorian boots, and the mini-skirts and the see-thru blouses and the red-Indian hairbands and lace-bottomed velveteens. None of it, by any stretch of the imagination, turned him on, as their phrase had it. He smiled to himself.

Snow caught the smile, and said, 'Joke?'

'Not really.' Abbott was annoyed at Snow's intuition. 'By the way, you didn't tell me what happened with Waters today?'

Snow's eyes blinked. 'He thought I might have a friend on the boat. Smuggling him in or out.'

'Who, Rowley?'

Snow blinked again, then after a pause said, coolly, 'No idea. Anyway, I hadn't, it wasn't even my boat. Belonged to a guy I used to know in New York. He lives down Florida now, fishes round here a lot. He gave me a quick run-out on the Sound and back. That was all there was to it.'

'I see.' Abbott went back to his food. He had not believed a word Snow had said. Angel looked at him enquiringly, but Abbott refused to catch her eye. At that moment, in the crowd, at the hall end of the room, Abbott caught a glimpse of a face he knew. He stood up quickly to get a better look, but the face was gone.

'Something?' Snow asked.

'Thought I saw somebody I knew,' Abbott replied.

They finished the food in silence.

A bongo roll brought the rattle of plates and the babble of conversation (the deep, easy laughter of the men, the high-pitched life-loving cries of the girls) to a halt. They looked towards the end of the room, where Harry and the very big man had pushed two long tables together, to form a rough platform. Bertha seemed to be protesting about possible damage to the surface of the tables (which were of unpainted cedar), but, as Harry climbed up on them, ignoring her, she threw her hands up in resignation, sat down, and was lost from sight. Harry, who was something of a natural comic, mock-overbalanced and almost fell into the audience. This gambit was greeted with a cheer. When it ended, the drumming of the rain on the roof could be clearly heard; and behind it, the growl of thunder.

'David is certainly sending it down out dere!' Harry rolled his eyes in the manner of Stepin Fetchit, and there was some laughter and one cry of 'Stop tomming, man!' Harry ignored it. 'You all is here in the dry, so you should worry! Now, listen people, the party's been goin' a while now, and everybody's a mite tired, I reckon, so I'm gonna ask two *lady* artistes we have with us tonight to each do a turn for us.' Abbott felt Angel's body stiffen. 'An' the first is a gal you all know ... Marie!'

The bongos began low and soft, but gaining power slowly and steadily, until the audience were clapping their hands to the insistent, throbbing beat. Then somebody put the lights out, all save a small table-lamp. The very big man, and Harry, brought a limbo-hurdle up on to the platform. There was extra loud applause, as Marie stepped on a chair and then on to the tables. She was wearing only a large red handkerchief knotted around her breasts, and a long black skirt, slit in front to the waist. Underneath were red bikini panties. The audience cheered as she moved, forward, then back, in short hip-swaying steps. This went on for a long time, two minutes or more. Again, this performance had little to do with the commercialised limbo Abbott had witnessed at the night club two evenings before. Effective as that had been, this was something else. The sweat glistened on the stocky, firm body of the girl. She was waiting, now, as if entranced. Harry adjusted the pole for her, then stepped down.

Marie danced to it as if to a man. Her gestures were bawdy and brought laughs from the audience, and her body subtly underlined the sexual strategy of the piece. Her hips thrust forward, in violent time to the music. As the beat quickened, her eyes closed, and she ripped off the long skirt and arched her body backwards, so that all the audience saw of her was her knees and the legs supporting them, and her bikini panties.

'Hey, Marie, what about the pants?' an unsteady male voice shouted, from the protective darkness. Marie straightened up, and, lifting each foot in turn, whipped the garment off. She threw it into the audience, but with (Abbott thought) no lack of deliberate direction. The pants fell on Snow's table. He left them lying there, and drew unmoved on his thin cigarette. The handkerchief bra followed it, wildly, into the audience. There was a cheer, and then a hush, as Marie's head fell back, her legs straddled again, and in the half-light, to the audience's rhythmic clapping and the pulse-beat of the bongos, her bare feet shuffled forward towards the rod, now held at around a foot from the table-platform. Suddenly, the very big man struck a match and it spluttered along the petrol-soaked rod. The sweet smell of burning cedar filled the room. Marie's body arched forward, the muscles silk under the black skin, towards the flaming barrier.

'*Do* it, gal!' cried a high voice, in the darkness.

Marie, very very slowly, began to pass under the burning rod: her legs first, then, to the frantic bongo-beat, the rest of her body, held at a horizontal angle, the nipples of her breasts almost touching the flame. There was a very long, breathless, moment as she was poised between savage burn and safety. Her feet shuffled, an inch at a time, along the floor. The audience stopped clapping. They sighed as one person, as her torso and head came clear of the flame and then she shuffled the last time, her body lurched, backwards from the hips, and she was under, and safe. Marie brought her nude body straight, to sudden, thunderous, applause and cheers. Her smile was to the table, to Snow and (Abbott thought) possibly Angel.

'Bloody tart,' Angel said. 'Had to take her knickers off to get a round.'

'It was still wonderful.'

'It was crude.'

'They'll ask *you* now.'

'They'll be lucky!'

'I don't see how you can say no, Angel.'

'Just watch me. How do I follow anybody who's just done a striptease?'

'It *was* a bit more than that, darling....'

The applause was unremitting, mingling with the thunder of th
rain on the roof. The sweet smoke-pall lay thick over th
audience, hanging steady in the airless room. Marie, nude in th
soft light of the lamp, bowed to the audience, proud and bitte
and somehow defiant. Abbott leaned over to Snow.

'Some girl.'

'She is.' Snow's voice was neutral.

'I think they'll ask Angel to sing. I think she'd rather not.'

'Why?'

Abbott shrugged. 'We have to be going anyway. It's pretty late.
Then his eye was caught by the face of a young man Marie wa
handing on to the platform. The audience, if they had been noisy
before, were deafening now. It was the man Abbott had seen i
the yard, at Snow's cottage.

The man raised his fist, and there was instant applause and a
low murmur, like sea-surf, from the men present. It was a stil
moment, as the man held up the bony black fist, and Abbott felt a
shiver down his back. The gesture seemed, obscurely, to be directec
at him. Nobody was looking his way. All eyes in the crowded
smoky room were on the thin figure in the faded and patchec
jeans, with the Afro hairdo and the huge, myopic granny-glasses
A comic figure, in some ways, and yet possessed of a latent powei
and drive that stilled any humorous fancy. The man was real, not a
figment of somebody's imagination in a Hampstead drawing room.
His voice, when he began to talk, was low and solemn and in nc
way religious. It was cutting, and lashing, and cruel. And so were
his words. 'You people like to enjoy yourselves. I can see that. You
like your rum and your sex and your food. You got all three, okay.
You're lucky. Every one of you, every single one of you, is luckiei
than if you just stepped in shit!' The sarcasm was heavy, and no
European orator would have dared address a crowd in that way.
This man was talking to people he loved and yet despised, people
in his own family. The ludicrous granny-glasses flashed, as he looked round the room, slowly, as if taking in every face. One or two
men near Abbott dropped their eyes, and regarded their smokes, or
their drinks. Rowley held the pause, his thin electric frame quiver-
ing. 'And a lot of you eat shit and you don't even know it *is* shit!
Or if you do, you don't care, because you got it made here in this
paradise isle, you got it nicely made, and you don't want it no
different!' Again, the flashing swivel of the granny-glasses, and
the low, insistent voice, almost a hiss, 'Am I right, shit-eaters?'

There was a long, shocked silence. Then somebody at the back of the room said softly, 'Man, you are right.'

Rowley looked at them all. His voice was very low, and his left leg shook. 'I know I'm right, I know I'm right because I've watched you do it. I've walked around the town and seen you do it. You all got nice jobs, don't you, waiting table, tending bar, driving hack? Okay, why worry about other people?' The long bony finger stabbed at them. 'Why worry about other people?' It was almost a scream in intensity, but the pitch was still low. 'Why worry about other people, what happens to them is their hard luck, that's how you all feel is it, you mothers? You *toms*!'

The audience did not move. This time nobody spoke.

Rowley shivered, his finger stabbed again. 'Is it, is that how you feel?'

There was absolute silence in the crowded, smoky place.

Rowley shook his head, as if in despair. 'You feel like that because you been taught to feel like that. To take second best, third best, to stand still for it. You been doing it so long you don't even know you're doing it. But your brothers . . .' Again, the stabbing finger. 'Your *brothers* ain't got it so easy in some other places. In some other places they starve, they don't have no nice houses and nice fat wallets, and enough to eat on the plate. They live like dogs.'

He took a breath and swayed and Abbott thought he might fall. He did not. 'You owe them. You *owe* them! While you sit here on your fat asses they do things. They are desperate, and they do things. You ain't desperate, so you eat shit and pretend it's sugar!'

The low voice at the back said, 'Man, that's true.'

The finger stabbed out in the direction of the voice. 'Yes, but what you doing about it? What are you doing about it, any of you? To help those other people, the desperate ones? How are you contributing, if at all?'

Nobody moved or spoke. The voice, low and whiplash, scourged them again. 'Okay, so what can you do, sitting in this lovely place, hanging about in the sun, what can you do? Like nothing, is what you say, as you reach out for the rum bottle and the plate of red snapper or maybe the piece of tail.' He waited, but nobody dared to laugh. The finger stabbed. 'I tell you what you can do. You can help. You . . . can . . . *help*!'

The word screamed around the room. An electric pulse went through the audience. Abbott looked at Angel. Her eyes shone, and they rested fixedly on the speaker. Her lips were apart and she seemed, like the rest of the audience, suspended.

'Help! They scream for it just like that. *Help*!'

The audience shuddered.

The voice dropped back to the low, hopeless key. 'But who's listening? Are you listening? Any of you?' The smoke drifted under the lamps, the rain hissed down on the roof. The soft voice at the back said, 'We're listening, man.'

'Right!' Rowley vibrated, the finger stabbing again and again. 'Then listen to me, because I speak for them. They sent me to speak for them. And I say to you, this is how you help. You give bread, but also—but *also*!—you got to *do* something!' The granny-glasses flashed, there was a suspicion of a fleck of foam at the side of the mouth, the finger, long, black, stabbed and stabbed again. 'You got to be ready to hurt and be hurt, you got to be ready for trouble and upset and violence and worse, because I tell you, and I been where it's *at,* I tell you the Man don't acknowledge nothing else, he don't listen to nothing else, it's all he knows, so you got to be ready!'

At that moment there was the sound of hammering on the front door of the cabin. The tableau on the platform froze. The whole audience stilled, the smoke from their cigarettes and from the burning cedar hanging still and heavy in the pool of light cast by the single lamp behind the stage. Harry's voice, in total anguish, could be clearly heard, even above the drumming, insistent rain on the roof, the voices of the men outside and the noise of fists and boots striking the front door. 'Oh, Lord Jesus help us, it's the law!'

'Come on, open up! Open up!'

Harry turned to the platform. 'What do I do? What?'

Rowley held up his hand. A babble of voices had started, but they stopped instantly. In a low voice he said, 'First, drop any evidence on the floor. Do it *now*! Second, don't open any door till I say! Then open *every* door and window there is, and climb out and run, and keep running. If anybody is caught, they knew nobody here! Okay, *go*!' At that, men ran to each window (there were several) and stood ready. There was much shouting and confusion.

Abbott grabbed Angel's arm, and Snow said, 'Keep still, we'll dash for the back door when he says!'

All eyes in the place were on the man on the platform. As the front door gave way under force (the wood splintered noisily, and

Bertha's wail could be heard all over the room) the man said, *'Now!'* The single light went out.

Snow said, hard and urgent, 'After me!'

Abbott put his arm round Angel. She was asking, 'It's only a party, why the hell do we run?' Nobody answered her. Abbott was too busy keeping his eye on Snow, plunging ahead of them. The great mass of the crowd was plainly unable to move, and Snow was skirting them by keeping close to the wall, walking over the tables towards the kitchen. Abbott pushed Angel close behind him, all the way along the room. This way they reached the kitchen, to find it jammed with people trying to get out of the back door. Snow pulled them both into a large pantry, and slammed the door behind them.

'What the hell . . .?' Abbott said.

'There's a pantry window. They may not cover it. I'll jump out first. If I say okay, you follow. Right?'

Abbott protested, 'No, why . . .?'

'Do you want to be arrested?'

'Not particularly, but . . .' Abbott stared at Snow in the gloom. The man's whole body was tense and tigerish. Abbott said no more. Snow turned, and opened the small window. He swung on to the sill, and squeezed himself out into the night. Abbott could feel the rain and darkness swirl in. The noise of surf was very loud.

Abbott said, 'I think, we don't do this . . .' But Angel was on the ledge quickly, and out into the night. He heard her fall softly into what sounded like sand.

'Come on,' she called. 'It's okay, quick!'

Abbott barked his shins as he got on to the ledge, and leaped forward into the darkness. The drop was only three or four feet, but he rolled over, swearing. Snow said, 'Shut up, for Christ's sake!' and pulled him to his feet, showing a sudden, brute strength. 'This way!' They followed him along a path of shale, and then they were on sand. Behind them, the noises of the night erupted: women's shrieks, the roar of male voices, the slamming of car doors, lights. They found shelter in the lee of rocks and Snow said, gasping for air, 'We go to the beach and walk along the edge of the water. There'll be nobody there.'

Abbott started to shout, 'What bloody rubbish! Let's go back and give ourselves up,' when he saw, in a flash of lightning, the excited face of Angel. She's enjoying it, he thought, she really is.

He said nothing. Snow led the way along the beach. Their shoes sank deep into the sodden sand, and the wind tore at their clothes. The spray from the sea, crashing against the rocks, and flung inland by the wind, soaked them as they ran. Finally, when he had judged that they were safe, Snow turned abruptly inland. The rain glistened on his face, and he was, Abbott saw, afraid and trying hard not to show it.

'Go along this track to the main road. There's a garage about a mile along to the left. Knock them up and phone for a cab to come out and pick you up. Deny it, if anybody asks you were you at the party. If anybody . . .' He hesitated . . . 'If anybody asks where you were, say with me, at my mother's place, all evening. That you started to walk home and got caught by the weather.'

'Look here . . .' Abbott said. But Snow had turned, and was gone into the night.

'If I had to hold an audience by taking my knickers off,' Angel said, moodily, 'I'd jack it all in.'

They started to walk along the waterlogged track, towards the road.

7

'You were at the party, Mister Abbott.'

It was a statement, not a question, the way Waters said it.

Abbott looked out of the window of the hotel bedroom. The sun shone, blindingly. The flags were limp on the pole at the end of the courtyard. Guests promenaded slowly by, on their way to the swimming pool, and the air came into the room, balmy and mild, from the open window. The storm was a thing of the night, and the night had gone.

'I don't know that I have to answer that or any other question,' Abbott said.

'You don't. But I have to ask them.'

'Ask away. It doesn't mean I'll answer.'

Waters sighed and rustled his notebook. Abbott had seen it as probably a deliberate gambit on the man's part. It was full of scribbled writing, presumably notes or statements taken in the night. It was now eleven o'clock in the morning.

'I understand you got into the hotel . . .' Waters turned the pages of his notebook, 'at one-thirty or thereabouts?'

'Yes, I suppose so.'

'And before that, for the two or three hours before that?'

Abbott said, 'We went to the cinema. Then we accepted a car ride from friends. Later we elected to walk home, and got caught in the rain. We telephoned for a taxi, and came back to the hotel.' That, anyway, was all true.

'Yourself and Miss da Sousa only?'

'Yes. That is all I have to say. If you persist in asking me any further questions, I will have to talk to a local lawyer and find out what my rights are before I answer them. That goes for Miss da Sousa, too.' Abbott turned and picked up the telephone at the side of the bed. 'I'm going to have some coffee. Would you care to join me?'

Waters shook his head. 'I know you were at the party.'

Abbott ordered the coffee before he replied. 'I don't know how.'

'I've been told.'

'Will these informants swear to it? In court?'

'Who's talking about court?'

'Nobody. But I presume you have it in mind?'

'Not necessarily. Of course, the people who own the house are in trouble. Mister and Missus Harry Pike.'

'I'm sorry to hear that.'

'You know them then?'

'I'm sorry to hear that anybody is in trouble. What's the charge?' Waters smiled. 'Allowing drugs to be used on their premises.'

'Is that serious here?'

'Very. We don't want that muck to get any kind of grip on the people of this Island.' Waters' face flushed, and he leaned forward. He seemed to mean what he said. 'It's the beginning of the end, in a society like ours. It's a harmful, dirty business . . .'

'You seem very sure of that.'

'I am. But it is only one of the things that puzzle me.'

'Oh?'

'The smoking's bad, but it isn't the whole scene.'

'Then what is?'

'Troublemakers. Outsiders. People who stir things up because it answers some long-term strategy.'

'Who are you talking about?'

'Don't you know?'

'No.'

'Then I'll leave you to find out, Mister Abbott.' Waters put his fountain pen in the top pocket of his blue blazer and crossed his Bermuda-shorted legs. The high socks looked very colonial, as did the pipe and the short bristly red hair, and Abbott was irritated by the image.

'A little freedom never came amiss. Why not let people go to hell in their own way?'

'That,' Waters said, 'is not what the law is about.'

'From what you've told me,' Abbott replied carefully, 'a few people were having a party. They enjoyed themselves in their own way, on a perfectly private occasion. I don't see why the law should intervene, so long as no harm is done to anybody.'

'The law,' Waters said, 'takes a serious view of what went on at that party.'

'What did go on?'

'I think you know.'

'Obviously I don't, because all you have said is that some people smoked pot. Now, I don't like the stuff, but you are only two hours' flight from New York on this Island. You are bound to get some of their weather.'

'We don't want that kind of weather.'

'But it's here. The jets bring it here.'

'Was there anything or anybody at that party,' Waters asked doggedly, 'that you were surprised to see? I don't mean Snow, or the girl Marie, I mean anybody else, anybody . . . unexpected?'

'I haven't the remotest idea what you mean.'

'I think you have, Mister Abbott.'

The waiter came in with the coffee. Abbott poured himself a large, black cup. 'You sure you won't have a drink or something?'

'Not till sundown. Hardly ever do.'

'That can be pretty late out here.'

'It's still a good rule.'

'Maybe they don't smoke till the sun goes down?'

'I don't think that's very funny.'

'Sorry, I do.'

'There's a difference, believe me,' Waters said heavily. 'The medical evidence is in about alcohol . . .'

'Some of it pretty awful . . .'

'. . . But not about this muck.'

'Was anybody on hard drugs at this party?'

'Three or four.' Waters referred to his notebook. 'But that is not my major concern.'

'No? Then what is?'

'Safety. Security. The priority of any . . .'

'Policeman?'

'If you like.' Waters lit a match, remembered that he was in a suite with a bedroom adjoining, and swung it out. 'We are a colony still, you know, and maybe a mite paternal towards everybody . . . but this is still a parish really, it isn't a vast stretch of, say, Africa, with mineral deposits and strategic importance and all that. We are simply a small island, open to wind and weather, as you say. We'd like to keep the storms out, that's all.'

'Is it possible to do that in nineteen-seventy-two?'

'It's possible to try. It would be criminal not to try.'

'Some . . . colonies have worked out their own salvation.'

'So they have, and a fine mess they've made of it. The democratic notion of one man, one vote, is going to cost Western civilisation its lot before it's finished. The people who take over from such as myself don't have such a care for democratic institutions, and I *am* talking about Africa.'

'What's the problem, do you see something like that happening here?'

'I don't know what'll happen here, I just go on from day to day, doing my job.'

Abbott drank his coffee. 'Well, I'm sorry I can't help you do it. But there you are.'

Waters picked up his notebook and got to his feet. 'Where will I find Miss da Sousa?'

'She's down at the pool, but I must — again — warn you that if you talk to her I'll insist on a lawyer being present.'

'And she'll only repeat what you've told me?'

'I can guarantee that.'

Waters put his notebook in his pocket. His mild blue eyes bored at Abbott.

'Your friend Snow does a lot of fishing.'

'Does he?'

'Out nearly every day.'

'Oh, is he?'

Waters nodded. 'Never eaten any of his catch when you've been up at the cottage? I'd say his mammy does 'em to a turn.'

'Yes, I have eaten fish there.'

'He uses a little rowboat with an outboard. Useful to get away from the rollers. You can't bring anything big, like, say, a cabin cruiser in close, you'd lose her.' Waters paused. 'So a little boat can be useful.'

'For fishing?'

'And other things.'

'Such as?'

'Oh, going out to bigger craft.' Waters' blue eyes still looked directly at Abbott. 'Some of the locals sell cabin cruisers bait that way. Then the cruisers go out and fish for the big stuff.'

'I see.'

'Yes,' Waters said. 'It's a shame about Snow's boat.'

Abbott looked mystified, which he was.

'Went missing in the storm yesterday.'

'Did it?'

'He tells me . . .' Waters looked regretfully at his loaded pipe, 'he tells me he had it tied up, and it must have floated away.'

'Then that's probably what did happen, isn't it?'

'Snow's too much an islander to lose a boat like that, but I expect he's out of practice.'

Abbott said nothing.

Waters waited a moment. 'Nothing at all to tell me, Mister Abbott?'

Abbott shook his head. 'No, I'm sorry.'

Waters loomed closer. He was tall, six feet two at least, and built in proportion. Abbott had a feeling of physical power, held in reserve. He understood why it was useful for a policeman to be big. Primitive, but effective. For a moment he felt overlooked, and he was not a small man.

'You don't know what you're in, you know, Mister Abbott.'

'I'm sorry, I don't understand.'

Waters tapped his teeth with his unlit pipe. 'If you tell me everything, I'll tell you everything.'

'Like two people with everything in common? Attitudes? Colour? Background? Interests?'

'Why not, we *have*.'

'I'm sorry, Mister Waters. Can you find your way out?'

Waters turned, at the door. 'You're not a realist, Mister Abbott. I thought perhaps you were, but you aren't.' His eyes took in the communicating door to Angel's room. 'But there you are, we are all what we are.' And he was gone.

Abbott finished the contents of the coffee-pot thoughtfully, smoked another cigarette; then he went down to the pool. Angel was lying on a long chair, eyes closed, her golden body spread to the sun, and her beauty made him catch his breath. He sat down next to her, loosened his sports shirt and let the sun soak into his body. Abbott felt weary, his sleep of the night (what had been left of it) had been fractured by vivid and unsettling dreams. Small wonder, he thought. They had simply been a preparation for what was to come, the visit of Waters, and the questions. He would doze now, and talk to Angel later, he decided.

'Don't sit like that.' Angel opened one eye. 'Put your sun-glasses on and try some oil. You'll burn.' She leaned upon one elbow and handed him some Ambre Solaire. He shrugged, and she commanded, 'Oh, take off that shirt.' He did so, and she spread oil on his body.

Abbott put on his sun-glasses and tried to look as if this was everyday. He could not entirely rid himself of the notion that he appeared ridiculous. Still, he suffered the operation, half-flattered, and only when she had finished did he say, 'As I expected, we had a visitor.'

'Oh, who?'

'Waters, naturally.'

Angel's hand stopped abruptly on his chest. 'What did he want?'

'Details of the party.'

'How did he know we were there?'

'Somebody told him. Somebody always talks on occasions like this.'

'Did you tell him anything?'

'No.'

'Didn't he lean on you?'

'He did.'

'What did you do?'

'Told him I wanted a lawyer.'

'And he left it?'

'For now.'

Angel leaned back and arranged her body to accept the sun. 'All that fuss because a few kids were smoking hash. Most of 'em for the first time, from what I saw.'

'I think there was a bit more to it than that.'

'Oh, like what?'

Abbott opened his eyes. It was an effort. 'That duffle-bag Snow gave me at the quay yesterday. The one I gave to him in the cinema.'

'Yes?'

'It had to be contraband of some sort.'

'Why?'

'Snow pushed it on to me. He must have been expecting Waters.'

'You mean the cabin cruiser smuggled it in?'

'Probably.'

'But how did Snow get on it?'

'Took a small boat out from that cove near his mother's place. But the weather blew up and he couldn't use his small boat to get back. So he had to come back in the cabin cruiser. With the stuff.'

'How do you know that?'

'I don't, it's just a guess. And something Waters said. But, another thing.'

'What?'

Angel was sitting up now, looking at him steadily.

'I gave him that duffle-bag in the cinema.'

'I know, I saw you.'
'He didn't have it when we got in the car.'
'You're sure?'
'I'm sure.'
'Somebody in the cinema . . . collected it?'
'That's what I think.'

Angel let it all sink in, then she leaned back and was silent for a few minutes. 'He's talked to Snow this morning? Waters?'
'I'm sure he has.'
'And you don't think he has any proof of any kind?'
'No, or he wouldn't talk to me. Why should he? He has to find the duffle-bag to have any proof.'
'Yes, of course.'

The sun shone down, hot, searching. Bodies splashed in the pool and the waiters hurried around with trays of long, iced drinks for people sitting under bright red canopies in the café area. A breeze wafted across the pool from the bay, and snatches of conversation came to them from people all around. Abbott waited.

Angel said, 'What do you think was in the duffle-bag? Drugs?'
Abbott pondered. 'I don't know. Probably.'
'Do you think Snow's *into* something?'
'It's likely.'
'Do you think it's serious stuff?'
Abbott shook his head. 'I don't know.'
'Is there more?'
'What?'
'Do you know any more?'
'Why do you ask?'
'I think you do, that's all.'
'It's just a hunch.'
'Tell me.'

Abbott said : 'I think we should get Snow back to New York as soon as we can. It'll be easier there.'
'What if he won't go?'
'Then I think we should go, Angel.'
'And forget *Paradiso*?'
'I think so.'

Angel made the reply Abbott had been expecting, or something very like it.
'Not sodding likely, unless you have more evidence than this!'
'Look, he's in trouble with the police . . .'

'Who wouldn't be, in his place . . .'

'What nonsense !'

'Abbott, I'm not going back until we have this thing set up with Snow. Without him, we have no show, nothing.'

Abbott protested, 'There are other directors . . .'

'Not for this. Not for me.'

'Angel, listen, we can go to New York tomorrow, say I have urgent, unexpected business. Ask him to follow. Do all we need to do there.'

'You sound afraid.'

'Angel, I think I am. I'm a law-abiding man, and I didn't enjoy last night.'

'No, I know.'

'What does that mean ?'

'It means I know you didn't, that's all.'

'How ?'

Angel gestured irritably. 'I saw it. You were scared witless.'

'Yes, I was.' Abbott was very irritated indeed, now. 'Don't you see this whole thing, whatever it is, could get out of hand ? Waters more or less threatened . . .'

'Oh, *him* ! That silly old poof.'

'He's not a poof ! *Is* he ?'

'Looked it to me.'

'Oh, come on, just because . . .'

'Abbott, I am not going to New York until we have this thing settled. It means too much to me. You go if you like. I'm staying.'

Abbott took a deep breath, but before he could say anything at all a figure came into view at the other end of the pool. Snow walked towards them, dressed, as he always was, in shiny black silk sports shirt and slacks.

'Hi, folks, how are we all this fine mornin' ?'

Over his shoulder was slung the duffle-bag. There was no lock on it.

'We are bloody awful,' Abbott said. 'Having just had a visit from the fuzz. I believe they talked to you ?'

Snow sat down and said, to a passing waiter, 'Carl, can I have a beer ?'

'Sure, Snow, coming up, man.'

'Angel,' Snow smiled, 'you look good.'

'She didn't have to talk to Waters. I did,' Abbott said.

'Relax, man. It was nothing. Just a lot of fuss over a few hash tokes. Forget it.'

'He asked a lot of questions.'

'So long as you didn't answer them, Jack.'

The sun was very hot and a lot of people were splashing in the pool. People dived often, but nobody seemed to actually swim.

'Did you?' Snow's voice was idle.

'No, I didn't, but it was very difficult.'

'It always is, with them.'

The waiter brought the beer and Snow said, 'How much is that, Carl?'

The waiter said, 'Too much, but your money's no good here.'

'Hell, no,' Snow protested.

The waiter said, 'If I can't buy a celebrity a drink, who can I buy a drink?' and he was gone. Snow sipped his frosted Budweiser and smiled to himself.

'What happened to you?' Abbott's voice was testy and he didn't care.

'Me?' Snow smiled tolerantly at Angel, including her in a conspiracy against Abbott's uneasiness, caricaturing it. 'I went home.'

'But they called round, the police?'

'Ten minutes later.'

'And?'

'Took a statement.' Snow sipped his icy beer, turned to the sun. 'Man, they love their statements.'

'What did you tell them?'

'That I was home all night.'

'Did anybody corroborate that?'

'My mammy did.'

'Did you sign it?'

'What?'

'The statement?'

'Sure I signed it.'

'Then you're in trouble.'

Snow laughed, softly. 'How do you mean, trouble? I'm in trouble if I don't make a statement, man, not if I do. They want a statement. So I give them one and everybody's happy.'

Abbott said, 'They know you were at the party. They know we were at the party. At least I didn't sign anything.'

'That,' Snow said, 'is because you are white, rich, and the gentleman likes you.'

There was another silence, broken only by the splash of bodies in the bathing pool and the soft surf of muzak in the café area. Angel broke it, impatiently. 'What happened to Marie and the others, that Harry and his wife?'

'Oh, Marie got away, too.'

'With the man on the platform?' Abbott asked.

Snow looked blank. 'What man?'

Angel said, 'Harry and his wife?'

'Oh, they had to go down-town. It was their house, see?'

'What a shame!'

'Yep.' Snow finished his beer. 'I guess it surely is.' He seemed to have tired of the conversation, for his eyes roved unhurriedly over the bodies of the girl tourists, lying in fleshy pink and brown ranks, all around the pool.

'They got a hard time out of it,' Abbott said.

'I guess they did, at that.' Snow was still looking at the bodies of the girl tourists. 'But they knew what it was all about.'

'Did they? All of it?'

'Sure.'

'And your mother, when she signed that statement?'

'She didn't sign no statement.'

'She didn't?'

'No, she didn't.' Snow turned to Abbott. He smiled, but not politely. There was something savage in the smile. 'Look, Jack, Waters didn't want me in the bag or her in the bag. We play our own games out here, man.'

'Don't include me in them again,' Abbott said. 'I mean that.' Unable to trust himself further, he got up and went into the men's changing room. He put on a pair of swim-trunks, and went back into the swimming-pool area. Snow was still sitting at the table with the duffle-bag on the floor beside him, and he was sipping another beer. Abbott plunged into the water, ignoring Angel's wave, and swam around to work off his irritation. He debated simply packing his bags and leaving, but he felt that Angel needed him more than she realised. Snow was a man who demanded his own way in all things. Angel was used to cajoling and conning the various people she worked with, charming them into her way of doing things. In a word, she was professional. Snow, at some level, Abbott thought, was an amateur; the best kind, but still, somehow, the kind of director who could hit or miss. If Angel was going to work with Snow she would need him around, as a

140

buffer. That much was clear. Abbott wondered if it was another excuse for giving Angel her own way, then decided it didn't matter whether it was or not. The relationship ran on Angel's terms because there was something she still wanted from the world. All Abbott wanted was Angel herself. He swam two lengths of the pool, pulled himself out of the water and padded across to the table. They were gone, but a scrawled note on a napkin said: *We're in the Night Club Room.* Just that. They hadn't even called him. Of course, he hadn't looked their way, and he had pretty deliberately contrived not to do so. Still, Abbott felt hurt. He crumpled the napkin and nodded to Carl, the waiter, who was clearing away the glasses. Snow had left him a five-dollar tip. Carl pocketed it with a smile.

Back in the hotel bedroom, Abbott changed into a light suit. He could not bear to hang around forever in sloppy casual clothes. He supposed it was some kind of hangover from his years in the city. The telephone rang as he knotted a dark blue silk tie over his light blue sports shirt.

'Jack, it's David O'Hara.'

'How are you?'

'I'm fine, what about you?'

'I'm all right.'

'I hear you're in a bit of trouble?'

'What?'

'With the police?'

'Oh, that.'

There was a pause, then David said, 'Go careful, Jack. You don't understand how things work out here.'

'I know that.'

'Well done.' David sounded relieved. 'Listen, I'm throwing a party for you.'

'For us?'

'Do no harm. Meet a few local people. Nice crowd.'

'When do you . . . ?'

'Tonight. My place. I have a flat.' He gave Abbott the address. 'I can rely on you both, eightish?'

'Well, of course.' Abbott was touched. 'It's really very kind of you, David, I must say.'

'Well, we have to rally round and all that, don't we?'

'I'm not sure I follow?'

'See you this evening. Oh, and not formal or anything. A suit, though. Okay?'

'I'll look forward to it.'

'And I'm forgiven by you both?'

'For what?'

'Well, the sea trip. It was my fault. I should never have taken you out, you know.'

'What absolute balls. We loved every minute of it.'

'Oh, well, that's okay then.' David hesitated. 'You been seeing something of that fellow Snow, have you?'

'Not much, but we do talk business with him.'

There was a pause, then David cleared his throat and said, 'Well, yes, well, I should keep it strictly to business if I were you, Jack. Curious fellow. Well, see you tonight. 'Bye now.'

Abbott replaced the receiver, slowly. Then he went down to the night club. The sound of bongos greeted him as he entered. The tables were piled at the rear, and a pianist he recognised as being from the local band, and the huge black man with the bongos, sat at the back of the stage. Marie stood in a rehearsal track-suit at stage-right. Snow was sitting on a hard chair, with what Abbott recognised as the manuscript of *Paradiso* in his lap. He was leaning forward, watching Angel move and sing. She was wearing a yellow shirt Abbott had never seen before, and black tights. To Abbott, she looked very beautiful.

Angel knew the lyrics and the music of *Paradiso* by heart. She had recorded them on tape, and she had played them back to herself, correcting faults of breathing or memory, far, far into many long nights. Now, she was singing one of the numbers, and Snow was listening in his savage, intent way. Abbott went to the back of the hall, and sat on a spare chair, deep in the shadows. The throaty voice moaned.

> 'I know what it's like to be shut out,
> I know what it's like to be hurt.
> I know what it's like to be a shadow on a wall,
> I know what it's like to be treated like dirt.'

Snow's 'No!' was violent. The bongo stopped at once, the piano a beat later. A smile played across Marie's lips, but she did not move or speak.

Angel said, mildly, 'I've only sung two verses.'

'I know that.'

'Then why stop me?'

'I couldn't stand any more.'

Angel shook her head wonderingly. 'You may not like the lyric but it's the only one I have.'

'I don't mind the lyric, darling,' Snow's voice was hard, hurting, low.

'Oh, well the music isn't much either.'

Abbott smiled to himself. Angel was not new at this either.

'I don't care one way or the other about the music!'

'Then what seems to be the problem?'

'The problem, *dear* . . .' Snow seemed to be having trouble with his voice. 'The problem, as you put it, is not the song. It isn't the words, although I don't love them too much at that, and it isn't the music, which I agree isn't Kurt Weill. No, darling, it's none of those things. The problem is the way you are singing it.'

'Oh dear, dear,' Angel said, 'what *have* I done wrong?'

It was an English put-on, and Abbott knew that the posh accent was used to cover the embarrassment that Angel was feeling. Its effect on Snow was instantaneous.

'I'll tell you what you're doing wrong. Everything!'

'Oh, do tell how?' But Angel blinked.

'This girl is singing about being poor, being lonely, being black.'

'Coloured.'

'What's the difference?'

'The difference, if you remember, Mister Producer, *is* the story.'

'Yeah, well, okay. So try to sing like the girl feels. Look, I know what you're doing, you're giving a nice conventional reading of how-you-think-this-big-star-would-sing-this-big-song! I don't want you to be a star, baby, I want you to be *this* girl!' Snow leaped on to the platform and confronted Angel. The tigerish image suggested itself to Abbott once more and it was all he could do to prevent himself calling out. He wrapped his legs around each other and locked his fingers. Angel would have to handle this. It was her business, not his. '*This* girl,' Snow was saying, 'she's what the words *say,* she's a shadow, she's nothing, people don't even *see* her when they pass by, so she's hurt, she's shut out . . .'

'I know that,' Angel said. 'I can read, y'know.'

'Okay, I believe you, but this kid, this hurt girl, maybe she couldn't read, you thought of that, maybe *she* could-not-read?'

'So what?'

'So, she's nothing, nobody, she can't relate to anybody or anything. She's got this . . . nothing quality. No projection. Just . . . nothing!'

'All right, I'll try to do it like that.'

'Okay, when you're ready.' Snow got down from the platform.

The piano player started again at a signal from Angel. She had sung only the first two lines of the lyric before Snow was on his feet again.

'No, no, no! Can't you feel it's phoney? Can't you feel it?'

Angel's reply was harsh, but she was still in control. 'No. Or I wouldn't do it this way, would I?'

'Okay.' Snow nodded to the pianist. 'Do it all through, and see if you feel it then.'

Angel sang the number all through. Abbott did not feel that it was in any way phoney. It seemed to him a perfectly sensible reading of the song and Angel, of course, *sang* it superbly. The pathos of the lines was hardly there, but Abbott knew enough about performers to know that the *sense* of any text was the last thing in their minds, that to what effective use the text could be selfishly put was what occupied most performers. He smiled to himself. It was a very old and honourable duel. The player working for himself (in this case herself) and the director working for the piece as a whole. When Angel finished singing, Snow said nothing. The pianist went on strumming and tinkling; and the big man on the bongos played a roll or two. Snow sighed audibly, and got out of his chair. He leafed through the script. 'Okay, Marie, let's do your dance.'

'Don't you want to talk about the number I've just done?' Angel asked, uncertainly.

'No, I want you to think about it.' Snow called to the bongo player, 'Okay, give us plenty.'

'Sure,' said the man.

'You don't want to discuss it?'

'No.' Snow waved to Marie. 'Okay, go!'

Marie moved to centre-stage, forcing Angel to give ground. Angel hesitated, and then crossed to stage-left and sat down, staring at Snow. Abbott was pretty sure that she could not see him, in the darkness of the auditorium. At the state of her feelings he could only guess. It hurt him to do even that. He tamped his emotion down. It was useless for him to feel too much. He could not interfere. It was the life she had chosen, and she must live by the rules of that life.

Marie danced (with sensuality and grace) a short solo to the song that Angel had just finished. Obviously Snow had choreographed it, and Marie danced to his exact pipe. When she had finished, Snow clapped and Marie, breathless, bowed and sat down at the edge of the stage. Snow looked at the script for a long moment, then called out, 'Angel!'

Angel crossed to centre-stage and stood waiting.

He let her wait.

Finally, she said, 'Yes?'

He looked up. 'Oh. Right. Have you thought?'

'About what?'

'Your interpretation of that song, what else?'

'I can't see what's wrong with it?'

'You can't?' Snow's voice was cutting.

'No, I can't.'

'Well, it's corny and it comes from other performers, not from life. And from life is the only thing that counts. Anybody can work out of other performers, other writers, other directors. It's the real, original thing, straight from *life*, that catches an audience. Life, life, life! You have to know that girl's poverty, know her hopelessness, know *her*! Can you do that?'

'I can think myself into it, I'm only just starting to work on the part, aren't I?' Angel was standing very still, her face and voice composed, but Abbott knew the agony she must be feeling. 'It'll take time, won't it, to get into the part?'

Snow said, 'If you begin wrong, you'll go on being wrong and you'll end very wrong indeed, baby.' He was standing, arrogant, hands on hips, staring up at her. 'You have to begin right, if anything is to come of it at all. You have to *be* this girl. I ask once more, can you do it?'

Angel said, 'As much as anybody can, I reckon.'

'Why do you say that?'

'Because I know how she feels.'

'You know how she feels?' Snow's voice was disbelieving. He looked at Marie, and she smiled.

The bongo player said, 'Oh man,' to nobody in particular, and the pianist waited patiently, as if he had been waiting for this cue all his life.

'*You* know how she feels? This girl, this poor lost girl, this shadow?'

'Yes, I do.'

There was a silence. Snow expelled his breath noisily.

'All I can say is, none of that is coming through, baby.'

'I'm sorry about that.' Angel smiled, a frozen wince. 'Maybe we should pack it up, try again tomorrow?'

'We've only just started,' Snow said. 'What are you running away from? Me?'

'No.'

'Then what? The part?'

'I don't know. Maybe.'

'Why, because you find it painful?'

'It is painful.'

'Because it isn't glamorous?'

'No, I don't think so.'

'It isn't a glamour part, you know that, you've read the script, you know it isn't a glamour part, it's a *sincere* part, it's about this poor raggedy girl, and there's no honest way of making her glamorous and attractive, there's no way of making whoever plays her somebody to be loved and desired and jealous of, is there? Which is what you are trying to do, baby. Make her lovable and desirable and it's shit, baby, it's all crap.'

There was the longest silence yet.

Angel refused to break it. She stood absolutely still, and stared straight back at Snow, beautiful and defiant, her dark eyes fixed on his face.

Snow threw the script on to a chair, and said, much more softly than before, 'You are playing it like a star. What I want you to do is play it like this girl. I want you to be this girl for me. But you can't do that. You can't.'

'I said I can, but if you want to forget it, let's forget it. You don't like my work, okay, I can live with that.' Angel turned and began to walk across the stage towards the steps leading down to the auditorium.

Snow's voice followed her, still soft. 'Baby, I said, what are you scared of?'

Angel stopped and turned. 'Not you!'

'But of success maybe, because if I take this one, we'd *go*! I know that.' He let her hesitate a long moment, unsure of whether to turn back or not. 'If we are to go to Shaftesbury Avenue or Broadway or both, this is where we set the whole thing going. I have to know, from the start, whether you can do it, because my name goes on it, as well as yours. This is the start, baby. Can you do it?'

'I said I could.'

'I know you *said* it. I want to know why you said it?'

'Because it's the truth.'

'You know how this girl in the story *feels*?'

'I said I did.'

'All righty! Tell me how you know, baby, tell me how?' Snow sat down again, propped up his legs on a spare chair and leaned back in the style of a man about to be told a very big lie. Abbott knew it was all an act, done for some supposedly professional purpose. He also knew that many of these kind of gambits by directors were simply power-ploys, that they enjoyed their omnipotence over the player, the really talented person, and that in an odd way, it was themselves they were hurting. None the less, he felt an almost overwhelming urge to walk up to the stage, hit Snow hard in the gut (and damn the consequences) and tell Angel to go and pack. He knew the futility of these thoughts, however. So he sat, and his palms sweated, and he could hardly bear to watch.

Angel was asking, 'Do you want me to do the song again?'

'I want you to tell me how you know so much about this kind of girl. I want to hear you talk about her. Then, maybe, later you'll be able to sing about her.'

Angel walked back to the centre of the stage. Snow continued to gaze up at her, the tilt of his black head expectant, disbelieving. The other three waited, curiously, eyeing the way she walked, ready, like Snow, Abbott thought, to find her reply wanting. He willed her to stop it all, not to be drawn by Snow's taunts, to refuse to sacrifice any hidden part of herself to this kind of hysterical examination. But he knew there was nothing that he could do.

'I know this girl . . .'

Angel's voice was low but clear.

'I know this girl because in many ways I am this girl.'

The four dark heads watching her did not move. Somewhere, away from the undersea atmosphere of the night club, voices sounded, cheerful and loud. Inside, the silence went on, until Angel broke it.

'I didn't select this story because I wanted to be a star, *Mister* Producer, even if you think so. I selected it because I felt that I could do it justice. All right, I've never been in the Islands till now, but you don't have to be in the Islands to be . . . deprived, okay?'

Nobody answered her. Nobody moved.

Abbott's palms were very moist now. He took out his handkerchief and dried them. He wished miserably that Angel would stop. What good did she think it would do?

'The girl in this story is an orphan. Okay, I'm not an orphan. I do have a mother. I don't know where she is right this very minute, but she'll be drunk in some room somewhere. She's always drunk in some room. That's how I was sent to a home for a while, *Mister* Producer, when I was a little girl, about seven years old. I stayed there a year, then I ran away, back to my drunken mother, in the room. They got tired of chasing me, so in the end they let me stay with her. We never had rent money, we never had milk money, we never had money for shoes or for dresses. You could say that we were piss-poor. The girl in the play isn't any worse off than I was, because she's in a beautiful place, all sun and sand and sea, and I was in the streets of a big, dirty city. And also, I had to look after my mother, best I could. Otherwise, I don't believe we had it much different.'

There was another silence. The ferry-boat hooted, out on the Great Sound. The four black heads were still turned towards the girl.

'You want to know where my father was?' Angel laughed shortly. 'The answer is I don't know. My mother never talked about him but then she'd be ashamed, because she was bog-Irish, and there was always a crucifix in the room. She never went to church though. And she never talked about my father. I never asked her. I never wanted to know. I don't want to know now, in the way this girl in the play does.'

Adroit, Abbott thought, she had brought them all back to business, reminded them all what they were there for.

'Apart from that one thing, I could be that girl, *Mister* Producer.'

Again there was the silence, but three of the black heads were now turned towards that of the fourth, Snow. Without taking his feet from the chair, he asked, lazily, 'It's a big point, baby. Why didn't you want to know who your father was?'

'I don't know.' Angel shrugged. 'I just didn't.'

'Afraid?'

'Maybe.'

148

Snow's feet hit the floor with a crack.

'That's gotta be the reason, baby!'

Angel held her voice level. 'What does it matter? The girl in the play is her, and I'm me. I only told you my own story because you thought I was some know-nothing smartass actress trying to get herself loved, at any price, not for the part, but for herself. I'm not that kind of artist, at least I hope I'm not.' She half-smiled, for the first time since she had begun to speak. 'Let's get on with the singing, shall we?'

The bongo player nodded his head vigorously, as if to himself, and gave a tentative roll on his drums. The pianist optimistically strummed a chord. Snow, however, did not move. 'I think it does matter. I think the fact that you, the artist, didn't want to know who your father was, could influence the way you'll play this girl. She wants to know. You say you didn't. I want to know why you didn't. I want to know what you were afraid of?'

Angel said nothing for a long, long time. 'I know what you are doing, *Mister* Producer, or at least I think I know what you are doing. You're breaking me down to nothing, so you can build me up again. Look, mate, it's been tried and I don't work that way.'

Her voice shook slightly, but Abbott thought, why wouldn't it? He admired her very much, at that moment.

'Never mind what I'm doing, don't attribute motives to me.' Snow's voice was whiplash. He was wrestling, Abbott knew, for the superiority he felt he must have, if he was to mould the entire production to his own taste. Abbott bitterly regretted the impulse that had taken him to Morris Simons, the agent. Better no show at all, than this.

He watched and waited, as sickly fascinated as the rest, for Snow's return to the attack. It was not long coming.

'You say you didn't want to know about your own father, and I ask you why?'

'Because I just didn't. He wasn't there, so he didn't exist.'

'But he did exist.'

'Not for me, he didn't. And I don't see what this has to do with anything . . .'

'Miss da Sousa, I'm the *prospective* director here, right?'

'Right.'

'And I am allowed to work my own way, right?'

'Right, but . . .'

149

'At the end of today, at midnight tonight, I want you to tell me if you want to go on with the project.'

'What about *you*? Do you want to go on?'

'I'll know then. I'll tell you then. We must both be able to say yes, and mean it, because if we don't mean it, this kind of mistrust . . .'

'There's no mistrust.'

'This kind of mistrust will come up again.'

Angel said, after a long pause, 'All right.'

'Before then I have to show you how I work. You have to be sure you can stand my methods, baby, because I work my own way . . .' The girl Marie suddenly giggled, and Snow's face turned towards her, his head pointed, snake-like. Marie fiddled with her dress, turned away, rebuked. Snow swung round again, towards Angel. 'You have to decide whether you can dig my methods, because they are the only ones I have, and it's them or nothing.'

'And if it's nothing?'

'If it's nothing, I'll respect you for making that decision.'

Snow leaned back and waited. He was relaxed, he had put the onus of withdrawal on the girl, he had asked for everything and given nothing, and Abbott wanted to shout, but did not. His shirt was sticking to his back, despite the air-conditioning.

'I can't make any decision yet, *Mister* Producer. Except to give it a go, and decide at the end of the day.'

'Great,' Snow said, easily. 'Then we can get back to work, okay?'

Angel nodded, imperceptibly.

'You maybe think my questions about yourself are personal and irrelevant. I can see why you'd think that, I really can.' The voice was low and silky now. 'But if you are going to play this girl I *have* to know how much you know about her, how much . . . ah . . . sympathy you have with her, *exactly* how much, okay? Then there is the possibility we don't have an intelligent reading of the part, but more like a real person up there on the stage, come opening night. That isn't very usual in the theatre, okay I admit it, it's all usually just a vehicle for the star. But you aren't a star yet, baby. You will be after I finish directing you, if I decide to do that. After you're a star you can take any part you like and ruin it by turning it into *you*, like all stars do. I don't mind that, I won't be directing you then. Now, I am.' Snow's voice fell even lower. 'So I ask you again, in no frivolous manner. Why do you *not* want to know who your father was? It's natural a girl would want to know that, why didn't *you*? What was there about him you were afraid of?'

There was the longest silence yet.

Angel's head, for the first time, dropped.

Snow's voice was almost inaudible. 'Well?'

'I don't know.'

'You do, Angel.'

'No.'

'Yes, you do. What were you afraid of about him?'

Abbott stood up and as he did so his chair fell over behind him. He stared at them wildly, foolishly, conscious of their surprise that he was present. 'Excuse me,' he said, in a loud voice, but nobody replied. Abbott walked out of the place, quickly, looking at none of them. The door slammed noisily behind him, and somehow he was in the foyer, conscious of the cooling sweat on his body, and of his own agitation.

'Hello, Mister Abbott.'

Waters got up from a seat, putting down, regretfully, a copy of *The Times*.

'Oh, hello.'

'Snow still rehearsing, is he?'

'. . . Yes.'

'He's cool.'

'I'm sorry. I don't understand you.'

'Are you all right, Mister Abbott? You look pale.'

'No, I'm fine.'

Abbott walked out of the foyer, into the sun. He hailed a taxi, from the rank. The driver asked, 'Where to, sir?'

Abbott pondered. 'The other end of the Island.'

'St. George's?'

'That would be fine.'

The car spun through the twisting, green lanes of the Island, but he did not see them. The palms of his hands were still wet, and the shirt was sticky on his back. He thought about nothing, except the anguish of Angel on the platform, and he tried hard to keep his anger in manageable proportions. He knew that if he had remained in the night club a moment longer, he would have spoken. Angel would not have wanted that. She must make her own decisions. The driver, after what seemed a very long time, said, 'Here we are, sir,' and Abbott got out of the cab.

'Want me to wait?'

'Will I pick up another cab to get me back?'

'Sure. At the livery over there.'

'Livery?'

'It's what *you* call a garage.'

Abbott paid the man; the cab turned in the main square, and was gone. It was very hot in the square, and few people walked about. He was surprised by the look of the town, stopped dead in the middle of the eighteenth century. A row of steps loomed in front of him as he walked, and he climbed them, asking an elderly black man sitting on a form, which church it was. The man said, 'Why, that's St. Peter's. Oldest church in the Western Hemisphere. Sniff good when you go in there. It's cedar you'll smell, from the rafters. Since the blight there ain't so much of it left on the Island.' Abbott went inside. Nobody else was in the church, and he wandered around, trying to forget the picture of Angel, standing firm on the stage under Snow's questions. He wondered again at the tenacity of talent. The inscriptions on the church's whitewashed walls told of yellow fever and shipwreck and skirmishes with the French. The sweet smell of cedar hung in the air like incense, and Confederate flags drooped dustily from the rafters, along with those of ancient British regiments of the line. It was, indeed, an outpost of Empire, Abbott thought. Men had died here to found a better way of life than they had at home. That their descendants should still believe in it should surprise nobody.

He sat in a pew, and noticed that he had stopped sweating. The church was cool (the walls looked six feet thick) and the scented air almost refrigerated. Abbott let his hands hang between his knees and wondered how much good he was doing Angel. If the musical worked out, and she decided to go on with Snow (and he with her) the sensible thing was surely to bow out, and leave them to it. The difficulty was, he would have money in the project, and his training was to stand sentinel over his money. It would be very difficult.

'You read the writings?'

It was the elderly coloured man, just inside the door. He looked retired from work, well looked-after (clean white shirt, linen trousers) and at a loose end. His pipe was carefully docked, and he had taken off a battered old straw hat. He pointed to various boards giving details of ships sunk, and men who had died young.

'Yes, I saw them.'

'A lot of lives lost to make this Island.'

'Looks so.'

'All those brave men. Some o' them Yankees.' He peered at Abbott through his cracked glasses. 'You American?'

'British.'

The old man smiled. 'We don't get too many these days.'

'No?'

'They used to come on the ships. But now it's all them jets.'

'That's right.'

'All tourists.' The old man lowered himself, slowly, into a pew. 'They don't see nothin'.'

'No?'

'Not the real place. Can't, less you live here.' He looked regretfully at his pipe. 'Don't suppose that's what they come for anyway.'

'No.'

'Them fellas round the walls, them fellas that got their names up there, there ain't any of our names there.' Abbott said nothing. 'No, we don't rate a mention, but we built most of St. George's, I mean, with our hands.'

'That's all history. How are things now?'

The old man smiled. 'Well, I tell you. They ain't bad, I got plenty to eat, enough to drink and smoke, and I got nice new clothes to sit in the square in. My daughter's proud, y'know? So she dresses me up. So I don't mind. I'm all through with life 'cept for sitting and maybe talking a while. So I'm happy, 'cos an old man don't need a lot, and I'm old.' He looked as if he wanted to spit, but swallowed instead. 'But some of our names should be up there.' Abbott nodded, and smiled, as the old man said, 'But since we mostly didn't have names, I s'pose it don't matter.'

'It's all past,' Abbott said. 'What happens next is what matters.'

The old man said, 'I don't want nothing to happen next. I like things the way they is. Change for the sake of it, that I don't want. Young folks always want that.' He peered at Abbott. 'You lived long enough to know better?'

Abbott nodded. 'I'm afraid I have. I believe in slow and sure, but I'm not certain I'm right.'

'Slow and sure. I like that,' the old man said, and got to his feet, as Abbott fumbled in his pocket. 'Nice talking to you.' Abbott took his hand out of his pocket, quickly. 'You should walk up to the Fort. It's a good view. Straight up the hill, can't miss it.' He went, softly, out of the church, and the door closed. Abbott sat there, in the cool, cedar-scented place and felt no religious impulse, but some sense of peace. Finally, he got up and walked out quietly, closing the door gently on the tattered flags of Empire.

The view from the old Fort, with ancient cannon pointing across the harbour to the south, and the open sea to the north, was worth the hard, uphill walk. Abbott perspired in the hot sun, but this time it was a healthy sweat. Calmed, he gazed across the bay, the gentle breeze in his face, and thought again of the fog of London and the smog of New York. The idea of never going back to these places struck him, momentarily, with extreme pleasure, but he was forced to grin wryly at the notion. Angel had battles to win in those grim cities, and he would be with her as long as she wanted him. He began to retrace his steps down the hill-path towards the town. There was really no need to get anxious. Angel knew what she was doing. He had got out of the rehearsal at the right time. All would be settled when he got back, one way or the other. Abbott relaxed, slightly tired, in the cab he found to take him back to the hotel, and smoked a cigarette. He felt a good deal better.

Waters was still in the lounge, still reading *The Times*, as Abbott walked through. He raised his hand in salute, but Abbott chose not to see it. The hotel was quiet, everybody was out enjoying the sun, and Abbott's spirits rose, as he thought of a plan for the rest of the day, after rehearsals had ended. He stopped at the restaurant, booked a table for the second sitting of dinner, and asked that some hock be put on ice for the meal. He talked cheerfully to the girl clerk, and marvelled at the way the native Bermudians had turned their English into something American, yet not quite. Then, his step light and confident, he walked down the thickly-carpeted steps into the night club.

At the door he almost cannoned into the bongo player, exiting, carrying his instruments in cases and looking very ordinary in his off-stage persona, as performers always do. He was followed by the pianist, who looked even more everyday. They nodded briefly, and hurried away up the stairs. Abbott went inside, and found Marie switching off the lights. There was nobody else in the echoing place.

'Oh, hello,' Abbott smiled, politely.

'Hi.'

Marie's eyes were sharp and black and lively, but not in any life-enhancing way. Abbott decided, in that moment, that she was a person hurt by life. He had known many hurt people in his time and he always felt sorry for them. He did not, however, like them.

'Is the rehearsal over?'

'Yes, sir, it's over.'

'Where ... er ... is everybody?'

'Everybody?'

Marie seemed to be enjoying this, so Abbott said, briskly, 'Yes, everybody.'

'Well,' Marie said, 'the two musicians just gone, and I'm here.'

'I'm talking about Angel.'

'And Snow?'

'And Snow.'

Marie laughed and flicked the last light off. The place was now lit only by the lights from the main staircase. Abbott, who could not see her face clearly, was irritated.

'Snow went. I dunno where.'

'And ... Angel?'

'Oh, she went too.'

'Where, to the room?' Abbott turned away.

'Don't reckon so.' The girl's voice was almost a laugh.

'Then where?'

'With him.'

'With Snow?'

'That's right.'

Abbott swallowed. His throat was dry. 'She ... left no message ... about where she'd gone?'

'Not with me.'

Abbott nodded, dumbly, looked directly at Marie's face. A shaft of light from the staircase illuminated it, momentarily. Now he knew why she was hurt. She was hurt by Snow.

'They have gone away to work on the play some more, I suppose,' Abbott said, his voice sounding hollow in his ears.

'Yeah, I guess that's exactly what they doing,' Marie said. 'They enjoying themselves some more, working on that ole play. Snow always do that, with all his girls.'

Abbott stared at her a long moment, and then he turned and walked quickly out of the place, slamming the door behind him so violently that a pane of glass shattered.

8

David O'Hara's party was crowded and noisy, and the first person Abbott saw there, after his host, was Waters. He did not see him too clearly, for he had fortified himself with a number of very large gins before leaving the hotel.

'We do keep bumping into each other,' Waters said, mildly. He was wearing a dark suit, like all the other men in the room. 'Glad you came along, though.'

'Shows the right spirit?'

'Something like that. How's your friend Snow?'

'He's all right.'

'Good. I hope this *business* thing you have with him works out to advantage.'

'Oh, it will, I'm sure,' Abbott said. 'But whose is another question.'

He accepted a large gin from David O'Hara, who asked, suspiciously, 'Been drinking already, Jack?'

'I had a fast couple. Like to enter a party two drinks ahead.'

David gazed round the crowded, chattering room. 'You aren't ahead of this lot. Where's Angel?'

'I'm buggered if I know,' Abbott said loudly. He was aware, as he spoke, of Waters' sceptical eye on him, and he added, 'She went out. Expect she'll be along later. I left a note for her.'

'Glad you came on, anyway.' David's eyes were anxious, fluttering around his guests. 'Come out on the balcony. It's cooler and I'll introduce you to some people.'

'We'll talk later,' Waters nodded.

'I hope not,' Abbott said, and followed David. Waters laughed easily, behind them.

'Look here, old Jack.' David took his arm as they pushed through the throng of drinkers, some of whom seemed familiar to Abbott, probably from the Yacht Club. 'Why fall out with Waters? He's a decent man.'

'He isn't, but let it pass.'

David pushed him into an alcove. 'Look, I brought you here to meet some nice people. You're the guest of honour, and you turn up half-pissed!'

'Sorry.'

'And without Angel. Didn't she want to come?'

David sounded hurt, so Abbott told him the truth. 'I honestly don't know where she is. She went out.'

'On her own?'

'Probably working. This play thing.'

'Working? It's eight o'clock.'

'They work by thinking, imagining how it'll be, all that stuff.'

'They?'

Abbott drank his gin off in a gulp. 'All these artistic people.'

David said, moodily, 'I wish she'd been here.'

'She might turn up yet.'

Abbott didn't believe it.

'Come and meet these people, anyway.'

'Who *are* they all?'

'Mostly local. I've met them all since I came to work here.'

'What do they do? What do I talk to them about?'

'Money, with the men. They're in banking, that kind of thing. Sport, sailing. Mind, they're experts.'

'Then I'll stick to money. The women?'

'Sex, as usual. Really, old Jack. You're losing your touch, aren't you? Where's the ram of Regent Street?'

'That was you, not me.'

'Still, there used to be some life in the old dog?'

'All gone, I'm afraid.'

'I don't believe you. I've seen Angel, remember.' David pursed his lips, looked into his drink. 'Tell me . . .'

'Yes?'

'That colouring of hers? So dramatic.' David looked up. 'You did say she's Spanish?'

'No, I said her name was.'

'Ah, yes. Of course, silly of me.' David took his arm. 'Come and meet people. And Jack . . .'

'Hello.'

'Go easy on the juice.'

'I'll be all right.'

'Nothing wrong, is there?'

'Why?'

'Not like you to booze without good reason, when I knew you.'

'It wasn't like me to booze at all, when you knew me. I'm a

different man now. Or, rather, the same man in different circumstances.'

'Yes, I suppose the traffic gets heavy sometimes.'

'What the hell,' Abbott asked heavily, 'do you mean by that?'

'Nothing at all, Jack,' David said, hastily. 'Simply all your money and no job to do, that kind of thing.'

'Oh?' Abbott pondered, a shade woozily. '*That* kind of thing?'

'Yes.' David took his arm again, with irritability and purpose this time. 'This way.'

The flat was not a large one, but David had furnished it with taste, mostly with antique-looking cedarwood pieces. He had found a few prints for the wall and a good carpet for that part of the floor which was not polished wood. The rooms—he seemed to have two large ones—were spacious and high-ceilinged, and the house was obviously at least two hundred years old, originally a planter's residence. The balcony was at first-floor level, but there were stairs from the lacy-ironwork verandah to the garden, in which the famous Island Easter lilies glowed creamily in the light thrown through the opened french-windows of the house. The people on the balcony were pleased to see him because he was British, and when the men heard that he was an accountant he was instantly accepted. Abbott recognised the type and the conversation, and it was only after he had been talking to two very astute money-men for half an hour that he realised how out-of-date his stock-exchange and financial knowledge was these days. But it was shop-talk, of the kind he had always enjoyed, and he listened with interest, and drank freely. One of the men, very British in name and manner, but with the slight American accent of the Island, finally said, 'And what are your interests now, Mister Abbott?'

Abbott puffed on the havana that one of them had given him, and said, 'Well, show business, I suppose.'

'Show business?' the man echoed, doubtfully. 'Oh, are you the fellow who ... ?'

David appeared from nowhere. 'Jack has substantial holdings in television back home. Fell into a gold-mine. Lucky sod.' The men laughed happily at that, and one of them invited Abbott to dinner.

'This play thing you're doing?' the first man said. 'Is it set on the Island?'

Obviously, there were no secrets, as Snow had warned.

'On a place a bit *like* this, maybe. But more like Jamaica or Haiti, I imagine.'

'Those places are a lot different from this.'

'In degree, certainly.'

'In kind.' The first man was bald, and had a military look. 'You aren't soft on the equal-society thing, I hope? Nearly all these writers and movie people seem to be.'

'I don't have ideas.' Abbott drank some more gin. 'Not my province.'

'But you'll be putting up the money?'

'Oh, that. Well, yes. Some of it.'

'Then you must hold yourself responsible for what is shown and said?'

'Not at all. I'm in the business of making a profit.'

The military-looking man nodded to that, but added, in a more reasonable tone, 'What if the play or musical or whatever it is stirs up more trouble than it sheds light, on a very difficult subject?'

'That isn't my problem. Audiences must make up their own minds about that.'

'By that'—the military-looking man was no fool—'by that, I take it this is yet another story showing the white man as exploiter of the black, a figure of awful tyranny and concerned only for himself?'

'Not exactly. I think it's simply a touching and probably truthful record of how it is to be a poor black girl in an island community, anywhere in the Caribbean.'

'That's enough for me,' said the second man, who looked as if he regretted the dinner invitation. 'I could probably write it myself, from the description.'

Abbott said, 'It isn't my fault if it's the kind of thing audiences feel in sympathy with.'

'Audiences in New York and London don't know a thing about it.' The military-looking man stared fiercely at Abbott. There was no mistaking his sincerity. 'If our ancestors, mine and his'—he indicated the second man—'if they hadn't come to places like this, and made something of them, from nothing, then half of New York and London wouldn't be there, because they were built on the profits and endeavours of people like our ancestors. It's a lot of soppy, liberal crap. The merchants and sailors who came out to this place were poorer than anybody in the Caribbean now. Half of them died of scurvy and starvation. But the survivors hung on, by their broken nails and aching backs. That's why we stand here and drink in comfort today, because of their efforts.'

'Hear, hear,' said the second man. He stared at Abbott with distaste.

'Look,' Abbott said, 'you are the victims of a very good propaganda campaign, but one with a lot of truth in it. It's trendy and *chic* to take easy radical positions in New York and London. To say out with the white planters, in with the blacks. I agree. But you make a bad case for yourselves. Surely you must have one?'

The military-looking man took another drink from a passing tray, with the air of somebody who needed it. 'You don't know the Islands, old man, or I wouldn't have to explain it to you. If you think we haven't a case . . .' He paused and looked at the second man, who sighed. 'Look, *our* case is we developed this place. It was a barren rock. It was full of birds and it had some water. That's all. It was uninhabited. There was nobody on it except a few hogs the Spaniards had let loose. Our ancestors farmed it, planted and reaped and sowed, and traded, and built, and made it what it is.'

'They imported slaves to help them do it.'

The military-looking man nodded. 'All right. I grant you they did. But it wasn't, to *them,* the reprehensible act everybody now thinks it is! To them it was a perfectly ordinary thing to do. The Spanish and Portuguese were doing it down south. The planters in Virginia were doing it. The Church said it was all right. The State had no law against it. It all looks barbaric and horrible now . . .'

'It was barbaric and horrible.'

'All right, I agree there, but what am I supposed to do about it three hundred years after the event?'

'Make amends, possibly?'

The military-looking man sighed. 'Have you looked at this Island? I mean, really looked? We have made amends. Black people here are better off, better paid, clothed and fed . . .'

'I've heard the rest of it,' Abbott said. 'All right, you aren't responsible for what your ancestors did, but you must see it from the other side.'

'We do,' said the second man, very quietly. 'But I think we may be too late.'

The military-looking man glanced at him. 'Not here. Further

down south, maybe. Here we're in time. Here we can work it out together.'

The second man said, 'Too late, Joe.'

'I won't accept that. I refuse to accept that. Carry the whole thing to its logical conclusion. Where would the black people on this Island be if they hadn't been brought here? A vast proportion would have died of disease in West Africa, or lived miserably under a tribal system, then on nothing much under the British colonialists, and on less under their present gun-toting dictators.' He flushed, as if he had said too much, then added, 'It's no use talking to you, I know, but if I tell you that the coloured fella could never have got this Island to where it is, that it took Northern European stock, with an ethic of hard work for small rewards from fishing and farmstead, I'll only have to hope you'll believe me. Left to our black friends, it could not have happened because they weren't at the culture level to do it. We ... the whites ... have brought them up towards that culture level. . . . Theirs was a tribal one . . . which, admitted, we didn't do enough to get them out of, but we are doing it now. . . .'

'Too late, Joe,' the second man said, sadly. He seemed to be rather drunk.

'Not too late,' said the military-looking man vehemently. 'Not if they'll let us help them, as partners, because now we have become a genuine democracy they outvote us, and that's the biggest joke since Rhodesia.' He finished his drink, in a disgusted way. 'If you knew the Islands, I wouldn't have to tell you any of this, but the coloured fella likes his booze and his girl and the sun. The Islands boy isn't a worker. I know it's unfashionable to say it, but just look around you. He likes an easy life, that's his tradition. He isn't northern and puritan and protestant. He's something older and deeper and darker. He'd ruin this Island, like he's ruined most of Africa, because he lets the other fella do it. It's his temperament to let the other fella do it. You look at everything that's ever been done in this Island, or any other in the Caribbean, and you'll see who did it. A white man. You may say shame, but it's the truth.'

'I don't say anything,' Abbott said. 'I'm just a money-man, like you.'

'My ancestors built this place.' The military-looking man finished his drink. 'I don't give it up without one bastard of a struggle.'

The second man looked deep into his drink, and seemed to be debating the next word. At last he said it. 'Amen,' he remarked, thickly, 'to that.'

They both stared glassily at Abbott, as if expecting him to say something, but he felt it wise only to smile and mutter, 'Better circulate, I suppose,' and moved away. His head was beginning to ache, the strain of sitting in the hotel room, waiting for Angel to ring, was beginning to tell.

David O'Hara intervened, again.

'I'd like you to meet some lovely ladies, old Jack.'

'Always delighted . . . to do that,' Abbott said, mock-gallantly. 'But . . .' He stopped. There was only one lady, and she was indeed attractive. Tall, blonde, implacably Anglo-Saxon, with a wedding-ring, hidden under diamonds, on her left hand. Abbott always looked at women's rings. He supposed it to be a sign of advancing middle age.

'This,' David O'Hara said, 'is Marcia Gray. Jack Abbott.'

Marcia Gray said, 'Oh, I've heard about Mister Abbott.'

'Call him Jack. Everybody does, except . . . Everybody does, don't they, Jack?'

'That's right.'

David pushed two large drinks into their hands. 'My boss is here, and I don't think he's even got a drink yet. Excuse *me*!'

Abbott sipped his new drink.

'You said you'd heard of me?'

Marcia smiled. She had very good teeth. She was very sexy, in a healthy, aggressive way. Just to look at her was a challenge, but Abbott was not responding to challenges. His eye fell on a telephone, on a side-table, back in the main room. Perhaps Angel would ring?

'You're here with Sam Snow, aren't you?'

'Well, I'm here talking to him.'

'I heard something about a girl singing. Is she to be in the show?'

Abbott drank and talked politely, telling her a little about the proposed musical, in the vaguest terms.

'Oh, is it set in the Island then? Is that why you're all here?'

'Not really, no, but I suppose it could be.'

'Well, Snow would be the man to do it, wouldn't he? He's done very well in New York.'

'Yes, he has, that's why . . . we asked him.'

'What's the story about?'

'Oh, a poor little . . . er . . . coloured girl.'

'It would be, I suppose.'

'It's quite touching.'

'I don't doubt it.'

'The sort of thing . . .' Abbott laboured. 'Audiences might like in New York or London.'

'Oh, I'm sure they'll like it there.'

'Can I get you another drink?'

'No thanks, I'm fine.'

'I'll just get myself one. . . .'

'I shouldn't.' Her voice was gently ironic, and somehow reminded him of Helen.

'What?'

'I really think you could use some fresh air, Mister Abbott.'

'Jack.'

'I think you could use some fresh air, Jack.'

'Then . . . let's walk in the garden.'

'Mind the steps, they're tricky.'

Several people were sitting on the crabgrass lawn, glasses in their hands. Moonlight filtered through the tamarind trees. The low buzz of music and conversation carried to them, on the balmy air, from the house. They found a cedar garden-seat and sat down, Abbott thankfully. Marcia looked at him with amusement. He noted her blue dress was very low-cut and her figure full, and her skin very white. In some way, she certainly did remind him of Helen. For one thing, she was thirty-five, at least.

'You're going at it hard, aren't you?'

'How?'

'You've had a good deal to drink this evening, I'd say?'

'Oh, sorry.'

'I don't mind.' Marcia Gray laid her large, cool hand on his. He froze, but it did not seem to be a particularly amorous gesture. 'You're feverish, I think.'

'No, just hot. Cooler out here. Nice garden.'

'It's the old Spiller place. It's let into flats now. I suppose, when they can, they'll pull it down and shove up another luxury hotel.'

'Nice lilies.'

'Bermuda lilies. Bloom every spring. They're going off a bit now.'

'They're wonderful. So are the red things.'

'We get them better than that.'

Abbott said, meaning it, 'This whole place. It's beautiful.'

'Yes, it's a pity it'll all go.'

'When?'

'When we get independence. Whenever that is.'

'Not going to happen here, is it?'

'Well, we *are* a colony. So it might not, for a long time.'

'You sound . . .' Abbott struggled for the right word, 'as if you fear it?'

'Of course I fear it. My family have lived on this Island for three hundred years. We farmed virgin land and built houses to live in, and went into trade, and sailed the Caribbean end to end. All from this place. If there was a war, we sent our sons. I lost my father in the R.A.F. This is our home, but I don't know how long we'll be able to hang on to it.' Marcia crossed her magnificent legs. 'Of course, we're small. We might not be noticed.'

'It's not the end of the world, even if it happened.'

'No, but it would seem like it.'

'Nothing could spoil this place.' Abbott's headache was gone, the air had done the trick, he felt calm, rested, with this woman, with her expectant sensuality and her common sense. It was rather like a conversation with Helen. 'It's too beautiful for anybody, however foolish, to want to change it.'

'Want to bet?'

'You'd stay on, would you, if anything like that happened? A change of the political scene . . .'

'Would I hell. I'd go to the Algarve, or to South Africa or Rhodesia.'

'You would?'

'Of course I bloody would.'

'And your . . . husband?'

'We're divorced. He lives in New York these days. With his dolly-bird.'

'I see. I'm sorry.'

'That's all right. I hope my bitterness didn't show?'

'Not really.' He smiled. It had. 'You've stayed on, on your own?'

'That's right.'

'Why?'

Marcia gazed round the dark green garden, at the silky white of the lilies, at the lights from the house and the crisp, unreal lawn, green as Christmas paper-grass in the moonlight. 'Because it's my home, and I don't want to live anywhere else.' She laughed. 'Of course, I won't meet anybody here, anybody I can . . .' She laughed again, a throaty, womanly sound. 'Anybody for a companion. People don't stay long enough. They come and work for a while and then they go away.'

Abbott studied his cigarette. 'I'm sorry.'

'Why be? I live in a paradise. I should be grateful for that, and stop bitching.'

Abbott stood. 'Would you like to go back inside?'

'I'd like another drink.'

'So would I.'

'Not sure you should.'

'That's why.'

Marcia laughed, and put her arm in his, and Abbott thought if only the obsession was for a woman like this, how much easier it would all be. Once on the balcony, he found them both drinks. The party was thinning out. Guests were saying their goodbyes to David O'Hara.

'Are people going on somewhere?'

'To dinner, most of them.'

Abbott was about to say the obvious thing (the hopeful tilt of the woman's head) when the telephone pealed shrilly in the room. David answered it and then his eyes roved around, looking for a face. Abbott stood clear of Marcia so that David would see him, but his gaze moved across Abbott to Waters, standing smoking, out on the verandah.

'Tony, for you. Business, I think.'

'Bloody people. Excuse me, will you?' Abbott heard Waters' deep voice and saw the shower of sparks from his pipe as he bumped against another guest, moving quickly towards the telephone. As he answered it, his eyebrows raised, and he laughed, and his eyes (Abbott could have sworn) searched for, and found, Abbott's own. He felt suddenly chilled.

'Were you expecting a call?' Marcia asked.

'I'm sorry?'

'A telephone call? Were you expecting one?'

'Oh, not really.'

'You looked as if you were.'

'Did I? Sorry.'

'Don't keep saying you're sorry. You make me feel like a wife.'

A black manservant passed with drinks and Abbott took two.

'They're champagne.'

'Who's counting.'

'You've been drinking gin.'

'What of it?'

Marcia sipped her wine. 'You'll be sorry.'

'That's later.'

Marcia laughed, and she looked a lot younger suddenly. Abbott thought, there's a young girl still left there, but she's well into her thirties now, and she feels she must act like somebody who has lived, loved, and been divorced. He drank his champagne, and it tasted very good indeed, so he signalled for another.

'Jack, go easy.'

It was a shock to hear her say his name so intimately, but he refused to be shocked.

'I will not go easy, Marcia.'

There. Once you said it, it was much easier.

'You know one thing, Jack?'

'What?'

'I think I should put some food inside you.'

'Do you?'

'There's nothing here but scraps.' Marcia snapped her handbag shut. 'Wait for me a minute, I'll just pop in the john, then we'll go and eat.' She smiled. 'That is, if you want to?'

'Certainly,' Abbott said, gallantly. 'Why not?'

David looked surprised as they left. 'Going already?'

'That's right.'

'Enjoy yourselves.'

'We will.'

'Show him the sights, Marcia.'

David's left eye closed, on Marcia's blind side, as Abbott left. What the hell, he said to himself, do you think you are doing, Abbott? In Marcia's Alfa, coasting up the road along Harrington Sound, with the dark sea calm on their left, he could find no easy answer.

The house was large, white, and colonial-looking, and stood in a garden not unlike the one they had just left. It fronted on to the Sound, and the steady slap of water could be heard in the dark night. There were no lights in the house. Marcia stopped the Alfa expertly and got out, without help.

'Is there nobody at home?'

'Only us.'

'I thought we were eating?'

'We will be. Hot soup and cold lobster suit you?'

'Sounds wonderful.'

It was. Especially a good cold Chablis, left in the fridge by Marcia. Who would have come back with her if he hadn't? Abbott wondered. He stifled the thought. He was here, that was the relevant fact, the only one that mattered.

'Nice room.'

'I like it.'

'The furniture's very striking.'

'All original. Some from my family. Some from my husband's.' Marcia faltered, then smiled, too brightly. 'He didn't take anything, not even crockery or silver. It's all priceless, but I suppose it would look pretty much out of place in New York. Besides, the central-heating would warp the wood.' All around them, as they sat, were grouped the priceless pieces of antiquity : a love-seat in cedar; an old map, on parchment, framed in cedar, on the wall; a seat of cedar, three hundred years old, with cushions in the English style; an ancient brass telescope; several old sea-boxes, dark as pitch. There was a good deal of excellent pewter and copper and silver, very old and heavy, and a harmony of wood and workmanship that nothing but age could bestow. 'Of course, I'm used to it, I don't see it. But everything is still used, it isn't a museum.'

'I'm sure.' Abbott smiled, to make the remark personal, and she reached out and touched his hand. This time it was not a medical touch; her nails bit ever so slightly into his skin. A momentary unease gripped him; he got up from the table, and took his coffee with him. 'You're very lucky to live in a place like this.'

'As long as it lasts.'

He hesitated. 'Do you mind if I use your telephone?'

'There's one in the hall.'

Abbott made the call quietly, his hand half-over his mouth. Angel was not in the hotel. He replaced the receiver, slowly. He felt the expected sense of loss and hurt, and an unexpected anger.

Marcia made no comment when he returned, but simply handed him more coffee, after a quick look at his face. She was an extremely civilised woman. Abbott thought how pleasantly domestic it all was, but that was all. The hurt and loss and anger nagged at him, as he talked to Marcia, trying to interest himself in the moment, waiting for his explosive feelings to dissipate.

'Have you lived on the Island all your life?'

'I went to school in England.'

'Did you like that?'

'Not much. Butch ladies, who didn't know they were, running the place, and a lot of silly half-les affairs going on. Very good scholastically, though. None of it was much use to me when I got back here. But in those days it was the thing to send sons and daughters to England for their education.'

'Oh? And now?'

'More like Vassar and M.I.T.'

'Why is that?'

'Oh, a feeling that the States is the place now. That could change, of course, but I doubt it. Anyway, most of the business interests here have States connections. It's useful to know the language. And you fly to New York in two hours. London takes seven.' Marcia's dress, cut deeply at the leg, slipped, revealing splendid thighs. She did not adjust the dress. Abbott willed his loins to stir. They did not. 'How does London look now, I haven't been for ten years, since . . .' she grimaced, 'my honeymoon.'

'London's changed a lot.'

'How?'

'Oh, it's not quite so aristocratic. The welfare state has made it look like New York, in parts. The British working class, now emancipated, like their hamburgers and pizza. London is now two places, aristo town and prole town. You take your choice.'

'I couldn't live there. I'd have to live somewhere in the Shires, if I went back.'

'You'd have a job to find them. It's all commuter country now.'

'Oh God, nothing stands still, does it?'

'No,' Abbott said. 'Least of all the things of our youth.'

'I mean, nothing turns out like you think it will.'

'Never does.'

'I used to like New York, but now I can't go there. It's no place for a woman to be alone in. Besides, I'm scared of bumping into them, you know?'

'You wouldn't.'

'Oh, I might. On Fifth Avenue. Or in a restaurant. Imagine how I would feel, to see them, arm-in-arm, or both sitting at the same table, looking into each other's eyes.'

'You'd live.'

'I suppose I would. I'd just hate to have it happen, that's all.'

'You'd be all right. All that is over, for you.'

Marcia shrugged, lit a cigarette, not waiting for Abbott's proffered lighter. She was used, he realised, to doing it for herself. 'I suppose it should be all over, but the trouble was, I loved the bastard. Of course, I guessed he was playing around on those New York trips, but I figured what the hell, after ten years it must get a little boring, the same woman, the same actions, everything, and all that stuff, like a man's a hunter, and that includes other women, and he'll do it anyway, can't help himself.' She smiled, ruefully. 'So, as long as he seemed cheerful when he came home, I put all that out of my mind. I trusted him. I don't mean not to *do* it, I mean not to let it matter. But . . .' She fell silent, staring at the carpet.

'It was serious?'

'With the dolly-bird? I don't know. He said it was. He seemed to mean it. He tried to give her up, then said he couldn't, you know the pattern?'

'Yes, I know it.'

'Sorry to bore you.'

'I'm not bored.'

She drew on her cigarette, in a pleasant, womanly way. 'Well, one day he flew off and didn't come back. His lawyer wrote, and there it was, all set out, the divorce settlement. It was very fair, he was always a fair man. I think he simply wanted his freedom. Oh, not just from me, but from the Island, the whole parochial deal. He wasn't just a businessman, he was artistic in a way, I mean he liked ballet and opera and plays. So, he's got what he wanted.'

'No children?'

'Girl at a boarding-school in England. She's nine. My old school, but they say it's changed. All progressive and permissive and sixth-form problems with pot. Sounds like a different kind of hell. He arranged that too, the bastard. Leaving me nothing.'

'You could have fought it?'

'Yes, but I didn't want to. It seems to me, in this world, you can have a husband or you can have children, but you can't have both.'

'The woman needs the children . . .'

'And the man gets left out?'

'That's the theory.'

'I tried very hard for it not to happen. But maybe it did.' Marcia refilled Abbott's brandy glass. He sipped, and the warm, sugary spirit helped. The hurt was beginning to go away. Everybody was hurt and hurt back, in turn. The thing was not to care, or not to seem to care, Abbott decided.

'Your husband has no wish to come back home, I mean to visit?'

'God no, he hates the place.'

'Then he's an idiot, it's wonderful.'

Marcia shook her head. 'He always hated it. He's artistic, I told you, home was always a place to get out of.'

Abbott thought about Angel, and nodded, but he said nothing.

'You ever been married?' she asked, after a pause.

'Yes.'

'For a long time?'

'It was, yes.'

'Sorry. If you don't want to talk about it?'

'Not at all. Nothing to say really. In many ways it's a little like your own story. I mean, my wife's side of it would be. Except there were two children.' Abbott smiled, painfully. 'All my fault, of course, I accept that. We'd functioned while I was struggling and working. Once I . . . Well, I had a little luck with money, and it altered things, that's all.'

'There was a girl involved?'

'Yes, there was, actually.'

There was a long silence. Marcia looked at Abbott quickly, but he said no more, and she got up again and refilled his glass.

'Hey, I'll be drunk.'

Marcia smiled down at him, tolerantly.

'Well, you aren't going anywhere, are you?'

Abbott looked up at her, but she was still smiling tolerantly, and, he thought, she had learned one lesson about men, and learned it, perhaps, too well. She now thinks they are all the same. He sipped his brandy, however, and felt the better for it. Marcia's story had brought back the desperate days of the eventual split with Helen, the last time he had left the house, the children white-faced and tight-lipped at an upper bedroom window. They were supposed to be in the garden but they had *known* (they had probably known for months) and Abbott had almost turned back at that moment, but the last words Helen had spoken had been, 'Go to your whore, then!' and it simply wasn't possible to go back after *that.* Besides, Helen had been behaving like a lunatic, shouting and yelling at him. He had never known her raise her voice before. He shuddered. All that, thank Christ, was behind him. Oh, not the obvious things, like the unforgiving children (maybe, when they were thirty?) and the occasional awkward meeting with somebody who hadn't heard, but the real hurt and fear of it. All that was gone, bought off as far as possible by the money. It had all been worth it, it had to be. Abbott drank the rest of his brandy.

'Do you always go at the booze like this?'

'No. Not as a rule.'

'Any special reason?'

'Not really. A bit low, I suppose.'

Marcia walked out of the room without another word, taking her glass with her. Abbott, after a hesitation, followed.

'Jack, in here.'

She was naked in the darkness.

'Just a minute, let me get my things off.'

'I'll do it for you.'

'No. Please.'

'Oh. All right.'

Her scent was Mitsouko. Helen had once tried it but had gone back to her favourite Chanel. Abbott's arms went around Marcia's soft body. She was firm and strong and her breasts were good, and her hips were wide.

'Jack.'

'Yes?'

'This is just between us. It has nothing to do with anybody else.'

'All right. . . .'

'I mean it.'

'Yes, all right.'

'You *do* want to, don't you?'

'Of course.'

'You . . . sure?'

'Yes.'

'But you . . .'

'I'll be all right.'

A long moment of indecision. Then, 'If I do this . . . and this . . .'

'Ah, no . . .'

'And *this* . . .'

Marcia did everything. It was the experience of many men, but there was no indelicacy or lewdness. Abbott finally responded, and it was all adroit and inevitable, and the preliminaries were not hurried, or too-long delayed, and the act itself was fierce and roaring, and a thing of thrust and counter-thrust, and at her climax Marcia said, 'Oh, I love you, darling,' and Abbott said nothing.

They smoked cigarettes in the dark.

'Was that all right?'

'Wonderful.'

'Was it, honestly?'

'Honestly.'

'Again later?'

'Later.'

She put out her cigarette, slid her arms around his neck, closed her eyes, and slept. Abbott lay awake, smoking, listening to the slap of the water against the jetty. Some time, about three o'clock, he gently disentangled her arms from around his neck and slid out of the bed. He went to the bathroom, washed, put on his clothes, drank a very large brandy, to clear his head and take the taste of sex and sleep away, made a telephone call for a cab, debated leaving a note, decided against it, and left. The night was still dark over Harrington Sound as the taxi droned down the driveway. A light snapped on in the house behind them as the car pulled away, but Abbott did not look back.

'Where to, sir? The hotel?'

The cab driver was, unexpectedly, the one who had driven them from the airport to the hotel when they first arrived. A tolerant smile played about his lips. On impulse, Abbott said, 'Do you know the Snow place?'

'Happy Snow's?'

At least he sounded surprised.

'That's right.'

'Yeah, I know it.'

'That's where I want to go.'

'This time of night, sir?'

'As fast as you like.'

'Still gotta be but twenty mile an hour.'

The cab droned through the night, as Abbott sat back in the seat and smoked a cigarette. This was the time for a confrontation, while he felt that any woman would do, that there was nothing wondrously specific about any one of them. Feeling as he did now, drained and empty and sad, he would be able to say the things that needed to be said, things he would never manage to say while his loins ached and his throat filled with desire and anger. Marcia, God bless her and be kind to her, had served a purpose, if only this. The cab drove on, across the moonlit, sleeping island. The sea was calm now, or as calm as it ever could be, in this ocean place, and the tropical shrubs at the side of the road stood bright and sentinel in the moonlight.

The cab stopped at the bottom of the lane. The driver half-turned.

'Want me to wait?'

'No thanks.'

'You sure? No phone for a long way.'

'Tell you what. I'll pay you for the journey and extra to wait ten minutes, right?'

'Right.'

'If I'm not back then, you go on, forget me.'

'Right.'

Abbott paid, and got out of the cab. The dirt road was uneven, and he stumbled a couple of times. His resolution hardened with every step. If there had to be some kind of decision, it must be now, not in two years' time. He could not share a woman. All right, it was old-fashioned, tribal, but it was how he felt. He could not play musical beds. The episode with Marcia had proven that.

The cottage slumbered in the moonlight. No lights showed, but as Abbott came up the path to the door, a bird moved in the tamarind tree. Abbott looked up and thought he saw a flash of red feather. Then the door opened, before he even knocked, and Happy stood there, a barrel-like figure in a cheap, quilted kimono, buttoned up to the neck. Abbott stared at her.

'Hello, Mister Abbott.' She did not sound surprised to see him.

'Did you hear the car?'

'No.'

'. . . Saw me come up the path?'

'No. Come in.'

Abbott's shoes scraped on the doorstep. The redbird in the tree cawed in protest.

'Shut up, bird. You got all day to sleep,' said Happy, conversationally. 'Not many of those old redbirds left, y'know. The place is full of sparrows, greedy little devils. But that ole redbird, he's been here as long as the Island.' She sighed. 'When they all gone, I dunno, maybe everything gone?' Abbott followed her inside. The room was empty. It was cool, and a Calor Gas lantern buzzed and shone. The brass-faced clock ticked in the corner. The face showed three-thirty, as near as Abbott could read the single hand.

'I like the old lantern,' Happy sat down, in her rocker, as if was three in the afternoon, and motioned Abbott into pride of place on the sofa. 'It's got a soft light. The electric's hard on the eyes.'

'You've been awake? Sitting up?'

'That's right.'

'You often do that?'

'When I think something's gonna happen.'

'And you thought that tonight?'

'Yes, I surely did. Oh, yes.'

Abbott said, 'I came because . . .'

But Happy talked on, as if he had not spoken. 'My grand-mammy had the second sight, y'know? I don't think I have. But there's something. *Her* mammy was locked up, for talking to the spirits. That wasn't allowed, see? I ain't got nothing like that gift, but there's *something.*' Her eyes closed, and she sat still for a long moment.

Abbott wondered if she had gone to sleep. The alcohol buzzed in his head, and he closed his own eyes. He had almost forgotten what he was doing there.

'Are they here?' he asked abruptly.

Happy opened her eyes, 'Who?'

'Angel and . . . your son?'

'Now, why do you ask that?'

'Because I telephoned the hotel, and Angel isn't there.'

'When did you do that?'

'Half hour ago.'

'Where was you calling from?'

'A . . . friend's place . . .'

Happy opened her eyes wide, looking at him.

Abbott said, 'She was supposed to be at a party. It was being given by an old friend. But she never turned up.'

'When did you last see her, Mister Abbott?' The old eyes closed, the rocker creaked, yet Abbott was conscious of an intelligence at work.

'This afternoon.'

'And you know she's with my son?'

'She left the hotel with him.'

'You see them go?'

'No, Marie told me.'

'Ah, that Marie.'

'No reason for her to lie.'

'There is, but never mind.'

Abbott swallowed. 'Look, all I want is to find out where she is. I want to know if she's all right. Is she here?'

Happy shook her head. 'That's not all you want to find out. You want to find out, is she a whore.'

Abbott was shocked. 'Not at all!'

'Yes, you do. And if she was, what would you do?'

'You mean with your son?'

'No, with anybody.'

Abbott just stared at her.

Happy rocked in the chair. 'You left your wife for Angel, right?'

'Yes.'

'Really, in your heart, you think she's a whore.'

'No, I don't.'

'You'd leave her. It would give you an excuse and you'd leave her. You'd do it to hurt yourself.'

'I haven't thought in those terms.'

'You'd do it to hurt yourself, to pay yourself back.'

'I don't see how you can know this.'

'Because I've lived a little time.' Happy smiled crookedly. 'Do you want coffee?'

'No, thanks,' Abbott said. 'I simply want your assurance they aren't here.'

'It's not my job to give 'surance, even if I could,' Happy said, getting to her feet. 'You look all done in. I'll get you that drink.' She got out of the rocker chair, leaving it moving, and waddled into the kitchen. Abbott rubbed his eyes. These kind of nights were no use to him. It would all have to keep until morning. He called, 'I have a cab at the end of the road. I'll go now.'

Happy came back into the room. 'Your cab's gone. Coupla minutes ago.'

'Did you hear it go?'

'It's gone, Mister Abbott.' She went back into the kitchen. Abbott sat down again. As he did so he thought he heard a shuffling sound upstairs, and a voice call, very softly, but he could not be sure. He walked quickly into the kitchen, and found Happy pouring milk on to the instant coffee.

'You take this back through and drink it. You'll find it's just what you need. You look pretty done in. What you been doing all night, besides drinking?'

Abbott took the coffee and sipped it, and, as he did so, detected a lingering scent of Mitsouko in the air, from his hair and fingernails, no doubt. It always stayed there longest. He felt dismayed and depressed. He went back into the living room and sat down. 'Nothing much. I'm tired, I've been tired since I came to this Island.'

'It's the air.' Happy followed him in, bringing her own cup. She sat down again, opposite to him. 'It's the air, and then it's the sun. Put the two together, it's too much, if you ain't used to it.'

'This will wake me up.' Abbott sipped his coffee. 'Then I'll walk down the road and phone for a taxi somewhere.'

'You'll have a long walk. No telephone around here.'

'Just the same, I'll have to get back.' The coffee was hot and sweet and Abbott was grateful for it. 'You still didn't say whether she was here or not.'

'Go upstairs and look, when you've finished your coffee.' Happy rocked, her eyes on him. 'You love that girl, don't you?'

'My feelings don't matter. I expect certain conduct. If it isn't there, then the only road is out.'

'You think that?'

'Yes, I do.'

'And you a man?'

'That's right.' You bloody hypocrite, Abbott, he told himself. 'Being a man, you should know better.'

Being a man, I am a hypocrite in these matters, Abbott thought. It's something I can't change. He drained his coffee. 'I know the kind of man Snow is. He told me himself, he slept with a lot of different people. He told me himself that he got into trouble, getting in the wrong beds, that he'd blown a few jobs on account of it.'

'That's his temperament, but it don't mean much.'

'It does to me.'

'You're determined it's happened?'

'No, I hope it hasn't. But *where* is she? It's . . .' Abbott read the brass-faced clock with difficulty. It seemed darker, rather than

176

lighter, in the kitchen, yet there was a streak of dawn at the window. 'It's four o'clock now. Where is she?'

'Prob'ly back at the hotel, fast asleep.'

'You *think* that?'

Happy smiled and nodded, as if to a child.

Abbott looked at her uncertainly. 'You *feel* that, do you?'

'You want me to say yes, Mister Abbott. I dunno why you bother y'self into such a sweat. You know what you want. Why kid y'self, why torture y'self, Mister Abbott?'

Abbott said, 'I don't know.'

'Your trouble,' Happy rocked comfortably, 'your trouble is you're still living by your old standards, your wife's standards. But now you gone from her. You in a different league. Where people live a different way. Am I right?'

'Yes,' Abbott yawned. He felt very sleepy. 'I suppose so, but . . .'

'You thinking about this Angel as if she's your wife, but she ain't your wife, not by a long chalk and never will be, I mean, maybe you'll marry her an' all that, but she ain't the same kinda woman as your wife was. Ain't no use treating her the same.'

'That's all right, but I expect . . .'

'Expecting ain't gettin', is it, Mister Abbott? I think sometimes it be wise to take what you kin get, not what you expect. You never get what you expect in this world, so why go on expecting it, why not live with what you got, enjoy it day to day, and stop worrying about it?'

Abbott said, 'I can't. I . . .'

'You love her? Okay, but why keep torturing y'self about it? You love her. Okay, maybe she loves you. But . . .'

'I don't think she does.'

'No?'

'She's always saying she doesn't want love, the old kind of love. She wants a relationship.' Abbott could not think why he was telling this fat old woman all this, except that he was still hung-over, and miserable and somewhat ashamed, and to talk was a relief.

'I know about love, I don't know nothing about a relation-ship. I don't believe nobody else does. A relationship is just an excuse for not loving somebody. It's what my son call a cop-out, right?'

'Probably.' His head was very fuzzy now, and he was really very tired. Happy's eyes were on his face, unblinkingly. The day outside was getting brighter, beating at the window. He must go soon.

Happy said, 'So I think maybe this is a girl who doesn't love, in the ordinary way, y'know? I mean, in the way most people do. Who gets love elsewhere, in some other thing, maybe? That ordinary love ain't enough for her. So she loves a lot of things, you, her job, herself, what's wrong with *that*? She just loves *more* things than most women.'

'She loves them all less.' Abbott noticed his speech was slurred. The brandy, he supposed.

'I don't think so. I see her, y'know. She got a lot of capacity.'

The redbird in the tree cawed to meet the dawn. Abbott's mouth was very dry. He tried to get to his feet, but waves of tiredness came over him. He yawned hugely, and shivered.

'Look, I tell you what,' Happy was saying softly, 'you're done in. You just lie there on that ole couch, and I put this here blanket over you, and you sleep a little. Then in the morning you get a taxi and go back to the hotel.'

'No. I . . .' Abbott did indeed feel very tired. His head lolled.

'No cabs now. You'll have to wait anyway.' Happy spread a blanket over Abbott, and he released his breath in a long sigh, leaned his head back against the prickly horsehair, and slept.

It was bright day when he wakened, and the house was full of music from Happy's transistor. The sun streamed in the window, and the smell of coffee was in his nostrils. Abbott felt enormously refreshed and optimistic. Happy came in, in her white apron, and gave him a cup of black coffee. He drank it gratefully, tugged at his rasping beard.

'There's a razor in the kitchen you can use. Can't get back to the hotel looking like you been out all night,' Happy said, ironically.

Abbott lathered and shaved and found himself whistling. Happy's eye on him was sceptical. 'You feel better today?'

'Yes. What time is it?'

'Nine o'clock. There's a taxi waiting for you at the bottom of the road. I walked out and rang for it for you.'

'Oh, thanks.'

'Ain't nothing.' She smiled, ironically. 'You want to look upstairs, case anybody's here?'

Abbott wiped the foam from his face. He grinned, a little shamed. 'No thanks. I'm sorry . . . about all that.'

'Don't be. My son laugh when I tell him.'

'Is he here?'

'He was. He's had his breakfast three hours ago. Gone out in his boat.'

'Oh?' Abbott looked at her quickly, but the plump black face was impassive.

'You'd better get off, get your cab.'

Abbott walked down the road and found the cab waiting. It was the same driver as before.

'You been around some tonight, sir.'

'The hotel, please.'

Abbott half-knew what he would find. Angel asleep in the large bed, nude, her arms around a pillow. He did not wake her.

9

'Where did you go?'

Abbott was trying very hard to keep the accusation out of his voice. The doubt and hurt, too. He was not succeeding.

'We went up the Island and had dinner.'

'Dinner doesn't take till three in the morning.'

'We sat and talked in the place till one o'clock.'

'About the play?'

'About the play.'

'And then?'

Angel tucked her négligée under her long, golden legs. It was very flimsy, and the contours of her breasts and her pubic mound showed clear.

'Oh, for God's sake put something on!'

Angel looked at him with wide eyes. 'Throw my robe over, please. It's on the bed.'

Abbott went into the bedroom and found the robe. It was made of the same kind of flimsy material as the nightdress, which Angel had put on after she wakened. It smelled faintly of Angel's scent and of her body. He held it in his hands, and groaned slightly. Then he went back to the balcony. The sun was beginning to get hot; it was almost noon. Angel had wakened thirty minutes before, but refused to talk until she had showered and eaten breakfast. Now she sat on the cane chair, protective dark glasses over her eyes, sipping her third cup of coffee. She seemed infuriatingly at ease.

'Just put it over my shoulders.'

Abbott did as he was bidden, and sat down again. The breasts and the pubic mound were still aggressively protuberant. He sighed. 'Look, you say you left the restaurant at one o'clock? What then?'

'Why the questions?'

'Because you left no note to say where you'd gone or anything. I was worried.'

'Only worried?'

'Among other things.'

Angel put the last piece of toast into her mouth. 'You were the one who left, Abbott. You charged out of that rehearsal like a wild thing. I didn't even know you were there. Nor did Snow.'

'You were hating him at that moment. Now?'

'Oh, I'm not afraid of him any more.'

'Why?' Abbott's voice was brutal in his own ears.

She shrugged. 'Oh, reasons.'

He averted his eyes from the nightgown, climbing up the bare golden flesh as Angel crossed her legs. 'Where did you go at one o'clock?'

'Oh, we drove around.' Angel poured herself more coffee. 'Then we sat in the car, talking. We talked the whole damn play through. All the way. We went over every scene, we discussed every character, every move, every motivation, we talked about the scenery, the words, the music, the theme, plot and characterisation. Mainly, we talked about my part.' Her eyes shone, there was nothing bogus about *this,* Abbott thought. 'He made me see that girl in the play, he made me feel like her, breathe the scent of her, *know* her. He's a wonderful man.'

'And you did all this till three in the morning?'

'Of course we did. It could have been six for all I knew.'

'You never thought about me, sitting here, waiting?'

Angel lit a cigarette. 'I was too busy listening to him, arguing with him, agreeing with him, everything. I tell you I was hoarse at the end, laughing and shouting. I was drunk on it all.' She expelled smoke. At least, it was an ordinary cigarette. 'Now I know why he's got a brilliant reputation. He imagines himself into people. He *was* that girl, when we talked last night. He talked her into being, and then into me. He gave her to me—Snow did that. I could go on and play her now, if I knew the book better. In short, a lot was done. We can go on with it.'

'You could have telephoned, at some point,' Abbott said, doggedly.

'How do you know I didn't?'

'There was no message at the desk.'

'Maybe I didn't leave one?'

'Did you ring?'

'Were you here all night?'

'You know very well that we were invited to a party at David O'Hara's.'

Angel threw back her head, and laughed. 'So that was what you were worrying about? Abbott, you really are a fool!'

'It was important to me, if not to you. I had accepted an invitation on behalf of us both.'

'Abbott, darling.' Angel leaned forward, and the beautiful breasts almost swung free of the restraining nylon of the nightgown. Abbott felt anguish. 'The whole object of our meeting Snow is to get him to direct *Paradiso*, correct?'

'Yes, but ...'

'No buts, darling. Did I waste my time getting him to agree or should I have been at the silly party with all the colonials and their wives eyeing my tits all evening?'

Abbott hastily averted his eyes. 'Not the point at all. The thing is, you didn't ring or even leave a note. How the hell was I to know what you were doing or where you had gone?'

'You weren't and why should you?'

'Why should I?'

'Yes, why? I was working, baby.'

'Don't call me baby. That's Snow talk. Why didn't you at least ring?'

'Because, like I said, I was working.'

'Eating, drinking, talking. If you were ...'

'Why do you say that?'

'What?'

'If I was, why do you say if I was?'

Abbott felt suddenly chilled at the note in her voice.

'Because his ex girl-friend was jealous, I suppose. Marie. She said you'd gone off with him, like all his girls do.'

'Did she? She said *that*?' Angel's voice was cool, and academic. Then, suddenly, she laughed.

'What's so bloody funny about it?'

'Everything. It's all stupid. Her jealousy. Your jealousy. Jealousy is always stupid.'

Abbott said, painfully. 'It isn't when it's justified.'

'You think it's justified? You think I went off with Snow to grab a little nooky?'

'Oh for God's sake, why put it like that?'

'Why not, it's just what's going through your mind, isn't it?' Angel's eyes were on his, oddly cool, he thought. They did not match the words. She did not care (he could have sworn it) which way the conversation went, she was occupied beyond it all.

Whether with memory of love, or anticipation of glory, he could not guess.

'You were with the man about fourteen hours, Angel.'

'Yes, darling, and I'll be with him another fourteen today, if need be.'

'Today?'

Angel looked at her watch, a present from Abbott, tiny and gold, on her slender wrist. 'In half an hour, to be exact.'

'He's hired the night club again?'

'He said he would. We meet him there.'

'We?'

'You'll be coming down, won't you?'

'I don't know.' Abbott stood up, his back to her, and looked out over the Sound. The water was a brilliant poster-blue, and people on a sailer waved towards the hotel. Bathers in the sun-lounge and around the pool waved lazily back. Abbott said, 'What did you say the name of this restaurant was?'

'I don't know, I never remember those things.'

It was true. She didn't.

'Ask Snow,' Angel said. 'He'll remember.'

'And where you sat talking for two hours? In the car? He'll remember where that was?'

'Yes, why not ask him? Excuse me, I must get ready, I've had enough of this shitty talk!' There was a rustle and she was out of the chair and into the bedroom. Abbott ran after her, seized her arm (conscious of the stupidity of the action, and yet unable to control it; oh you bloody fool, he thought) and twisted her back to face him. 'Did you let him bang you, is that what happened, is that why you're big friends now? When I left that rehearsal yesterday he was cutting you to pieces so neatly, I couldn't stand the sight of it one moment longer! That's why I had to get out!' Abbott realised he was yelling, but he could not help it. 'Is that what happened, *is* it? Did he bang you?'

Angel twisted her arm free. She looked more sulky than hurt or angry.

'Is that what you think of me? You talk as if I'm a whore.'

Abbott said, 'I didn't say that. I asked you a question, and you haven't answered it.'

'Look, Abbott, any time you want to leave me because you think I'm a whore, do it.' Her voice was weary.

Abbott thought, with a pang of sharp compassion, she's played

183

this scene before, she's been deserted before. It isn't new and it isn't even what I want, but I have to know. He said, 'I don't think *that . . .*'

'You do. I told you about some people, actors, I've lived with. So you think I'm a tramp.'

'No, I know you aren't, but . . .'

'But what?'

'If there's somebody else, I'll get out. I'm only standing by holding your coat—most of the time, anyway.' Abbott felt his voice getting out of control, but it had to be said. 'I'm pretty useless, because when I got the money I stopped having a reason for living and working, except for you. Now I've probably been all kinds of a bloody fool for putting all my emotional eggs in one basket, but at least I have to know if it's the wrong basket. You owe me that. Don't sod about with my affection for you, because it's real, I sometimes think it's the only real thing about me these days.'

'Abbott, don't talk such cock . . .'

'If you want Snow, have him, have all he can give you, but let me out, let me go. Just tell me.'

Abbott stopped shouting and there was a silence between them, like something solid. Angel drew on her cigarette, looked at her watch, and sat on the small couch. She patted it. 'Sit down, Abbott. I want to talk to you.'

'Talk away. I'll stand.'

Abbott did not want to be too near her. The golden breasts and the soft arms were too much. He might not be touching them again. It was best to start getting used to distance. He swallowed. His throat was very dry.

'You said I was having a bastard time with Snow yesterday. He didn't like what I was doing with the part. Right?'

'When I left he was going on like every megalomaniac director I have ever seen rolled into one.'

'Right. And he got worse after you went.'

'Not possible.'

'It was. It was. He did it.'

'If you say so.'

Angel was sitting on the edge of the couch now, and there was nothing left of the relaxation there had been on the balcony. The long limbs were tense, Abbott thought, and why not? If people lied, they usually went tense while they were doing it.

'Abbott, I had to do something, darling. Otherwise, Snow was going to tell me to forget it. I was fighting him, I wasn't taking his instruction. Oh, I would have, but he put it in such an insulting way, y'know, personal . . .'

'I know, I saw him.'

'Well, either I gave in, or he would go. I could see that. But he wanted to break me down in front of the others, Marie and the musicians . . .'

'He'd want an audience, he's that type.'

'It's how he works.'

'Then sod him, there are a hundred other directors.'

'None of them as good, Abbott.'

'What difference will it make, in the end?'

Angel shook her head. 'A lot, probably everything will depend on it. And Snow has the critics in his pocket, they think he's Mister Integrity this month. And they matter, they really do, in the theatre. It isn't television, where the show's already *gone*. Theatre critics sell tickets. It could mean the difference between a success and a failure. You know that's true.'

Abbott shrugged. 'All right. I admit we want him, but there's such a thing as price. If you went out and laid . . .'

'Shut up and let me talk, for Christ's sake, won't you, please!'

Angel did not raise her voice, but the intensity cut through Abbott. He wondered if it was deliberately histrionic, and doubted it. It sounded sincere. But then it would, under the circumstances, for a number of excellent reasons.

'All right, I've shut up.'

'Like I said, I had to get him off my back.'

'So you turned over?'

'Abbott, *you* bastard!'

'All right. Go on.'

Angel seemed very small, and hunched, on the couch. Her voice, when she spoke, was low. 'You heard him going on at me, about how the hell could I know anything about the part of this little coloured girl, I hadn't had her experience of poverty, and all that?'

'I heard you say you had.'

'Yes, but after you'd gone—and I think you being there upset him. Anyway, he started again, and he got at me, saying I didn't know anything about being poor and spat on.' She stopped, her shoulders sagged. 'When I have actually, Abbott . . . I have actually hawked my ass in the streets.'

Abbott just stared at her.

'No!'

'Oh, yes, but I couldn't *do* it, don't worry.' Angel's laugh was dry, forced. 'I was fifteen years old, and it was my mother's idea. She was ill, and there was no money to pay the gas bill and no food or fire, so what the hell, you don't want to know all that...'

'Fifteen!'

'Fifteen!' Again the dry laugh. 'It was late, for the district. Anyway, I didn't do it, I went and got a job in a shop where the manager used to feel my bottom every time he passed. I learned to smile at him, Abbott, because I'd walked along that street, and I hadn't liked it much. All the men did was stare. Irish, Paks, Indian, white—you know Stepney? Nobody spoke to me. I don't think anybody knew what I was doing.' Angel lit a new cigarette from the butt of the old one. 'So I got to the end of the road and then I turned and walked back again. It seemed to take a long time. The men all stared, again. I suppose I looked too young. Jail bait. Then I was home. I cried, and my mother slapped me, and I slapped her back. For the first time. Next day I got the lousy job from the manager because I let him touch my tits. Making it cool, like it was an accident.'

Abbott felt a surge of pity so strong he could hardly speak. 'You told Snow all *this*?'

'Did I shit. It would have been wasted on him.'

'Then...' Abbott's voice faltered. 'You went out with him... and you...'

'Abbott, he went on at me and on at me, and at last I told him I'd been young and poor and that...' She looked up at him, her eyes wide. 'You remember what he said about my father, kept asking what I was afraid of about him...?'

'Yes,' Abbott said. 'But I don't want to know, let's leave it, Angel. This is no good.'

'No, you asked, and I'm telling you.' Angel looked away, seemed to shrink even smaller on the couch. 'I told him why I was afraid of finding out about my father.'

'Yes?' Abbott said, dully.

'Because my father was part coloured.'

Outside, the people round the pool shouted to each other.

The sun poured in from the balcony.

Abbott said, 'And was he?'

'You'd wondered?'

186

'Yes.'

Angel suddenly uncurled, threw herself back on the couch, and laughed. Her legs were wide and the skin on her inner thigh soft and golden. Abbott looked down at her, painfully.

'You *wondered,* Abbott?'

'Yes, naturally. With your looks.'

'And you never said anything?'

'What was there to say?'

The laughter stopped, as abruptly as it began. Again her eyes look serious. 'I like you, Abbott. Do you know that?'

'What did Snow say to all this?'

Again Angel almost choked, with sudden mirth. 'He was knocked out, really high, he went wild! It was all kisses and hugs. And then off we went and ate and . . .'

Abbott stopped her. 'Never mind that. Why tell *him*?'

Abbott meant, before you even told *me*? Yet he had never asked about her life. He knew she had come up a hard road, with dancing-lessons and singing-lessons paid for by going without breakfast; bit parts and walk-ons and finally the television panel game; and the four-letter word. Details, he had never asked for. And now, for an advantage, had she used it to sway Snow? He looked at her with new respect, but, also, with rising anger. 'Why tell *him*?'

'Because-I-want-him-for-the-show!' Angel stood up. She was still laughing, and she danced towards the bathroom, raising the skirt of her nightgown above her knees in a mock-dance.

'And for *that,* you told him . . . your . . . ?'

'Dread secret, yes. I'd have done more than *that,* darling!'

'Angel, for God's sake, it's not a joke . . .'

'No, honey, it isn't.'

Abbott waited. Angel turned, at the bathroom door. 'You see, my mother simply never knew *what* my father was. He was a sea-man, and he said he was Spanish, from oh, somewhere, one of their colonies. Or maybe Portuguese. That's all she knew, just that and no more, and she wouldn't talk about him. Oh, not for any deep reason. I don't think she saw him more than a few times. She never really knew him.'

'So what you told Snow . . . ?'

'Was a lot of cock, dear.'

'*Was* it?'

The bathroom door slammed. Water roared. Abbott sat, and

smoked a cigarette. Then he rubbed the sleep out of his eyes, looked at his watch, sighed, and went slowly downstairs to tell them that Angel was going to be late for the rehearsal.

Snow did not seem surprised to hear it. He greeted Abbott with a wide smile, and said, 'Angel tell you we got a good way to getting it together?'

'She said you'd done a lot of work on it, yes.'

Behind Snow, on the dais, Marie sniggered. The bongo player laughed, richly and briefly, as if to himself. The pianist just sat, waiting.

Snow said, mildly, 'What's so funny back there?'

Marie giggled again.

Snow did not look round. 'Shut up, silly bitch!' He said to Abbott, 'I think we may have ourselves a winner here, Jack. If I can get it right.'

Abbott held down his new, rising anger. The big *I*, he thought. 'Does that mean you will definitely want to do it?'

'I don't know. I haven't made my mind up, y'know? I mean, I keep getting this kinda feeling we're constricted, that we should be making a movie, not a musical, that the story's more important than the music? That we should be outside, telling the real story of this girl, shooting wild-cat, y'know?'

'No, I don't know,' Abbott said. 'And I haven't a lot of symfor that point of view. What we are offering you is a musical, a small musical with a London opening, possibly New York later, if it does well.'

Snow smiled. 'Is that what you are offering me?'

'It is.'

'Well then, I might just take it. But, Jack, let me say this. I'm an artist, and I go by feel and touch, and I like to wait to hear the cameras turning for me, or to see in my head the stage-lights going down, or whatall. Jack, I think this might not be a musical, y'know? I mean, I think the music's okay but not, I think, great great. But the story is great great, and with a little rejigging here and there...'

'By you?'

'Who else? With that, I think it could be a straight piece. It could be important, it could matter.'

'Angel is a singer, not a straight actress.'

'Then we make her one.'

'I can't see the point.'

188

'The point, Jack,' Snow said, patiently, 'is that we may have a second-rate musical on our hands. Or a first-rate, serious, work of art.'

'I'm sorry, I'm just a money-man, I can't be expected to understand all that.'

'You've been around, Jack. You know what I mean.'

'There is no finance for a movie.'

'It would only need to be a cheap one. We could do a deal, maybe?'

'No, I don't think it would be any use to Angel. She needs a career as a singer. It's what she *has*. A one-off part in a movie isn't using her real talent.'

Again Marie giggled. Snow turned round slowly and looked at her. Marie turned away sullenly, and bent down, showing him her trim bottom, in skin-tight rehearsal gear. The bongo player laughed. The pianist waited.

'Jack. Angel is an artist. She has all kinds of ability she doesn't know about.'

There was another muffled snort from Marie. Snow ignored it.

He shifted to another tack. 'You were pretty well out, last time I see you,' he said. 'Snoring away on that couch.'

'Your mother kindly put me up last night.'

'She said you called by, late.'

'I was looking for Angel.'

'She was with me.'

'I knew that. I thought you might be at home.'

'No, we ate and talked. She tell you?'

'Yes, she told me.'

Snow waited. Marie's head came up. The bongo player stopped playing and stared. Even the pianist seemed to be looking at him. You bloody coward, Abbott, he told himself, but a sense of self-preservation held him back. He did not want to know, he realised. It was as simple as that. Depressed, he turned to find a seat at the back of the room. At that moment, Angel entered. She was wearing light blue leather hot-pants and a roll-top, armless sweater, and the inevitable soiled white tennis pumps. The effect was considerable. The bongo player rolled his drums. Even the pianist tinkled a few notes. Angel waved her hand. Abbott's breathing stepped up, at the very look of her. He resisted an impulse to speak, and went to the back of the room, found a racked pile of

P.—N

chairs, took one, and sat down. It occurred to him that Snow must be paying for the hire of the room, and that would not be cheap. Well, if he was interested enough to spend his own money, then he might do the thing after all. Abbott lit a cigarette, and watched Snow and Angel kiss, like two professional artists, on the cheek.

'Sorry I'm late, darling.'

'That's all right, baby.'

'Where do we start?'

Snow handed Angel a book. 'I thought we'd try the song we did yesterday. Show Abbott how much work we've done on it.'

Marie giggled once more.

Snow said, slowly, 'Marie, will you go?'

Marie stood up, the skin-tight track suit bursting with young flesh. 'What you say?'

'I said, will you go, please?'

Snow sat down, propped back on two legs of his chair, took out his shiny tin, and ignored her. His back was all she could see.

'I'm sorry, I . . .'

'Just go, will you, please?'

'Oh sod you, you lousy mother!'

Snow smoked, looking at nobody.

Marie stood, hesitating. Then she walked abruptly off the stage, and out of the door. The shattered glass was already replaced, but it almost cracked again with the violence of the slammed door. Nobody spoke; they all waited.

Snow said, easily, 'Okay, everybody, shall we start?'

The pianist struck up the notes of the music, and the bongo player fell seriously to work. There was no more laughter.

Angel moved into centre-stage and began to sing.

Abbott was astonished at the difference. The day before, Angel had been parodying the song, making herself (as Snow had said) seem like a star who just happened to be singing about a small, deprived girl but who could, by no stretch of imagination, *be* herself. It had been (Abbott realised now) cool and professional and removed. Today, it was uncomfortably alive and real, and Angel was singing the banal words as if they really meant something, as if, in fact, she *was* the girl. Abbott felt uncomfortable under the intensity of the projection, the half-sobs and the hurt of the piece, and he had only one real criticism. If ordinary audiences reacted as he did, that is to say, *uncomfortably,* then it was indeed too real. Snow had done too good a job, the piece had ceased to be trivial, it was now beginning to look suspiciously like art; and Abbott was not sure that was the point of the exercise. A musical had to entertain, first and last, and entertainment, in the brash terms of a musical, could mean tear-jerker, but did not, could not, mean real tears. The whole thing was too good. It was as simple as that.

> 'But the sun always shines in the morning,
> And the moon always glows in the night.
> And I know if I pray every night and every day,
> Then one day it will all come out right.'

Angel stopped singing, and bowed. For the first time since Abbott had known her, Angel broke sweat while she was working. Usually, the matt studio-make-up remained firm, dry and un-crackable. Also, there were no nerves, only exhaustion. This was something else. Sadly, Abbott knew the problems of performers who equated effort with effect. Angel would not be human if she did not feel that what she was doing was *right*. She had to feel it. She was putting so much effort into it.

Snow was equally entranced.

'You were great, baby!'

'Thank you, Mister Producer, sir.'

Angel actually did a curtsey, and put her finger to her chin. Abbott despairingly reminded himself that this was a business situation, as far as she was concerned, and tried to smile to him-self at the idea of Snow (almost certainly amorously) thinking of her as part-coloured; even a tiny part would make her respectable! He tried very hard to feel contemptuous of Snow because of this, but failed. All he felt was an uncertainty, and a deadness.

They all were turning to him, and calling for his word.

'Well, how was *that*, Mister Backer?' Snow called.

'Great.'

'You really think so?' Angel craned forward, looking blindly out of the floods.

'Great interpretation.'

'Better than yesterday?'

'Different from yesterday.'

Snow said, 'I detect a reservation somewhere there, Jack?'

'No, no reservation.'

'No?'

Abbott had to say it. He made it sound diffident, casual. Or he tried. 'Unless it's a mite too real, I dunno, maybe it is a little? I mean . . .' There was a long frozen silence, and then Abbott said, 'Uncomfortable?'

'It's meant to be that,' Angel said, loud and impatient.

'If it is, then fine,' Abbott replied, evenly.

'No, go on, Jack. Expand.' Snow had turned, and was shading his eyes in Abbott's direction. He did not sit down.

'Nothing to expand, really.'

'Must be.'

Abbott coughed. 'Well, all right. Just this. If it's a musical we're talking about, then maybe this realistic interpretation is, I don't know, a mite too much? Ah, let's put it another way. It shouldn't —maybe?—get any more real than it *is*.'

Angel said, 'You're suggesting, soften it?'

'I'm not suggesting anything. You asked my opinion.'

'It's a crummy opinion! What do you want, sugar dusted all over it?' Angel lit a cigarette, and sat down on a chair at the side of the stage, crossing her legs away from Abbott, dismissing him. He winced.

'Then why the hell did you ask for it?' he said, angrily.

'Oh well, if you're going to be like *that*!'

Snow interrupted. 'Jack, look. Don't you *like* it?'

'I like it. I'm not sure an audience would . . .'

'Take no notice of him, he talks crap.' Angel was hurt.

'Shut up, Angel, I'm talking to Jack,' Snow said, meaning it.

'I think,' Abbott said, 'that you are probably right. This is a movie treatment. It's real. It's too real for a musical.'

'What balls!' from Angel.

'No, he could be right,' from Snow.

A roll on the drums from the bongo player.

Nothing from the pianist, who waited.

A waiter put his head through the door. 'Mister Jack Abbott?'

'Here.'

'Telephone call for you, sir. Urgent. In the phone booth in the lobby.'

'Thank you, just coming.' Abbott tried to take the sting out. 'That's how it hit me. Excuse me, will you?'

Abbott followed the man out. He heard Angel say, 'Look, let's ignore all that, let's not ask opinions, it only screws us up!' Abbott knew that he was meant to hear it, it was a reminder of his position. To hell, they had asked him, and it was his money.

'It's a lady on the line, sir,' the waiter volunteered. 'In booth three.'

Abbott gave him a tip. 'Thanks.'

'Sir.'

In the booth he steeled himself, and picked up the telephone.

'Operator here. Mister Abbott, your call, sir.'

'Thank you.'

'You're through now, Mister Abbott. Speak now, sir.'

'Hello, Marcia,' Abbott said.

'Hello?'

Abbott said, 'Yes?'

The voice said, 'Jack?'

'Yes?'

'It's Helen.'

'Oh?' Abbott swallowed. The small booth seemed to spin round. 'Helen, is something wrong?' A sweat broke out across his back. 'Are the kids okay?'

'They're fine.'

'You're sure?'

'Yes.'

'Then . . . how is everything, okay?'

'Yes, Jack. Everything's okay.'

'You're well?'

'Yes, Jack, I'm well.'

'You're sure?'

'Yes, I'm sure.'

'Where . . . are you ringing from?'

'Home.'

'Home?'

'London.'

'Oh, yes. Of course.'

Helen had stayed on in the house, with the children. Abbott tried to visualise it: the chintz on the chairs; the worn stair-carpet; the children's toys all over the living room. He had always meant to confine them to a nursery, but never had. Now, of course, they were at boarding-school, and older, and the house would be neat and quiet. He said, 'It's nice to hear your voice, Helen.'

'Yours, too, Jack. How's life?'

'It's . . . fine. I think. I mean, I'm just living it, and it seems okay.'

'You never were an enthusiast for life, Jack. I hope it's better than it sounds, wherever you are. You've been through enough to get there.' She paused. 'We all have.'

'Yes, I'm sorry.'

Helen ignored that. 'I had quite a performance getting your whereabouts. The company wouldn't tell me, I mean, till I talked to the chairman.

'You talked to old White?'

'Yes. I had to find you, you see, Jack. As I say, I hope it isn't an awkward time or anything. You are six hours' difference out there, aren't you?'

'Helen.' The sweat was beginning to dry on Abbott's back, and he was becoming nervous and irritated. 'You said there was nothing wrong. This call must be very expensive, and I'd really like to hear why you made it.'

There was a long pause.

'Hello?' Abbott said. 'Are you there?'

'Yes, Jack. The thing is, I've met somebody.'

Abbott echoed, stupidly, 'Met somebody?'

Another long pause.

'Somebody I want to marry, Jack.'

'To marry?'

'Yes.'

This time it was Abbott's turn to be silent. It should not have hurt, for it to hurt was ridiculous, after all they had gone through, after the bitterness and the last harsh unspeakable words. He did not, in those seconds, recall those later moments; the impression was of an earlier emotional time. 'I'm glad,' he said at last. 'Very glad for you.'

'Are you, Jack . . . really?'

'Of course I am.'

'Well, you can afford to be tolerant, can't you?'

'I'm sorry?'

'Well, you've got what you want, haven't you? You're happy? Or, I mean . . .' Helen laughed, the sound was familiar and heart-touching, and it was as if she was in the stuffy booth with him. 'As happy as you are likely to be?'

It had always been a joke between them that he was a miserable person by temperament, whereas he had really been miserable with her, and (more probably) his circumstances. Well, that had all changed now. He said, stiffly, 'I'm fine. Do I know the man at all?'

'No, I don't think so. His name's Harry Sarden. He's an architect.'

'Oh, sounds a solid person?'

'He is, except . . .'

Abbott waited. A woman of Helen's age. On her own. Two children. With a little money. The field would not be large. The choice might be strange. Finally, he said, 'This must be costing a fortune, Helen, is there anything more to say?'

'Well, yes, there is, Jack . . .'

'Then for God's sake say it.'

'Don't shout, please, this is difficult enough as it is.'

'What's difficult about it? You've found a fella. Congratulations!'

'It isn't quite as simple as that, Jack.'

'Oh, I thought it was.'

'No.'

'All right. I suppose I pay the telephone bill anyway, so what does it matter?' Abbott had meant it as a joke, but it did not come out as one.

'In a way, that's the point, you see?'

'No, I don't see at all, Helen.'

'Well, actually . . .'

'Yes?'

'Harry is a little younger than I am, Jack.'

'Is he?'

'Yes, he's just thirty-three.'

'I see. And?'

'He's got a lot of talent . . .'

'Has he?'

'Oh God, are you really going to make me say it all?'

Abbott said, 'For Christ's sake, I don't know what you are leading up to, Helen. If you have something to say, I do wish you'd say it, dear.' He had never called her dear before in his life. It was a showbiz word, for older, less attractive ladies, used by such as Snow. He was instantly ashamed. He added, using their old, dated word, 'Darling, this is me. Talk straight. You were saying Harry has talent.'

The line buzzed and faded, and when he heard her voice again Helen was in the middle of a sentence, '. . . and he needs capital if he is to go out on his own, and it's now or never for him . . .'

Abbott said, 'Out on his own?'

'He's . . . he's a junior partner in a firm at the moment, and he wants to go out on his own and that means . . . well, it means capital, Jack.'

'Oh, does it?'

'Well, of course it does.'

'All right, how does this affect me?'

'Well . . . Really it's a matter of . . . Oh, Christ.'

The sound of crying was too much for Abbott.

'What is it you want, Helen?'

Helen blew her nose three thousand miles away.

Abbott waited.

When she spoke again, her voice was harder, and somehow, weary.

'I knew this was not going to be easy. But I didn't expect you to make it quite so difficult.'

'I'm not making anything difficult. I'm asking you why you're calling me. We're divorced. There's no earthly reason why you should call me about your boy-friend.'

Helen said, tartly, 'Except that he'll be stepfather to your children. Presumably you'd be interested to know who he is?'

'I now know. Is that why you called?'

'Partly.'

'All right. Now I know who he is, I suppose I'll do the usual thing, make one or two enquiries, ask some people about him . . .'

'Don't you dare do that!'

'What?'

'Put private investigators and people on to him!'

'I didn't say I would do any such thing. Why, has he something to hide?'

'No, he hasn't.' But Abbott detected something.

'Has he been married before?'

A long pause.

'Once. When he was twenty.'

'Oh, and what happened to that?'

'His wife . . . died.'

'Just . . . died?'

There was the longest pause yet.

'You really are a bastard, aren't you? You'll never change.'

'You rang me, Helen. This expensive conversation is all your idea, not mine. You don't have to say anything you don't want to.'

196

'Don't you care about your own children, at all?'

'Of course I care, that's why I'm asking you how his wife died.'

'God, you're worse than my mother.'

'Why? Did *she* ask?'

'If you must know, Harry's first wife . . . suicided.'

'Suicided?'

'Yes.'

'All right. So long as I know.'

'He's been in analysis. He's very level now. But he went through a very bad time.'

'He's lucky he found you, Helen.'

'Funny!'

'No, I mean it.'

Helen took an audible deep breath. 'Jack, he'll be all right with the kids. I'm sure of it.'

'He'd better be.'

'Not that he'll see much of them. Being away at school.'

'No.'

'He likes kids.'

'Does he?'

'Yes, very much. They've met him and they like him.'

'I'm glad to hear it.'

'Are you being sarcastic, Jack?'

'No.' He tried once more. 'Are you happy, Helen? Is this what you want?'

'Yes.'

'Then there's no more to say, is there? Except to wish you luck?'

'Jack, will you stop being so bloody defensive and listen, *please*!'

'I'm listening. I've been listening all the time.'

'Harry . . . he's at the crossroads in his career. . . . He has to get out on his own now . . . and marriage. . . . It would be an extra expense at a time . . . at an awkward time. . . .'

'It always is.'

'Jack, please don't be glib. Please.'

'Oh, get on with it, Helen!'

'Well, he's . . . worried . . . about keeping us.'

'He's worried . . . about *keeping* you?'

'You make it sound indecent.'

'If he can't keep you he shouldn't marry you, should he?'

'I could go out to work, Jack. All I could be is a typist, but I'd do it if I had to.'

Then why ring me? Abbott thought. But he said, 'That would be rather unfitting.'

'What, for the ex-wife of a very rich man? People might talk?'

'I hadn't thought of that, but they might.'

'Jack, as things stand you give me an allowance, right?'

'A handsome one.'

'I want it to stop.'

'Oh?'

'I don't want your cheque coming in every month. It would be too embarrassing and humiliating, really, for Harry.'

'He won't be living on it, why should he be embarrassed?'

'Well, he would be. Besides, I think we'll sell this house.'

'Oh, why?'

'He isn't keen on it, it's too far out of town, and, besides, well, it has sad memories for me.'

Shrewd, Abbott thought, what *can* I say to that? 'All right, you don't want my allowance, so you sell the house to raise capital for Harry's business, and you move to London and live in a flat?'

'You make it sound as if he's a sponger.'

'Aren't those the facts?'

'No, they are not.' Helen's voice was icy now.

'All right, but I insist on paying the children's school bills, and seeing they are all right.'

'No, I don't want that, either.'

'You're very independent, Helen, and I admire that, but aren't you being rather foolhardy?'

There was a silence. Then Helen said, in a low voice, 'This is my one chance at happiness, Jack. Don't deny it to me. At least you owe me that much.'

Abbott said, 'Helen, I'll do all you ask.'

'You haven't heard all I ask yet.'

'Oh? Is there more?'

Helen said, clearly and distinctly, 'Jack, if I asked you, would you keep up the allowance I now have? Even if I marry Harry, when, by our legal agreement, your allowance stops?'

'You just said you didn't want it.'

'I don't.'

'Well, then?'

'I'd like it in cash now, instead.'

'In *cash*?'

'Yes.'

'Why, for God's sake?'

'Never mind why. I'm asking you a favour. It's nothing to you, which way I get it. I'm asking for five years' money, now, that's all, just five years' allowance now.'

Abbott said, 'To help Harry with his business?'

There was a long pause. 'Yes.'

'That is why you telephoned? The only reason?'

A longer pause.

'Yes. Of course it was. Why else should I want to talk to you?'

Abbott felt the booth close in on him. He gazed at the water-fall in the foyer. Some tourists, newly-arrived, were throwing coins into the water.

'Jack, are you there?'

'I'll instruct my lawyers. Goodbye, Helen.'

Abbott put the telephone down and pushed his way out of the booth. He walked through the foyer of the hotel, and out into the sunlight. The warm air was soft and fragrant, and he walked into the grounds of the hotel, round the bungalows set away from the main block, and inevitably he was looking at water again, the boats bobbing against their moorings across the bay, and the fins of the sailers as they glided by. Abbott willed the tranquil peace of the scene into himself. There was, after all, no reason to feel shocked. It had always been on the cards that Helen would find somebody else. The man she had found did not sound like the choice anybody would have made for her : but he had, presumably, been the only candidate. Abbott recalled a conversation in a London pub with Masterson, his lawyer, after their divorce case had been heard. Abbott had been shocked by the procession of tight-faced, oldish, unhappy, *used* women in the court, and had said as much to Masterson. 'What happens to them all for God's sake?' Masterson had looked into his glass, and replied, 'Nothing, usually, if they haven't any money. If they have, a fella with one leg, who wants to be a painter, and has to spend six months a year in the sun, doctor's orders because of his health.'

'Only he's a bloody *architect*!' Abbott said, aloud, to sea and sky.

'Talking to yourself, Mister Abbott?' Waters rested his elbows on the stone parapet. The smoke from his pipe wafted away across the water. He was wearing a blazer and Bermuda shorts and look-ed like a tourist, apart from the fact that he had no tan, just a reddy skin, white under the collar. A lifetime in the wrong climes had not turned him even slightly brown.

'Oh, hello,' Abbott said, heavily. 'This wouldn't be accidental, would it?'

Waters contemplated his pipe. 'As it happens, this meeting is fortuitous.'

'Is it?'

'Yes. You were a long time in that telephone box?'

'Talking to a relative, not that you couldn't find out.'

Waters tamped down the tobacco in his pipe, drew on it evenly. The smoke wafted away across the water, again.

'How is Marcia Gray?'

'All right, I imagine.'

'I admire your taste.'

'Do you?'

'Fancy her myself, actually.'

'Only you can't take the risk.'

'Not in my job. Besides, I'm married already.' Waters puffed on the briar. 'Not like you, you lucky sod.'

'Oh, I don't know.'

Waters sighed, swung his pipe in an arc, embracing the Great Sound, the fronded islets, the sky. 'Lovely. Hate to see it all spoiled.'

'Think it might be?'

Waters turned towards Abbott, his grey eyes heavy and serious. 'Yes. It might be. But not if I can help it.'

'Commendable, I'm sure.'

Waters turned away as if to hide his irritation. He smoked in silence for a moment. 'You still don't see things our way, do you?'

'I don't see things any way. I'm a stranger here.'

Waters waved his pipe, taking in the clustered, pastel houses, the bright water, the soft edges of the far shore. 'There are some elements who would spoil all this.'

'You mean change it?'

'It's the same thing.'

'Not necessarily.'

'I think so. There are examples, elsewhere in the world.'

'Elsewhere isn't here, and anyway, things seem very quiet.'

'I want them to remain so, which is why I'm talking to you.'

'I thought you had a liberal policy?'

'We do. But in my experience, liberal policies need defending by conservative powers. If they aren't, they fold up. And a nastier, much more conservative power inevitably takes over, usually holding a gun. I could give you examples of that too, but no doubt you can think of them for yourself.'

Abbott's head was beginning to ache and he was not surprised. He said, 'I came out here for a little peace, not to talk politics.'

'We aren't talking politics, we're talking law and order.'

'Oh, are we?'

'Yes.' Waters turned his earnest grey eyes to Abbott again. 'Without it there will be no politics, only tyranny.'

'You truly believe that, don't you?'

'Yes, Mister Abbott, I truly do. And not just here.' Again, the wave of the pipe, the gathering-in of the still beauty of the bay. 'Anywhere in the wide world. Apart from those places where the gun already rules. It's too late for them. They'll have to work out their own salvation.'

Abbott said, irritated, 'Look, you didn't follow me out here by accident. What do you want?'

Waters looked surprised and a little hurt. 'Co-operation, that's all.'

'It's another way of spelling treachery.'

'I'm sorry you think that, but let me try to explain.'

'I wish you could.'

Waters took a deep breath, whether for medicinal purposes, or because he was again irritated, Abbott could not tell. The face was meaty, and expression had long been trained out of it. If the man was sincere, it would be impossible to tell. If he was insincere, it would be impossible to tell. It was an occupational face, like, Abbott thought, every face in the world that had been around for longer than forty years. 'Sir,' Waters was saying, formally, 'we have had it very easy here. One or two upsets. Nothing much. Owing, partly, to there being very little discontent on the Island. From any quarter. But . . . there are always people who are not content to leave well alone. There are always those who want to . . . spoil things. And not just spoil things. To take action of a violent nature.' Again the earnest grey eyes turned to him, the stolid reddy face. 'When I use that word, I use it advisedly, I really do. And that action I intend to prevent.'

'How on earth can I help you do that?'

'By telling me what you can.'

'You asked me that before. I was very annoyed then. I'm even more annoyed you've asked me again.'

'Mister Abbott.' Waters' eyes were unblinkingly fixed on him, and Abbott felt a pang of uneasiness. 'You may be the only person who can help me. There is somebody special . . . on the Island, and I think you may have seen him. I think I know *where* you may have seen him. I want you to telephone me at this number, day or night, if you see him again.' Waters took from his hippocket a small pasteboard card. Abbott said, 'No . . .' but Waters pushed it into his shirt pocket. 'No promises necessary, Mister Abbott. You see, I said a day or so ago that you were not a realist, but *now* I think you are.'

'What happened to make you change your mind?'

Waters shrugged. 'The way you have reacted to various events.'

'Like what?'

'Oh, in your personal life, let us say, shall we?'

Abbott felt chilled. 'In connection with what?'

Waters smiled blandly, evasively. 'It doesn't matter.'

'It does to me. Do you mean Snow and Angel?'

'Snow and Angel?' Waters' face was impassive now. 'They work together, don't they? All this rehearsing and so on?' His eyes sought Abbott's. 'Why, is there some trouble there?'

Abbott looked hard at the reddy face. It was without warmth, or hate, or any other emotion. 'If you have been listening to any telephone conversations, or hired anybody else to do that, I warn you, I can cause trouble . . .'

Waters held up his hand. 'I'm not looking for trouble. I'm trying to prevent it happening. I think you are a realist now, that is all. And I hope you can help me find the person I seek.'

'That is very unlikely.'

'Perhaps. Still, I hope.' Again, the arc of the pipe, taking in the warmth of the sun, the cloudless sky, the tropical foliage behind them, the sun-washed houses on the mainland, climbing behind the hotel on to the central ridge of the Island. 'Because you see, sir, I meant every word of what I said. When I used the word violent . . . I meant it.'

Abbott stood, in the dazzling sun, looking at the man. He felt very weary. The impulse to take out the small white card and tear it up came to him, but he was drained of the emotion needed for such gestures. He simply said, 'You'll excuse me?'

Waters smiled and waved his pipe, but did not speak, and Abbott walked slowly into the hotel. In a quiet bar he ordered a large brandy, and sat down at a brass-topped table, amid interior shrubs and palms. Outside, in the mock-English garden, grew ordered rows of sub-tropical vegetation, and a private man-made stream which, he realised, ran the mock-waterfall in the foyer of the hotel. He remarked on it to the waiter, who, taking him for a genuine tourist, said, 'You'll be going to the Flower Pageant to-morrow, sir?'

'I don't know.'

'Oh, you mustn't miss it. Biggest day of the year. Everybody there.'

'Where is it held?'

'In Hamilton. You be there early or you won't see a thing.'

Abbott thanked the man, left an American-sized tip, and sipped his brandy like a medicine. The spirit glowed in his empty belly (he had not eaten breakfast, waiting for Angel to wake up) and he was, suddenly, very hungry.

'Is lunch on?'

'Yessir. Just started.'

Abbott thought : to hell. His headache was worse and he needed time to think. Also, he needed food. The restaurant was only half-full—the golden sun was keeping people outdoors—and Luigi was pleased to see him, at his regular table.

'For Madame also, sir?'

'No, she isn't lunching.'

'Ah, no? She is singing?'

'Singing?'

'In the night club? Rehearsing with . . . er . . . the gentleman . . . Snow?'

'Yes, she is, actually.'

'I hear this, yes, sir. Now, to begin, sir?'

'Oh, just a steak rare and some salad.'

'And to drink, sir?'

'A red. Half of something. I'll have it now.'

Abbott sipped the Beaujolais (very expensive here, he noted, but it would be, the import duty would be so high) waiting for his steak. Luigi hovered around, and finally asked, 'Madame is a good singer, no?' Abbott detected the true Italian contempt for all vocalists not Italian.

'At what she does, she is very good.'

'*Popular* singer, they tell me?'

'Yes.'

'Not the opera, sir?'

'No, not the opera.'

'I have a cousin training the opera.'

'Your cousin must be talented.'

'Of course. The family make many sacrifices to send him. I also contribute.'

'Very good of you.'

'Oh no, sir. It is proper. He is family.' Luigi's eyes fell sadly on to the sunlit scene outside the long window.

Abbott said, 'Where are you from?'

'Napoli, sir. You know?'

'Indeed I do. Do you like the Island?'

'Oh verra much, sir.'

'No, I mean really?'

Luigi looked indignant. 'Oh verra much. I have good job, good pay. I do not have this in Napoli. There many slums and much poverty. Here is no poverty. Here, everybody well off, you know, if he work.'

'You find that?'

'Oh, yes, sir. Here I have place to live, wife, kid. No chance of that in Napoli, you know, sir.' The steak arrived and Luigi served it as if it was a Neapolitan dish, with the care and dignity due to so much protein on one plate. 'Here, I like, sir. It is one of the places of the world, no? Here, also, I play the golf.'

'You play golf?'

'That is so, sir. A good game, no?'

'Very good for the character.'

'Sir? Oh yes. Very. Of course, sir.'

Luigi, like any good waiter, withdrew as Abbott began to eat. The steak was very large, in the American fashion, and Abbott ate it with appetite, refusing to let his thoughts wander. The events of the morning, and they had been considerable, could be gone over later in a leisurely way. No point in worrying at any of them while he felt thus stunned and irritated. This, he thought, must be how women mostly live, without the steadying, dulling, influence of work. It must be why most things that *happen* seem more important to them than they really are. The wine was good and, although there was simply too much of the steak, he ate most of it, and drank his coffee slowly like a convalescent. On reflection, he had another brandy with it, and a cigar. It is not, he told himself, every day that your wife tells you she is to re-marry. The only thing to do, plainly, was to celebrate, or pretend to celebrate. He finished the brandy and the coffee, signed the check (after scrutinising it carefully) and walked, replete, down to the night club. If he did not feel entirely well, he reflected, he certainly felt better. Or more numb. Numb being the way to live, he decided.

They were still at it. Angel's voice was, incredibly, going through the song again.

> 'Yes, I know what it's like to be shut out,
> Yes, I know what it's like to be hurt.
> I know what it's like to be a shadow on a wall,
> I know what it's like. . . .'

She stopped, in the middle of the line, as soon as Abbott walked in.

'Oh, hello,' Angel said.

'Hi,' Abbott said, gravelly.

Snow nodded; he seemed relaxed and easy. 'Jack, we've been killing ourselves here. Sit down, we're knocking off for a while.' He turned to the bongo player and the pianist. 'Okay, fellas, take an hour, right? Get yourselves beer and sandwiches. Put them on my tab.'

The two men went out, and Angel came down from the stage. Her face glistened with sweat and there were dark patches on her sweater, under her armpits. The dark eyes glowed. She was, plainly, supremely happy.

Abbott said, 'How is the rehearsal going?'

'Great, absolutely great. We've been through all the key scenes, and, Abbott, it's really going to be *great*!' Angel put her arm around his neck and kissed him on the cheek. There was, obviously, enough happiness to go round.

Abbott said, 'I'm glad to hear it,' disengaged himself, and sat down.

Angel slumped into another chair, and took a mouthful of beer from a can. She stretched her long golden legs. Abbott averted his eyes, with an effort. 'I know this is going to be something wonderful. I just know it is, Abbott, I just know it will make a great show.'

'Yes, but what kind of show? Is it still a musical?'

'Abbott, I don't know, honestly, baby.' Angel leaned forward, and put her hand on his. Abbott winced at the 'baby', but he waited. 'It's such a great story, the way Snow has it mapped out, but I dunno if it isn't too good for the mink mommas of the musical comedy circuit. I think it's beyond them. I think it's something for the kids, it's a *now* idea, not a *then* idea! ... Oh, hell, I'm not saying this very well.'

'Ah, but you are,' Abbott said. 'You are saying it very well indeed. You are saying that it isn't a musical, but a movie, which is where I came in.'

Angel threw the empty beer can down, and half-turned away, sulkily. 'Can't you see what I'm talking about at all, Abbott?'

'Not really, no. I have the machinery for a musical set-up. I don't have the machinery for a movie set-up. It's as simple as that.'

'For God's sake, you've enough money to do what you want to do.'

Abbott said nothing to that.

Snow looked at Abbott curiously. 'You been drinking, Jack?'

'I had a couple. I also ate.'

'Was that telephone call important?' Angel asked, suddenly.

'It doesn't matter.'

Angel looked concerned. 'Who was it?'

'Helen, actually.'

Her eyes found his. 'Everything ... all right?'

'Everything is fine. Just fine.'

Angel's eyes stayed on his face. To break her gaze, Abbott turned to Snow. 'Are you sold on making a movie of this?'

'Not, y'know, absolutely. But it's what it should be, Jack. I mean, y'know, artistically?'

'Tell me why?'

'Because I can cut around the place, that way, I can tell the story in pictures. Oh, there'll be a song, the song you heard Angel sing earlier, but it'll be the only song in the movie, the *only* one, and I'm not entirely sold even on that. I mean, maybe we'll use it over the credits, that kinda thing, it won't belong in the context of the story as we'll see it, if we go for a movie. And I really honestly think we should, Jack. It might not make money, who could say, who can ever say, but it would be a very respectable piece of work to be connected with, as director or artist, Jack. It would be certain to be respectfully received by the New York critics and by the London critics, too, and, Jack, I could do it on a shoe-string. I'd be prepared to give my services free, that is, work for just expenses, till such time as there were any profits. And if there weren't any, well, shit, who cares, so long as we do something we, y'know, *believe* in?'

Angel said, 'Jesus, Snow, you're so right.'

Abbott realised that they were both looking at him in an expectant way.

He stood up, nodding now and then, as if he was thinking about it, and walking around abstractedly, until he reached the door. He turned back to them and said, evenly, or as evenly as he could, since he felt very, very tired, 'I've listened to all this, but my deal with the author is for a musical comedy, and not a movie. I have the backing for a musical comedy but not for a movie. A movie, financially, would be out of my class.'

'Balls, Abbott . . .' from Angel.

Snow said nothing, his eyes on Abbott, not blinking.

'Out of my class, because I don't understand the financing, and I haven't time to learn. So I am afraid, kiddies, it is a musical or nothing. Very sorry.' Abbott went gently out of the place, closing the door softly behind him. He went up to the bedroom, put the 'Do Not Disturb' sign on the handle of the door, locked it, and took off his trousers and shoes. He selected two of Angel's sleeping pills from a bottle at the bedside, and swallowed them. Then he pulled the coverlet over his head and fell instantly asleep. At some time in the night, he thought he heard, faraway, a woman's voice and knocking on the door; but it seemed like something from a dream, and he did not waken.

10

The sun struck Abbott in the face, bright and pitiless. He wakened with a loud groan. The watch on the bedside table showed ten-thirty. He relaxed, and lay in a sleepy haze. Plainly, he had slept all the way through the previous afternoon. Since he had only cat-napped on Happy's couch the night before that, the long rest was simply a catching-up, a necessity of the unconscious, to get every-thing into order. Helen; the situation with Snow; Angel. Thus he reasoned, but as he thought of Angel a shock of memory went through him, and he got to his feet, and padded across the car-peted room in his shorts and shirt. The connecting door was open, but there was no sign of Angel's room having been used. The bed was untouched, the curtains had not been drawn. Abbott sat on the neat bed, and stared at the jumble of Angel's clothes. A white linen suit thrown carelessly over a chair, the wardrobe open, dis-playing packages of gifts bought by Angel in Hamilton. Shoes, kicked off, scattered across the carpet. Abbott looked at all these, recalled the woman's voice in the night, and lit a thoughtful cigarette. Angel was not in the room because he had locked her out. Plainly, she had tried to get in, but could not, and hadn't asked the hotel desk-clerk to open the door. Abbott felt depressed and guilty. He debated showering and shaving before he thought anew, but instead he picked up the telephone and asked for the desk.

'This is Mister Abbott in three-three-seven. Is Miss da Sousa in the hotel, do you know?'

'One moment, sir.' A pause. 'Isn't she in three-three-two?'

'She is, but she's out. She didn't book into any *other* room in the hotel last night?'

'One moment, sir.' Another pause. 'I'm afraid not, sir. I can page her? At the pool? In the lobby, and around the bars? It will take only a few minutes, sir.'

'If you would. Oh, and try the night club, would you, in case they are rehearsing? And then ring me?'

'Certainly, sir.'

Abbott went into the bathroom and showered. He tried not to think, but the hot water on his skin brought his mind painfully alive. He had only himself to blame, that much was obvious, but there was, after all, a limit to how much he was supposed to take. If his relationship with Angel was to prosper it must be on the grounds of mutual interest, and not remain one-way traffic. He soaped his body, still brown and firm he noted with a small satisfaction, much unlike the flabby white sorbo-rubber covering of his years with Helen. Yes, there were things to be said for his way of life with Angel. Youth-feeling and fitness were two of them. The ice-cold jet swished away the soap and Abbott towelled himself dry, in a more optimistic mood. Angel would be in the hotel. She would have behaved sensibly, probably gone to another hotel for the night rather than raise a fuss. He was almost finished shaving when the telephone rang. He now felt rested and able to face the day. The internal sleep-computer had done its work. Everything was in its pigeon-hole. Whatever shocks were to come, he would, at least, be ready for them.

'Yes?'

'The desk, sir. We did not raise Miss da Sousa, I'm afraid, sir. She does not seem to be in the hotel.'

Abbott's spirits dropped abruptly. 'You tried the night club?'

'Yessir. Apparently it *was* booked, but Mister . . . er . . . Snow cancelled it.' Odd, how they never liked to say his name with 'Mister' in front of it.

'I see. Thank you.'

The room seemed very empty. Abbott smoked another cigarette, then walked about the place for a few minutes in his bathrobe. If she wasn't at the hotel, then where was she? Another hotel? With Snow, at the cottage? Somewhere else altogether? He pulled on a sports shirt and trousers, and combed his hair. Then he sat and smoked another cigarette. Then he rang for coffee. His appetite for food seemed to have gone. When the coffee came the waiter knocked and waited for Abbott to open the door. The 'Do Not Disturb' notice still hung on it from the previous night. As Abbott tipped the man, he remembered Snow's dictum that waiters know everything that happens in a hotel.

'Do you know Miss da Sousa?'

'Oh yes, sir.' The man's eyes gleamed. 'Very pretty lady.'

'Would you have any idea where she is now?'

The dark eyes flicked away. 'No, sir, I ain't seen her. You tried the desk for help? Maybe she's at the pool?'

Abbott said, 'You have no idea?'

The man looked evasive. 'I haven't *seen* her, sir. Like I say, the desk . . .'

'That's all right, thanks.'

Abbott sat on the balcony and drank his coffee black. The sunlit scene below him was lively with the movement of brown bodies gaily clad, the splash of water, and the cries of youthful voices. Abbott saw none of it. The faces of his children came, unforced, into his mind, but he could not retain them. Two years, it had been; they would both look different now. Whatever he had done, it was over, and there was no going back on it. They had their mother, and, soon, their new stepfather. Sometime, in the far future, he would talk to them truthfully. Till then, no doubt, a few neutral visits would be arranged, but he dreaded them. Perhaps it would be better not to see them at all? It would be upsetting for them, and probably for him. No real good would be served. Better to leave it until they were in their late 'teens. Then they might need his help. He would play it by ear. Abbott took pencil and paper and wrote out details for the settlement suggested by Helen, giving her all she asked for. He found some small fulfilment in this, for it was work. The telephone did not ring.

Abbott picked up a copy of the local paper, brought with the coffee, and leafed through it. The Island was a parish, and the paper was a sternly parochial one. A good deal of play was made of a recently-solved stoppage at the docks, and even more of the great event of the year, the Floral Pageant. Details were given of the number of floats taking part, and of the re-routing of traffic through the small town. Everybody was advised to be in their seats early. He read it all without really taking it in. The telephone did not ring.

Abbott pushed his cigarettes into his pocket and went out of the hotel. He found a taxi in the rank, and directed the man to Snow's cottage.

'Last time I drove you up there it was night, sir. Night 'fore last.'

Abbott stared at the driver. 'Yes, we keep meeting, don't we?'

'Well, I usually work from the hotel, sir.' The eyes flicked away.

'Do you know a Mister Waters?'

The man's face went stolid. 'Can't say I do, sir.'

'Just an idea. Thought you might.'

'Waters? Can't say I do. Nice ole day, though, sir?'

The man was plainly willing to talk, but Abbott felt wary. These days the only people he seemed to talk to were waiters and cab drivers, and others who served and serviced his life. Before the money he had known many kinds of people; he had often used public transport, he had gone to football matches, he had, from time to time, talked to people who did not know, and didn't care, whether he had money or not. It was one of the penalties of the money. There were others, like the way everybody was pleasant and seemed to be prepared to put up with a good deal, from a comparatively rich man. The Victorians, he had been told, equated riches with goodness. He could not see that any of this had changed. People still had that special expression come over their faces when they were told he was rich, as if he was a favoured person. It had happened with the local businessmen at the party the evening before. Abbott looked, unseeing, at the spectacular beauty of golden beach and foamy sea, as it was revealed behind hills of sand and long spiky grass. He did not feel rich or favoured.

The cab came to a stop at the end of the dirt road.

'Want me to go on up?'

'No, here will do.'

Abbott paid the man, then saw that his eyes had not left his face. 'You know Snow pretty well, sir?'

'Yes, I suppose so.'

'He's a very clever young fella, they tell me.'

'Yes, he is.'

'All them New York shows an' that?'

'Yes.'

The driver put the car into gear. 'Still an' all, he's a little wild, know what I mean?'

'Yes, I think so.'

'I mean, this changing the world and all that?'

'Yes.'

'Lot of misery here already. Can't see the point in adding to it.'

'Snow's not political. He's theatrical.'

'I dunno.' The man shook his head. 'All this talk.'

'What talk?'

'You heard it, same as I have.' The man looked up suspiciously, the white eyes huge in the dark face. 'You know what I'm a-talking about, if you up seeing Snow like you is.'

'No, I don't. What sort of talk?'

The car engine roared. 'Mister, if you don't know, I ain't a-telling you. So long now.' The cab wheeled round, and disappeared in a cloud of fine yellow dust.

Abbott shook his head, and started to walk up the uneven road towards the cottage. The sun was very hot, and only the fresh breeze from the sea saved him from sweating. He was glad when the cottage came into sight. The front door of the place was open, and pop music carried to him on the warm air. As he walked up the path, the cardinal bird cawed uneasily, in the tamarind tree. At once the music stopped, and as Abbott entered, a tall man in denims, wearing granny-glasses, stood up quickly, looked at him, and, without a word, walked out into the kitchen. A door slammed at the back. Abbott said, 'I'm sorry, did I interrupt something?'

Angel looked quickly at Snow, who was sprawled on the couch. He did not get up. 'Hi, Jack,' he said.

'Hello.' A haze of pot, Abbott noticed, hung in the air.

Angel straightened herself up from the rocker-chair. She put her arms around his neck, and kissed him on the cheek. 'Hello, bad temper. How did you sleep?'

'Fine. I took some pills.'

'That and the booze. We couldn't wake you.'

'No, I'm sorry about that.'

'Sit down, Jack, take the weight off your feet.' Snow smiled, lazily. 'A drink?'

'No, thanks.'

Abbott sat down, his legs weak. The relief of seeing Angel was more than he wished to show. She puffed on the reefer, and he noticed blue bruises beneath her eyes, the sure mark (with her) of exhaustion. He wondered what had put them there. He decided, defensively, probably the heavy rehearsals, all the talking and thinking. Angel, like most performers, was not a talker and thinker, she was a doer. She said, 'Happy put me up for the night.'

'She seems to make a thing of it.' Abbott meant it to come out as a joke, but it did not.

'Well, I had to sleep somewhere, and I was bushed. We rehearsed until seven o'clock, here, then later we went out, ate and talked. I rang but you didn't reply to the phone in the room. It was one in the morning when I banged on your door. And I didn't want to raise the desk, seeing the delicate situation.' Angel laughed, and her lovely teeth showed, and there seemed to be a serene relaxation about her. The work, Abbott thought desperately, it has to be the work. 'So Snow brought me back here.'

'You could have knocked harder.'

'We nearly broke the door down as it was. Anyway, I didn't think you wanted to see me.'

'We?'

'Snow was there.'

'Sure,' Snow said.

'You could have telephoned this morning.'

'I could have.' Angel stubbed the reefer out. The sweet scent was too much for Abbott. He got to his feet and opened the door, letting in the warm, balmy air.

'Why didn't you?'

'Because I knew you'd feel better once you got over your tantrums.'

'My decision of last night,' Abbott said, heavily, 'was no tantrum. I meant it. I haven't the money for wild movies.'

Angel looked very quickly at Snow, and he smiled and looked up at Abbott. 'Then we may have to look elsewhere for our backing, ole Jack.'

'Not with this. I hold an option on the copyright.'

'Would you stand in Angel's way, if it was what she wanted to do?'

Abbott sat down, hopelessly. 'No. But I don't think she should do it.'

'That would be for her to decide.'

Angel looked at her hands. Abbott said, 'Well, Angel, do you want to do it that way?'

Angel looked at him with enormous eyes.

'I think Snow's right, Abbott, I really honestly do.'

'You'll make it where?'

'I dunno. Here, maybe.' Snow drew on his thin reefer and the room was again full of the pungent scent. 'But first we'd have to go to New York and raise the capital. Anyway, raise enough of it to begin shooting.'

Angel said, 'Abbott, won't you think again about the money? We've been all over the story. We've talked it out, I mean, really *out*. And it's a great chance for me.'

'As an actress?'

'Yes.'

'Is that what you are? An actress?'

'I'm a performer, what's the difference?'

'Enormous. I hate singers who can't sing. I hate actors who

can't act. I'll put my money on singers who can sing, and actors who can act.'

'You don't believe in me?' Angel's voice was very cold and distant, and he felt desperate hearing it.

'You know that's not true, or I wouldn't be here.'

'No, I'm sorry, Abbott.' Angel impulsively put her hand on his knee. Abbott tried to will himself to ignore it. 'Listen, Snow can make me a good actress.'

'No, he can't, he can only make you *look* one.'

'What's the difference, for God's sake!'

'With trickery and camera-angles he can make you *look* great. Being great, that's another thing. Ask him.'

Snow shrugged. 'Genius takes longer.'

'There you are.' Angel's lips tightened. 'You don't believe I can do it.'

Abbott sighed. 'No.' He looked at Snow. 'You'll be going on to New York about money?'

Snow first glanced at Angel. She shrugged, looked away. Snow took up the point direct. 'So. No hope at all from your end, Jack? Financially?'

'None whatever, I'm afraid.'

'Tough.'

'If the idea's as good as you say it is, you'll get backing.'

'We certainly mean to try, yes sir!' Snow said, to nobody in particular.

There was a long silence.

Angel said, 'I think you're mean, Abbott. Mean and close-minded.'

'Probably.'

There was another silence.

'Don't make up your mind now, darling. Think about it. Please.'

Abbott averted his eyes, kept his voice level, with an effort. 'We arranged to leave tomorrow. I intend to do that. I have business in London.'

'What business?'

'To do with Helen.'

'Oh, *her*.'

Snow made a small motion of warning to Angel that didn't escape Abbott. He said, 'Jack, we'd have something very special, and if you like I'll talk, but all I can really say is, I believe it would make a better movie than a musical.'

'I want to ask you one question,' Abbott said.

'Shoot.'

'Is it as good a business proposition?'

Snow looked at the joint in his fingers. 'Honestly?'

'I'd appreciate that.'

'Honestly, no it isn't.'

'Thank you for that, at least.'

Angel said, desperately, 'At least, take today to think.'

'No, I . . .'

'For me? Just today?'

'Today, all right,' Abbott said, heavily. 'Not tonight.'

There was another silence.

Angel broke it. 'Abbott, listen, this thing could be wonderfully visual. We thought of doing it here, on the Island. Using local occasions, y'know? Like the Floral Pageant in Hamilton today?' She got up, kissed Abbott on the forehead. 'Come down with us. Come see it! You'll see what we mean.'

'I don't know,' Snow said, doubtfully, 'leave Jack to make up his mind, huh?'

Angel looked surprised. 'You just said it's wonderful. You said we might use it?'

'Well, it is wonderful, Angel, but Jack's said his say, he'd be bored. Let him go away and think.'

'At least let him see the kind of scene we want to shoot!' She seemed surprised. 'At least he should do that!'

Snow stared at her, seemed to debate, then smiled and shook his head. 'Okay. Come on down, Jack. Why not!'

Abbott said, slowly, 'That man who was here just now?'

'Man?' Snow looked mock-surprised. 'He was just a neighbour. He had to leave in a hurry.'

'That man,' Abbott said, 'was Rowley. He is wanted by the police.'

Snow looked at Abbott for a long moment. 'You're wrong, Jack.'

'No, I don't think so.'

Snow stood up, crushed out the joint. 'Come on, we'll have to move if we're going.'

'You don't want to talk to me about him? Rowley?'

Snow shrugged. 'There's nothing to say, Jack.'

'Nothing to say, or nothing I'd understand?'

'Both maybe.'

'I'm open-minded.'

There was a half-amused snort from Angel at this. 'You've just proved it.'

'I'm narrow-minded about money. That's my training. But we weren't talking about money.' Abbott turned to Snow. 'Were we?'

'No.'

'Then why not tell me where Rowley fits in, because he fits in somewhere?'

'Not with you, Jack.'

'Meaning it's none of my business?'

'Meaning that, if you like.'

'I was told that he was dangerous, possibly violent.'

Snow drew on his reefer. 'I can guess who told you.'

'Never mind who told me. Is it true?'

Snow shook his head. 'Why mix in things that don't concern you?'

Abbott stared at Snow, seeing (he fancied) a meanness and a strength he had not suspected. 'I was told violent. And that could mean people hurt. Do you go along with that?'

Snow smiled. 'It may never happen, Jack.'

'But do you?'

'Like I say, it may never happen.'

Abbott turned to Angel. 'Do you know any more than I do? You've been here, you've talked to the man?'

Angel looked quickly at Snow, then shook her head. 'We just talked about music. You're worrying yourself about nothing, Abbott.'

Abbott said, 'I was in Malaya. I saw people dead. I don't like violence. Nobody wins. Except, eventually, the wrong politicians and generals. It's best not to have it.'

Snow said, patiently, 'I know it's best not to have it, Jack, but sometimes people won't pay attention to anything else, will they?'

'That's an assassin's argument, it always was.'

'Okay, then that's what it is.'

'And you're supposed to be an artist!'

'You never heard of committed artists, Jack?'

'No. Just artists.'

'But then . . .' Snow smiled, tolerantly, and got to his feet. 'You're only a money-man, aren't you, Jack? That's what you always say?'

Abbott did not stand up. He felt weary to the bone, and sick to look at both of them, sick to feel the fragile skeins of understanding between them. Was it simply business, or was it *more*? He could not tell. He said, 'How deep are you in whatever Rowley is in . . . ?' But there was no answer to come, for in the doorway stood Happy, hands on her hips and a smile on her face. 'Hello there, Mister Abbott, now don't you start talking politics. I'd of thought you was too sensible for that.' She waved her hand. 'What you smoking? That ole pot agen? Gawd, I dunno why you bother.'

'Happy, you never smoked it, how can you know?' Snow's Uncle Tom act was on again, and Happy brushed his words, and (Abbott thought) his manner, impatiently aside. 'I been smoking the stuff when I was a girl, I had it from that useless father o' yours, oh, he try anything, that man, he try that as well.'

'Happy, you're a *liar*!' Snow laughed.

'Well, I dunno how you can say that, since you weren't around.' She opened the door wide, and a window, too. 'Angel, get this no-good fella outa the house for a while, why don't you, take him down to Hamilton to see the flowers.'

Abbott recognised the note of familiarity with a sense of sickness. Yet, inevitably, came the counter. Angel had been staying in the house all night, it was an innocent familiarity, that was all. Also, Snow might have told Happy of Angel's (possibly real?) background. That, too, could make a difference in the way the older woman saw her. Yet, there had been a rapport between them, from the start. Abbott did not know what to think, except that he wanted to get out of the house, and soon. Angel and he must talk, alone. He said, 'I don't mind going to this thing if you want to.' To Happy he added, 'Are you going?'

Happy shook her head. 'I've got a whole heap of washing to do that won't do itself.' She looked at Snow, a long, easy, but, to Abbott, faintly interrogative look. 'Besides, you're all young, enjoy yourselves.'

Snow said, slowly, 'Come if you like.'

Happy just looked back at him. 'No.'

Snow turned away, quickly, pocketing his shiny tin of makings, but to Abbott the gesture seemed to carry another meaning for the older woman. He could not guess what.

Angel said, brightly, 'All right? Let's go see this wonderful show you think should go in the movie.'

Snow was still looking out of the window. 'I don't say it should definitely go in. I say it's the kind of scene that maybe might.'

'You don't sound so sure now?' Angel looked puzzled.

'I dunno that I want to go. It's commercial. It's a drag.'

'But you said . . .'

'Let's forget it, eh?'

There was a silence.

Abbott took Angel's arm. 'All right, let's you and I go down. We need to talk and this would do.'

Angel said nothing to that. Her eyes were on Snow's back. At last he turned. 'Okay, let's go down, look at the shindig. Marie's old machine is out back. We can go in that.'

Happy came to the door to wave them off. Abbott dawdled his departure, and said, as the others climbed into the battered Chevvy, 'You've been very busy, putting up strangers this week?'

Happy folded her hands under the white apron. 'They ain't strangers.'

'No, but first me, then . . . Angel.'

'You slept like a baby . . . and Angel ain't no trouble.'

'You asked her . . . to stay? Last night?'

Abbott was conscious of how jealously foolish he sounded, and of the heat, and of the roar of the defective car engine. He could also feel Angel's eyes on his neck. Still, he waited for the woman's answer.

'She ast me. She was welcome.'

'You like her?'

'I like everybody.'

'But Angel, especially?'

Happy shrugged. The tiny eyes gleamed in the folds of black skin. 'She's had no proper folks, you knew that? Only that ole mother, a no-good one, that. Maybe I liked her 'cos of that. I got a special feelin' for them kinda folks.'

Snow honked the horn. Abbott said, hopelessly, 'Last night . . . *did* she . . . ?' He could say no more. The sun was very hot on his back. Snow honked again.

Happy said, kindly but bland, 'Now, you just stop botherin' so much, Mister Abbott, you just take life a bit easier. Don't expect too much, huh? Then maybe you be satisfied with what you get, right?'

Stung, Abbott said, 'And, of course, your other visitor?'

'Other one?'

'Rowley?'

'I dunno any Rowley. Nobody by that name.'

'Any name, it's the same thing.'

Snow spoke, quietly, at Abbott's elbow, 'Jack, I thought you wanted to go?'

Abbott said, ironically, 'Well, thank you, Happy.'

'For what? I didden say nothing.'

Abbott got into the car. It still smelled of cheap scent and burnt oil. Snow revved the engine. Angel waved, but Happy, in the doorway, did not wave back. They bumped slowly down the dirt road. Abbott said, 'This is Marie's car?'

Angel said, 'Yes.'

'Where is she?'

Snow did not seem to have heard the question. His eyes were on the road ahead, but his whole body seemed tense, and Abbott, in the back seat, thought that he detected a movement of Snow's body away from Angel, in the front passenger-seat—a quick, involuntary gesture that seemed (or did he fancy it?) to bring a stiffening of Angel's body. She, too, sat up and looked firmly to the road in front of the car, and Abbott sat behind and watched the back of their heads. Nobody spoke at all, all the way into Hamilton.

They parked the car on the outskirts of the town and walked in. The narrow streets were a ferment of bodies. It did not seem possible that the plantation-town could hold so many people. Every tourist on the Island seemed to be in the streets, camera at the ready. The locals, for whom the event was really staged, according to what Abbott had read in the morning paper, crammed on their balconies along Front Street, facing the serried ranks of gaily-shirted tourists, jostled into the stands that backed upon the harbour. Down at the front, sitting or standing, and most closely-packed of all, sat locals who were not influential enough to obtain balcony-views, mostly black, a great many of them resembling Happy. There were many hundreds of children at the very front, sitting cross-legged, more or less patiently in the hot sun, waiting for the proceedings to begin. Uniformed policemen in khaki, wearing the traditional helmet of the British bobby, stood idly along the route. Abbott listened to the far-off brassy strains of the band of the Royal Bermuda Regiment, and thought : this is a family day, it is an outdoors celebration, a fête, one of the things that television and cinema and all indoor packaged performances cannot touch. For nobody, outside in the free air, ever knows what will happen. There is always an air of unpredictability about such events, which is their basic attraction. The thought, for some obscure reason, did not cheer him.

Angel clapped her hands together. 'What a scene!'

Snow stood, rather morosely, whistling through his teeth. 'It's pretty commercial, as you see.'

'Oh, I dunno.' Angel didn't like the thought. 'Everybody looks happy.'

'They're easy made happy.'

'Don't be such an old grouch.' Angel touched his arm, and Abbott looked quickly away. They work together, he told himself, these things mean nothing.

'Okay, what do you want to do?' Snow waited, the hesitation very apparent now.

'I want to see it. I want . . .' Angel waved towards the stands. 'I want a good seat! That's all I ask.'

'Jack?' Abbott was surprised that Snow's voice held an appeal. 'Do you really want to see this thing? It's a tourist attraction, that's all.'

Abbott said, 'Why not, what else would we do? I thought you said it would be a great scene, if you shot the movie here.'

'I changed my mind. It's crappy. It's jingo. Who needs it?'

Angel said, 'I do. It looks great.' She indicated the tiers of spectators. 'Why not get us a seat up there?'

Snow said, 'Okay, I'll try.' He walked reluctantly towards the pay kiosk at the entrance to the tiered seats. Bunting blew along the route of the procession and the strains of the band grew nearer. Angel jumped with childish excitement. 'They'll be here soon!'

Abbott said, abruptly, not looking at her, 'Is there anything between you two?'

The whole moment was stilled: the expectant hum of the vast crowd, the music, the cry of the startled, circling seabirds in the harbour behind them: the hot sun encapsulating it all. Angel said, her eyes very wide, 'Well, of course there isn't.' Abbott still looked at her, and she added, 'In *that* way.'

'That's a qualification, Angel.'

'It's all the answer you're getting.'

Abbott waited, and she added, 'Is that really what you think of me?'

Snow walked back towards them, and the whole scene began to move again. Abbott merely nodded (he could not trust himself to speak) and turned towards Snow, who shook his head. 'No use. All the tickets are gone.'

'All of them?'

'So the man says.'

Angel's mouth drooped, and she rubbed her eyes irritably. She was really disappointed. Abbott didn't know whether to laugh, cry, or walk away. At that moment he caught the eye of a woman signalling with a programme from the front row of the stands. With some dismay, he realised that it was Marcia Gray.

'Excuse me.'

'What?'

'I've seen someone I know.' Abbott turned away from them and hurried over to the stands, pushing his way through the close crush of bodies. Finally, he was near enough to call. 'Hello. How are you?'

Marcia looked at him, with only a hint of a smile on her lips. She was beautifully dressed, in a way that suggested good flesh pressing against soft material, and wore a large-brimmed straw hat with a sash ribbon trailing. Marcia had style. It was different from the younger, trendier non-style of Angel (who was wearing a T-shirt and jeans) but it was, for Marcia, extremely valid and fetching into the bargain. Abbott said, again, 'How are you?'

'I'm fine. You?'

'I'm with friends.'

'So I see.' Marcia's eyes gleamed, past him, amused.

'I meant to be in touch.'

'I'm with my aunt.' Marcia indicated an elderly lady of absolute composure, who was gazing, birdlike, through dark glasses at the rest of the crowd. 'She's eighty-four.'

'Oh, I see.'

Marcia's eyes darted across towards Snow and Angel. 'You'll want to get back to your friends? You'll have to hurry to your seats. The procession will be here any time.'

'That's our problem. We haven't seats.'

'You don't?'

'No, I'm afraid not.'

'You won't see anything from street level.'

'No, but it doesn't matter....'

Marcia seemed to be debating. Then, 'Tell the man at the pay box you're sitting with us.'

'What?' Abbott craned forward. Around him, bodies, pressed. He wondered if he would ever get out. Nearer, the band's music drifted on the cheers of distant crowds. 'I'm not sure ...'

'Marcia Gray. Just tell him that. It'll be all right.'

'Will it?'

'Yes, there's room.'

'Oh, that's very good . . .'

'Hurry up, or you'll miss it!'

Abbott nodded and turned and pushed his way out of the crowd. It left him perspiring and exhausted. He walked across to Snow and Angel, who stood back from the press of people, hard against the harbour rails.

'Jack, never thought we'd see you again.'

'Come on, we can go in.'

'Where?' Angel's eyes shone.

'In the stands, front row!'

'No!'

'Yes.'

'Great!'

Snow said, 'I'll stay down here.'

'But why?'

'Look,' Snow said, 'you were asked. I wasn't asked.'

Angel said, 'Oh, what crap, was he asked or wasn't he?'

'The lady saw us all, we're all invited.'

'Who is she anyway?' Angel asked, looking curiously towards the stands. Marcia was craning forward. The band noises were nearer.

'Met her at David O'Hara's party the other night.'

That, at least, was true.

'She looks attractive.' Angel looked quickly at Abbott. He composed his face. 'Did you take her to dinner?'

The instincts of women.

Abbott said, indignantly, 'No, I did not.'

Angel smiled. 'And *you* talk to *me*.'

'I hardly know her!'

Angel said, ironically, 'And she offers us seats?'

'Are we,' said Abbott, heavily, 'taking advantage of this kind offer, or are we standing here talking?'

'Why not?' Angel said.

Snow said, doggedly, 'What for? Who wants to sit gawping at all those flowers, and silly girls on dray-carts?'

'I do,' said Angel, promptly.

Moisture appeared on Snow's brow. Abbott had never seen him perspire before. 'Forget it all, why not, it's not worth the rush.'

'I'm going up. See you later.'

And Angel made her way towards the stands.

Abbott said, 'Oh, come on.'

'Don't go up there, Jack.' Snow's voice was low.

'Why not?'

'Just don't.'

'But for God's sake, why not?'

Snow just looked at Abbott a moment. The band was very near now and a shimmer of expectancy ran through the crowd. 'Okay, Jack. Suit yourself. But . . .'

'What?'

'Nothing.'

Abbott looked back at him, perplexed. 'She did include you, you know.'

'Okay, okay.'

'You'll come?'

'I'll stay down here. You go. I'll be fine.'

'You sure?'

'I'm sure.'

Angel called, 'Abbott, come *on*!' and Abbott turned, and pushed his way to the pay box. The man said, 'Come on, sir, I'm closing this gate, want to see it myself, you and the lady here are sitting with Miz Gray, right there!' He pointed, and closed his gate behind Abbott.

Angel was already in her seat and she waved to Abbott, who, with many apologies, navigated the row towards the three women. 'I introduced myself,' Angel said, ironically.

'Oh, good,' Abbott said, with false cheer.

'Isn't your other friend coming up, Mister Abbott?'

Marcia, Abbott was pleased to see, was keeping the thing on an impersonal level. He was glad of that, even if she had had some practice in the art. A lady, he said to himself, a cultivated and decent lady. It seemed impossible he had been to bed with her.

'Snow didn't think you meant him, for some reason.'

'Oh, what rubbish, of course I did.'

'That's what I told him.'

'Silly fellow.'

The old lady turned her birdlike gaze on them. 'Snow?' she asked, in a voice of reedy authority.

'My Aunt Maud, she's very old,' Marcia said, smiling hastily.

'Snow?' said Aunt Maud. 'I know his mother. Used to be at the old Barratt place.'

'Yes, that's right, Aunt.'

'Thought he went to New York?'

'He did. He's back on holiday.'

The old lady looked down the road towards the noise of the band. 'They always come back.' Her teeth champed. 'Wise ones never go away.' She turned to Angel. 'Don't I know you, gel?'

Angel was very still. 'No, I don't think so.'

'Funny. You remind me of somebody.'

Marcia said, quickly, 'Aunt, the floats are here.'

'I can see that,' said the old lady. 'Not blind, my dear, not yet.'

'I'm very sorry about her.' Marcia leaned in to Abbott and he caught her scent, and his senses responded, ritually. 'She's, well, you know?'

'Don't apologise for me, Marcia,' said Aunt Maud. 'Apologise for yourself, if you have to. Not for me. Not on this Island. I know everybody on the place. By *that* . . .' She leaned over, and her long index finger prodded Abbott's ribs. It hurt. 'By *that,* I mean everybody who is anybody, and when I say that I don't just mean white, I mean old people, people been here long enough to count, people got their folks buried in the ground here. And their folks' folks. *That's* what I mean.'

'Yes, I'm sure,' Abbott said, and Angel laughed. The old lady turned to her. 'You Portuguese stock?'

'My aunt's talking about the people on the Island . . .' Marcia said. 'Aunt, this lady is from England. Watch the procession.'

'I know her from somewhere, that face.' Aunt Maud sighed. She pointed the long, beringed forefinger at the approaching band. 'Bagpipes. They never sound right to me, but people want 'em. Like so many cats.' The massed pipes and drums of the Bermuda Regiment passed in full and stately review towards the dais, further down Front Street, on which sat the Governor and his lady. The band was received with loud applause and cheers, and marched, perspiring, with measured tread. In the loud noise, as Angel and the old lady fell into conversation, or rather Angel listened (with, Abbott saw, a smile) to her criticisms, Marcia again leaned forward, and Abbott had to remind himself it was not deliberate, surely, that her thigh touched his. He groaned inwardly.

'Don't worry, Jack. I'm not going to seduce you.' Her eyes were smiling.

'I'm glad to hear it.'

Her eyes went to Angel. 'Trouble with the girl-friend?'

'Not really.'

'Oh, I would have thought so.'

'Why?'

'Otherwise, why me?'

'Oh, that . . . I'm sorry. . . .'

'Don't be. I'm not.' The pressure left his thigh, and he breathed deeply, relieved.

'I'm glad it happened,' Abbott said, gallantly.

'So am I. But it's over, yes?'

'Well, I . . .'

'That's all right. So long as I know.'

Marcia did not say more, but Abbott felt that a certain tremor went through her. He looked up to see Angel's eye on him. He smiled at her, but she was listening to the old lady and did not smile back. She merely looked at Marcia and nodded, as if to herself.

The old lady was talking.

'This is for the tourists, but in the old days, in Snow's mother's day and my day before that, ah, we had some times. It was all slower then, you had time, no jets and no noise. . . .' Abbott was reminded of the taxi driver's words, on their first drive from the airport: 'They always come back.' He looked ahead to the first float. It bore the legend of a local church, and was an intricate design of Easter lilies, all a perfect and shimmering white, with a girl in a white gown atop the whole display, waving a single bloom. The girl, of course, was white too, and instantly identified by the old lady. 'Joan Pitter,' said Aunt Maud. 'Pretty but they never get any place, the Pitters, they don't like hard work.'

'That isn't Joan Pitter,' Marcia said, 'It's Audrey Milton, Joan Pitter's daughter.'

'Same thing.'

The second float—and those that followed it—were a blaze of colour. Honeysuckle, bougainvillaea, morning glory, and roses of every colour were entwined in designs, often on bamboo cane, backed by the maidenhair fern of the Island, so intricate that sometimes it was hard to tell what the design represented. A wondrous scent hung in the clear and balmy air, wafting across the spectators in a gentle mist. Each massive, flowery float received a due meed of cheers and applause, with very little increase in volume for even the most impressive ones. Abbott realised why. Despite what Snow had said, this was a family event. All the floats had been worked upon in equal measure by all concerned, every child, black or white, perched atop the enormous banks of sweet-smelling plants was some local person's child, known to the watchers. There was praise for everybody. Everywhere, all along the crowd, people's mouths were open, their teeth shining, their faces creased in pleasure.

'The judges will pick the first float, the Bermuda lilies,' Aunt Maud said. 'Bound to.'

'Why do you say that, how can you know?' Marcia asked, a shade irritably.

'You wait and see.'

'Oh nonsense, Aunt Maud.'

'Wait and see if I'm right.'

A detachment of the Bermuda Regiment marched by, in dark blues and reds, in good formation, Abbott thought, though his army days seemed a long way behind him now. He had had little of the barrack-square training that had brought such precision to these part-time soldiers. It had been six weeks at Aldershot, and then jungle-training, and finally, the jungle itself. All Abbott knew of soldiering was life and death, the smells and wounds and the treacherous mud of Malaya. He had done what he had to do, as the others had (he had fired a lot of rounds but rarely *seen* the enemy) and now he did not often think of those times, which seemed to belong to a far distant past, his youth. Some of it he had left in the steaming jungles of Malaya, for he had known many disturbed dreams after he returned to London. They had gradually ebbed away, after his marriage. Helen had always been terri-fied by the violence of them, and he had need to reassure her when he came to, pyjamas soaked, after re-living the ambush in which his best friend had been killed; seeing the villagers staked out in the market-place; or dead, lying like discarded rubbish in the corners of their huts.

'You all right?' Marcia was looking at him sidewise.

'Yes, yes. I'm fine.'

'You don't look it.'

'Don't I?' Abbott was genuinely surprised. 'I am. Don't worry.'

'I can't, can I, you aren't my property, are you?'

Abbott said nothing to that but simply stared ahead at the floats drifting by, breathing in the wafts of scented air—mimosa, yucca, oleander, scarlet hibiscus—trying to forget the village, and the scattered bodies lying around, and the blood. Why should he think of that now? It was all in the past, a forgotten skirmish in a forgotten war.

'I'm sorry,' Marcia said, low. 'I shouldn't talk like that. Especially now you've patched it up?'

Abbott let the question lie. There was no point, so far as he could see, in replying to it. Aunt Maud spoke up, in a shrill but even voice, 'It's good, but it's not as good as last year. The lilies were better last year.' She turned to Angel. 'The lilies were brought to the Island from China, nearly two hundred years ago. My father's father grew them. He was one of the first to have a crop big enough to give to his neighbours at Easter. Now they send them to New York by air. They call that progress, my dear.'

Abbott's eye ranged idly along the applauding crowds, thicker and more tightly-packed towards the dais, and suddenly his eye was taken by a movement that did not belong in the normal, forward-pushing, craning pattern of the flux. A man's face, turned away from the crowd, something familiar about the shape of the dark head, a flash of arm, and a sudden violent splintering of glass as a shop window shattered; a sudden over-bright flash of flame; a report simultaneous with the flame, and fragments of bright glass fizzing, deadly, through the air. First, the sharp cries of individual impact and pain. Then the sudden, panicked, mass voice of the crowd.

The individual yells of fright and anger died in a slow, inexorable movement away from the area of the flame and the report. The movement fast became a blind rush, with people trampled and thrown down. Men in uniform ran from all points towards the happening, pushing the crowds back, linking arms to do it, straining and thrusting. A senior uniformed man ran out into the middle of the road and, with uplifted hand, halted the procession. Everything stilled, as the senior uniformed man raised a megaphone to his mouth, and his reassuring words fell on the ears of the watchers in the stands, and those others nearer the report and the flame. The watchers stayed where they were, safe, but the panicked ones strained against the human wall of men-in-uniform holding them back. Their rush forward, Abbott saw, would have thrown them across the procession route, and, gathering momentum, fatally into the crowds opposite : the children sitting cross-legged, and the adults standing. It would be a crushing encounter, for these people would have nowhere to retreat, being pinned by the sea-wall behind them. The moment was full of desperation and danger. Abbott watched, helpless. The man with the megaphone called for stillness, again. And again. The people in the stands, Abbott and Angel and the others, all stood and watched the event, but could see little, for the crowd was too dense and the flux of it too violent and sudden to make any comprehensive pattern. Yet Abbott had seen something, the shape of the head, the raised arm, something bright in the hand held aloft. Smoke eddied above the solid mass of bodies.

'What is it? A fire?' Angel asked, her voice low.

'Something like that.'

Aunt Maud said, 'I heard glass go. It was glass, wasn't it?'

Marcia's hand was on Abbott's arm. 'Oh, God. It's started.'

Abbott disengaged his arm. 'Not yet.'

'It has, I know it has.'

'No.' Abbott stared across towards the ring of uniformed men. Their legs were apart, and braced, and their heads were bent, and their hands were tucked into their belts. Their arms were entwined, and they gave ground to the press of bodies behind them grudgingly, in inches. The senior, uniformed man called again through his megaphone, this time more urgently, for the crowd to stand still, to keep calm, to remain as they were. And something in the tone of his voice held them, and they stood still, and the uniformed men relaxed, and did not need to give ground any longer. Slowly, the crowd began to move back, settle once again to the contemplation of the scene, as, at a wave from the senior uniformed man, the floats began to move once again. The band struck up, overshadowing the nearing wail of a klaxon horn, and the people in the stands began to sit down, one at a time, then in dozens, until only the most curious were still staring across at the flux of the crowd opposite. Abbott was of this number.

'What *was* it?' Angel asked.

'Somebody broke a window, probably,' a man behind said, without much conviction. Several people agreed with him, with even less. One said, 'What about that smoke, though?'

'Sit down, young man,' Aunt Maud told Abbott.

'I beg your pardon?'

'Sit down. I can't see. All the nonsense is over, isn't it?'

'Oh, yes. Yes, of course, I'm sorry.' Abbott was about to sit when he saw a figure dart across the path of the procession. It was one of several that had eluded the cordon held by the men in uniform and it melted into the crowd immediately below the stands. Abbott stood again, in dire indecision. The wail of the klaxon was very loud and near now. Abbott said, 'A police van?'

'An ambulance,' Marcia said. 'Somebody must have been hurt. I told you it had started.'

Abbott saw the ambulance men running along the path of the procession, past the slowly-moving floats, with the girls now simply still and frightened, and all eyes on the scurrying figures. They disappeared into the crowd opposite, and, as Abbott still stood, they came out with forms on the stretchers, calling above the music for gangway. Four times they did that, and in the sunlight, there was bright blood on some of the blankets; the faces of the suc-couring men were set and grim; the crowd murmured, like a great unhappy beast. Then the klaxon started up again, in the side-street, and then, slowly died away. The crowd opposite re-formed; the girls on the flower floats stood up and smiled and waved, once more.

'Do sit down, young man. Have you never seen an accident before?'

'I'm sorry,' Abbott said. 'Excuse me.' He began to move out.

'You can't do anything . . .' Marcia began.

'I just have to talk to somebody down there.'

Angel called, 'Abbott, where are you going?'

'Back in a moment.' He waved his hand.

'Oh? All right.' Angel sat down again, unhappily. As Abbott went, he saw Marcia shoot a long, searching glance at Angel. The way women *look* at rival women, he thought. He pushed his way through the crush. He found Snow at the railings, staring down into the blue waters of the harbour, his back to the happenings of the afternoon.

'Has he gone?'

'Who?'

'Rowley, who else? He came this way. Where is he now?'

Snow's face was expressionless. 'Jack, I don't have an idea what you're talking about. Angel still up there?'

'Yes.'

'Isn't she coming?' Snow's eyes were wary, withdrawn.

'Not now.'

'Oh, well, I'll call it a day, I reckon.' Snow turned to go.

Abbott grasped his arm. It was very hard and muscular. 'You heard that bang?'

'Sure.' Snow looked up, straight at Abbott. 'What was it, a firework?'

'It was a bomb of some kind.'

'No?'

'Some people were hurt. Flying glass.'

'How do you know?'

'I've seen flying glass before. People on stretchers. People bleeding.'

'Tough.'

'Is that all you have to say?'

The sun glinted on the water behind them. The seagulls shrieked, settled momentarily on the masts of boats, flying off again in the eddy of the disturbed murmur of the crowds. Snow said, carefully, 'What else should I say, Jack?'

'That you hate it as much as I do.'

'What, people being hurt?'

'Yes.'

'Well, I do.'

'Do you?'

'Yes of course. Jack, tell me, what the hell is all this about?'

Abbott's shirt was sticking to his back now, but once he was saying them, the words came easily. 'It's about the fact that Rowley's here, in this crowd. I think he has just spoken to you.'

'You're always going on about Rowley, Jack. I dunno any Rowley.'

'You do. He's been staying at your house.'

Snow said, 'Could you swear to that?'

'Not earlier today. But now, I can. And I will.'

'What changed your mind?'

'I saw him run from that quarter. Where people were hurt.'

There was a long pause. People pushed by, talking in low tones. The band was still playing, and the bunting swung in the warm breeze, but something had gone out of the air. Snow said, even more carefully, 'It wasn't planned anybody would be hurt, Jack.'

'But they were.'

'It wasn't planned they would be.'

'Then why chance it?'

'Not my decision, old Jack.'

'You help, don't you?'

'I do,' Snow said, 'what I feel I should.'

'It's wrong.'

'It could be all there is.'

'If it puts one innocent person on a stretcher, it's wrong.'

Snow said, low and urgent, 'I can't believe that, Jack. And even if I did, I couldn't do anything about it, because nobody would believe me, or believe in me. People get hurt anyway, Jack. Not necessarily dramatically, like those unlucky people out there, but one way or the other. Wounds aren't all made by flying glass, Jack. There are other kinds, baby, and they bleed just as much and they hurt just as much, only it's inside. And I tell you, old friend . . .' Snow's brow was wet. Abbott thought, he believes this, he really does. '. . . None of those people hurt, in that *accident,* would care if they knew the pattern it was part of.'

Abbott said, 'I don't believe that. I can't believe that.'

'Of course you can't. How could you?'

'You mean, because I'm white?'

'Of course I mean because you're white.'

Ah, it was all out at last. Abbott said, 'You're an intelligent man. Your life belongs in the arts. Why even touch *this*?'

'Because I was asked, baby.' Snow moved further along the rail, so their words could not be heard. 'I didn't volunteer, I'm no hero. But I shot my mouth off a little here and there, and I was heard. And I was put on the list. And I was asked, baby. It was put up or shut up.' Snow stared at him. 'So I put up, okay, not much, a coupla things, easy things.' He shrugged. 'I did it because I was asked.'

'You were a mug.'

'I don't think so.'

'I've seen terrorists before. I've seen what they can do.'

'Not these people.'

'Anybody with a gun or a bomb. I've *seen* it! I've seen the kids' guts trailing on the floor. *I-have-seen-it*! Maybe you haven't. If you think a wounding remark is in the same street, go and ask to see one of the victims' guts, at the hospital.'

'Jack, it was an accident.'

The sun was very hot. Snow waited.

In the end, Abbott said, 'I will report having seen him. I have to.'

'Okay, Jack. Do what you have to do.'

'Before he does anything else.'

'Don't apologise to me, Jack.'

'I'm explaining.'

'Don't. You don't need to.'

Snow turned away towards the sea, and Abbott said, 'I'm sorry,' and turned to go. Snow's voice came over his shoulder, low. 'That sea-bag of mine, Jack.'

Abbott stopped. 'What about it?'

'It had the gelignite in it. You brought it ashore.'

'*I* did?'

'Yes. I handed it to you, remember? You gave it back to me in the cinema.'

Abbott felt very chilled. 'What bloody difference do you think that makes?'

'None. But I thought you'd like to know.' There was a hint of a bitter laugh in Snow's voice. Abbott pushed his way out of the crowd. On impulse, Abbott turned, began to run. He went towards Pitts Bay Road. The sun was hot, and his clothes stuck to his back. The streets, away from the Front, were deserted. Abbott ran quickly, and was glad of his new-found fitness. Two years ago, he could not have done this. His present regimen and the loss of the pounds had brought him back to something near his army weight. He turned off Pitts Bay Road where, down an alley, they had left the battered Chevvy. He was somehow not surprised to see a young woman sitting behind the wheel of the car. He knew before he was close enough to be sure, that it was Marie. As soon as she recognised him, she got quickly out of the car, and called, 'Oh, hello there. I'm borrowing the car back, didn't Snow tell you?'

Abbott said, 'No.' He looked around the alley. There was no sign of Rowley. At the end of the alley, the blue sea created a spectacular backdrop, and there was a sandy path leading down to the shore. Marie stood, trying to smile and make conversation, glancing at her watch. Abbott noted that there was a valise in the back of the Chevvy. Marie looked at him looking, and smiled nervously. 'I'm going to stay with a friend.'

'I'd forgotten it was your car.'

'Oh, I don't mind Snow borrowing it. But I need it myself, now.' Marie moved, as if to get back in the car. 'I have to go, I'm afraid, I'm late for an appointment.'

'I had the impression you were waiting for somebody.'

Marie's lips closed. 'You are wrong, Mister.'

'I don't think so.'

Abbott pointed. Rowley was walking up the sandy path towards them.

Marie said, 'You are a fool.'

Abbott was ready to run but Rowley did not run. He walked, cat-like and very lean, towards them. There were black patches of sweat, Abbott noticed, in the armpits of the faded denims. He seemed very tired, but rested, like a man who has recently made love. Nothing, Abbott thought bitterly, so harmless.

'Hello, there.' Rowley's voice was lethargic.

Marie said, 'Cool it. This man thinks he knows something.'

Rowley asked, unsmiling, 'Like what?'

Abbott let himself relax, as he had been taught in the army. 'Like somebody threw a bomb and people got hurt and it was you who did it?'

Rowley was a long time answering. Abbott realised that this man was nearer forty than thirty. From the body of the hall, at the party two nights before, Abbott had guessed him to be no more than twenty-six. He wore the uniform of youth, but it did not truly belong on him, for he was no longer young. It was a disguise.

'Friend,' Rowley said, wearily, 'keep out. This isn't your fight.'

'Why?'

'Why what?'

'Why *that*! Down there? Those people?'

Rowley stared at him through the tinted granny-glasses, the only expensive item, apart from a large, dull metallic wrist-watch, on his person. 'Because there's no other way.'

'There's law and order and voting.'

Marie said, 'We have to go,' in a conversational voice. Abbott might not have been there.

'Right, get in the car.' Rowley's voice was even. He would face desperate situations often. Nothing of this would be new to him. Abbott relaxed his body again, as he had been taught.

'What about him?' Marie asked, not even looking at Abbott.

'What about him?' Rowley answered.

Marie looked at Abbott, shrugged, and laughed. 'Okay.' She got in the driving seat of the car, and started the engine.

'I'm getting in the car,' Rowley said, patiently.

'I don't think so.'

'Stay out of it, Mister.'

'She can go if she wants to. You stay here.'

Rowley shook his head, and carefully took off his granny-glasses. He folded them into a case and put them into the top pocket of his denim jacket. Abbott knew that, classically, he should have struck then, when the man had both hands occupied. Rowley blinked myopically, and said, 'Be sensible, keep out,' and Abbott knew the moment had gone. Also, he knew that he could not allow Rowley to get into the car.

He said, 'I know some karate. I don't want to harm you. Just don't get in the car.'

At that moment, Angel shouted from the top of the alley.

'Abbott!'

As Abbott turned to her, he knew that he had done something irrevocable. The blow had to come and come it did, hard and with a lot of weight behind it, but only a fist without a weapon in it. Abbott doubled up, and rolled as he fell, remembering not to keep still, to roll and scramble long enough to get back his senses and prevent his opponent from using his feet. He rolled and scrambled in the red dust, and the blackness and nausea began to clear. Somewhere, a door slammed and an engine roared. Abbott sat up and retched, his vision blurred. He forced his eyes open and looked along the alley towards the road. The Chevvy was turning, on two wheels and with a protesting scream of tyres, into Pitts Bay Road, heading up the Island.

'Abbott! Oh, my God! Are you all right?'

Angel was looking down at him. Behind her, Snow stood, hardly out of breath. Abbott shook his head clear and, hanging on to the wall, somehow got to his feet. A feeling of physical humiliation, such as he had not experienced for a very long time, came over him, and he pushed away Angel's proffered hand (she was trembling, and her hand was cold, at least there was *that*) and brushed the fine red dust from his clothes. His head hurt behind his ear where Rowley had hit him, and there would be a swelling, but, he thought, no real harm was done. It had been messy, like any street-fight between people who did not know how to fight. Abbott remembered the Scots instructor at Aldershot (the seamed, age-less face, the stink of tobacco and alcohol on the breath, any time of day or night) and recalled, across the years, the words, 'Nivver tak yer eyes off the other fella!—Nivver! Or ye're *daird*!' He waited a moment, refusing to look at either of them, until his head had quite cleared, and then he began to walk up the alley towards the road. His legs were very weak.

'Jack, you're a fool!' Snow said. 'Keep out!'

Abbott walked on.

Angel called, *'Please,* Abbott!'

'Oh, stick to your bloody friends,' Abbott said, his voice unsteady. Angel said no more, and Abbott did not look back. He walked steadily into the town, making small repairs to his appearance as he went. The Flower Pageant was going on, to its end, pretending nothing had happened. Abbott pushed his way to the front of the crowd, ducked under a barrier, and crossed the road between two massive floats. The scent of mimosa was overpowering. Before an irate policeman could reach him, he ducked into the crowd on the other side of the road, and, patiently, pushed his way through it. He found Waters staring at a shattered and burned-out shop, his feet crackling in powdered glass. Firemen were still applying foam to the blackened floorboards of the place. There was blood on the pavement.

'Oh, hello, Mister Abbott.' Waters looked down at the blood.

'I've seen Rowley.'

'Oh, have you?' The pipe snatched quickly from the mouth was the only sign of excitement. 'Where and when was that?'

'Four or five minutes ago.'

'Why the delay?'

'Let's say I was making up my mind.'

'Whether to talk to me?'

'In a way.'

Waters gestured to the burnt wood and the splintered glass. 'This is *him,* you know. At least, I think so.'

Abbott said, 'I thought that.'

'Bloody pathetic.' Waters waved his pipe. 'Any ideas?'

'I've seen him at Snow's place.'

'Recently?'

'This morning.'

'You did?'

'He may have gone there now, I think.'

Waters stared at him, mouth open, and then he shouted, 'Tommy, the jeep. Quick! Come along, Mister Abbott!' And Waters started to run down a side-street. Two other men, the two young men Abbott had seen on the jetty three days before, followed them. Abbott, his legs leaden, ran too. On Front Street the noise of the band was suddenly quieted. An official voice boomed. Somebody was awarding prizes.

11

The Land Rover sped along the coast road, having navigated the crowds in the town itself. Abbott sat in the front with Waters, who drove well in excess of the twenty-mile limit. Waters had finished talking on his R.T. set, giving details of how Rowley was dressed and telling all his units to keep a look-out. His voice, as he arranged all this, was in no way excited. To him, such action was everyday. Abbott sat next to him, trembling and chilled. It was a long time since he had been engaged in such desperate activity. He was, he supposed, in some sort of shock. He hoped that Waters would not ask questions, but, of course, it was more than could be expected.

'You have seen this man more than once?'

'At least twice.'

'Since I asked you to help us?'

'Once. This morning.'

'Then again at the flower pageant?'

'Yes.'

'When was the first time you saw him?'

Waters' voice was neutral. The countryside flashed by. Now, it did not look so domestic. Abbott thought he knew how informers felt. He still considered that there had been no choice. He owed Rowley nothing. About Snow, he was not so sure. He had done what he had done in an emotional moment, the moment he had seen the bright blood on the blanket, as the ambulance men ran with the victims, calling for gangway. 'The first day I was here, but I did not recognise him then. I thought he was a neighbour.'

'Did Snow's mother see him?'

'Unless she was blind she couldn't miss him. I think he must have been sleeping at the house.'

'She was not sure,' Waters mused, 'to know who he was.'

'I don't suppose she did,' Abbott said, carefully. 'Not for a minute.'

'That would be my first thought,' Waters replied.

Something, anyway, had been salvaged.

'About Snow himself, what would you say?' The question was asked in the same neutral tone, but they both knew the import of it. Abbott sat in silence, the air cold on his face, and felt chilled, as he had never felt chilled in the swamps of Malaya. He said, 'I wouldn't say anything. You'll have to ask him yourself. All I can tell you is what I've already told you. I've seen Rowley, and I know he must be violent, because he performed a violent act. I didn't actually *see* him do it, but I saw enough. I think he did it, and it may or may not have been intended to hurt people as well as property, I don't know. I don't give a damn about property, but if there's a possibility he's going to do it again, and people are going to be hurt, then if I have to shop him, I'll shop him. That is what I have done, and you'll have to make do with it, because there isn't any more.'

Waters merely nodded, as if Abbott had not spoken, and said, 'But you must admit your story is full of holes? I mean, what makes you so sure about Rowley? You must have seen him actually throw the bomb?'

'Nothing more to say.'

Waters ignored that. 'The obvious thing would be you'd talk to Snow about it, if you suspected he was connected with the whole business in some way. Did you do that?'

'I have helped you as much as I can.'

'And that leads on to another interesting thought.' Waters pressed on the accelerator. The narrow road was empty of traffic. All the tourists were in Hamilton. Here and there an old black man or woman sat at an open door, face to the sun. 'A lot of people have to know about a thing like this. All kinds of people. You were with Snow a lot this last week. Can you think of anybody he met who might be interested?'

Abbott said nothing. The Land Rover cornered noisily. The cart-tracks of the early settlers had been turned into narrow, twisty roads. They were not suitable for driving at this speed.

'Did you, for example, meet anybody at that party? Can you recall if Rowley was there?'

'I can recall nothing.'

'Later, maybe?'

'No. You've got my co-operation thus far. That's it.'

The R.T. chattered and Waters, driving with one hand, answered it. He listened carefully to the message (too faint for Abbott to catch) and simply replied, 'Yes. Keep looking.' He turned his head to the two young men behind. 'No sign of him yet.'

'He may be gone,' one of them said, without emotion.

'Maybe. An ocean-going boat brought him in, and then he was collected by somebody in a smaller boat. Probably the way they brought the jelly in, they wouldn't risk bringing it through customs, it's tricky stuff to handle.' Waters added, almost courteously, to Abbott, 'But of course you knew all that, or you must have guessed it?'

Abbott did not reply. The Land Rover purred, Waters sounding his horn at every corner, which was about every fifty yards, as they progressed along the spine of the Island. From time to time a very black small child waved from a garden or a window but nobody in the Land Rover waved back.

Waters asked, 'Which war were you in, to see people hurt like that?'

'How do you know I was ever in a war?'

'How else would you care?'

Abbott said, 'I was unlucky enough to be in Malaya. As a conscript infantryman. In an unfashionable county regiment.'

'Oh, which one?'

Abbott told him.

Waters nodded, agreeably. 'A good mob, I hear tell.'

'We did our best in a bad situation.'

'Somebody had to do it.'

'I suppose so.'

'Anyway, they aren't there now. You shifted them. About the only place anybody's ever shifted the bastards. I reckon Templar did the job of all time.'

'He had the locals on his side. That was what did it for us.'

'Yes, I suppose there was that.'

'Too bloody right there was.'

The R.T. chattered again and Waters answered. He listened, again, then, 'All right. Tell everybody to look out for her. No charges again. Not yet. Just hold. Out.' Again, he half-turned to the silent young men sitting behind. 'The lady Marie is not at home and nobody has seen her today. May mean something, may not.' Neither of the young men replied.

Waters said, 'I suppose you know the lady Marie?'

'If you mean the girl dancer, yes, I do. We've been rehearsing together.' Until Snow threw her out, he thought. Yet today Snow was driving her car? Abbott tried not to show anything.

'Did you have any thoughts about her?'

'Only that she is an excellent dancer.'

'Used to be Snow's girl-friend, but you knew that?'

'Not my business.'

'Oh? I should have thought it was.'

'Why would you have thought that?'

Waters did not reply, directly. 'Snow's a bit of a boy. In all ways. Trouble is, he mixes art with reality, like all these artistic people. Doesn't know where one ends and the other begins.' To Abbott, it sounded an acute judgement, but he simply said, 'My dealings with him are on a purely business level.'

'Oh, and how is the business doing?'

'I don't think it is.'

'Fallen through?'

'I'm afraid so.'

'Not surprised. Snow's clever but he has to run everything his way. Probably works all right for him. Of course, it would be a very different thing if he got mixed up in something bigger than himself. Then he would have to take orders and he wouldn't like that.' Waters seemed again to be waiting, but Abbott said nothing, and he mused in the same neutral voice, 'How did the girl—Angel, isn't it?—get on with him?'

'Oh, all right.'

'Very attractive.'

'I think so.'

'Did he think so?'

Abbott let the words sink in, absorbed them with enormous difficulty, and refused to reply. Waters sighed, and concentrated on his driving. They turned up the dirt road. Clouds of dust rose around the wheels of the Land Rover.

There was a small crowd of people around the door of the cottage. They were mostly old, probably those neighbours who had not gone down to the flower pageant. They were excited and agitated, and as Waters braked the Land Rover he cursed under his breath, 'Jesus God! What now?' The two young men were out of the vehicle before it stopped moving, clearing a way for Waters to walk through. He asked no questions of the chattering crowd, who fell silent at his approach, simply staring at him in a bemused way. It was only then that Abbott saw that the windows of the cottage were shattered. He followed Waters in the door. One of the young men stayed outside. Abbott could hear him begin to ask questions.

239

The room was dark and Abbott's feet crunched on broken glass. It had fallen on the room like hail. It glinted everywhere, in the sofa, on the table, in the very walls of the place. In the middle of it all, in the rocker-chair, sat Happy, with an old neighbour-woman, terrified and wordless, at her side. At first look Happy seemed to be sitting in an ordinary way, and Abbott moved forward to speak to her. Waters took his arm, gently. 'Don't touch her.'

Abbott looked again. Tiny fragments of glass were sticking out from the plump arms and from her forehead and cheeks. There was no blood, just the tiny glinting particles. 'Good God, how!'

Waters pointed to the ruins of the brass-faced clock in the corner. 'I'd say somebody who didn't know much about jelly stowed some there. It got too warm. Maybe he was coming back for it and got delayed. Anyway, it blew, the glass from the clock went everywhere, and she got most of it.'

'Is she going to be all right?'

'Mostly shock, I think. It must have been a hell of a bang.' Abbott knelt down and spoke to Happy. 'I'm sorry,' he said, 'I'm very, very sorry.'

Happy's glass-encrusted hand moved, in a soothing gesture. Her voice was low and hurt. 'Why should you be sorry? Ain't your fault.'

'It could be.'

'You didn't put the bang stuff there.'

'The ambulance is on its way. Don't touch that glass. They'll do all that at the hospital,' Waters said, in an official voice. He added, 'Has anybody else been here? Before us?'

Happy's head came up, and she just looked at him, a long haughty moment. Waters stared back. 'Well, have they? Rowley and the girl? They did come, didn't they, but no time to do anything, so they went off without the jelly. Or did they take some of it, and leave this lot, the overripe stuff, the stuff that banged after they disturbed it?' He waited, in the gloom, for Happy to speak, but she simply stared back at him, impassive, and his eyes dropped and he said to his young assistant, 'Yes, well, get statements from anybody who saw anything, not that I expect any of them did.' As the young man moved, he added, 'Get some cars out, up this way. I did say alert the Coastguard, didn't I, and the Radar Station, and say to ask for an air-sweep from the field?'

'Yessir.'

'All right, carry on.'

'Yessir.' The young man went out. Waters gestured to the old neighbour-woman to go, and she looked questioningly at Happy. Happy nodded wearily (all her gestures seemed a beat slow) and the woman left. Waters knelt down to Happy's level, in the manner of a miner, on his haunches. It was a skilful physical thing, and it gave Abbott a vast impression of strength and adaptability.

Waters said, 'Happy, do you want to help your son?'

'How? Is he in trouble?'

'I'm afraid he could be.'

Happy looked dully at Waters. Then, her eyes closed, but whether in pain or sorrow Abbott could not tell.

'How is he in trouble?'

'Well, I'll tell you.' Waters' voice was low and friendly and regretful, and for all Abbott knew he might be all of those things. He was, to Abbott's certain knowledge, above all a policeman. 'There's been a bit of trouble in town and I think he's connected. Also connected is this man Rowley. Now, I'm not interested in your son if I can get Rowley. It's Rowley I want. Rowley is dangerous, he's no use to his own kind, never mind himself. Rowley can cause damage, here or somewhere else. Of course, if he's gone, then that's that. I think you know whether he's gone or not. I think you can tell me if you want to. If I get Rowley, there's no questions asked, I won't want to even talk to your son, there'll be nothing to talk about.'

Happy's face was impassive, the tufts of glass sticking from her forehead glinted in the light. Her voice was soft.

'What do you want me to tell you, Miz Waters?'

'Oh, where Rowley is, or if you don't know, anything you heard him say. Anything like that.'

'Jest that? That all?'

'That's all.'

Happy sighed. 'I sure don't want that boy in no trouble, now he's got his career goin' over there in New York City.'

'Naturally. This way you'd help him.'

'He's not a bad boy.'

'I know that or I wouldn't be trying to help him.'

'He's got some funny friends.'

'Like Rowley?'

'I dunno their names, Miz Waters.'

'Try to think. Any name would help.'

'My head's a bit fuzzy. Musta been the bang.'

'Yes, but try. Any name.'

Happy was silent, her brows knitted. The particles of glass glinted in her arms, as she moved.

'Tell me about Rowley, then,' Waters pressed.

'Rowley?'

'He was here, wasn't he, he was staying in this house?'

'Rowley was?' Happy looked wide-eyed. 'That name, I dunno it, Miz Waters.'

'No?' Waters did not move. It showed enormous fitness to be able to sit like that, on his haunches, to wait, and think, some kind of self-imposed physical test. Abbott said, 'Happy, I shouldn't say anything more at all, anything more of any kind. Leave everything until you feel better. Don't talk any more now.'

Happy's eyes glinted. 'I think that's a right good idea now, Miz Abbott.'

Waters stood up. Abbott thought the man might strike him. But in a very low and still neutral voice, he merely said, 'And I thought you were one of us.'

Happy mused, 'Rowley was it, you say?' in a distant voice.

Waters turned back to her. 'Yes?'

'No, I don't think I know that name.'

'And he wasn't in this house, ever?'

'Nobody of that name here. 'Course, all sorts stay a night or two. Friends of my son, mebbe. I never ask who they are, and if they tell me I don't remember. I'm bad on names these here days.'

Waters' face tightened. He lit his pipe in a gesture of resignation. 'All right. We'll talk about it tomorrow.'

'Ain't no more to say, Miz Waters.'

Waters snorted, and said to Abbott, 'Outside?' Abbott followed him out. Waters gestured for the trembling neighbour-woman, who stood by the door, to go back in. 'Stay with her, Alice.' His voice was surprisingly soft.

'You know her?'

'In this place you know everybody.'

'Then how could Rowley get lost?'

'Easy, if nobody wants to tell you. They'll make him a village secret.'

'Will he be off the Island now?'

Waters stood outside in the sun, tapping his pipe against his teeth. 'I don't know why I should tell you, in view of your attitude, but probably. Fast boat, waiting offshore. Of course, that may be what he wants us to think. So we'll look, obviously.'

'What did he hope for?'

Waters shrugged. 'What do any of them hope for? Shock tactics. Probably aimed at the dais, but he couldn't get near. I had a cordon of police.' The blue eyes blinked. 'I was not entirely unprepared.' Waters sighed. 'So he chucked it into the shop. It had to go somewhere, he couldn't carry it around, could he?'

'He would have killed, you think that?'

'Who knows, with them? Anyway, the idea is, scare you. Next time a little more. You'll be that much more afraid. That's the theory. Won't work here.'

'You seem confident.'

'I am. This man is a loner. I think. Anyway, I hope. You see, these people have priorities. This place isn't one. Not for a long long time. Possibly never. I hope never.' He frowned. 'Can't weigh you up. Whose side are you on?'

'I wish I knew.'

'You seemed tough enough about them before? You've seen Happy in there?'

'Yes, but if I hadn't raised the alarm they might not have rushed back here and mucked about with the gelignite.'

Waters' eye glinted. 'Who else did you tell? Snow?'

Abbott shook his head, and looked at the ground. Waters turned to one of the young men, who had a notebook out. 'Any luck?'

'None of them saw anything, so they say.'

'What else?'

'Some footprints at the back there. Marks of car tyres in the sand. Two different lots. Might mean something, sir.'

Waters puffed on his pipe. 'Might.' He seemed resigned, in a cheerful way, as if he would now simply do what had to be done. 'Clear all these people back home. Tell them it's over. Ambulance on its way?'

'Be here any minute.'

'Good, good.' Waters called to the neighbours, in a raised but friendly-enough voice. 'All right everybody, off you go, back home. All over. Nothing to see.' None of them moved, or even blinked.

Waters said, 'You see what we're up against?'

Abbott said, 'What about me?'

'What about you?'

'Will you need me here?'

'Planning to leave?'

'Tomorrow.'

Waters took his pipe from between his teeth. 'You can go, I won't detain you. If you give me a statement now, down at my office, that is.'

'I will only say what I've already told you.'

'Come along, my dear chap, you can do better than that?'

Abbott made no reply. He was looking at a cab that had turned into the dirt road. It stopped and Snow got out, looking very lean and striking, but somewhat haggard, in his black shirt and trousers. He looked at the crowd and at Waters and then at Abbott. He walked fast and cat-like towards them, his face expressionless.

Abbott said quickly, 'She's been cut by flying glass but she's all right. Ambulance is on its way.' He wanted to ask where Marie's old Chevvy was, but he did not, because he knew. Or at least, he thought he knew. Behind Snow, at the cab, Angel was telling the man to wait, her eyes on the group, shocked.

Snow said, stonily, to Waters, 'All right for me to go in?'

'Of course. Carry on.'

Snow nodded and went into the cottage. One of the two young plain-clothes men, at a glance from Waters, followed. An ambulance turned into the dirt road, klaxon whining, and struggled up towards the cottage. Two uniformed men jumped out, carrying a stretcher. They ran into the cottage without looking at anybody.

Abbott walked across to Angel. 'You all right?' She nodded. Her face was drawn and tired, with the incredulous look of the young when nerves and body give out unexpectedly. The shirt and jeans looked genuinely crumpled, for once.

'Should I go in?' she whispered.

'No point now the ambulance people are here.'

'Oh God, what a mess!'

'It was always on it would end this way. These sort of things often do.'

'Abbott, what do *you* know about these sort of things?'

Abbott was stung by the tone of her voice, but he said, 'Perhaps more than you think.'

'I doubt it.'

'How can you know?'

'Oh, I don't know. I feel . . .'

'Sympathy? For the Cause?'

'You make me feel a fool, Abbott. Sympathy is all I have to give them.'

'It's wasted, and anyway they don't want it.' Abbott would have said more, but the men came out, helping Happy into the ambulance. They did not use the stretcher, but the group moved very slowly and carefully.

Happy looked round at them all, but she showed no sign of recognition. She simply said, 'I should of sold that ole clock, when I was offered twenty-five dollars for it.' Then she got into the back of the ambulance; one of the men got in with her. The doors closed, and the ambulance set off from the uneven dirt road. A cloud of red dust followed them.

Waters said, sadly, to nobody, 'They'll have to pull that glass out with tweezers, one piece at a time.'

Snow stood in the doorway of the cottage. He asked in a harsh voice, 'Well, who's giving me a lift back to town?'

Waters opened the door of the Land Rover, with an ironic gesture. 'I think I have that honour.'

Snow threw down his cigarette, and climbed silently into the back of the Land Rover. Waters got in beside him, and one of the two young men got in the driving-seat. The vehicle followed the ambulance down the unmade road, twinning the thick red dust of the ambulance. The crowd watched, rapt and silent. Behind them the cottage stood, blind and windowless, in the hot sun.

Angel had waved her hand, but Snow had showed no sign, his face set forward. Now, she turned to Abbott, and her eyes were very slightly moist. Abbott was shocked. He had never seen her cry. She touched his hand. 'I'm sorry, Abbott.'

'Why?' Abbott asked, lightly, his love for her choking in his throat. He guided her into the cab. She moved slowly, like somebody puzzled and remorseful. The second of Waters' young men held the door open for Abbott before he got in himself. As he slammed the door of the cab, Abbott heard the cardinal bird caw in the tamarind tree. He leaned back in the seat, and closed his eyes.

12

Abbott slept fitfully on the top of the coverlet. He was glad to see the dawn. Despite the chilly air-conditioning of the room, he felt feverish and unreal. The night before, Angel had finally taken two of her pills, and climbed into bed. They had not spoken of the events of the day, at his request. 'You're shocked, I'm shocked, the thing to remember is I'm going home tomorrow. What you have to do, is sort out if you're coming back with me, right?'

Angel had been in bed by this time, the coverlet tucked up to her face, her eyes closing with the impact of the Soneryl. She said, 'Abbott, I wanted to talk to you about that.' He had interrupted her gently, touching her lips with his finger. 'Tomorrow. You'll know tomorrow.'

'Snow still wants me to go to New York.' Her eyelids drooped. 'He thinks it's the right thing to do with the idea.'

'I know he does. Only that lets me out. And anyway, he may have changed his mind, after all this?'

'I wonder why we didn't see him?'

'Probably kept him apart from us deliberately. Go to sleep.'

'Talk in the morning, okay?' She smiled, and he touched her cheek; then her eyes closed and she slept. Abbott had not slept. He had lain on the coverlet and smoked, shoes kicked off, a large whisky in hand, going over the events of the afternoon. They had waited for an hour and a half in Waters' outer office, a plain room with a very pretty girl-secretary bringing them coffee every twenty minutes, profuse with apologies. 'I hope Mister Waters isn't going to be long. But I imagine you know how busy he is, and first things first.'

'Let us make our statements or whatever, and then let us just get out of this place.' Angel's nerves were beginning to go.

The girl had blinked. She was sun-bronzed and reddened, but basically Anglo-Saxon and it showed in her reply, which was, 'I'm sure Mister Waters will be as quick as he can,' and a sympathetic glance for Abbott.

He had not complained, he had simply decided to say no more. Angel had sat nervously, on the edge of her seat, and looking at her, Abbott was reminded of the awful story she had told about going into that far-off street, on that far-off day, looking for men. Was it true? The incident did not belong with the Angel he knew, but how much did he know? How much had he ever known about her? Abbott dismissed the question. Angel existed for him as she was. What she had been was no part of his present relationship with her. Yet, if any small part of the story was true, she must have no love for authority of any kind; a situation like this must stir up old anxieties, old humiliations. If it was true?

'Well, what are you going to say, Abbott?' She was bone-tired, he could see, and yet, boldly rolling one of her cigarettes.

'Nothing, except that I saw Rowley.'

'Rowley?'

'That's right.'

'You expecting me to tell Waters anything?'

'You must do what you want to do.'

'Don't bet on it, I will!'

At that moment one of the young men opened an inner door and said, 'Mister Waters can see you now.'

'Both of us?'

'Yes, please, sir.'

Waters was sitting behind a leather-topped desk. The late-evening sun glinted into the room, which was plain and could have been that of an old-fashioned lawyer. The air in the room was thick with tobacco smoke, some of it from cigarettes. Waters' pipe was out, and his young assistant was not smoking. Abbott guessed that the long session, the low hum of voices that had faintly percolated out to them as they sat on the old leather couch in the waiting room, had come from a long interrogation of Snow. Waters rubbed his eyes and indicated old leather chairs. They sat down. Abbott accepted a cigarette from a cedarwood box held by the young man. Deliberately, Angel lit her thin roll-up. She said, 'I've been waiting an hour and a half. I'm, personally, sick of waiting. What do you want?'

Waters leaned back. 'I'm sorry, I was busy. Talking to a person we all know.'

'I don't suppose you learned a lot.' Angel crossed her legs.

Waters' glance dwelled on them a long, regretful moment. 'Miss da Sousa, all I have to ask *you* is whether you can tell me anything about this man Rowley?'

'Why should *I* know anything about him?'

Waters looked at a piece of paper in front of him. His voice was even more regretful, a slight apologetic incline of his head towards Abbott. 'I see here that you spent last night and one night earlier this week at the Snow cottage. Rowley was there, we have reason to believe, some part of that time. It seems hardly likely you could have failed to meet him?'

Angel refused to meet Abbott's eye, and said promptly, 'There were one or two people around, but I don't know who they were. Who *is* this Rowley anyway?'

Waters drew on his pipe. 'I'm afraid you are not being very helpful, Miss da Sousa.'

'You bet you life I'm not! Now, can I go?'

Waters smiled, a slight apologetic nod, and said, 'Take Miss da Sousa back to her hotel, Tom.'

'Yessir,' said his young aide.

Angel hesitated. 'What about...?'

'He'll be along.' Waters smiled. 'In a few minutes.'

Angel stood up and looked around the office, at the musty files and the old, battered desk and the wooden model of the Bermuda clipper on the window-sill. 'I used to like policemen. Maybe I didn't meet enough of them.'

And she slammed out.

Into the long silence, Waters said, 'You have yourself quite a handful there. But a very attractive young lady, no doubt of it.'

Abbott said, 'What has happened to Snow?'

Waters ignored the question. 'I have had your statement typed out.' He pushed a paper across the desk and Abbott read it, slowly. 'Is that what you told me?'

'Yes.'

'I want you to reconsider not being able to definitely identify Rowley as being the man who threw the bomb.'

'I can't do that,' Abbott said. 'It just looked like him, but I wasn't absolutely sure it was even the same man I saw at the cottage until I saw him run across the road.' The words hung in the smoky air, and finally Walters said, 'So you cannot add to that?'

'No, I'm afraid not.'

'I'm sorry to hear it. Try to think again. Try to think back to that moment, when you first saw the man, with his arm raised, and something in his hand, something bright. Was that man Rowley? Don't answer now. Think how he was dressed. Was he dressed like the man who crossed the street, a few moments later, the man you are absolutely certain was Rowley?'

'I never said I was absolutely certain it was Rowley. I said it was the man I saw at the cottage.'

'It was Rowley.'

'Have you got him?'

'No.'

Abbott shook his head. 'I really can't add to this. I'm sorry. Do you want me to sign it?'

Waters looked at him steadily, as if debating more talk. Then he waved his pipe, in a gesture of mild disgust. 'At the bottom.'

Abbott signed the paper and stood up. 'Can I go tomorrow?'

'Will Miss da Sousa be going with you?'

'I don't know.'

'You don't?'

'No.'

Waters seemed to consider this for a moment. 'Well, I suppose like cleaves unto like.'

'I don't know what you mean by that remark.'

'I think you do, Mister Abbott.'

Abbott said, coldly, 'If that is all?'

Waters did not stand up, or offer his hand. 'I'll telephone you tomorrow morning at nine. There will still be time, then, to cancel your flight if need be.'

'I can assure you,' Abbott said, 'you will need very good reason to detain me. I am not without resources. I can get excellent advice and help.'

It was rarely that Abbott used his money, and he was always surprised at the response. Waters said, 'I know that you can, and I hope it will not be necessary.'

'So do I.' Abbott nodded, and went out of the room. The polite girl-secretary said, 'Good evening, sir,' and Abbott said, 'Goodbye,' and then he was in the street. The town had closed down. It was evening, and lights were coming on across the harbour. Abbott smoked a cigarette, looking out to sea, across the astonishingly beautiful vista of the Great Sound, all soft mist and water in the last rays of the sunset. Then he walked back to the hotel. He found Angel in a bath, very exhausted, and at that point he decided to insist on a truce, on their both having time to think. Surprisingly, Angel had agreed, and had eaten a supper on a tray in her room. Abbott had not felt hungry, but he had gone down to the restaurant. An omelette was all he could manage, and a half-bottle of white wine. When he returned, Angel had taken the pills and was already in bed, looking ill, and very young. It was in no way to be wondered at, and Abbott sympathised. Angel had worked very hard to get *Paradiso* off the ground. That she wanted it more than anything in the world, he was in no doubt. Given her temperament, that was inevitable.

He had held her hand until she slept, and now it was morning. Abbott looked at his watch. Quarter to nine. He yawned and went into the bathroom and splashed water on his face. Then he put on his bathrobe, and switched on low lights.

'Abbott?'

She was sitting up in the bed, wearing, he saw, touched, one of his pyjama jackets. Normally, she wore nothing at all. She pushed a hand through her hair and said, 'Is there any news?'

'Of what?'

'Has Waters telephoned?'

'Not yet.'

'He will though?'

'In a few minutes, I expect.'

'Give me a cigarette, will you?'

Abbott lit it for her and sat down in a chair. Angel poured herself a glass of water and drank it at a long swallow. Even this small action touched Abbott, but he merely said, 'How do you feel now?'

'Better.' But she did not smile. 'I want to get away from here, Abbott.'

'That can easily be arranged.'

Angel drew on the cigarette. 'I know, I know.'

Abbott said, carefully. 'We have to talk.'

She frowned. 'Why? How does talk help?'

'I have to say what I think. Whatever you want to do, after I've said it.' Abbott felt the words coming easier than he had feared. They should, he thought. He had been rehearsing them most of the night. 'I care about your career, and I have had a small part in it. I'm not an expert, because nobody is, or everybody with a good adviser would be a star, and they aren't. I think you have a good, popular, voice, Angel, possibly a great one, and I don't think you know just how good you really are. Of course, you know you're good, but not how good. So a musical of *Paradiso* was, and is, always *on,* for you. I don't see why we can't

250

go back to London and start it all again. Look for another director, I mean?'

Angel said nothing.

Abbott took a deep breath and tried to smile. He failed. 'Now we come to Snow, who is brilliant but unreliable'—he raised his hand before she could protest—'of course he is, we've seen evidence of it. But he wants to make a movie of it, all hand-held and cineverite. . . . All right. That may be the right thing to do. But he has no backing. Maybe he could get it. Maybe. Then, if you went into it—if he still wanted to do it—you'd be an actress. Or rather you'd be a *person,* because Snow sees you as the girl in the story, he's seen you as the girl in the story ever since you told him about your father. And . . .' Abbott paused . . . 'I don't know if that story is true or if you just told it to Snow to con him, and I don't care. All I know is that Snow will not use you as an actress, as an artist, he'll make you *that* girl. He'll break you down until you *are* that girl. He's strong enough and talented enough to do it. But whatever he does, you won't come out of it as a singer, or as anything you really are. You'll come out of it as his creation.' Abbott dropped his voice. 'If that is what you want, total domination, fine. It may be the right decision to take. I don't believe so, but it may be. You have to make up your mind what you want to do, Angel, and I'm afraid you have to make up your mind now.'

Abbott sat back in his chair. He was perspiring, and yet cold and clammy. He wondered if Helen had felt this way when she had realised there was no hope of reconciliation. He thought: as the Arabs say, take what you want and pay for it.

Angel said, in a low voice, looking away, 'I like Snow. I don't love him, Abbott.'

'No?'

'Maybe I couldn't love anybody. I mean, not in that old-fashioned-all-my-life way, y'know?'

'Who's asking for it?'

'Sometimes I think you are, Abbott.'

'No,' Abbott lied.

'I'd hate to hurt you, later.'

'I'd rather be hurt later than be hurt now.'

Angel drew on her cigarette. She said, academically, 'I'm not going to talk about Snow, you know.'

'All right, if you don't want to.'

'*Is* it all right?'

251

'Yes.' Abbott swallowed, drily. 'What do you want to do?'

The telephone rang and Abbott answered it. Waters said, 'Good morning. This is just to tell you that we have no objection to your leaving today. Either you or Miss da Sousa.'

Abbott said, 'Thank you. Is there any news at all?'

'Of Rowley, none. He's probably away.'

'How is Happy?'

Waters said, 'I've just talked to the hospital. She had a good night. She should be all right.'

'I'm glad,' Abbott said. He was. 'What about Snow?'

'Snow?' Waters echoed. 'Oh, he went to New York on the early morning plane. My idea, I need hardly add.'

'And that's it, as far as he is concerned?'

'I sincerely hope,' Waters said brusquely, 'that is it, as far as everybody is concerned. Have a good flight, Mister Abbott.' He rang off.

'You heard that? Snow's gone.'

'Yes, I heard.' Angel had swung out of the bed. She padded towards the bathroom. There was a certain spring in her step. Abbott felt an insane urge to touch her, but he somehow did not. Instead, he called, 'You could find him in New York easily enough. His agent will know where he is.' He waited, as bath-water roared, looking out of the window, over the sun-soaked, changeless Island. A large redbird, survivor of the thousands on the Island when the terrified negar first landed, soared from a tree in the hotel grounds, an exotic flash of crimson against the sheer blue of the sky, and flew away up the Island.

Abbott thought, I can help her, I know I can, but even if she stays with me it may not last. If she is successful it will change her, and if she is unsuccessful it will change her, as the money has changed me. But then, if one thing does not change us in this world, another will. He knocked on the bathroom door and called, 'What do you want to do? I have to ring the airport.'

In answer, after a very long moment, Angel came out of the bathroom, naked.

'Oh, Abbott.'

Before he kissed her, he locked the door.